PRAISE FOR LAUREN DANE AND HER NOVELS

"*Inside Out* is tender, romantic, and unapologetically sexy...Lauren Dane writes with an emotional depth and authenticity that always leaves me breathless. Simply put, I love her books!"

—Lara Adrian, *New York Times* bestselling author

"Hot, hot, hot with the right mix of tenderness and depth! In other words, don't walk, run to read!"

—Carly Phillips, *New York Times* bestselling author on *The Best Kind of Trouble*

"*The Best Kind of Trouble* is a great example of what Lauren Dane is known for—strong family ties and confident characters with an extra touch os sexiness for good measure!"

—*Fresh Fiction*

"The perfect combination of sexy rock-star fantasy and emotionally tender romance."

—*Kirkus Reviews* on *The Best Kind of Trouble*

"Most remarkable is the fierce power of Dane's uniquely confident heroine, whose strength gives this story power... Dane's mastery of her characters and their emotional complexity shines, making it a book fans will savor."

—*RT Book Reviews* on *Broken Open*

RECKLESS

LAUREN DANE

FOREWORD

Dear readers,

Welcome back! Reckless is the first in a new contemporary romance series I'll be publishing. Within it there'll be Brown Family and Hurley Boys next generation, along with some faces from Ink & Chrome and Whiskey Sharp.

I did a slight adjustment of age between Miles, his little sister Poppy, and his cousin Xander, so if you're fans of my Brown Family books, you might notice that. Nothing foundational is changed from the original series. I just aged them up a few years.

I hope you love Harlow and Miles's story!

Lauren

CHAPTER
ONE

Miles opened his email with the link his aunt had sent of a live performance of a band he was thinking of having open up for Earthquakes on their upcoming US and Canada tour. He'd already heard their new studio length release but live was a different story.

Blue, you've heard their produced sound, but Jeremy sent along this video of a recent live performance to give you an idea of what they're like live. Love you. Come take me to lunch soon. Xoxoxo, Auntie E.

No one but his aunt called him by his middle name, Miles thought as he smiled at her message, making a mental note to drop by and take her to lunch the following week. Jeremy was his agent too, and had sent him the video as well, but Erin sending it meant even more.

Grabbing his headphones and synching them with his laptop, he flicked a fingertip over the return key to open the link and start the video.

Harlow Martin was a punch to the solar plexus. Blue lights splashed over her skin, shoulders, and the line of her jaw as she sang, full throated, body rocked forward as she played guitar. The intro was good. The guitars built seamlessly upward, catching the barb of the drums.

She owned her space on stage. Knew her angles, flirted just over the head of the audience. An ideal without being a tease. An act every bit as much as any male lead ever was.

The snarled whiskey of her voice filled his head, swirling like a sharp-edged tornado to his gut where it seemed to shift something. Unlock the dam he'd carefully constructed against his baser impulses.

Then she shifted into a new song with three jumps sending her breasts high rather delightfully as she stayed on beat and never got winded. She made it look effortless as she hit one of her pedals, turned and gave the other singer a coy look as she handed the lead over to him.

Their show was high energy. Twelve songs and they only slowed it down twice. He checked the date and information attached and noted that it had been seventeen shows into their current tour and they weren't tired at all. Weren't phoning it in.

Harlow Martin loved what she did.

Miles sat there, absolutely ensorcelled by her. Yes, absolutely Above Me could hold their own on stage opening for Earthquakes. Yes, this person had whatever quality it took to handle the intensity of attention and expectations from their position.

His heart thundered to the point of slight dizziness as a knowing seemed to settle into his bones. He'd been burned badly a few years before. Bad enough that he'd been licking his wounds and had kept his personal life locked the fuck down to keep from making any more painful mistakes with beautiful people who made his dick hard.

But this one? *This* beautiful person? Harlow Martin not only made his dick hard with her fiery, self-assured sexual attractiveness, she was talented as fuck. Creative. She co-wrote the band's smart, insightful, clever songs. She was interesting.

She didn't need anyone else to get ahead. Didn't need to attach herself to someone else's star or bask in the light of another sun.

And he knew her.

Her father wasn't just a successful musician. Richie Martin was heavy metal royalty and had dominated that part of the music world for decades.

So because Miles's dad was also a successful musical act, he and Harlow had bumped into one another backstage at festivals and the like and had created a friendship. As the kid of a rock star, Harlow knew him and their life in ways that created a deep intimacy from jump. An intimacy he should be wary of, but instead found himself intrigued by enough to want more of.

He hadn't seen her in person in about six years. Since a giant radio station show their dads had played. Back then he'd thought she was pretty and funny. He'd liked her but there hadn't been enough of her in his life that he'd pursued more. He'd gone on to build his own career and apparently, she'd done the same.

But right then? Harlow set fire to something inside him. Made him want to haul her close and kiss her on the mouth. Smear her lipstick and get drunk on her taste. Something about her called to him on levels he hadn't known existed.

Which made her a threat he had no way to counter. And he...well, he didn't want to.

Before he thought about it any further, he forwarded the footage to his bandmates. They'd already heard—and given their thumbs up on—Above Me, but he figured it couldn't hurt for them to see the other band in action.

Miles rolled into their rehearsal space a few days later. Nearly everyone else had already arrived so he got himself a mug of tea. The last thing he needed was to strain his voice before they'd even left town.

He'd forwarded a copy of Above Me's album to all his bandmates when he'd put them in his top three a few weeks prior. Earthquakes was a democracy. Though he was their leader, they generally made decisions as a unit. It kept a sort of cohesion and unity he saw in bands that survived the long term.

Which band opened was a choice he definitely wanted everyone to make as a group. And, as he'd figured, each of them had responded back with Above Me ranked at the top. That'd been before he'd sent them all the concert footage. After that, they'd all doubled down on their support.

"By the way, I've been listening to Above Me all week. I like their sound a lot. Harlow is a beast as a frontwoman," Maddie Hurley told him as he strolled over. She led the band at his side as the rhythm guitarist and he valued her opinion a great deal. "That footage, yo. I need to make her my new best friend. I think we're roughly the same size. That would double my wardrobe." She laughed like she already didn't have a ridiculous amount of clothing courtesy of a mother who ran a series of clothing boutiques.

"She's got this edge that plays with girly but wraps it in barbed wire. It's...effective." Heat slid through his system. There was something about the way she wielded her appearance that made it even hotter. Smarter. Sharper.

That something deep inside him that Harlow had awakened—that sense of recognition—had already begun to take up space.

Maddie looked him over through narrowed eyes. "Why do you have a tone? What does it mean?"

Fuck. This was what happened when a person worked with family. They knew you pretty damned well. "I have a what?" He smeared cream cheese on a bagel and draped a slice of tomato and some lox over that. "Where did these come from?" *Yes, oh yes*, the chew alone told him they were likely not from anywhere local.

"How should I know? Your sister came in, dropped food off, talked to me about some album and tour stuff and left again. *Focus, Miles.* When you talk about her band, or, maybe specifically about Harlow Martin, you sound different. Interested?"

Miles snorted. If he admitted anything he'd never hear the end of it. Bluntly, it wasn't any of Maddie's business if he was interested in Harlow. Or why. Maddie would want to try to draw parallels between anyone new and his last serious relationship.

No one knew better than Miles that nothing was the same, least of all him. Harlow was a musician too, and in a way that was so joyfully confident that it rung his bell. It got under all his well built and very jaded defenses and made him feel things.

Just from some video and audio. Christ. What would it be like when they finally got face to face when the first show of the tour rolled around in two months? Something good, he hoped. Certainly something to look forward to.

He might have a growing something for Harlow, but more importantly, Above Me was perfect to open for them. One thing he would not do was make this about his dick. He wasn't an asshole. This business was hard on everyone, but young talent coming up like Above Me most especially. Miles knew it wasn't vanity that he understood what a potential break it was for them to open on an arena sized tour. The exposure could catapult them into the next level of their career.

Maddie knew him well, so he kept it genuine and hoped she backed off. "Interested first and foremost in her band opening for our band during our upcoming US and Canada tour." He finished off the second half of his bagel As Omar Marquez, their lead guitarist, and Silas Best, their drummer, came in. Miles paused to say hello to two of his oldest friends.

Omar tipped his chin. "Morning. Feels like it's going to be a good day. Flirted with that cute dude who moved into the condo across the hall. Turns out he's a radiologist at Swedish. My mother will finally be happy if I manage to date a doctor. She doesn't care if it comes with a dick. It's the degree."

Knowing Omar's very driven mother, Miles was more inclined to think she just wanted Omar to be happy, but there was no denying she was very opinionated in her desire that he date someone with an *actual* career since he was out there *wasting his potential playing music like a teenager instead of being a grown up.*

"We're talking about Above Me," Maddie said as Silas joined them, grabbing some food.

"Still a total yes from me," Silas said before he gulped some juice.

"Definitely a yes. Was there a problem?" Omar asked Maddie.

"No," Miles answered with a look at Maddie.

"I was just saying it had seemed he had a tone talking about Harlow. I mean, she's gorgeous so it's not like I'd have blamed him. I was just trying to figure out what was happening," Maddie said.

Troublemaker.

He rolled his eyes. "I like her. I'm fairly confident you all will too. Maddie hasn't met her because she didn't travel as often with her dad, but I've hung out with Harlow several times backstage. She knows this world and appears to have worked hard to achieve the success they have so far. As a band they know what it is to be on tour. This is going to be just fine. And, as Maddie mentioned and I'm sure you two noticed since you've seen the video of their concert, she's not hard to look at. I think it'll be easier on us all that they won't have as steep a learning curve." Miles shrugged and hoped they'd move on.

Maddie and Miles had grown up together, part of an extended family spanning two states, two rock and roll bands—now three—a cookbook author, several artists, and no small number of tattooists. They were a big, noisy, colorful bunch who loved one another fiercely. There was a protectiveness the adults of the family acted with toward these children, now adults themselves, who were out in the world making art of their own. Miles knew he could get advice from anyone in Maddie's family just as easily as his own. It meant something.

No. That wasn't entirely true. It meant everything.

Sometimes it was like being from a country most people thought they knew about but felt mostly made up. Being the child of famous people held a spotlight on you, shaped your personality in ways most others could never truly understand.

Citizens of that crazy nation were small in number but fierce in presence. It was a group Miles was proud to be part of, though he still struggled at times with the responsibilities and stresses of life in the public eye.

Harlow was one of them. That got to him even though she wasn't the first famous person's kid he'd known. Something about her just stuck in his brain even though he'd known her before.

Things were different for them all than it was when they were teens backstage at whatever festival their fathers played in. *He* was different.

"I say we contact Jeremy so he starts working on that and get back to rehearsing," Silas said. They'd had six months off before they'd started working on their most recent album and were currently in the build up for a summer tour and a fall leg in Europe.

All of them had that restlessness found in the weeks leading up to a tour. That sense of anticipation laced with anxiety and celebration that got a person through the long nights to come.

Finishing up the last of his food, Miles made a quick call to Jeremy, who promised to get in contact with Harlow. Once that was finished, he turned off the outside world.

Their rehearsal space was north of Seattle in Edmonds. It was an easy enough drive for Miles, who lived on Bainbridge Island, and the others who lived, at least part of the year, in the Seattle metropolitan area. It happened that a mutual friend had leased it for several months and the band who'd been slotted in had imploded and broken up. The space wasn't fancy. It was located in a weird little warehouse district within easy distance to an excellent pho place, a deli and a Greek diner but close to nothing else really, so they were left alone and could come and go whenever.

It was unreal. That's what it was. More than anything else, the fact that he was there with his band, rehearsing for a multiple months long arena tour had been a result of hard work, yes. But it was just magic. Plenty of bands worked hard. For years and years. Grinding away and it just never came together.

He hoped to never take it for granted.

Miles snapped open his guitar case and pulled his bass free, pausing to attach a new strap before slinging it on so he could tune it up and be sure all was well.

It was, of course. He'd never allow it to be otherwise. But it was the ritual of it. The step by step of making himself and his instrument ready to create that mattered to his process.

For a few minutes they tuned and tightened and got themselves situated before Maddie called out, "Wake Up," not as an order, but as the song they would start playing.

It rolled over him as Omar's guitar started off with Silas's drums and he slipped in, laying the bassline that would take the open into his lyrics.

On tour he'd use an earpiece to help keep his brain on lyrics and his bassline, but during rehearsals he relied on his internal monitors and the cues he'd been trained to keep on track. Wake Up was a full-throated roar of a song and it would get the crowd revved from jump.

But it was a song he had to give his all to. The chorus was powerful, delivering the emotions of a song about solitude, loneliness, and forgiveness. He'd written it in the aftermath of his last breakup when everything and everyone he'd counted on had felt so far away. He'd been lonely and so fucking exposed but unable to just...fucking deal with it all. Music had saved him. As well as family who'd simply shown up whether he'd asked or not.

He leaned close to the microphone to whisper and then amp up to a full-throated roar.

Threadbare and torn apart, exhausted. So close to giving up, broken hearted. I can't, can't stop, get up be something more than alone.

Maddie's voice came in then, nudging his along, carrying through to the bridge where Silas's drums were waiting as the guitars rose and fell again.

The emotion behind the words would always be part of him. But it lacked the ability to hurt him anymore. He'd taken it and used it. Created something so much better. That alchemy had enabled him to plow his energy back into his life, his music and career and leave his ex and those mistakes in the rearview.

CHAPTER
TWO

Above Me ended their solo tour on a Wednesday and would be opening up for Earthquakes on the start of their US/Canada tour the following week. Which was that very day.

Harlow rolled out of her temporary bed in a borrowed house in San Francisco, where she and the rest of her band were staying the few days before the concert.

She'd barely had two days at home in Seattle before they set off again to San Francisco. At the house they currently stayed in, there was a great rehearsal space. It was a nice thing that her dad's keyboardist had decided years before to diversify his investment portfolio with property and had offered it up to them for the very low price of tickets to the concert when it rolled through Los Angeles toward the end of the summer.

She'd have done that anyway. Just like he'd have let them borrow his house anyway. But that he wanted to be at her show was pretty much the best thing.

Down in the kitchen, Nora was already at the

coffeemaker while Brian rustled through the giant fridge. "Morning," she said, pausing to look out the kitchen windows at the vista beyond. The San Francisco Bay glittered in the pale sunshine off in the distance and from one part of the room she could see the distinctive red of the Golden Gate Bridge and the other she could see the Bay Bridge leading to Oakland.

"Just got coffee started," Nora told her.

"There are biscuits in the oven and I'll start the gravy in a few," Brian told her as he put ingredients on the large island. "Big day needs a big breakfast."

"Like I ever need any excuse to eat biscuits and gravy," Harlow teased him. "Can I help?" she asked.

"Nah. We've got it handled," Nora answered absently as she puttered.

Nora and Harlow had met on the first day of sixth grade as they'd both started at the arts middle and high school they'd both attended and had hated one another the first few weeks until a random cafeteria incident had found both on the same side of an argument and they'd ended up cleaning the floor with their competition.

That had been it. Nora Abelard had been Harlow's soul mate from that day on. Brian had come along a few years later. He'd imprinted on Nora and they'd lost a guitarist in their band so they'd gained a new guitarist and the third to their weird little family, and he'd gained a Nora and Nora's best friend.

They'd been asked a dozen times if they were a throuple, to which Brian always groaned and said he had enough to manage with Nora. He was the brother of Harlow's heart and that suited her down to her toes.

"We'll move to the hotel later today," Harlow said as she looked over the daily sheet their tour manager had dropped off for them first thing. The dailies were their lifeline for the rest of the tour, detailing where they needed to be and when. On tour there were long stretches of time where every day tended to feel very much the same, so having some direction kept Harlow on track and gave her a measure of control.

"Phil says our clothing arrived with the rest of the gear," Nora said, putting a steaming mug of coffee in front of where Harlow sat at the sunny breakfast nook.

"Thank god." A pallet of their gear had gone missing. All their clothes except for the day to day stuff they kept with them at the hotels was nowhere to be found for two days. Long enough that she and Nora had gone out the day before to take care of a few days worth of gear at the very least. "Not that the stuff we grabbed yesterday isn't going to be perfect to add to the wardrobe I already have and all."

"If this music thing doesn't work out for you, a business where you scout an area and let people know which thrift stores have the best stuff would make you a million dollars," Nora said. "You have supernatural thrift radar."

"Blame Marcella."

Harlow and her aunt hung out a lot while her father was working. Marcella—who she was closer to than her biological mother—had gone out of her way to keep Harlow interested while they were out on tour. Her father's youngest sister, she'd only been twenty two when she'd moved in with them and became Harlow's caretaker so Richie could make a living and pay all those bills.

Her aunt had a great sense of style but she, like Harlow's dad, had grown up pretty poor so at first, thrifting had been a way to attempt to be fashionable in a world where seventy-five dollar jeans were simply not achievable. Then, because her aunt was at heart an artist in most every way, thrifting had been a way to teach Harlow to style an outfit, how to upcycle the clothes to make them into something altogether new and unique.

"She's the GD best," Nora agreed.

Her aunt had sent every review of every show of Above Me's tour. Well, the good ones. Harlow knew there were bad ones out there, though she did her level best to avoid them. But after each show there'd be texts and emails with little things she'd found online. It never ceased to fill Harlow's heart to overflowing to be loved that way.

Interestingly enough, Marcella hadn't been the only one who'd sent links to reviews. Once Earthquakes had asked them to open, Miles Brown had started to send them along with cheerful little notes. *Hey there! Saw this review of your show in Tucson. I know if it was one of ours, I'd want to see it. Congratulations and see you in a few weeks. M.*

Just seeing his name in her texts gave her a little flutter. Why was obvious. He was gorgeous. Talented. His energy was deliciously sexy. Naturally she'd get a little flushed at his attention. Still, he hadn't said one damned inappropriate thing. Just supportive, friendly stuff and it was absurd to have butterflies over it.

Not that her libido cared.

Part of her excitement about that night was that she'd see him again after several years. She liked him, or the person she'd known as they were growing up, hanging out backstage at festival shows their fathers played.

Soon enough, breakfast was ready and they ate, chatting

between bites as the day fully woke up. Harlow's phone rang and when she noted it was their agent, she answered and told Jeremy she was putting him on speaker with everyone.

From the beginning, it had been important to the three of them to make as many decisions as they could as a unit. They argued and cajoled, sometimes they didn't talk for a day or three, but no matter what, they always presented a united front to the outside world.

"It's not the first time I've been backstage at an arena show," Harlow muttered as she tried not to gawk because it might not be the first time she'd seen the organized chaos of a live rock and roll tour show, but it was the first time it was *her* arena show.

Giant crates called work boxes had the band names stenciled on them along with other letters and numbers that would enable the load out of all that gear so it could be set up in a very specific order. She'd always found that part fascinating. The way the show went up in one order and was taken down in the opposite order. And it worked!

Harlow had decided to walk around so she could enter the arena as a fan would. There were hours before their soundcheck so she had plenty of time to find a seat up and out of the way and watch.

She took photographs and some video as first, trucks arrived to help place protective flooring over the arena polished wood. Then the stage was set up to one side and midway through that, people began to scramble up ladders, climbing up into the complicated foundations of the set. Then the light and sound booth set up center on the floor.

Given the complicated rigging that had gone on with giant white sheets of fabric hanging at the rear of the stage, with hanging video screens alternating between them, Harlow figured Earthquakes would have great visuals to go with their set and was really pumped to see them live.

Maybe one day Above Me would have such a complicated and amazing set to go with their show. Certainly a goal to work toward. But their lack of such a thing wasn't a reason for her not to celebrate the fact that Earthquakes had come this far already in their career.

"These would be some great seats, huh?"

She turned toward the voice, already smiling as she recognized Miles. "I was just thinking that very thing. Hi."

He opened his arms and she stood, moving to hug him, lingering longer than she'd planned to, but he smelled good, and he didn't actually loosen his hold immediately either.

"It's good to see you, Harlow," he told her, settling into the seat next to hers.

"Same. Thanks again. This is..." She waved a hand at the giant speaker stacks that were currently being built and then the black cases with Above Me emblazoned on them just waiting to be unpacked.

"This is our first arena tour too. I'm blown away by just how big everything is. Between you and me? I've been part of the process of building the stage and the overall show with the designers and I'm dying to see it all in play tonight." His grin rendered some of the edge into softness due to the joy on his features.

Miles Brown was beautiful. She sat at his side, both twisted to face the other better, so she got the full impact of his physical nearness and his looks. He wore jeans with a T-shirt. Nothing fancy. It was the man inside them that did all the work.

Green eyes fringed with dark lashes took her in with open interest. He had a ring in his septum piercing and her gaze kept returning to it over and over again because where it met his mouth and the dark caramel lushness of a beard so perfect he had to have just had it trimmed up, well it was perfection. The entirety of him, so big and delicious smelling did something to her pulse. The watch he wore on his left wrist drew her attention. Classic. Elegant without being ostentatious. And it went well with the fine dusting of dark hair and the muscles and tendons of his forearms.

Charisma and charm rolled from him and over her. Damn it. She was no stranger to super compelling people. She'd grown up with and around them her entire life, so why was this man so...alluring?

"My goddess, Silas's drum kit is incredible. Nora is going to have kittens when she sees it." Even though Above Me was going on first to open, their gear would be set up after Earthquakes's was. As the other band's set up dominated the stage it wasn't that big a deal.

"It is. And like every other drummer I've ever met, he'll be happy to talk about drums with Nora at length any time she wants." Miles snorted a laugh. "I probably don't even need to ask if you're ready for tonight. You just got off your solo tour right?"

"A week ago yesterday. Then we went home for two days, washed clothes the whole time, watered plants and headed down here. We've been here since Monday." Rehearsing all day. Meeting their various techs and their sound engineer. "By the way, Kenya, our sound engineer, she tells us your people have been great about coordinating with her and front of house. Appreciate it."

Earthquakes was a hot property earning a lot of money so being able to make use of their sound was a huge bonus. Most headlining bands were good about sharing, but there were some who were *proprietary*—stingy in Harlow's opinion—with everything and the openers had to scramble to make do.

"Makes no sense to us not to share that resource. We've got a great engineer and he's grumpy with everyone but other engineers. Oh and my mum, but that's due to them both being English and my mother being impossible not to like." Miles's blush brought those damned butterflies back. "There's no fucking reason to be a dick. This industry is hard enough so I can't see the point in playing dominance games. If Kenya has a problem, or any of your people, let me know. Please. It makes no sense to have something that's supposed to make things easier actually making things worse."

Surprise and then pleasure slid through her at his request. They were a far less powerful band and it would be easy to run them over to serve everything else that favored Earthquakes. But she believed Miles. To her toes. He truly wanted to be sure they were okay.

"Thank you," she said.

"You look really good," he said and then paused as if to gauge her reaction—which was wildly flattered. "Can't lie, I've been looking forward to being able to see you in person. Not a disappointment."

She'd been wearing the same leggings and t-shirt for the last few days as they'd rehearsed and hung around the house, but when she came to the arena that day and knew she'd be seeing Miles she'd decided to put on pants with a zipper and a blouse that flattered while remaining comfortable and easy to move in. "You'd never know they lost the crates with our clothing in them, huh? Found this morning, thank goodness."

"You could just wear hotel robes the whole tour." He laughed. "Super comfortable."

"Too hot. Plus it gaps open and as my clothes were gone, they'd see a lot more than the price of their ticket can buy," she told him around a snicker.

"We'd certainly sell out every night." He winked.

Then...well her hand was in his and she couldn't recall when that had happened. Only that it felt natural to have her fingers tangled with his.

He turned her wrist over, examining her forearm. "Goldfish?" he asked of the five small, scattered goldfish she had inked around it.

"Two things. One, keep fucking swimming," she murmured as she looked at their joined hands and then tried not to feel lonely when he let go to trace a fingertip across each tattoo.

"I can get behind that," he told her, his head still bent. And then he sang, "They say goldfish have no memory, I guess their lives are much like mine. And the little, plastic castle, is a surprise every time."

He straightened and let go of her arm. She took a deep breath but it was full of his scent and that didn't help her racing pulse either.

She grinned at him. "That was the second thing that inspired the ink. Love that song so much. Love everything Ani DiFranco does really. My aunt introduced me to her along with Bikini Kill. I got to introduce her to Le Tigre so it's a lovely circle."

"My aunt Erin plays Ani all the time. Grew up hearing Erin sing along while cooking or whenever the mood struck."

"I admire the sort of control and independence Ani's built for herself and her career. I want to say something with what I do and the work I produce. In my own way, of course, but I think that's her jam anyway. Be yourself doing what you're passionate for."

Harlow watched the work on the arena floor just beyond and decided to share a thing she'd been thinking about.

"Also, it's just so...weird and wonderful that you're sitting here talking about your aunt but Erin Brown is one of my icons. She's not only a great songwriter, the production stuff she's done with your dad has been stellar." Harlow stopped herself, not wanting to gush any further and make Miles uncomfortable.

He guffawed. "There's no one in the world like her. I'm so lucky to have her in my life as such a mentor. She and my dad have given me a master class on how to be successful in the music industry."

Without a doubt, Adrian Brown and his sister Erin had been an indelible part of the alternative rock scene and then later when Erin stepped away from performing and Adrian went solo, that next level career had exploded and catapulted him into superstardom.

"I like that." And she did. Harlow loved that she got so much from her father in the same way.

"We can't all learn how to shred from a metal god," Miles teased her.

Harlow's dad was a metal hero and most definitely her own personal one, "He's taught me a lot, for sure. We're pretty fortunate to have the musical examples we do. When we passed through LA on our tour, he and I spent hours just jamming together at his house. Honestly? I love watching him play guitar. He's...magical." She'd probably never in her life be as good and as natural as her dad was when it came to guitar playing. But what a joy that he'd passed it on to her.

"He absolutely is magic," Miles agreed before his phone made a sound. He looked down at the screen and then back to her. "The rest of Earthquakes is here. We'd love to meet you three in person. Do you have the time right now? Are Brian and Nora here?"

"Yes. I left them in our common room to come out here to watch load out." She sent him a smile as she stood. "I'd love to meet everyone."

"Your dressing rooms are just down from ours. We can stop by to grab Nora and Brian on the way if that works for them," he said, walking at her side.

"It should be, yeah. You all ready?"

"We'd better be," he said with a snort. "From today until late September we'll be touring. Hell, you've already toured three months and you'll be out until the end of summer?"

"We just scheduled two new shows this morning, as it happens. Looks like once we're done with this tour, we'll hit the festival circuit that takes us into September. We haven't done any shows in Europe for two years so we'll most likely schedule some shows in at some point." Though certainly not the size of the tour Earthquakes was taking to Europe.

"Awesome," he said, nodding to security who gave them both access to the performer spaces backstage. They recognized Miles immediately but gave the badge she had on around her neck a quick look before waving her through.

At their dressing room Miles paused. "We're just up there." He pointed. "Come on over when you're ready."

"Okay. See you in a few."

He took her hand and then halted, obviously surprised by his actions. Harlow squeezed to give him some cover and also to give herself a few breaths once he let go.

She'd planned to watch him walk away but he remained facing her, taking backward steps so she let him see the sway of her hips as she went in to find her bandmates.

CHAPTER
THREE

Miles had to pause a moment once she'd gone through the doorway and out of his sight. The impact of just a few minutes with her fucked with his head.

He'd wondered what that first time they saw one another again after all these years would be like. If it would be awkward or lacking the chemistry he'd hoped for. But he'd been looking forward to finding out.

After making a quick stop in the venue business offices to sign a few things their management needed to have couriered back immediately, Miles had headed down to where their hospitality room space was.

He too had paused on a mezzanine level to take in all the chaos. Vehicles, techs, construction workers and a dozen other types were down there where his band that he'd started a version of in middle school would open a nationwide stadium and arena tour.

As he'd been watching, Miles he'd caught sight of her sitting and doing the same thing he'd been and he'd started loping her way before he'd consciously decided to. Her dark hair had been pulled up into a braid, exposing the beauty of her face. And the wonder on her features.

During their twenty minutes or so, he'd taken her hand twice. Even now he felt her skin against his.

Just that closeness and the touch of her had nudged that placed within him that had already begun to wake and stretch after he'd watched her perform. Woken it further so that he was already thinking about when he could touch her again.

Grinning, he spun on his heel and arrowed through the main door of their green room space.

"Signed those papers," he told everyone. "Ran into Harlow. Told them we wanted to meet them, so they'll be here in a minute."

"Cool," Silas said.

"Make sure to invite them to eat with us," Poppy said.

When his sister told him she wanted to be his tour assistant Miles had turned her down.

He'd argued that she was too young to be out there dealing with the kind of bullshit that happened backstage. He sure as hell knew that firsthand and he shuddered to think about that touching her in any way.

She'd begun an entire campaign for the job that had involved her just sort of...taking over his life but in the best way. She got things done efficiently and to his specifications even when he didn't know she was about to do something or other until she'd completed the task.

Then she got their parents involved over the Christmas holidays and it had turned into a big Brown family thing and half his relatives were involved in a very lively discussion that had ended in Miles offering Poppy the job she'd already been doing really well.

And there she was being great at it yet again.

A few taps on the doorjamb and Harlow came in with the other two members of Above Me. She raised her chin in greeting, along with a waved hand.

"Hi, everyone."

Miles moved to her side and faced Nora and Brian. "I'm Miles Brown. That's my sister and my assistant Poppy. Omar Marquez, lead guitar. Silas Best, drums. Maddie Hurley, rhythm guitar."

Harlow grinned at them all. "I'm Harlow Martin, guitar. Nora Abelard, drums and Brian Green, bass. We're really glad to be here. Thanks for having us."

There was a bit of back and forth as everyone bumped elbows or shook hands and Miles breathed a little easier because so far so good.

Maddie and Harlow stood chatting with Poppy and Nora and he made his way over.

"I saw you sing on stage with your dad's band six or so years back. I can't even remember what festival it was, but I do remember it was at the Gorge and I was drinking a beer so I was legal. The sun was setting and it was purple and orange and you came out," Harlow told Maddie. "It was "Everything", from the *Star is Born* with Barbra. It was just fucking amazing. You said it was for your mom and that was lovely. I've never forgotten that."

Maddie blushed and took Harlow's hands. "You don't know what that means to me. I'm so...thank you. My sister and I used to always sing that one when we were growing up. My mom still cries if anyone ever brings that night up."

"Small world," Miles said. "I was there that night too with Silas and Omar. That's when we swooped in and told her she had to be in our band. I don't remember seeing you that day though."

"I was there as a concertgoer. No backstage. Sometimes you just want to be a fan, you know?" Harlow said and became a thousand times more sexually attractive. "I love that it was when the four of you became Earthquakes."

"Hey listen," Miles said, "Maddie's aunt, who is also my aunt too, but by choice rather than by birth, she used to go out with Sweet Hollow Ranch as their personal chef. She and her friends created a catering company that travels with touring acts. They have a load out of a whole ass kitchen before each show. Just in case you were expecting a packet of crackers or room temperature deli meat," he said. "They also have a post show meal. Something easy and portable most often as they have to tear down every night too."

"I'll have it added to your dailies," Poppy told them.

"Thank you. We'll definitely take you up on that," Nora said with a smile.

Harlow poked her in the ribs.

"What? They invited us!" Nora hissed at her friend.

"Just because we think a thing doesn't mean we have to say it out loud immediately," Harlow told her in a sing song voice.

"Whatever. Fortune favors the bold." Nora rolled her eyes and the two friends started to laugh.

Brian just sighed, clearly used to it.

.   .   .

"Do you mind if we sit in on your soundcheck?" Harlow asked Miles.

"Only if we can watch yours," Maddie said.

"Yeah, that," Miles agreed.

"Sure. It's during your meal break though. So we get it if you choose to eat instead," Harlow told him. Lots of musicians didn't eat a big meal before the show so it didn't slow them down performing. Harlow had found that a good meal about an hour or so before they went on helped her keep her energy, leveled out her blood sugar and mood. A hungry Harlow was an unpleasant Harlow.

"We'll work it out," Miles assured her, and she got the distinct feeling he'd do whatever he wanted whatever the case.

"I assume you have a ticketed soundcheck?" Brian asked, and Harlow wanted to laugh but didn't. Brian was always thinking about different aspects of the business and what could be done in each to further the band's aims.

"Yeah. Just started this tour. It's a fan club perk," Omar said. "There's a lottery system for the tickets each date. They're not sold via ticket agencies so there's no issue of a single agency buying all the tickets and selling them for more than most of our fans can afford."

"We were considering doing the same thing." Brian and Omar settled in for a long discussion, so Nora and Harlow left them to it.

Poppy directed two people to put several large boxes on a nearby table. "Promoter sent us cookies and mini quickbread things. Score." She tipped the delivery folks and then began to poke around, holding out various sweets and demanding someone try it to give a thumbs up or down.

Harlow watched the scene as she tried chocolate chunk caramel cookies and banana bread.

"No one seems horrible. I like them all so far," Nora said quietly. "And I think Brian is going to leave me for Omar now."

"Omar *is* really handsome," Harlow teased. "And seems as obsessed with all this stuff as Brian is. But. I think the lack of cute boobies might be a deal breaker for Brian."

"He's ours." Nora shrugged. "No one else can have him."

Snickering, Harlow put her head on Nora's shoulder for a moment.

The three of them excused themselves to go get dressed. They'd do soundcheck after Earthquakes and so she preferred to dress for their set in advance. Between soundcheck—and being after a headliner meant they'd be dependent on Earthquakes not taking up that whole time slot before the doors opened at seven—and trying to get a meal before their set, it was wise to be ready to go.

Harlow could admit she wanted to look gorgeous not only for the fans, but for Miles. Only to herself, but she could admit it.

Nora braided Harlow's hair and helped pin it into a crown while Harlow did her makeup with a dramatic eye, saving lipstick until after she'd eaten. Nora's hair was pixie cut short so she just ran styling product through her hands and pulled it up into a deliberately messy style that showed off the royal blue tips against the ash blond of Nora's natural hair color. Nora chose a halter that'd leave most of her back bare, in bright magenta that matched her sneakers. Denim shorts would keep her cooler and the embroidery up each side echoed the color of the top.

"You look like a piece of very dangerous candy," Harlow told her. Nora beamed. Her best friend was crunchy in so many ways—crystals and meditation and all that stuff—while also having a natural sort of edge she always seemed to effortlessly style. "If I didn't love you so much I'd hate your guts."

Nora laughed. "If we were on a housewives show, *looks like a piece of very dangerous candy* needs to be in my tagline. And we could have microphones instead of diamonds or peaches."

"I'll save the butterflies for right before we go on stage," Harlow said to Nora's reflection in the mirror. Part of that particular outfit were jeweled butterflies that tucked into the braids wrapping around her head. Pinks, purples, blues, and oranges, they caught the lights and made her feel beautiful. They echoed the butterfly on the back of the delicate looking —but truly sturdy—topper she wore over a purple slip dress. Also to wait until right before the show to put on. Fishnet tights that were performance style so she could wear them for several hours without discomfort, came next. Last, she pulled on boots that zipped up the side. She used to have lace up boots with thicker soles, but it was easier to control all her pedals with a thinner sole or barefoot, and once she'd taken a header on stage when her boot had come untied so that had been the end of laces.

Once they'd finished most of the preparation, they headed out to the floor to tuck off to the side to catch Earthquakes's soundcheck.

Kenya, their sound engineer, sat in the booth with Earthquakes's guy, Ned. She didn't appear to be annoyed, which was a good sign that she wasn't having any issues with access.

There was a nice sized group of fans standing in front of the stage. They celebrated every noise the band made, cheering even when a song would pause just a few seconds in to adjust sound.

They were all still in the same clothes they had on earlier, not going on for several more hours. And yet, Miles didn't need that anyway. Her gaze and attention was drawn back to him over and over.

Plenty of yells of his name, most with I love yous involved. He just smiled and told them he loved them too.

"It's like a sex bomb detonated," Nora murmured of Miles and his ridiculous charisma.

Sure felt that way in Harlow's panties.

She did resist that reply because it was public, Brian was just on Nora's other side, and she wasn't ready to admit it out loud. Her bestie would figure it out soon enough.

They finished up by six fifteen, Harlow and the others heading stage left so they could watch closer but be out of the way as Above Me's stage plot was laid out according to the plan Brian had sent over in advance.

Set up wasn't new. Playing live music wasn't new. There was a comfort in the way she'd seen this happen countless times. A confidence that won out over the nervousness that always came before a show.

And yet as she walked out to meet her guitar tech and she looked out from the stage at the vast arena beyond, this step was astonishing. She sent Nora a grin and devil horns and Nora gave a few beats of the drums in response.

Chick, her tech, and Kenya spoke back and forth as they

tuned and adjusted the sound of Harlow's guitar. Another tech tested microphones while Brian and Nora conferred with their people.

Lights were tested as the technical part of their performance was run through its paces and sharpened.

It wasn't until she stepped forward to her spot, guitar slung over her shoulder to test the mic herself that she noticed Miles and the rest of Earthquakes in front of the stage and hoped he couldn't see her blush from there.

And she didn't really think about him again until the process was finished and she handed off her guitar.

"Good job with time," Phil, their tour manager told them as they left the stage at five minutes to seven. "Anything you need from me?"

Brian had some technical thing he wanted to talk about so Nora and Harlow left them to it and left the stage.

Poppy waited for them with a bright smile. "Hi! You sounded great. Miles and the rest went to eat but I said I'd come grab you."

The room they'd converted into a small dining area was full when they arrived. Miles was up and at her side immediately and Harlow wasn't the only one who'd noticed.

"Hey," he said. "Everything go okay with soundcheck?" He led them to the table where the prepared food had been laid out.

"Yes, thanks. Sound is great." Though she knew theirs would be better. They had better gear and that's how it went. Still, through her earpiece, things worked well and she was confident they'd sound fantastic.

The meal had a fish option, a meat option, and a veggie option. Something for everyone, Harlow figured as she chose salmon with roasted veggies and instead of the pasta she wanted—and knew would make her want a nap in an hour —she chose the tabbouleh. Filling and good energy. She'd have that pasta later.

Nora looked at her carefully once they'd settled in at the small table Miles had led them to. "Be right back," Miles said. "I'll bring some water for the table."

"Let it go," Harlow whispered.

"For now," was the only guarantee Nora gave as she dug into her food.

"Come back here after the show. There will be box lunch type things for everyone," Poppy told them as she joined them with her full plate.

"It's very handy to have an aunt who starts a tour catering business, huh?" Harlow teased.

"It really is! I wish so much that Mary, that's our aunt, was with us. But our cousins are in high school and they're doing baseball so there's all sorts of stuff they don't want to miss being out on the road. You'll meet her at the end of the tour. They live in Hood River, Oregon. It's not very far to the Gorge so I think she and my mum are going to plan something big. Browns, Keenan-Copelands and Hurleys never do anything halfway." Poppy's tone and her eyeroll were laden with affection and Harlow liked her even more for it.

They made small talk for awhile until it was nearing their set so they cleaned up and headed back to their dressing room to add the finishing touches to their outfits.

Miles had been in and out of the dining room while they'd been eating but Harlow understood. He was responsible for making sure everything went well for Earthquakes. There was media stuff too.

She still felt a phantom tingle where he'd put his hand on her elbow as they'd entered the room the first time.

Harlow had Nora help her slide the topper, which was a series of crystals hanging in chains, over her slip dress. On the back there was a butterfly detail that she'd used as inspiration for the glittery butterfly hairpins she'd stumbled on at a flea market in Nashville a few months back. A quick smooth of her hair and careful application of deep red lipstick and she was ready to go.

She and Nora stood side by side, looking in the large mirror. "We look awesome," Nora said.

"Totally."

Brian came in as they took some selfies and then it was time. Phil came to collect them and walk them through the maze of hallways to the stage where they'd enter from the rear instead of stage left.

Chick and the other techs waited, stepping in to hand over instruments and earpieces. Harlow didn't wear hers the whole show. She liked to hear feedback from the crowd so she took them out from time to time. But they protected her hearing and helped her pick through all the noise to find her guitar and stay on beat.

She knew they were hooked in when she tried the opening to Billy Squier's, "Lonely Is the Night" and heard the crowd react.

After a quick grin at the others, they brought it in, touching foreheads the same way they had since eleventh grade. These friends would never let her fall. They'd hold her up and kick her ass when she needed it.

"You ready to do this?" Harlow asked them.

"Fuck yeah," Brian said, echoed by Nora.

"Let's gooooo," Nora called out, separating from them, grabbing her sticks from her tech, and slipped through the curtain that took her out on stage.

The audience cheered. Nothing crazy just yet. They were the opener. Hell, half the ticketholders weren't even there at that point. Still, this was their chance to triumph or fail, so hopefully Harlow could get them to the end of their set and have made some new fans.

Nora settled in behind her kit and made a quick pass to let Brian know he was up next. And it helped them to get an idea of the time it took her to get there. Brian timed his entrance a few moments later, and when his bassline began, wrapping around Nora's drumbeat, it was time for Harlow.

One last deep breath past her nausea and Harlow moved through. From backstage to center stage. She left her fear and her anxiety behind that curtain and embraced her badassed persona. Harlow had wanted this for as long as she could remember, and she was going to give it everything she had. Center stage Harlow didn't worry about failure, pretended not to even notice those in the audience who weren't even paying attention. They were hers to capture or not.

When she jumped up and down a few times once the driving beat of the song had begun, hit her distortion pedal, and grabbed their attention. And didn't let go until she was ready.

. . .

Miles stood watching them play, impressed and beyond attracted to Harlow. The woman he'd hung out with earlier had turned his head for sure. But this? This was Harlow at a fifteen. She moved on stage with joy and confidence.

The confidence was what shot straight to his cock. Christ she was fucking amazing. She flirted with the audience but made it charming and funny instead of gross or cringe. They tossed the spotlight back and forth between the three in a way he knew took practice and thought, but made it look effortless.

At his side Maddie danced with Poppy as Silas watched Nora drum. Omar just took the whole scene in with the same ease he did everything else. But they all were into Above Me's performance and clearly saw their hard work.

The light bouncing off the butterflies in her hair made it look like she was a flower and they fluttered around her head. The sparkling thing she wore over the purple dress she'd had on at dinner echoed that. That purple dress had called to his hands. It had taken all his willpower not to touch her and that silky fabric that had skimmed over her body.

Beyond that craving that she'd awakened when he'd watched that video six weeks before, there was something so professionally produced about them while they remained rebellious and young. Miles hoped the industry didn't kill that. Harlow's fire was delicious enough that he wanted to get close enough to scorch.

He needed to get his head on his own performance, so he gave Harlow a thumbs up when their set was over to very eager applause, but he and the rest of his band headed to their dressing rooms to handle last minute issues. Each of them had their own pre-show process and rituals so he found a quiet corner, put his headphones on and closed his eyes to meditate and focus.

It was an hour later when he changed into his performance gear and met the others for the walk up with Poppy guiding the way. His baby sister was utterly unflappable as she navigated them through, holding off hails and questions that weren't urgent.

For the dozenth time that day alone he was glad she'd manipulated him into hiring her.

Once they'd gotten to the immediate staging area, their intro began to play and they were surrounded by techs helping them gear up. When he'd been seventeen or so, watching this happen to his dad, it had always felt like a gladiator getting ready for battle and that's the emotional energy Miles tried to bring to their live shows.

Fans paid a lot of money to come to shows. They took time out of their daily lives to drive to an arena, pay another huge amount to park and then everything else inside the arena except water and the bathrooms cost more money. Miles didn't want any of them to walk away feeling like they'd been cheated. Earthquakes owed them their absolute best every performance, no matter what, and that's what they all committed to do.

They jumped in place as Omar chanted what Miles thought of as their battle cry. Essentially a checklist of what they needed to do.

Play hard.

Play loud.

Give it a hundred.

Over and over as the four of them did a call and response until they cheered and were ready to get out there and do it.

The intro music died down and the crowd cheered and then got silent as the panels behind Silas's drum set slid apart to show them standing there.

Omar teased the open of three different songs as they all came on stage. The silence erupted into monstrous applause and the booming vibration of stomping feet.

This was magic. This moment was unlike anything else he'd ever experienced and he was so damned grateful for it. The crowds, the lights, not an empty seat. He'd loved playing live music since he'd been a teenager and getting to do this so many times every year was the best thing ever.

"Hey there, San Francisco," Maddie said and then they launched into "Cuts Me Up", a hard and fast number from their first album and a fan favorite.

They sang along, the crowd knowing every pause, every word and snarl.

When he held back on the chorus of "Shine Though" the audience took over every sigh and growl. Joy was a bright, warm sun in his belly when he turned and caught sight of Harlow off to the right. She'd changed into jeans and a t-shirt, but the butterflies were still in her hair as she moved her hips to the music and sang along.

Something she'd already awakened in him stretched out a little more, pleased as fuck that she was there enjoying herself.

Two hours later, a sweaty, tired, but very happy Miles and the rest of Earthquakes debriefed with their sound engineer and techs before heading off to shower and change into regular clothes.

He saw Harlow at the end of the hallway and called her name, jogging over.

"You were on fire tonight. Holy shit. Good job," she told him with a smile that made his stomach tighten. "Fans loved it. An excellent start to this tour, yeah?"

He took her hand. "Thanks. It felt really good. You were all amazing too. What are you up to right now?"

"Grabbed some food so we're headed back to the hotel."

He wasn't ready to let her go for the day.

"Did you need something?" she asked once she saw his expression.

"If you want to wait about forty-five minutes or so, we can all ride together," Miles said.

"Thanks for offering, but Phil's arranged a car for us. Enjoy your night. Celebrate this! You deserve it. We'll see you tomorrow."

He frowned again. Normally people did what he suggested. There was chemistry. As he still held her hand and she looked up into his face with an openness he knew wasn't manufactured, he was certain he wasn't imagining it.

Harlow called out her congratulations to the others and then slipped her hand from his.

"Oh! Wait. I forgot to tell you what I thought of your show," Miles said with a grin, pleased he'd found a way to keep her there just a little longer.

"Terrible right? You're going to fire us?" Harlow teased and damn if he didn't want her even more because of it. She knew they'd done well and wasn't going to pretend otherwise.

"Really awful. I'm sorry you're so out of tune and homely."

That made her tip her head back to laugh and he arrested his attempt to step forward and kiss the exposed skin of her throat.

"I'll see you tomorrow, Miles."

She caught up with Nora and Brian and Miles stood there watching her walk away until she'd turned the far corner.

CHAPTER
FOUR

Two days later they needed to drive from San Francisco to Sacramento for the next show, so Harlow had packed her stuff and been ready but when she checked the peephole and opened the hotel room door, it was Miles standing there.

"Hi! Are you lost?" she asked, stepping aside to admit him.

"Your ride is here," he told them.

"I thought you'd be flying or something," Harlow said.

"We're driving between cities for most of the shows. Makes more sense that way and I'm going to be honest and admit that it's just so much less costly in most cases we prefer it."

True or not, what Harlow wasn't sure of was why he was there. Surely, they didn't want to share their private transport with their opening band and she said something like that but nicer.

"We're just musicians like you are, Harlow. It's a seriously nice bus we'll be using the whole tour and you're invited. You're three people, not forty."

"Stop trying to talk him out of it, for fuck's sake," Nora said as she hefted her small suitcase and overnight bag and went into the hall.

"Yeah, stop trying to talk me out of it," Miles said with a smile, liking Nora more every moment. He bent close to Harlow's ear. "I already told Phil you'd be coming along with us. He says he'll see you in a few hours. I want to hang out with you. I like being around you."

Oh.

She hoped she wasn't blushing but the heat on her skin told her that was a vain wish. She wore her emotions on her skin. Mad, happy, or sad, she blushed, flushed, and got splotchy.

"Is that okay with you?" he asked oh so quietly like he hadn't just snuck under her defenses and gotten right up in her space. And he was so big. In more than only physical terms.

Miles was used to being in charge. Used to people following his leadership. Getting involved romantically or sexually with someone like that was something she usually avoided. Harlow was her own strong personality used to being in charge.

For the last few days, she'd been thinking about that. Thinking about the way he made her react. The way she sought him out when they were at the venue and the way he did the same. This was dangerous territory. They were on tour together and letting herself get caught up in Miles was a hugely ill-advised idea.

But she nodded. It had only been a few days after all. What could be the harm if she was careful? Just a little taste.

Then he brushed his lips over the shell of her ear before he grabbed one of her bags and headed into the hallway before she could respond.

Miles paused at the door so Harlow could get on first. Which gave him a great view, his reaction to he was glad to hide behind sunglasses.

Some part of him had eased in, patient to slowly seduce her. Greedy to know her more. Spend time with her. Here she was in his space for the next few hours.

Poppy waved a hello. "I'm so glad you're coming along. Once we get moving, I've got smoothies and coffee and a bunch of breakfast sandwiches and wraps. Come sit."

His perfect sister directed Harlow to the spot next to the one Miles had staked out. Miles sent her a discreet nod of thanks.

Within a few more minutes they'd finished stowing the luggage and everyone had loaded in. The bus lumbered out of the city and on to the next one.

Soon enough there was food and coffee and several different conversations. Brian and Omar had bonded over D&D and were talking about the people on the crew who'd be up for a weekly game. Nora pulled out a deck of cards and was in the process of explaining a very complicated set of rules to Poppy and Maddie.

"What was the first song you learned to play?" he asked Harlow.

"One Divine Hammer by The Breeders. You?"

He grinned at her, a scorching blast of heat. "I love that. For me it was Creep."

"Radiohead. Well played."

"When my dad came into my life—and the instant he knew about me, he was a consistent presence—part of how we learned each other was through music. He helped me, well, me and Silas, learn the song in the garage of the house I'd grown up in."

It remained one of his favorite memories of his father.

"You've been playing music with Silas a long time."

Miles looked at his oldest friend. "Yeah. We went to the same elementary school and didn't really hang out. But in middle school we were both in the jazz band and that's when we became friends."

"It was the food. My house was always chaos, but Gillian, that's Miles's mom, she always had great food in the house and didn't care if I slept over three nights a week," Silas said from his perch across from them.

"Mary, that aunt Maddie and I share, she ran a catering business so she's the reason our house was always over-flowing with food. Mum took care of Mary's heart and Mary took care of Mum's health and me," Miles explained.

"That's the age Nora and I became friends. I honestly can't imagine my life without that nosy bitch. She's my soul-mate," Harlow said.

In the midst of the card game, Nora held up devil horns in agreement before turning her attention back.

"She's the one who will tell the server if the food is wrong. And she does it without making anyone hate us," Harlow joked.

"Every friendship needs that person," he told her. "Why a Breeders song?"

"I love the Pixies and through them I discovered The Breeders. My aunt introduced me to more music than my dad has. She had these binders of CDs and I'd page through, choose something at random and we'd listen. My dad's the one who helped me learn the chords though."

"Is he cool with you going into music too?"

Harlow nodded. "He's very proud of us. Always has been a big support. He and Brian's aunt produced our current album in his home studio. Wants to see all our contracts just to be sure we aren't being taken advantage of. Even though his agent is at Jeremy's agency, and he likes and trusts Jeremy."

"In a weird way, Jeremy has always been like family," Miles said of their shared agent—and his aunt's ex-husband.

"If my dad thought anything but that Jeremy was helping, he'd say so loudly and insistently. He's very mellow in his personal life but when those lines are crossed, he can go off." Harlow snorted a laugh. "I know people assume he's a wild man with the way he is on stage. But that's a persona. He puts it on like a costume. When he's not onstage, he's taking my three-year-old sister to her dance lessons and playing with her in the pool. I just always wanted to be a musician and he always supported that."

Miles liked the way she spoke of her family. Another connection, he realized.

"Your mom?" he asked.

"Isn't really in my life." Flat words closed with a period like a door slam.

He'd back off. Until he got to know her more and could

poke around without fear of hurting her feelings or making her feel uncomfortable.

"This is a very nice bus," she said shortly after that, to underline the subject was closed.

"We don't do overnights in it, but we'll be using it to drive from show to show. There'll be a few dates where we'll end up flying and the bus will meet us at the next stop just because of distance."

"I can't sleep in a moving vehicle without terrible nausea. Affects my performance," Omar said, reminding Miles that just because they were all involved in multiple conversations, they were still listening to what everyone else was saying.

And he for sure caught Silas's narrow eyed stare when Miles had leaned close to Harlow. His friend wouldn't be silent about it forever. But right then Miles didn't really have any answers to give about it anyway. He just knew he wanted more of her.

Harlow got up to go sit next to Omar and tell him about a medication she took for her nausea while traveling but then came back to Miles so he didn't have to manufacture a reason to follow her.

"Miles Brown is hot for you," Nora said once they'd checked in to the hotel later that afternoon.

"He flirts with everyone. It's not personal." Harlow rolled her eyes, heart thundering.

Nora scoffed. "You're a liarpants! Yes, he's friendly and has that charming flirty energy with everyone. But he didn't corner anyone else on that bus. Just you. And then he watches you like he's starving and thinks no one notices."

Harlow growled. "Okay so there's some attraction."

"He's a lot. I searched online. His dick is pierced. Did you know that?" Nora asked.

Harlow clapped a hand over her mouth for a moment. "How did you know? Did you search for that very thing? Hussy."

"Some ex of his apparently got very chatty after they broke up a few years back. Told the gossip sites about their sex life and stuff. It's a Prince Albert." Nora picked up a pen and pointed to the underside of the cap at the top, indicating the position of the piercing.

"Were there pictures?" Harlow whispered.

"Not that I saw, and Brian already frowned at me for googling him anyway. He thinks I should back off and let you make your own choices. I think he's acting like we just met yesterday. Of course, I'm going to get in your business."

"We've got over two months to go so at this point, my choice is just to enjoy whatever it is. Flirting is fun. He kissed my ear," she confessed, telling Nora about that moment earlier that day when they'd left San Francisco.

"Just don't overthink," Nora warned, pointing at Harlow.

"I don't overthink."

Nora just stared at her.

"Okay so I do. But I like Miles. As long as this stays private and casual, things will be fine."

"He's one of the biggest rock stars out there right now. He's in commercials and has had movie parts already. Everyone is curious about him. How do you think this will stay private?" Nora demanded. "Don't go destroying this thing before it's even truly started."

"You and I both know if the gossip sites get hold of this it'll inevitably be twisted into me using him to get this gig for our band." Harlow could deal with most criticism, but the way women in the industry were so often accused of fucking someone to get ahead really pushed her buttons.

She worked hard to be successful. Gave up a lot. Invested time and energy and every spare penny to make this career happen. That anyone questioned that because she was considered pretty was a thing she absolutely dreaded. It always seemed to be the voice she heard, even though it was rarer than other voices that lifted her up and saw her talent.

"It's ridiculous that no one would think he was blowing me to get ahead."

"To be fair, he's way more famous than we are. But I get it. And I know you enough to know you'll let this get to you. So please, give yourself a break. Have fun and remember who the fuck you are, Harlow."

"Your soulmate?" she teased as there was a knock on the door.

"Obviously!" Nora tossed back as Harlow checked the peep hole to see who was knocking.

It was Miles.

"Hi there," Harlow said as she opened up.

"I just wanted to let you know we'll meet you here in the elevator lobby at four to head over to the venue," Miles told her.

"Oh, we leave about ten minutes before that. But I'll see you there."

"Ride with us. Makes no sense to waste gas and time, and

your per diem on a ride when you can just come along when we do. We leave at four and get there in plenty of time. And we can ride back together."

"Sometimes we will. Other times we will come back on our own for one reason or another. Same with getting to the arena. There are days when we have media and will make our own way there," she found herself saying, realizing that she had to set boundaries with this one.

He frowned and she was reminded of Ryder, her baby sister, when she got told no. Like she was astonished anyone would ever actually refuse something she'd asked for.

At her back, Harlow could hear Nora's barely smothered snicker and it lightened her heart.

"Have you had lunch yet?" he asked.

"Um, we just got here half an hour ago. No chance yet."

"Want to come get something to eat with me?" he asked.

A thousand reasons to say no. A hundred more to say yes but to have Nora along. Or anyone else so it wouldn't just be the two of them.

"Sure," she said. "But you're going to get recognized. Maybe we can do take out? I'll go in to grab it and we can bring it back here to eat?"

"There's a food truck place. Go there," Nora called out. "Bring me and Brian back something good. You know what we like."

"You both can come with," Harlow said, turning to Nora.

"You can be gone for a while. You know, enough of a while so Brian and I can *catch up.*"

"Okay. Put the do not disturb thing out until you're um, done catching up so I don't walk in on my parents doing it."

Nora giggled. "Deal."

Brian came out of the bathroom and looked back and forth between Harlow and Nora. "I don't want to know, do I?" he asked.

Miles grabbed her hand and tugged. "Nope you don't. Enjoy your catching up," he called out. "Get your things," he said to Harlow, who paused to give him a look. "Please," he added.

"See you two later. Open the window or something when you're done," Harlow called out after gathering her purse and allowing Miles to tug her from the room where she hung the do not disturb sign herself.

She came to a halt as she saw the car with a driver already waiting.

"This way we can eat and someone else drives," Miles said. "And I get recognized when I drive. It causes more attention than having a driver. I know it's weird. Do you think it's weird?"

It must be hard to be so recognizable, Harlow thought. That loss of the ability to do even the most basic stuff without causing a scene would hurt. And maybe it made other people think about him differently. She sure as hell got that second guessing everything she did and wondering if that made her look a certain way even though her intention wasn't that perception.

"I don't think it's weird," she told him as he held her door so she could slide into the back seat first. "You have a strikingly handsome face. Even if you weren't a celebrity people would look twice. It's harder to be Miles the average guy when you look like you do."

He settled beside her, closer than he needed to be, but she had no real complaints.

"I'm going to look up what trucks are there so we can know in advance what we want. That will keep the process shorter," she mumbled as she began to search on her phone.

Forty-five minutes later they were seated at a picnic table at a nearly abandoned park that stretched out next to the river.

"You're an internet research master," he told her as he dipped his burger into a container of blue cheese dressing.

"Ha. What I am, is someone who just spent nearly three months in a van driving across the country for our tour. These food truck lots are the best, and we ate at them as often as we could. Great variety, usually local vendors, cheaper than restaurants and way more mobile. And to keep the van from smelling like onion rings, we tried to find little parks here and there, so we got our vitamin D and some fresh air and a break from driving."

"I think this is a great idea. Fresno is next. Be my lunch date again?" he asked.

"Let's see how this one goes first. What if I'm terrible and you find out and then you're stuck eating a burrito with me?"

He laughed. "Goddamn, I really fucking like you, Harlow Martin."

Pleased, she smiled at him before going back to her cold noodle salad. "I'm very likeable. I guess I like you okay too," she teased with a wink.

"You'll turn my head with such effusive words of praise."

He was really smart and funny. Sexy as fuck and magic on stage. A combo that left her weak in the knees.

"What are you listening to right now and don't say Above Me," she said.

"Why not? I like your music."

She rolled her eyes. "Thank you. That's nice to hear. But this is Harlow and Miles getting to know one another, right? I'll go first. I'm listening to Wolf Alice and Earth, Wind & Fire. I think it's impossible to be in a bad mood while listening to Earth, Wind & Fire."

"It is Miles and Harlow getting to know one another, yes. Totally agree about Earth, Wind & Fire. I'm on a Who kick lately so I'm on "Quadrophenia" just now."

They finished up their lunch and headed back to the car for their return to the hotel. As they drove under the building to a rear entrance, Miles took her hand and squeezed it. "Thanks for coming with me today. You're really okay with riding to and from the venue with us? It's a sincere offer and I want you to, but I don't want you to feel pressured or anything."

"It's a very nice offer and I appreciate it."

Miles noted the slight pause but when she didn't say anything else, he waited until they were standing in a back service elevator lobby. "There was a but just now."

"What?"

Her confusion delighted him for some reason, and he leaned forward quickly to brush his lips over hers. "Sorry. When you said you appreciated the offer of the ride. There as a slight pause. An unspoken *but*. Tell me."

"I just have to be aware of what people do or don't do for me or around me. And whatever perceptions or assumptions come from that."

"Say that again but like I'm not bright," he asked.

"When women achieve things like, say, opening spots on arena tours, many people are happy and celebrate that.

There are people who lift other women and their successes up. But there are people who watch for any excuse, any reason to assume she didn't earn it like someone else – usually a man—would have. Those people see me taking rides and letting you kiss me as me fucking my way to where I am."

In her tone he knew she was speaking from experience. He wasn't ignorant of the double standard in the industry on so many levels.

"Fair enough," he said. "I won't remind you that Above Me is already plenty successful before now because that's a fact. As for the rest. Plenty of bands share stuff like transport to the venue. It's not unusual really. Sure, there are plenty that don't, but it's not going to raise eyebrows. We won't make a big deal of it." He paused and took a gamble. "I like being around you."

"And what if you don't in a week?"

"You're already writing fuck you break up songs about me and I haven't even used my tongue when I kissed you yet. That hardly seems fair."

The tension she was holding in her body relaxed and she laughed a little as she got onto the elevator with him.

"You and I click," he said quietly. "We liked each other before this," he waved a hand back and forth between them, "so I think in a week I'll still want to spend the hours and hours of transport time with you."

They reached her floor, and she got off, taking the bags with Nora and Brian's food with her. "See you at four."

Yes, she most definitely would be seeing him at four. And if he broke her heart, she would most definitely use that to write a fuck you break up song.

Harlow made him laugh. She treated him like a person instead of a celebrity. There was something so confidently self-assured about her but here and there he'd catch a glimpse of a more vulnerable Harlow. That Harlow who'd just shared that bit about perception? Genuine interactions like that outside his very close circle were rare and he wanted more of that Harlow even as he craved the badass version. Wanted her to trust him even more than he wanted to kiss her again.

That's what made him pause a little as he headed up to his room. This wasn't just physical attraction. He kept finding new things about her to be fascinated by. She made him greedy for more in a way that felt different than anyone else.

There was a vein of worry, some terror even, that this path he sped on toward the heart of Harlow Martin could end up in a terrible mess. But by the time he got inside his room and flipped the latch, he knew he wasn't going to shy away from this thing building between them. It just felt right in ways he couldn't really articulate at that point. Every time he'd ignored his gut feeling about something it had bitten him in the ass.

At the very least, there'd be songs written one way or the other. And what he hoped, even if a romance fizzled, they'd have a deep friendship by tour's end.

CHAPTER
FIVE

Though Harlow wasn't as disciplined and fit as Nora, who took her yoga very seriously, she loved the way it was her wake up ritual on tour. Loved the way it helped her focus on her body and mind for that time she was able to carve into the day. It was easy enough to do anywhere she could put a mat down and since she hated most other types of exercise but needed the strength and endurance to tour, yoga had become a regular thing.

In Salt Lake City, they stepped off the elevator on the lobby level because Harlow wanted to refill her water bottle and bumped into Maddie and Poppy.

"Hi! What are you two up to?" Poppy asked.

"There's an intermediate yoga class downstairs. Hotel says it's for all guests, so we figured we'd hit it up and see," Harlow told them.

"Really? Do you mind if we come too?" Maddie asked. "Poppy and I were just talking about how we needed to do something. We've got mats already."

"We'd love for you to come with us. It doesn't start for

another ten minutes. We'll meet you there and save you space," Nora said.

Harlow really liked both women. She and Nora had a lot in common with them. They were down to earth, especially given their place in the world.

Harlow also liked it that while Poppy was super yoga person like Nora, Maddie was more her speed. Stretching, muscle strength, focus and a way to keep moving, was all she'd wanted too.

Afterward, they all grabbed breakfast in a café not too far from the hotel.

"How are you liking everything so far?" Poppy asked once the food had arrived.

"The crowd has been great every night. The sound is fantastic, and our engineer is over the moon," Harlow began.

"And we just got news that we've got two singles charting now," Nora added. "Being out on the road is a lot at times, but the exposure is helping so we can't complain at all."

"Socially everything is fine?" Maddie asked.

"What do you mean?" Harlow wasn't sure.

"She means is everyone being nice and making you feel welcome," Poppy explained.

"Ah! Yes. It's fun being on tour with another band. More people to chat and hang out with. Usually." There were exceptions, Harlow knew.

"We've all traveled with *that* band," Maddie said with a snicker. "Thank goodness you're not like that. We love you and are so glad you're here."

"Definitely," Poppy said. "By the way, after the show tonight, we're all invited to a late dinner if you're interested. Which I hope you are because otherwise it'll be a bunch of dude rockers who Miles and Silas have been friends with since I was a kid. They're nice, don't get me wrong. But I'd like it if you were there."

"Miles would too," Maddie murmured.

Nora's brows lifted and before Harlow could stop her friend, she said, "Yeah. I've noticed. What's that about?"

Harlow sighed.

"What? Like you think they aren't curious?"

"Is it so shocking he'd be interested in my company?"

Nora halted. "It's not shocking. Look at yourself! He's lucky you look right back at him. Curious doesn't mean shocked. You know I'm always team Harlow."

Harlow put her head on Nora's shoulder a moment. "You're right. Sorry."

Nora knew all her buttons and triggers. She also knew all the work Harlow had done to overcome them. She was so very lucky to have Nora in her life.

"I know what Nora means," Poppy said. "I *am* curious. And I know Maddie is too. Obviously, you're someone he'd look twice at. But that's not really it. He's around beautiful people all the time. She's more than that. And I think Miles sees it and can't help but be interested. He's not...he doesn't usually do more than flirt with people around him as he's working. This is different."

"It's only been a week. I'm...interested too. But this is dangerous. We're on a tour together. He's the leader of the headlining band we open for. I just don't want the negative attention. The whole assumption by some that nothing is organic and real, but a way to manipulate via my vagina so I can get what I want is hard for me to not listen to," Harlow admitted.

"Yeah, that sweet, sweet next to nothing pay for opening on an arena tour," Maddie teased with an open smile that Harlow was grateful for. "The first year I was in Earthquakes there were all sorts of opinions that I must be boning Miles or Silas. Then it was that I was chosen because of who my dad is. Who my uncles are. It never fucking ends."

Maddie's voice was magic. She was quite clearly talented, and it burned Harlow's gut to know that sort of bullshit happened to women no matter what.

"Well that sucks," Nora said.

"My mother is a former model. She's tall and blonde and absolutely breathtakingly gorgeous. She's also a smart businessperson with a thriving chain of boutiques. She ran two of them before she even got back together with my dad. And still people liked to say she was coasting on the Hurley name. It's depressing to know it's never about who the woman is or what she does. It's always about the person who brings that nonsense up to attempt to destabilize her. All women really. Because they hate to see us succeed, Harlow. Fuck them. I succeed! Not gonna lie and deny part of my success is from sheer spite."

"I really like you, Madelyn Hurley. You're very smart." Harlow winked. "I'm glad we bumped into you both this morning."

"We are too," Poppy said. "Look, Miles is going to do what he wants to do. There's no way to manipulate him anyway. Trust me, I'm his little sister and I've tried! He's um."

"Bossy," Maddie interjected. "He's bossy and used to being in charge and, to be honest, he usually takes that and protects people."

"I did notice he seemed unfamiliar with being refused," Harlow said with a snort.

"He was really shy until he hit like seventeen or so. Then, I don't know, he just leaned into himself. If he pushes too hard, you have to just flat out say you're not interested. He'll back off then. Otherwise? He's going to be in your business trying to take care of you. Which is nice but also annoying," Poppy told them. "Our dad is the same. He's a caretaker."

"Thank you for the insight." Harlow was grateful to hear from others that her initial impressions of Miles were correct. She didn't get womanizer vibes from him, and after the last dude she dated, her womanizer radar was finely honed. But it was good to have her own intuition underlined.

"We'll definitely be at the dinner," Nora added. "We rarely turn down offers of food."

They headed back to the rooms shortly after that because Maddie and the others were off to do media before that night's show.

"Let's go ahead and pick you out a super cute outfit. We'll bring it to the venue and you can change after our set." Nora bustled into the room and began to rustle through Harlow's clothes.

"Do you think I should back off?" Harlow asked, knowing Nora would tell her the truth.

"Do you?" her friend countered.

Harlow snarled a little. "If we have this chemistry now, we will in a few months, right?"

"Maybe. Or maybe shoving aside what so truly *is* will slowly strangle it and, by the time the tour is over, you two won't be interested in each other anymore. In which case, the real question is, are you willing to lose this thing by backing off? Is backing off what you truly want or are you asking because you want to pursue him, and you need me to reassure you?" Nora pulled out a sleeveless teal halter type blouse and tossed it on Harlow's bed.

"I don't want to make a mistake with someone's feelings."

"What about your feelings?"

"Why are you answering my questions with questions?" Harlow demanded.

"Because you know the answers already and you want me to validate you. But if I had a problem with this, you'd know it." Nora dropped a pair of well-loved jeans next to the shirt. "Jeans will be fine."

And just like that, in her Nora way, she'd gotten Harlow to focus on herself and her choices without judgment. It was what she'd needed, naturally, and of course Nora had understood.

"You're going to be a great mom someday," she told Nora.

"I'll settle for being a great friend right now." Nora grinned. "Plenty of time for babies later. Still, it'll take practice." She waggled her brows at Harlow, who snickered.

"Practice makes perfect, I'm told."

"Poor Brian," Nora said. "Sometimes I want him so much I think I might just wring him dry."

"He appears to like it, so I don't know that he'd consider himself *poor Brian*. I think he believes he's *lucky Brian*."

"Aww. I really do love that guy."

"He deserves you." Not many would, in Harlow's opinion. Nora was a fantastic catch.

"I think he does. I hope I deserve him. He's the best." Nora shrugged with a smile.

Harlow had watched Nora and Brian grow up and into their partnership. They'd stumbled here and there, like anyone else did. But they seemed to share a bone deep commitment to putting in the effort to keep their relationship strong and healthy.

It gave Harlow a visible reminder that cynicism aside, the thing she wanted so deeply was possible.

"You two are sappy as fuck and I love it." She hugged Nora to her side a moment.

"I can't believe you hung out with her for hours and didn't invite me," Miles grumbled at his sister after she'd informed him how she and Maddie had spent their morning.

"I just brought you a smoothie and lunch, so you'd better find your gratitude." Poppy managed the same level of hauteur as their mum when she got riled up. It worked on him too.

"Thank you for bringing me food," he told her.

"Of course, I didn't invite you. You were still asleep at seven thirty when this yoga class was." She flipped him off before tossing herself into a chair. "You're not a morning person, Miles."

She wasn't wrong about that. It was a thing by that point that if they had to be anywhere before ten the others in the band would leave him be to avoid his crankiness for the first hour. Though he'd love to see Harlow in yoga pants, he didn't really want to get up early and exercise to do that.

"She's not just yours," Poppy said after a bit.

He grunted as he began to eat.

"I invited her to the after thing tonight," Poppy told him as she looked through her calendar. "She's very nice and she likes you. Maddie and I approve, but she's our friend too. We warned her that you were bossy and that you'd be in her business."

"Why? Are you trying to chase her away?"

She just stared at him, deadpan for long moments. "She's an independent person and she takes that independence really seriously. It's good for her to know up front. She'll manage you I wager. A weaker person wouldn't last a week with you. You're not meant to be with someone who doesn't want to walk at your side."

"What do you mean?" He knew, but he wanted her to say it. Needed her to.

"Whatshername wasn't your equal. She was never going to walk at your side. She wanted to warm herself in your celebrity glow, drain you of everything she could and if she destroyed stuff on the way out, so be it," Poppy said of Sophie, his ex. Their whole group of friends generally refused to use her name after the breakup when she had set fire to his privacy on that way out his sister just mentioned.

"Maybe I just didn't take care of her enough," he said.

"Really? You think that? Because if you do, I'm going to punch your Adam's apple."

"No," he admitted. It had taken him the better part of a year to truly process all the things that'd gone down between them, but he was at the point where he knew she'd never been as into him as he was her. Her attraction to him was about his access and that had been easier to accept than the way he'd let himself wallow in bullshit behavior during their relationship.

"I don't want to talk about her. Back to Harlow. It just feels like I've known her forever. And I don't mean in the way we have known one another since we were teens. I'm comfortable around her in the way I am with close friends and family. Not that I know as much about her as I do all you. But I feel like I can be myself. Like she doesn't expect anything but that."

"So, be yourself and try not to be too bossy while you're at it," Poppy told him like it was obvious.

He supposed it was. But what others thought of as bossy he considered protective. He liked taking care of people. "We'll see."

The house wasn't very far from the venue, but Miles had no intention of not sitting his ass down next to Harlow on the ride over.

"I'm glad you three came along tonight. You'll like Jeff and his wife Malorie." Miles was still buzzing from their performance. Tired but in a satisfied sort of way. They'd swapped out some new material into the setlist and it had been a hit and had given the spotlight to each member of Earthquakes.

Harlow had changed out of her stage gear, and he was a little sad because she'd been wearing a body skimming dress that came to her mid-thigh and had gone without shoes as she'd moved with such aggressive self-discipline and unhidden joy, he continued to catch memory flashes of how she'd looked even hours later.

Conversation swirled all around them as he took her hand and she looked up at him briefly and went back to what she'd been talking about, leaving her fingers clasped with his.

Silas looked over and one eyebrow rose briefly. He'd hear more about it when he and Silas were alone, Miles was sure.

Ten minutes later they were being invited inside.

"So you said Jeff and Malorie like you meant random people with those names and not actually Jeff Speck and Malorie Priya," Harlow told him after introductions had been made and they'd gone into the back of the house where the sliders were open to the night beyond. There was a pool that had been artfully lit and a comfortable common area just beyond.

"He's just Jeff to me," Miles said of his friend who currently dominated that part of country music that mingled with rock and roll. He sang rough edged songs about booze and sex and until Malorie had come along, he'd been plenty happy to live those songs out. But the equally powerful and successful photographer had changed Jeff's life, though not his songs. He knew his strengths just like any other artist who wanted to continue to do what they loved.

There was a huge amount of food and ice-cold beer to go with it. Music started up in the background as the ebb and flow of people began and he settled in to catch up with some old friends he didn't see often enough.

He couldn't always sight Harlow, but he heard her laugh or caught the sound of her voice and that was enough. Until it wasn't. Until he'd been off in a corner with Jeff and Silas and he'd just *missed* her enough to want to seek her out.

Miles found her outside, sitting at the edge of the pool, jeans rolled up, feet in the water. Her back was propped against the wall of the hot tub and her gaze looked out over the valley below.

"Hey," he said quietly, not wanting break the late night

quiet, the hum of the gathering inside was in the background.

She turned slightly, smiling when they locked gazes. "Hey there. Come cool your toes. It's a warm night." Harlow patted the place next to her and he eagerly took her invitation, letting his hip brush hers as he rolled his pants up and joined her.

"Doing okay? We'll probably be leaving soon. I'm sure you're tired." He found himself thinking about her comfort frequently.

She lifted a shoulder. "It's nice out here. Smells good. I'm surrounded by people but also just steps away I can be by myself."

"I should have come to look for you sooner."

"I've only been alone for like five minutes. Nora was out here with Malorie. They just went inside before you came out here. Plus someone named Tim chatted me up."

Miles sent her a sidelong glance. "Chatted you up?"

"He was nice. Flirty. Offered to show me around tomorrow."

"Are you messing with me?"

She tipped her head back on a laugh that caressed his skin. "Are you surprised?"

"No. You're gorgeous and you smell good and people like being around you."

"That and you've been chatted up more than once that I've seen," she teased.

"Regardless, I know for a fact you didn't see *any* chatting back." It made him grumpy that anyone would hit on her when she was so obviously meant to be there with him.

"That's because you have very good taste, Miles."

He certainly did. After some painful lessons, but there she was, a reward for coming through it and out the other side. "And are you going sightseeing tomorrow?"

"I told him I was interested in someone else. He still offered to take us on a hike if we wanted though. I thanked him but said we had other plans."

Oh. Well, that was a good thing.

"Good idea. Tell me something else about yourself. You said you always wanted to make music. But how did you get from there to here?" Miles asked.

"I started doing session work while I was still in high school. Lots of kids there had gigs in the entertainment industry. You went to an arts-based school too, right?"

They'd shared that in common as well. "Yes. Plenty of kids, especially in my junior and senior years had outside gigs in local or even national theater programming. I was able to get credit when I went on the road with my dad. That was pretty sweet."

"Okay so you get that part. I began to make a career for myself. Build my professional reputation apart from being Richie Martin's kid. I have my own talent," she told him, sounding a little defensive.

Maybe more than a little. It sounded very much like she was speaking from a place of painful experience.

"No argument from me. I come from a whole fucking family of talented musicians and artists. I know what it feels like to need to prove you're succeeding in your own right. And I know firsthand how talented you are. It's why you're on our tour."

He wanted to lay her down on the grass just beyond and kiss her under the stars. He wanted her in *so many ways*. It was so reckless but there it was. He wasn't going to wait. If he were to admit it, he hadn't really considered it. The only thing that would stop him from pursuing her at that point was her telling him to stop.

He cocked his head and quirked up the corner of his mouth. God. His mouth. He was just so much. Dark brown hair, longer on top. Thick with caramel highlights in the sunshine, she'd learned the week before. His eyes were green like his father's, but more hazel. They shone in the lights strung all around the trees and gave him the type of filter effect people on social media would scramble for.

Harlow then tried to pass off a raw truth as a joke, "I might be a little sensitive on the subject of my success and ambition." She flapped a hand. The one he'd been holding.

And he...he took it back, drawing it to him and kissing her knuckles and then her wrist before letting it go. She held it there, stunned for moments. He watched, carefully, assessing. Making sure she was okay with the direction their interactions seemed to be taking.

He took her hand back, again, this time tucking it between his.

"It's okay to be sensitive about something that's important to you. I get it. I can tell you all day just how talented you are, but it's more about here," he tapped his chest, over his heart with his free hand, "than here." He pointed to his brain. Tell me more about you," he said quietly.

Behind them, sounds of happy people filtered from the house. Laughter, singing, music. It was a pleasant, comfortable sound and an excellent part of an excellent night.

Harlow cleared her throat. "After high school my dad had begun to be very serious about the woman he'd been seeing, Jenna. I stayed back in California when he toured by that point. Continued session work and then I sold a song. Little bits and pieces that helped me build some savings so I could move out when Jenna and my dad got married."

"Wow. How did you feel about that?" he asked.

"It wasn't like I was ten. I was twenty years old, and I needed to move out and start my life." Her dad had been struck stupid with love and he deserved to have that time with Jenna.

"Nora and Brian and I decided to rent together because we could cover the rent on a nice enough place near the studios Brian and I were working at. He was getting solid engineering gigs. Nora worked at a law firm. We jammed regularly, but it was informal garage practice type stuff. Brian's aunt has a really swank recording studio and she let us use it when it was open. But she used to sneak in and listen to us. Before long, she started to give us tips. Taught us things. Helped us learn how to write our songs together. She encouraged us to book some gigs. And we did. It took a while and more than one garage or backyard party. But I didn't want to tell my dad until we had a real show booked at an actual venue."

He smiled and nodded. "You wanted to know you did it on your talent and not who your dad was," he said, telling her that he'd listened to what she'd said earlier.

"Yeah, that." She shrugged. "Not that I haven't taken his help plenty. It's a great thing to have, don't get me wrong. But when I called to tell him we were playing a show and that we'd been rehearsing and writing our own music for months, he could have been hurt or annoyed I hadn't said anything. Instead, he said, *right on, Punky*. He's a good dad, you know? We've played way better places since, and a few worse, but that was the start. My dad passed our music on to Jeremy's agency and we signed with them. We recorded an EP. It did well enough that we were able to keep going. We decided to move up to Seattle after I booked a bunch of studio work there and realized we could thrive. Music scene is great as you know. At first Brian and I worked plenty of studio jobs to pay the bills so we could make music and play gigs on every break we got. About a year ago we began to put together material for a full length release and when we were ready, my dad's studio had been remodeled—I suspect for us to use—and he offered it along with his rehearsal space and pool house. It was a whole family affair, I shit you not. But what we ended up with was good. The best thing we'd ever done by far and we didn't have to go into a thousand years' debt to the label. Jeremy has worked with enough small bands trying to break that he's got a lot of great ideas. The label already wants more from us, but Jeremy is using the tour as a way to get us a better deal. So thanks for that. And for listening to my very long and convoluted story about how I decided to start a band with my art school best friends."

"I like knowing things about you," he said softly.

"Even if I never get to the point in a straight line?"

His smile made him even more attractive. Mainly because it was just for her.

"I like how you meander. You got there eventually."

This was the oddest sexually charged conversation she'd ever had.

"God damn, you're so fucking beautiful," he said, and she

nearly gasped with the unexpected pleasure of his words. Words she couldn't un-hear. Her reaction something she wasn't willing to forego a repeat of. Harlow let herself want him fully, damn the consequences.

"You should kiss me," she said, all in. A real kiss. More than the sweet brush of lips he'd given her. She wanted heat. Craved his taste.

He moved ever so slightly and on a sweet exhale, his mouth brushed against hers and lit her system up.

Her lips opened as he moved to make another pass and his taste seemed to slide into her like smoke.

He slid his hand over her bare shoulder and around the back of her neck, holding as he deepened the contact, his tongue stroking hers, making her think of other things he could do with his mouth.

She had to squeeze her thighs together against the throb of her clit in time with her pulse as she turned enough to get her hands on his shoulders and then around his neck.

He sucked her bottom lip, grazing it with his teeth as he did, sending a shiver through her. Her skin tingled, hyper aware of him. Attuned to his presence and awaiting his attention.

The absolute mindless pleasure that washed over her as he kissed her like the world was going to end swamped her, left her nearly boneless in his arms.

Inside the house someone called his name, and he tore his mouth away on a curse.

Harlow blinked several times, coming back to herself and the realization that they were at a party full of people making out by the pool like teenagers.

Miles had to clear his throat. "Out here," he called out. To her he said, "We'll continue this soon." He stole another kiss and then stood as he had to shift a little to move his dick. His hard dick with a piercing. "You taste better than I imagined. And I've imagined a lot."

Glad it was dark enough to hide her blush, she took his offered hand and stood, heading back into the house.

CHAPTER
SEVEN

"So you gonna share what happened between you and Miles last night or nah?" Nora asked as they ate their lunch by the hotel pool, lounging just out of the direct sunshine. "I think we can agree that I have demonstrated a great deal of self-control not making you tell me before now."

"When I look up self-control in the dictionary, your photo is right there," Harlow teased and then looked around carefully to be sure they weren't overheard. There was a small, fan club only show for Earthquakes that night so Nora and Harlow had done their yoga and then headed out to the pool to enjoy a day off. Brian drove out to look at natural wonder type shit and hike a nearby canyon.

Harlow admitted, "He kissed me. Like a real kiss with tongue and teeth. He's really good with his mouth."

"God. You're never going to get rid of a guy who's good with his mouth," Nora said. "Neither would I." She waggled her brows and Harlow snickered.

Brian would pass out from embarrassment if he was part of their conversation.

"I thought he was going to pin you to his chest like a medal or a blue ribbon," Nora said with a smirk.

"Miles? What? Why would you think that?"

"You two were gone for at least forty-five minutes and when you came in Miles was all puffy chested and proud you were at his side. I mean, obviously he should have been. But it was very much clear he'd made some sort of claim and as your lips were swollen and your lipstick was gone, I figured you were okay with that."

"I made out with him under the stars on a warm summer night. Honestly, I started writing a song about it when his tongue was still in my mouth," Harlow confessed.

"Excellent! You slutty multitasker. I love it. You don't seem guilt ridden about it. Good."

"It was kisses. Not a marriage proposal. We're fine as long as no one makes a big deal of it."

Nora rolled her eyes. "Harlow, eventually someone will make a big deal of it. You and I both know it. But what's important is what *you* think. And what he thinks. So, when the inevitable comes and some dishrag of a person pops up in the comments with some nonsense about you riding that dick into the sunset for whatever he gives you, I will kick you in the face if you let yourself believe it for more than one second."

"Tough love?"

"Listen, I gave you a second to feel bad, didn't I? But that's all it merits." Nora's glare her way told Harlow her friend was serious.

Harlow wasn't about to argue because Nora was right. "Anyway. It was nice. He's a great kisser and he definitely listened to all my signals to be sure I was still on board with everything. He's a lot, but he understands consent. Sexy as fuck." Harlow fanned herself. Because Miles was sexy, but also because it was a thousand fucking degrees.

"It's a good thing Brian is amazing in so many other ways because this outdoors hiking shit under the nuclear sun is weird. I love him, so I'll sit here in the shade and judge him behind his back," Nora said.

Harlow laughed. "I love that you made him promise to come to the pool when we got back."

"He loves the heat and he loves the outdoors. Again, he's amazing in so many other ways and he never makes me go hiking with him. So he can go hiking and nerd it up with his D&D and all that as long as he doesn't expect it of me, which he does not."

"That's love."

"It is." Nora nodded. "I'm very lucky I found him so early in my life. If I had to use dating aps I'd die alone."

Harlow felt that to her toes.

Miles looked at the text Harlow had just sent with a smile and then regret that he wasn't there. She and Nora were in the pool while someone else—Brian he hoped because Harlow was in a bikini and looked delicious—had taken the picture.

Swimming then dinner. Hope tonight's show is amazing.

He took a selfie, angling the shot so she could see the

intimate stage set up behind him. *Looking beautiful. Wish I was there with you. See you tonight after the show?*

Miles wasn't used to this uncertainty with a romantic entanglement. Normally he just saw what he wanted and went for it. Which, he could admit, was what he was doing anyway, but with Harlow he wanted her to be feeling this uncertainty too. What he felt was so intense it left him off balance and vulnerable.

Text when you're done so I can be awake. Say hey to everyone and that we wished you all good luck tonight.

I will. If it's too late, I'll see you in the morning for the trip to Vegas.

I'll be awake.

Pleasure rolled through him at her words. At the way she'd accepted his need to see her, he hoped because she felt the same.

"Harlow says hello and have a good show," he told the other bandmembers.

"Why didn't you invite them tonight?" Silas asked from the stage where he'd been working with his guitar tech. His friend had known him long enough to assume everything Miles did was his business too. And it was a good assumption because Silas was very much like a brother.

"I did. She told me it was good for us to be all about the fans and if she was here she'd just be a distraction or in the way."

Silas paused and then nodded. "I like that."

"So, this is an official thing now?" Omar asked. "Not even going to wait until after their dates on the tour are done? You're not usually so...reckless."

Maddie gave him a measuring look but kept working.

Reckless? At times it did feel reckless. He knew Omar wasn't using the word in a pejorative sense. But Miles, especially after his last relationship had died, tended to be more careful.

That had been two years and a tour ago and he'd learned a lot about himself and self-control in the time since. Mostly the hard way, and chances were, he'd have scars for the rest of his life. But pain was instructional sometimes, and in the case of him and whatsherface, he had to touch that hot stove to learn his lesson.

But Harlow wasn't an unstable fame-hungry monster wearing a pretty face. She was something else. Something he'd never experienced before. Something he wanted more of so much his skin itched.

Something so far away from what it was with anyone before he popped up into her life, he could do nothing but pursue it. Because this was lightning in a bottle. A unique combo he knew to his toes was special. And, perhaps, fate.

This recklessness was in him not waiting. Like he should. Omar hadn't been the first to bring it up, Maddie had too. And they were right to call him out. But anyone who knew him as well as they did would see the difference.

"Just, she's maybe not at the Miles Brown level of involvement. Don't break her," Omar added.

It was his baby sister who came to his rescue. Poppy turned to glare in Omar's direction. "I like her. *And* Miles isn't a dickbag. He's not going to use his power to sex up some helpless person and then walk away."

Omar's hands went up immediately. "Obviously I trust and respect Miles, and don't think he'd take advantage of Harlow to get laid. I like her too. I promise! It's just we're all together for the next eight weeks. What if it goes horribly wrong? We all remember whatsherface," Omar said.

Miles snickered at Omar's continued refusal to use his ex's name. "She wasn't on tour with us. She's not anything like Harlow. And she wanted to cause drama so she could get clicks. Harlow has a job she seems to do really well. Without my influence or involvement. The Miles and Harlow deal is on equal ground." Which had turned out to be more important than he'd realized until it was happening, and his soul was happy about it.

"We don't need to worry about Miles breaking Harlow. Sophie broke you," Maddie said softly. "Sophie took something private and turned a spotlight on it. She took your trust and she hurt your family and friends as well as you. You felt responsible for that."

"She didn't break me permanently. Just for a while. Maybe to get me ready for Harlow." Miles paused as he realized maybe that part wasn't a joke after all. "As for what Sophie did and how it blew up all over my family and friends? It's my fault. I *am* responsible for it."

Omar made a rude noise, and a drumstick sailed his way that Miles was barely able to avoid. "How the fuck are you responsible for what she did? That's totally on her and I'm not going to let you wallow in something you didn't do. When you fuck up, I'll say so. You drank too much with her. You did too many drugs. You forgot yourself for a while. I assume the sex was fantastic."

"Why didn't you all say something then?" Miles demanded.

"Ha!" Silas shouted. "Fuck off. You weren't up for hearing anything anyone had to say about her. So, we called you out when you showed up to work high. We called you out when you invited her fucked-up friends to stuff. But you had to find your own way out of your relationship with her. The Miles you were at that time wouldn't have heard a damned thing we said."

"I'm sorry."

"You apologized back then. There's no need for you to keep doing it. Who among us has not fucked with some folks we shouldn't have? And found out?" Maddie snickered. "All of this is just us making sure you're thinking about outcomes with Harlow that might affect the tour. We like her and we love you."

"All right. I did think about waiting. And then I kissed her the first time and now I want more. Not just the sexy stuff, but I want to know her better. I promise you all I'm doing my best to think about how this might impact every-thing so I'm stepping carefully."

At his side, Poppy huffed a quiet breath of impatience and he loved her for it even more. Still, his friends were being his friends. Keeping an eye on him and speaking up when they were concerned. Which, given what they'd just said about why they didn't call him out over Sophie, meant they trusted him more than they did then.

Shame washed through him. No matter that they'd all told him he wasn't responsible, nor did they hold him so. The way Sophie had exposed their private life to the world, the way she'd taken the small things she knew about his family and had used that to raise her own profile, not caring about the wreckage it might have left was enough for him to finally let the dying gasp of their relationship go.

Still, she'd been allowed access into his inner life and

he'd trusted the wrong person. And he hadn't been the only one to be punished for that mistake.

"Folks are queued up outside if everyone is ready," Poppy called out after she squeezed his shoulder briefly.

They headed backstage and at his back, Miles heard the beginning of what would be a packed show at an intimate venue. He could see faces and interact more. The pressure still there, but different because these were their most active fans. Many had been with them since the very first few months of their fan club. Miles and the rest of the band wanted to give their all to these people who'd been supporting them since the start.

And afterward, he'd seek Harlow out even if just to say good night in person.

She got his text at nearly midnight. Harlow was still awake and waiting and at the buzz of her phone, happiness rolled through her.

Are you around?

She typed back, *Yep.*

I know you're sharing a room with Brian and Nora and I don't want to disturb them. Would you be weirded out if I asked you up to my room?

No. But I'm not fucking you tonight. Frowning, Harlow deleted that last bit. Though it was true, and she was for sure not going to do the sexytimes with him that night, it seemed a bit presumptuous.

She settled on, *No.*

I'm in 2401.

Be there soon.

Brian was still up reading so Harlow told him she was going out but would be back shortly.

"What's his room number so we know where to look if we're worried?" he asked her quietly.

"I'm just going up there to say hello and probably let him kiss me a lot. I'll be back soon. We have an early day tomorrow."

"You don't need to explain yourself to me, Harlow," Brian said with a smile. "I like this guy and the way you're responding to him. It never hurts to be safe. We love you and want that for you."

"Aw. You're awesome and I love you too. He's in 2401. Nora has Poppy's number so you can text her if you need anything. She's right next door to him." Harlow hugged him quick before heading out.

Miles waited at the elevator, leaning against a nearby wall and looking like a GD snack.

"How'd the show go?" she asked him.

He took her hand and they walked to his room. Suite.

Harlow spun to take it all in. "Very nice."

He blushed. "Some of the rooms we're in on this tour are pretty luxurious, I can't lie. The promoter has some deal with a few different hotels. Anyway. Hi."

Suddenly shy, Harlow looked up into his face as he stepped closer, pausing just short of contact.

"The show went great. We don't play in small venues very often anymore, but I do love it when we can. Especially a fan club gig. When I can see the audience better you know what I noticed?"

She shook her head.

"I kept looking for all that gorgeous dark hair and glitter

and couldn't find it. Even though I knew you weren't there, I kept seeking you out."

Her heart pounded hard enough to hear it in her breath.

"And then once we came offstage, all I could think about was getting back here to see you even if it was for just a few minutes."

He reached up to cup her cheek briefly.

"I'm kind of all about you, Harlow. That going to be okay?" he asked. "Not just for a quick kiss in the dark by a pool. I want more."

She waved a hand back and forth between them. "This is a bad idea while on tour." There. She'd said it and now could ignore it, or he'd listen and decide she was right and that would suck.

He laughed and then leaned in closer. "Yeah, well. I like to think it's actually a great idea. Unexpected. But then again, this thing between us is unexpected. I like that. Anyway, I don't always do what I'm supposed to. Not when I want something. Or someone."

A full body shiver slid over her skin at the way his voice went silky at the end.

"But." He reached out and caught the curl that had escaped from her braid and tucked it back. "Never if they don't want to be caught. It's no fun if everyone isn't interested."

Harlow licked her lips as she tried to think logically but realized there was no logic to this chemistry between them. Christ. She bet he knew lots of fun things to do while naked. And she couldn't really find the energy to push it away. Because she wanted him too. Timing could have been better, but sometimes, hell, most of the time, the best things came when you weren't expecting them. And having fun in a carnal way with this gorgeous man standing in her line of sight wasn't something she wanted to pass up. Reckless definitely. Delightful? She had a very strong feeling based on a handful of kisses and caresses that was a yes.

"I can't work up any arguments as to why it would be a problem to have you be all about me. I mean, I can make up a lot because it's silly and we both know it." She grinned at him. "None of them matter really because I'm in. I'm all about you too."

In a breath, he had leaned in and the scent of him rolled over her senses. Corduroy and sunshine and sex.

Her heart raced as she tipped her face up slightly to meet his kiss. The other kisses they'd shared had been nice, but this was something else entirely. This was decisive and full of barely leashed sexual power.

He banded an arm around her waist and slid his palm over her throat until he cupped the back of her neck as he continued to devastate her senses with lips and tongue and the bite of the edge of his teeth over her bottom lip.

He smelled great, but he tasted even better, and she warmed from her belly outward, softening into his hold.

Harlow was tall, over 5'8, but he topped out at about six one or two, so he still managed to make her feel powerful and petite all at once. He held her like she was precious, but it wasn't overly gentle. More like he…like he was pleased to have her there against him. Pleased with her body and the feel of her. Not using his size or strength for anything but pleasure.

They stood in the living room part of the suite, wrapped

around one another, tasting, kissing, and caressing until she was nearly boneless.

In the back of her mind, she knew if they took two steps they'd be at the couch and then...well then there'd be naked stuff and it was way too late to stop this thing between them, but also too late at night or early in the morning after she'd just decided to take this leap and she needed to rest and get herself together before sex.

It would happen. Very soon.

He broke the kiss, chest heaving. "It's after one. We've got a drive to Vegas in the morning. I'm going to walk you back to your room before I ask you to come into my bedroom."

Harlow found her voice as she put a hand on his chest. "I'll go on my own. You don't need to walk me."

"I'm not tossing you out at one twenty in the morning after having my mouth all over yours and making you walk alone to your room."

She put a hand on his arm a moment. "You're right. This isn't tossing me out. I need to sleep. You need to sleep. We'll see each other in like nine hours. What we don't need are any spectators to Miles Brown walking me to my hotel room at this hour."

He frowned and she knew he was going to be a handful.

Heh. More than a handful if that pressure against her belly from his cock was any indicator.

"I'll text you when I get in the room. So you know I got back okay." She went to her toes as she grabbed two fistfuls of his hair and pulled him down for a quick kiss. "See you later, bossy. Thanks for the kisses."

She let him walk her to the elevator because there was no

stopping him and he pointed out that the only rooms they passed by were Poppy and Maddie's so who was going to see and tattle? Back in her own room, shared with Nora and Brian and it still felt...lonely. Shoving that away, she quickly changed into pajamas and got into bed, knowing her dreams would be full of Miles.

CHAPTER
EIGHT

"Time to go," Phil, their tour manager called out.

There was something about the moment in between things that had always held a fascination for Harlow. And at that moment as they walked toward the stairs leading up to the stage, with the sound of the crowd just a few feet away, the stickysweetness of weed, kettle corn and beer hung in the air, it felt like a rock and roll fairytale.

Nausea, always present before she walked out onto any stage, was a metallic weight in her gut that Harlow swallowed past, breathing through her nose and out through her mouth. It would pass as the adrenaline and dopamine took over and she let herself just experience the utter surreality of what was happening.

At the base of the steps, they turned toward one another, touching foreheads and then they broke, Nora going up first, then Brian, their music calling her. And at the top of the steps, she turned and caught sight of Miles as he rounded a corner.

They'd had a fun drive from Salt Lake City and then had lunch together with everyone when they'd arrived. Things had subtly shifted from even the day before and there was a rhythm between Miles and Harlow that felt very much like a relationship.

He smiled when he saw her, so open and pleased. She gave him the devil horns and turned, taking her guitar as she stepped into the spotlight and began to sing.

He tipped his chin at her as they came offstage and then took up at her side. "You all sounded fantastic," he told them and meant it. Holy fuck, Harlow was just so utterly herself, confident, aggressive, every time she flirted and charmed and snarled her way across a stage had blown his mind.

Never in his life had he wanted to kiss someone more than he did right then. Obviously that wasn't going to happen as they were in a crowded hallway, but he'd definitely take that jangled, anxious uncertainty and use it on stage when they went on.

It felt *good* to be in that place with her. Sweet and sexy as hell.

"Afterparty tonight. You'll be there, right?" he asked.

"Yes, definitely. Thanks for the invite."

Nora and Brian headed straight into their dressing room, but Miles hung back in the hall with Harlow. He needed to get moving soon. Earthquakes would be starting their set within the hour.

But he wanted a little more time with her first. "I want you to save me some attention and time at the party tonight," he said softly.

"It's not hard to give you attention, Miles." Her mouth curved up into a smile.

"That's what I like to hear. I'll be sure to be worthy of that opinion," he told her.

Someone called his name a few times and he leaned close enough to be awash in her body heat but not close enough to kiss. "Gotta go."

"Break a leg," she told him. "See you out there."

The kisses in his room the night before had fully awakened something within him. An awareness of the depth of his greed for her and an acceptance of that.

He may as well enjoy it and fold it into his music.

After two encores he and the others stumbled off stage and down the stairs. Sweaty, amped up with adrenaline and that sexual charge he only found right after a performance, he looked around the area but didn't see Harlow anywhere though he had watched her on and off all show long out in the audience.

"They went back to the hotel to clean up," Poppy told him as she caught up. "I've got the van already waiting so once you and the others are ready, we'll go."

He gave her a questioning look.

"She's fine."

"Thanks," he told her.

"I said I'd be useful on this tour, and I think we can agree I've already been that and more."

"You're right. You're doing a great job." He slung an arm around her shoulders and hugged her to his side as she tried to push him away.

"You're sweaty and gross! Ew."

"Felt good out there tonight."

He nodded at the people who'd found ways to line the hall leading to their dressing rooms. Most he recognized as crew but there were others there, he knew searching for a good time to be had with a famous person.

He wanted a good time too. So he'd get himself cleaned up and head over to the bar they were holding their after-party at and find a way to get himself alone with Harlow.

At the party things were already in full swing and he was swallowed up by well-wishers, a drink put in his hand and refreshed each time he emptied it.

Music—thankfully not theirs because it would have felt masturbatory—pumped out of speakers. Local musicians filled the room, and he didn't fail to notice the way Harlow always seemed to be surrounded by people trying to get her attention.

But this was part of the business and Above Me could use all the connections they could get. Those connections were what often helped a band get to the next level. It didn't hurt that she was tall, drop dead beautiful, and projected a confidence nearly as sexy as the rest of her. But she was charming too. Had an ease with people.

He liked the way Brian and Nora stood with her, each contributing to the whole. Harlow wasn't going to be the type who'd abandon them if she got a better opportunity, and the comfort they had with one another was a sign they all knew it. And wanted onlookers to know it too.

She tipped her head back, laughing and Miles felt the tug in his gut at the sight.

"Easy there," Maddie said quietly. "The whole room is going to see the way you look at her."

Poppy snorted.

He shrugged. "Not a problem. Who'd be embarrassed to look at her this way?"

Maddie rolled her eyes. "It's cute that you conveniently forget *she's* got to prove she's more than the pretty face and the famous dad. For someone who has the same struggles, that's sort of ridiculous coming from you."

Oh. Yeah.

Miles sighed. "Okay, you have a point. But I don't want to hide it like she's a secret or something to be embarrassed about."

"Fair. And I'd have thrown my drink in your face if you were embarrassed because she's, well, she's above your weight class."

That made him laugh. "I thought you were wary about me starting anything with her while on tour."

"You're an artist, she's an artist. Lots of passion between and around you. I just don't want to see either of you get hurt. This business can be hard on your heart. That's all," Maddie told him.

"If this is about Sophie, I already told you, this is different," he said of his ex.

"Well sure. Anyone who knows you understands that. I was there during the whole thing, remember. I said today that you were acting reckless, but with Sophie you weren't reckless. You were out of control."

That was actually a really good distinction.

Maddie continued as they both watched the room, "The crash with you and whatserface was inevitable. And it was also inevitable she was going to blow it out of proportion and use it to build her own social media base. She never lied about what she was."

"I hate that none of you told me how you felt about her," Miles said.

"Fuck off, Miles. I could have told you in detail and you'd have continued to put your dick in her and do too many drugs and drink yourself into a stupor. It's the path you chose for a while. Put it on like a coat until you realized it didn't fit. My dad was the same. Lots of pretty boy musicians are. You grew up."

Maddie's father, Vaughan Hurley, had been quite the pretty boy rockstar in his day and had ended up divorced and alone for several years until he'd finally gotten over himself and put in the work to win his family back.

And Miles's father, too, had been one of those pretty boy rockstars, though he'd generally been able to keep himself under control with the help of Miles's aunt Erin and his uncle Brody. The Browns were tight. United. But they wouldn't hesitate to call one another out.

Maddie said, "So we waited until the thing between you and whatsherface burned down and were there when you needed us to kick your butt into shape. Harlow is a different thing entirely. She's a real deal, could be *the one* type of person. You gotta earn that. Get to know her. Learn her, and won't it be wonderful if it works out past the tour and you two end up together? Try not to forget that people like to take pictures of you because you're Miles Brown, rock and roll royalty. And Harlow Martin is a similar version of that.

The two of you together will sell laundry detergent and pizza pockets for any gossip site. But she's going to get twice the scrutiny you do because that's how it goes when you're a woman in this industry so don't make being with you harder than being without you is."

She was really smart. "Thanks for saying stuff even when it's not comfortable and I take it wrong."

"That's what family does. Like right now I see Omar flirting really hard with that dude near the dessert table. He's married and I doubt O knows it or he wouldn't be flirting. So, I'm just going to cruise over to say hello. Do the same to Harlow, why don't you?"

He hugged her to his side, kissing the top of her head. "Okay. Night, Maddie."

She headed toward Omar and he shifted his attention back to where she'd been standing but she wasn't there any longer and neither were Nora and Brian.

Miles tried to look nonchalant as he scanned the room but didn't find her. He texted asking if she was still at the party.

I'm about to leave. Nora and Brian are walking me to the car. I'll see you tomorrow. You were great tonight.

He texted one word as he headed out the back door. *Wait.*

CHAPTER
NINE

“ have to have you,” he mumbled while dropping hot kisses to her cheek, temple and down her neck.

Harlow made an inarticulate sound, a moan, an entreaty for more, agreement that she wanted him to have her as well. There weren't words for it all and they didn't need them anyway.

Their hands said it. His mouth on her skin said it. The way he hesitated here and there to give her a chance to stop, to be sure she was still with him was searingly hot. The whole thing between them felt so out of control, all action driven by desire and an intense need to connect. But each time he hesitated she knew it took his control. He did it on purpose because it mattered to him that she was there, pinned against the wall by his body, as enthusiastically as he was.

At her back, he managed, one handed, to get the keycard pressed to the right part of the door and it opened, sending them tumbling into the foyer. He saved them from crashing to the marble floor and spun her, still holding her waist, his mouth finding hers.

Stealing her breath.

She grabbed the hem of his shirt and yanked it up, only breaking the kiss when she had to get it over his head.

Even wanting him so much her pulse beat in her eardrums wasn't enough to forego the slow examination of his upper body. Wide shoulders she already knew about. But all the ink she'd uncovered was striking and sexy.

A long lick over the head of the dragon coiled up over his chest made them both gasp. Black and gray in what appeared to be a Celtic design. She'd ask about the ink later when the blood flow was back to her brain instead of her nipples and clit.

He hadn't done anything to the hair on his chest—her last lover had his waxed regularly—or the line leading from his belly button down into the waist of his jeans. She traced a circle around his navel and then followed that downy soft arrow south to the waistband and stopped. Teasing. Delighting in the intake of breath in response.

"Now you," he said, flicking open the top two buttons of her blouse.

"God yes, now me," she echoed with a solemn nod.

He laughed and bent his head to lick over the curve of breast swelled above the line of her bra and it was her turn to suck in a breath at the heat of it.

"So glad I wore the pretty bra for the party instead of the grungy super comfortable one," she said as he artfully and quickly popped the last three buttons and the material slid to her sides, exposing her upper body.

"Better than I imagined." He traced over the visible lines

of the clematis tattoo from her side leaving goosepimples in his wake. "You'll tell me about this. After."

"After."

He indicated she stay where she was while he put the do not disturb hanger on the door and locked everything up tight. "I'd go to jail if someone came in to disturb us and I had to punch them for it."

Miles stalked back toward her, the pale light from a single lamp in the main living area drew him in shadows and angles as she held her breath, watching.

One corner of his mouth slid up very slowly and she couldn't wait to find out if he had that sort of muscle discipline with other things he did with his mouth.

She had to squeeze her thighs together to ease the ache.

"You okay?" he asked her, drawing her close.

Beyond words she nodded and to underline it, she dragged the edge of her nails up his sides, over his ribs until he groaned.

Miles wasn't entirely sure anything in his life had ever felt so intense. In his arms she was a barely leashed fire. The heat of her skin seemed to blast over his body. Her scent, the shampoo she used, he thought, the earthy perfume she wore, and the spice of her desire rose and tightened all around him, pulling him in and snagging all his focus.

He glanced at the couch in the living room. Just that afternoon he'd caught sight of the arm and wondered if it would be a good height to bend her over and take her from behind.

But what he craved right then was to spread her out over

the bed and touch every part of her. Explore what made her toes curl.

"Are you thirsty?" he asked as he stepped far enough to take her hand and pull her toward the adjoining bedroom.

"That's the most random question," she said, following along.

"I don't want you to get dehydrated. I need you to keep your strength up."

"Well. Put that way. I should drink something."

She looked around the room when he let go of her hand and moved to the mini fridge to get some water for her, and by the time he'd turned around, her shirt was off and her hands were at the buttons of her pants. "Multi-tasking," she said and made him snort.

"Whatever you want to call it, I'm game." He handed her a glass of water and she drank it down in several deep gulps before handing it back.

"Are *you* thirsty? Because I'm about to wring you dry."

Surprised delight hit him, snagged between amusement and desire. But he drank water because he hoped she was serious.

And as he did, she shimmied from her pants, exposing more skin and ink.

"You're going to need to catch up or I'll be forced to have fun all alone," she said.

He was out of his jeans and boxers in record time, and he really dug that they both laughed as they went. He liked it even more that she turned another lamp on as she munched the chocolate she'd stolen off his pillow.

The long line of her throat called to him, and he gave in, drawing his mouth and fingertips over the delicate skin there. All while he petted down her shoulder, to her elbow which he held to steer her back to the bed.

When she tipped back and fell to the mattress, he stole long moments to simply take her in. Long, strong legs, bright blue toenails that matched her fingernails. And when he slid her boyshort style underpants down she made a sound that shot straight up his spine.

Her bra was one of the ones that closed in the front. He liked that. Liked even more that the little clasp was a heart. Her tits, freed of the bra were so pretty. He didn't have a favorite kind of breast. He liked them all. But hers were a pair he'd be happy to be able to see as often as he could.

"Pierced," he said softly as he reached out and gave the pretty bar running through her right nipple a twist to one side and then the other.

That worked given the arch of her back and the gasp of pleasure it evoked.

When she lifted herself enough to grab his cock at the root and slid her fist up and over the head. "Pierced."

He grinned. "Glad you like."

"Well, I mean." She squeezed gently for emphasis. "You've got the raw material to get the job done. The Prince Albert is just a delightful surprise. I've never checked out that particular dick from the library before."

How he could snort laugh while being ridiculously turned on he didn't know. But he dug it.

"I hope it'll be your favorite dick ever," he teased, but he meant it too.

"We'll have to take it for a test drive just to see."

He knelt over her body because he needed to kiss her

again. Needed to kiss and kiss and kiss her until she craved him as much as he craved her.

What was it about the way he cupped her throat, gentle but firm at the same time? It sent desire racing through her system. Well, *more* desire because she was already lightheaded from all the blood in her body settling between her thighs.

As she'd thought, a naked Miles Brown was...well, quite a sight. One she'd probably not forget. She hoped.

He looked at her like...like he'd never seen anything he wanted more. She didn't know what to do with it other than like it a lot. She'd think about the rest of it later.

Right then she had a gorgeous, naked man with a pierced dick, and she was all about it.

He kissed her like there was nothing more to be done on a Thursday night. Like the way she tasted was something he *had* to have.

She'd had partners who were hot for her before. Always a pleasure. But this was deeper and pushed all her buttons.

There was no tour, no band, nothing but Harlow and Miles and wow, how about that?

All other thoughts flew from her head when his mouth skated to her nipple, the pierced one. He didn't hesitate to play with the bar, tugging it sending sparks of white-hot pleasure against her closed eyelids.

She dug her nails into his sides, just above his hips and he groaned against her skin. A real-life pulse hit her pussy. He was a sex wizard, obviously. She might have popped her pussy a time or two, but pulsing? Only in her favorite books.

And now a dear diary moment. Score.

He settled against her, body to body and they both stilled as that skin-to-skin contact soaked into their bones.

"Christ," he mumbled as he kissed over to her other breast and down her ribs, licking and nibbling until she was shivery and witless. "You taste so fucking good."

Which he then proved by settling between her thighs and taking a long, slow lick of her pussy.

He hummed, a sound full of relish and it made her feel gorgeous. Harlow refused to close her eyes, not before she looked down her body at the sight of Miles, head bent over her like a penitent seeking benevolence.

His dark hair tousled from her fingers was soft against her inner thighs. The lines of the tattoo leading down his right arm seemed to pop where he cradled her hip and held her in place, her skin a pale backdrop.

Miles turned his head and nipped where her thigh met her body. It was so unexpectedly hot she shuddered, arching into his hold.

He lifted his head and locked his gaze to hers. "Hm. Liked that, did we?"

She nodded probably longer than she should have, but she *really* liked it.

"Let's see what else you like then, hm?" he said as he spread her open fully and began to devour her with licks, nuzzles and a few nips of his teeth in the right places.

As much as she wanted to come, he drew it out, pulling her to the very edge and pausing until she was just about to reach down and finish things herself. That's when he gave her one last look and then turned all that focus on her clit, circling it with the tip of his tongue with just the right amount of pressure and orgasm broke over her, sucking her down.

Miles had binged on Harlow enough that he was drunk with her. And wanted more. Especially when she managed to sit up a little and push him to his back. When she climbed up and straddled him, he nearly blacked out at how intensely good it was.

Her eyelids dropped to half mast, slumbrous and satiated. She smiled down at him. "That was delightful."

"Glad to have been of service," he choked out when she ground her pussy, so hot and wet against his cock.

Harlow reached up and undid her hair, sending it tumbling around her shoulders, a mass of dark curls.

Miles gave in and buried his hands in it, pulling her down to him for another kiss. He loved her mouth. Her lips, perfectly soft, fit with his like they were meant for him. He already had the taste of her in his system and her soft moan when she realized that made him harder than he already was.

She rocked slightly, sliding herself over the length of his cock, paying special attention to the bead at the top of his piercing, slowly driving him crazy with the intensity.

But when she tried to scoot down as she kissed her way down his throat and over his chest, he stopped her. "I want to be in you."

"I was on the way," she said with one raised brow.

"Don't think I'm complaining about that. Because I'm not. But I meant I want to be in your pussy. Deep."

She pouted, which...fuck, only made him hotter for her.

"Condoms?" she asked. "I assume they're okay with the piercing?"

"Yes, I'll put it on carefully. The ring is smooth so it won't rip. But the condoms are in a bag in the bathroom and I'm laying here beneath a gorgeous woman rubbing her pussy all over me so I'm having trouble with motivation to move."

Her laughter was something he realized he was going to crave when they were apart, and he tightened his grip on her hips.

But not enough to stop her when she rolled away and strolled into the bathroom. "FYI, though I'm sure you know this, this bathroom is the size of my entire hotel room. In this black bag with the red zipper accent on the counter?"

"It has a red zipper?"

She came out holding the bag, laughing. "You didn't notice the red zipper against the black of the bag itself?"

"The gear is a gift from my parents. Luggage and the like for the tour. More about this not-anything-about-me-fucking-you topic after I actually fuck you." He sat up and took the bag from her, unzipping the yes, bright red zipper, and rummaged until he found the square foil he was looking for.

She frowned when he tore it open with his teeth. "That's bad for your teeth."

"I have a dentist. Again, not the topic I want right now," he muttered as he rolled the latex on carefully.

"You're very bossy about topics," she said airily, looking at her fingernails.

He waved his dick at her. "Come on over."

She grinned and scrambled atop him again, grabbing the root of his cock to angle it as she slowly lowered herself.

He exhaled, trying not to wheeze at the tight heat of her

all around his cock. Trying very hard to think about the new strings he'd started using and whether or not it made any real difference in sound or playing.

Better that instead of coming forty-eight seconds after he got inside her.

And then she squeezed her inner muscles around him, and he slammed a fist down into the mattress to fight the sensation.

"Liked that did we?" she said, parroting what he'd said earlier.

Miles considered flipping their positions but then she rose up slightly and slid down his cock three times and he forgot everything but that moment between them.

"What's not to like?" he said with a slight squeak at the end when she pulled up and nearly off and lowered herself again.

The weight of her was just exactly right. They fit, and their rhythm clicked right off as he arched, not wanting to leave her pussy and then she met him and rose and fell again.

The bounty of her breasts was right there for him to see, to touch and with a little stretching, to kiss them as he took their weight in his palms.

It was her turn to arch then, pressing her breasts into his hold and when he took her nipples between his finger and thumbs, her pussy fluttered around him, getting so hot he felt it easily through the latex.

He traced over the lines of her tattoo to her hip and then shifted enough to find her clit and stroke it slowly as she rode his cock.

She drew a shaky breath and exhaled on a soft moan of pleasure.

Because the bedside lamps were on, he could look his fill at her as she rose over him. Her features were blissed out, eyes sleepy with pleasure, mouth slightly open, her hair wild around her shoulders, sliding forward over her collarbone. Making him want to find that very spot and kiss it.

Making him realize he'd remember this moment and follow up to make sure he kissed that spot. More than once.

Fuck. He was a goner for this woman.

In more ways than one. She squeezed her inner walls around his cock until his eyes nearly watered as he tried to hold back his climax.

He sped the lazy circles he'd been making around her clit, and her breath caught. Her gaze—so dreamy—cleared as she locked her attention on his. It was a race to see who came first. And wasn't that fucking awesome?

He knew he had her by a slight edge when her movements became less rhythmic and she tipped her head back.

The lure of her throat was more than he wanted to resist so he cupped it with his palm, gently so as not to harm, but enough that she remembered he was there.

Her orgasm, so hot and wet, rolled through her and tightened around him so much there was nothing to do but let himself go with a snarl, trying to get as deep as he could.

"I'm starving," she said some minutes later after they got their breath back.

He'd pulled her to his side after returning to bed, so he continued to twirl a lock of her hair around his fingertip.

"You did work very hard. Bound to wake up your appetite. I'll order room service."

She sat and looked down at him. "You are so fucking handsome. Providing food and orgasms is pretty irresistible. And, that ring in the head of your cock? Well, it certainly woke up all sorts of places in my pussy that I might have thought imaginary until you and your magic wiener."

"Pleased to serve all your voracious appetites." Snorting, he rolled to his feet and went in search of the room service menu.

She dragged a French fry through ranch dressing and ate it, thinking before she asked, "Did you always know you wanted to make music?"

"I liked music from an early age. Started playing bass and loved it. Had a garage band with my friends, Silas is one of them," he said of his drummer. "I've known him since middle school. But I figured it'd be something I did on the side while I did, well, some other job that could pay my rent, you know?"

She nodded.

"And then I met my dad." He shrugged. "That was a big turning point. Because my mum plays piano so I figured I got my musical talent from her side of my DNA. And then when my dad came into my life it made sense to me. I got it from both of them. He was so great, you know? He would jam with us, a bunch of kids in a garage playing covers. And then he and my mum got together, married and all that, and I started going out on tour with him. Which is where I met you."

She lifted her half-eaten cheeseburger in cheers.

"I saw that it could be a career. More than a hobby on the

side. But the center of my life. It obviously helps when your dad is a rock star, and I know you get that part."

Did she ever.

"Anyway, you know the other parts of the story. We started out at small clubs and worked up to larger ones. Made an EP which got us picked up by the label, like you did. Erin and my dad served as producers. I still use them to this day because they're so smart about all this stuff. We gained traction from the EP and then our first full length album. Then the follow up. Lots of touring. And now this new album is doing great and the ticket sales for this tour are, I'm told, outstanding. So I guess I'll get to keep doing this as my job. Thankfully. I love music. I love making music. I even love the chaotic energy of touring, though I have to admit, I do wish this tour had a break between North America and Europe so I can recover a bit."

He looked over to her and winced. "I'm sorry about that, by the way. I guess maybe we should have gotten that over with before we jumped into bed."

There'd been a push for two other European based bands to open for Earthquakes on their Europe leg and Jeremy had come to Harlow in person to talk with her about it. She hadn't been angry at all. The US leg would give them a lot of exposure, but they had their own tour to run, and they'd actually be in Europe at the same time toward the end of Earthquakes's tour, just playing far smaller venues.

"I'm not fucking you for a spot on your Europe leg," she told him and tried not to wince at the emotion behind her words.

"Uh...I didn't think you were. It's just that the possibility of a spot for that part of the tour had been spoken about and then it went in a different direction." He shrugged.

Harlow rolled her eyes at him. "Do you think I'm unaware of the differences between our spot and yours? We aren't ignorant of the process. Earthquakes is a much bigger, hotter property. You need to make decisions that align with that. European tour, British and Dutch bands make sense." She took another bite because cold cheeseburgers weren't as good as hot ones. "Jeremy already spoke to us about it. If I had a problem, you'd know. And I wouldn't be riding your dick. That's a good sign that I'm mad at you. Not riding your dick, I mean."

"Okay, okay. I just remember what it was like trying to break to the next level." He tucked her reaction away for future reference. He didn't want to hurt or offend her. He just wanted to be careful of her feelings.

"You can pay for the room service," she said easily.

"Deal."

She finished up her meal still naked, but once she finished, she got out of bed and began to reassemble her clothes, putting them back on in order.

"Going somewhere?"

"It's nearly three. I need to get some sleep since I got all tired from sexercize with you." She grinned.

He frowned. "You can stay here. I'm not kicking you out or anything."

"Well, that's good, because that would be terrible manners after I let you touch my boobs."

A laugh burst from him, satisfying her in a way she didn't want to look at too closely just then.

"I do have very good manners. And a king-sized bed. I even have a breakfast order coming. I'll share my bacon with you or order you more."

"Are you attempting to bribe me with bacon, sir?"

"Whatever it takes."

"As much as I do love breakfast cooked by someone else, especially when it includes bacon, I need to go back to my own room. I've seen fans in this hotel looking for you. And I've seen plenty of gossip mag fodder about you in the past. Getting snapped sneaking back to my room in the morning wearing what I had on last night seems like daring trouble."

"You embarrassed?"

She stood near the foyer and put a hand on her hip. "Oh, is that what's going on here? You're going to insult me for bringing up a very real issue?"

He growled and she realized this guy had probably very rarely heard no in his life. Harlow was all about education and not at all about responding to any of this baiting. He was struggling with something else. She wasn't sure what it was, and she didn't know him well enough to guess at that point.

"I apologize," he said as she sighed and turned, heading to the door.

She stopped and turned to face him.

"I got a little snotty. It's because I want you here with me. But you're right. For now. Let's see how it feels the next time or the time after."

"You're very sure there will be another time or the time after that."

His cheeky grin changed into something naughty and

uninhibitedly sexy and a responding pull low in her belly agreed there would be a next time.

He was standing so very close to her just moments later. He pulled her close and kissed her. "I like you, Harlow. I want to get to know you better. And I want to have a lot more sex with you."

"I like you too, Miles. We can definitely get to know each other better, including sex." She kissed him long and slow before stepping away and looking out the peep hole to be sure the coast was clear before she went outside the room.

He let go of her hand after kissing her fingertips. "See you tomorrow. I'd ask to walk you to your room, but you'll only say no."

She grinned. "See, you're learning already. Goodnight, Miles," she said and left the room while the hall was empty.

CHAPTER
TEN

Poppy had begun to deliver Above Me's dailies to them after Las Vegas. She got them to everyone in Earthquakes first, also making sure they were awake and were going to eat something before she and Maddie headed down to Harlow and Nora's room to bring theirs and then go do yoga. Usually in Poppy or Maddie's room as Above Me's was far smaller and contained a Brian who was sometimes sleeping.

After yoga, it had become part of their day to have a cup of tea and breakfast as the four women chatted for a while. Sometimes Miles would come down pretending to look for Poppy for some reason or other, but really, he just wanted to hang out with Harlow too.

Which was more and more all right as the days passed.

That morning—a quick look out the window of her hotel room reminded her she was in New Orleans—she and Poppy were joined by Maddie and Nora in Harlow's room for breakfast because for that city they'd booked connecting rooms.

"By the way, thanks again for the laundry duty," Maddie said.

The day before, right after they'd arrived at the hotel, Harlow and Nora found the laundry facilities in the hotel basement and had offered to run a load for anyone else while they were there. Maddie had jumped at the chance and had repaid the favor by bringing them chocolate croissants and chicory coffee she'd picked up on the way back to the hotel after a media thing.

"No problem. I've got enough to go about ten days without needing to wash anything, but I don't want to run out of underpants." And she sweated through her clothes when she was on stage under the lights, and no one wanted funky clothes.

She was having sexytimes on the regular with Miles so she had an even better reason to keep ahead of the dirty clothes monster. A person liked to smell good when a very gorgeous other person was kissing up on them.

He still didn't like it that she left his room every night. She didn't much like it either by that point. It was a lot easier to stay in his bed where it was warm, and she was pleasantly loose and sleepy from all the orgasms.

But there had already been pictures taken of them. Backstage, at a restaurant in Dallas and even inside the hotel. There'd been comments about the way Miles had been looking at her from the one taken at the restaurant. And at the time he'd been holding her hand under the table and was probably thinking about boning her. Or going down on her. Damn, the man loved eating pussy and she couldn't be happier about it.

They couldn't keep it quiet forever. Eventually, if they

continued with this…relationship or whatever it was, they'd either get caught or would have to be open about it to get ahead of a story. Until then though, she was enjoying herself with him in those stolen moments after the show each night.

She was sitting on the bed, guzzling coffee and listening to her friends chat when her phone buzzed.

"I need to take this," she said, getting up and going through the connecting door to Brian and Nora's room since Brian and Omar were off on a comic bookstore date.

"Hi there" she said when she called the number on the text.

"We got your message," her brother Hector said.

She'd left a voicemail to let him know she'd be in Atlanta for a few days and that she'd like to see him and their other brother Louis while she was there. It had taken her two hours to decide on the proper wording of a short voicemail and then she'd worried for the next day that she'd said things wrong.

"Oh good," she said trying to keep her voice calm and not betray any emotions.

"Come for dinner at our house on that Monday."

That brightened her mood considerably. Unless Gloria would also be in attendance.

"Louis is coming too, bringing his boys."

A heavy weight of the unspoken lay between them. Harlow had long ago given up expecting her brothers to understand the difference their mother had made between them her whole life. All they saw was that she got to go on tour with their father, that she went to a very good school and had regular contact with their stepmother and baby sister. To them it was on Harlow to patch it up. To Harlow, it shouldn't be her job to make her mother, a grown woman, not be dreadful, distant, and cold as fuck.

She *had* asked. She *had* tried. More than once. But eventually, she just gave up. Because she had her own life to live and parents and other family who did love her and want her around. And because she had to protect her heart from the repeated attacks that always came from Gloria if she was in Harlow's presence for more than two minutes.

So Harlow wasn't going to ask her brother if their mother was coming to dinner. That would be up to her mother because she was done carrying that particular burden.

It still hurt. So she did her best to look on the bright side and be grateful for the mother she had in her aunt, who'd given up years of her life to help raise Harlow, and for her dad, who had always been there for her. Her brothers... well...she loved them both, but they lived in suburban Atlanta and she was on the west coast so they didn't see each other very often. She wasn't invited to family events on that side, not by her aunts or cousins or even her maternal grandparents. So it was when she was in Atlanta, or when they were in LA to do theme parks and they came to visit with their dad and she came down from Seattle.

"Perfect. Can't wait to see you all. Should I bring anything?"

"No. Mindy has it all handled. Can you find the house okay?"

"Yes. I've got the address. I've been there before so it shouldn't be a problem."

Hector laughed. "Okay, good."

"Oh, and if you want, I can get you and Mindy and Louis tickets to one or both nights in Atlanta to see the show." She hadn't decided one way or the other as to whether she'd invite them, but as she'd just blurted it out, the choice was made, and she had to hope it worked out.

"I don't think we can swing both shows around work and the kids, but the Tuesday night show would work. Thanks."

She made a note on a pad of paper at the nearby desk.

"I'll see you all for dinner that Monday then."

"Great. Uh, you can bring someone to dinner with you, Mindy says. Or two if your bandmates want to come. But, we saw the pictures online so I'm guessing you have a boyfriend. He's welcome."

Pictures? Ugh. Harlow wasn't the only one who'd seen the photos of them together apparently. "Thanks," was all she said. She spoke to him a while longer before disconnecting and wandering back into her room.

All her friends stared at her when she came back. "Everything okay?"

"Yes, fine. I was just talking to my brother about seeing him next week when we're in Atlanta."

Nora's eyebrows rose, but she said nothing. Harlow knew she would though, once they were alone.

"That's nice. I didn't know you had family in the south," Maddie said. "How old are they?"

"They relocated with our mother back when I was like seven or so. Hector, the oldest, he's got a wife and three kids. Two boys and a girl. Louis is divorced and he shares two sons with his ex. They're co-parenting and it seems fairly successful. They're thirty-one and twenty-nine. My brothers, not their kids."

"I don't have brothers, but I have male cousins and Miles is like a brother since our families are all so close. My dad has three brothers and they're all married with kids so there are cousins all over the ranch where they all live. I love to hang out with them up in the farmhouse my grandparents built. They've spoiled us all terribly, thank goodness," Maddie said with a laugh. "If you weren't already hooked up with Miles, I'd totally introduce you to a few of them and they'd love me for it forever."

Poppy snorted. "I think Miles is enough to handle without adding Hurley cousins to the mix. Also, I think he's already called her. I don't make the rules, Maddie."

"Called her like she's the front seat? Not that you're biased," Maddie said with a wink.

Harlow laughed.

Poppy snorted. "Ha. I *am* totally biased because Miles is amazing. He's a great brother and I like the way he is when Harlow is around. Plus have you seen them together? It's ridiculous how gorgeous they are."

A blush heated Harlow's cheeks at the praise. Maybe she'd ask Miles if he wanted to go to dinner with her at Hector and Mindy's place. Or maybe that was stupid, and she should invite no one to be there to see if something went bad because Gloria showed up. But the kids would be there, and she seemed to love her grandsons, at least the few times she'd seen her mother with her nephews. Harlow hadn't met her niece yet. She was only eighteen months old, and Harlow had sent presents and checked in on her health and life regularly even if at times she felt like a stranger in her own family.

It was sad that Hector had a daughter only slightly younger than their sister Ryder, but neither of her brothers had seemed that interested in a relationship with her. But damn it, she couldn't take ownership of what her brothers, both grown people, did or thought. It wasn't her job to raise her brothers into men who were caring and loyal to their family as a whole instead of just one person.

"What's the plan today?" Harlow asked as she deliberately set that aside.

"Free play until four when we head to the venue," Poppy said. "Want to go to Bourbon Street? Do some touristy stuff?"

"Yes! As long as we can go to Royal Street so I can check out the galleries. I'm looking for something for the walls in our bedroom," Nora said.

Maddie cheered. "Yay! Let's meet back here in forty-five? Then we can go out and have lunch and then be back in plenty of time."

When Poppy and Maddie left, Nora closed the door and turned back to Harlow. "Is *she* going to be at this dinner?" Meaning Harlow's mom.

"I don't know. He said Mindy, his wife, was making dinner and that Louis would be there with his sons too. No mention of anyone else."

Nora said, "I can see on your features that you're not going to ask any of us because you think you have to face this on your own. But you don't. And if she's there, it will be awful. She won't want to resist the chance to berate you and make you feel bad. You need someone at your side because your brothers are too weak when it comes to her. I'll go with you."

"Thank you." She hugged Nora. "But you hate her and she knows it. Which is a nice thing for me because she deserves it. But it'll be uncomfortable for you and everyone else. And honestly, I'll be mortified if she starts something.

At least if no one else is there I'll be the only one embarrassed."

"You have nothing to be embarrassed about! That woman is shit. She is terrible and awful, and I'd like to high five her face. She could be a good mother, support you, be proud of you, love you. That's what mothers are supposed to do. *She* is unnatural."

So relieved to have a friend like Nora, Harlow hugged her again. "Thank you. For right now I'm going alone. But I will think about everything you said."

"Okay. I'm going to get dressed for the day. You do the same. Let's day drink," Nora called out as she went next door.

"I'll need a nap if I do," she muttered but that wasn't really an argument against day drinking.

"You're trying to steal my girl, Pop," Miles groused at his sister when she returned that afternoon after she'd spent hours and hours with Harlow. But was he invited? No. Did he really want to be or was it about missing Harlow and feeling totally off balance because of it?

"She's totally adorable, so I might if I wanted to, and she wasn't all moon eyed over you. But I did steal her for the day, and we shopped, and day drank and bought art. I regret nothing. We even found a few funky clothing places where we picked up some used and new stuff. She's fun. I'm getting to know her too. Mum and Dad will want to know details and I can tell them all positives. And you're with her every night after the show. There's enough Harlow Martin to go around."

"I should go down there to see how she is," he said.

"She's napping. I told you there was day drinking. We'll all see one another when we leave for the venue at four. Now I'm going to lay down awhile to rest up for tonight too." She bent to kiss the top of his head and dropped a white bag full of fresh beignets into his lap.

"Those are from Harlow. We stopped for a snack to fortify ourselves and she got extras for you," she called out as she left.

"Are you spying on me for Mum and Dad?" he called out but she either didn't hear or wasn't going to reply so he just growled to himself as he opened the bag and the scent of fried dough hit and made him feel better.

Still, he considered as he ate, making a huge mess with powdered sugar, it'd be better to have eaten these with Harlow.

And he said so when they got into the van just a few hours later to head to the arena. "Thanks for the beignets. I'll probably be sorry later, but I ate them all in one sitting."

She laughed. "I did too. Plus, I had a lot of rum. The nap has revitalized me. Now I'm ready for more food after the show is over. Everywhere is open late here, which is pretty flipping awesome."

"Wait for me. I want to come too. I mean if you don't already have other plans," he amended.

Harlow nodded, clearly pleased. "Okay. There's this restaurant we checked out earlier today and made reservations for tonight. Chef's table because he's some friend of your family?"

"Ah! Yeah. Two of my aunts are into art which is how Cora Silvera came into our lives. She runs a family gallery in

Seattle. Her husband is a chef. That's how Poppy must have gotten the name of the chef here."

A group rather than just the two of them so he'd be sure to broach the subject of one-on-one time again more in advance of the next city. Until then he had to share her with her friends and his too.

He looked over to her as she listened to some stupid story Omar told them all for the dozenth time. But she hadn't heard it before and the smile on her face said she enjoyed it and so that was nice.

Nice. Well. Whatever.

He wanted them to all get along. Because he liked it that they got her, that they understood why—beyond the obvious good looks—he liked her so much. If they could see why he dug her so much, they'd relax about the new relationship Harlow and Miles were building.

As Miles had taken a seat next to her in the back row, he took her hand and she leaned a little bit closer to him, squeezing his hand.

"Poppy said you all had a good day today."

"We did. I had to let my aunt know I was having some stuff shipped to her house and that I'd pick it up after the tour ends."

"Yeah? What'd you buy?"

"A bunch of stuff at this funky new and used clothing shop. I have a friend, one we all went to school with," she said, indicating her bandmates, "and she makes outfits for tours and appearances, that sort of thing. I'll send the clothes to her and I'll go see her the next time I'm in LA to get an idea of what she'll create for me. I also bought a painting, a small one of a street scene. I have an alcove in my house. I want to put it there."

"That's a cool way to remember where you've been."

"It is. That alcove is where I put various things I pick up while traveling, Stones, picture frames, I've got ornaments and glass of all types. The painting will be perfect there. Eventually after that one fills, there's another alcove on the other side of my living room."

"When I'm home and you're home at the same time, I want to see it. Your actual and metaphorical alcoves."

She snickered, but he couldn't say much more as they'd arrived and Omar turned back to talk to Miles as they all loaded off.

He kept her hand as they walked from the van to the double doors leading to the backstage areas they'd use. And he never heard the sound of pictures taken with someone's phone.

CHAPTER
ELEVEN

"What are you doing tomorrow?" Miles asked her as they lay curled up in his bed a few nights later. They'd had the first of two shows in Atlanta and the following day was totally free.

"Nothing until the evening."

He paused, wanting to ask what she was doing in the evening even though it wasn't his business.

"Want to go exploring? I've been in Atlanta multiple times but usually because I'm here to perform. I don't know much about the city otherwise," he said.

"How about thrift shopping? There are several thrift stores I want to hit. My brothers live here so I have a general idea of where everything is."

"Okay, that sounds fun. Can we do lunch and stuff too?"

"Sure. Buying things makes me hungry."

That made him laugh and pull her a little closer so he could kiss her shoulder.

"You're going to need to uh, mute yourself a little. Downplay all that Miles Brown. Otherwise, you'll get recognized within five minutes."

"Mute myself?"

"Yes. Wear a cap and some sunnies. That way you'll look more like one of your fanboys than yourself."

He harrumphed which only made her giggle and then roll from bed.

"I think if you stayed all night here but brought a change of clothes with you, you could leave in the morning, and no one will know you slept in my bed except me, and I really like that idea."

She looked at him, taking a long leisurely visual stroll from his toes to his head, both of them. "Okay. That might work. But not tonight because I don't have a change of clothing. I'm doing yoga in the morning with Nora and Poppy so they'll be waking me up at nine. That's six hours from now. I need the sleep and we both know if you and I are naked in the same bed, neither of us is getting any rest."

That was true and he couldn't deny it. He couldn't keep his hands off her when they were together this way. He could barely resist not touching her in public and had forgotten why he shouldn't, and they'd held hands more than once in front of others. Usually just the other band members, but still.

They needed to have a conversation about next steps in their relationship. He hated having to hide it. He wanted to put an arm around her shoulders after the show ended. Wanted to be able to kiss her when the mood struck.

"We've got media tomorrow, but we should be back by the time you're done with yoga. Then we can head out?" He'd have a car service reserved for their day. So they could have lunch drinks and not have to haul their purchases with them all afternoon.

He got up to walk her to the door, trying to mask his annoyance that they were still doing this. Annoyed by himself. There'd never been any of this with the others who came before Harlow.

And still, he found himself backing her against the closed door and kissing her senseless. Told her all he felt about her that way until he stepped back, satisfied by the dreamy look she wore.

"Goodnight, beauty. I'll see you in the morning. Text me when you get back to your room."

After they'd finished their workout, Nora, Harlow, and Poppy took a swim and then came back to Harlow's room to have some juice and chat for a bit. Maddie was off doing media that morning so it was just the three of them.

"I have to get ready for my day with Miles," Harlow told them and darted into the bathroom for half an hour to shower and put on some makeup.

"You look cute," Poppy said when she came out a while later. "Miles already thinks you're gorgeous, but there's no harm in reminding him."

"Are you asking him to go with you tonight?" Nora asked like it was totally cool to bring that up in front of Miles's sister.

"Ooh, invite him to what? He's got great manners even if he comes off like a big head sometimes," Poppy said.

"Big head?" Miles's head seemed to Harlow to be in pretty much perfect proportion to the rest of him.

"Our Mum calls it a swelled head. Like you know, when a person knows how handsome or talented they are, so they let it go to their head? When I was little, I just called it big head. My brother knows he's a good musician. He knows he's talented and handsome. But he's also still grounded most of the time."

"My brothers live here in Atlanta. I'm going over to my oldest brother and his wife's house for dinner tonight," Harlow said.

"They said you could bring someone," Nora said.

Harlow looked at her friend like she wanted to lock her outside the room.

Naturally Nora ignored that and continued talking. "Harlow didn't grow up around them, or their mother, who dumped Har off with her dad when she was two. So, dinner there is complicated because they act like it's impossible to see why their mother is a fucking monster. But she's an absolute horror show. And Harlow is too nice to them and doesn't want to make waves. So, I think she needs to take a backup with her. Someone who will protect her. It can't be me, according to Harlow, so it should be Miles. If she took Brian they'd start asking when she stole her best friend's boyfriend."

Harlow just sighed. There was really no way to rein Nora in when she was protecting someone. And she was right on the mark about what would happen if she took Brian.

"I *definitely* think Miles should go. In fact, I think if he hears you went alone and finds out how terrible it might be for you, it'll make him sad. Not that you should let your partner rule your life that way," Poppy added. "But he digs you so much. And he's really good at saying stuff that isn't an insult on its face, but it so totally is."

"The songwriter in him," Harlow said with a laugh.

"I'm sorry about your mom. That's got to be really hard." Poppy squeezed her hand briefly and let go.

Thank god someone knocked on her door before Harlow had to talk any more about it.

It was Miles, who had a ball cap in his hand, along with a pair of sunglasses. "Do I pass the Miles Brown Fanboy test?" he asked before kissing her soundly in front of everyone.

He had on an Editors tour t-shirt, jeans ripped in the right places and looked totally gorgeous. He put on the hat and glasses.

"Okay, yeah you tipped from Miles to one of his fanboys. Where did you get those sunglasses? I love them," Harlow took them off his face and tried them on her own. "Super cute."

"You can have them at the end of tour when I don't need a disguise. And what's yours?" he asked.

"My disguise is that way less people know about my band than yours. I'm just one of many chicks with this look out and about."

Everyone laughed.

"Let me get my backpack," she told him, but he followed her into her room completely and started chatting with Nora and Poppy.

"Maddie wanted you to know she was changing quickly and would be down to join you all shortly," he said.

"Oh are we all going shopping?" Poppy asked just to poke at her brother, which made Harlow snicker.

"Sure. Just in different places." He took Harlow's hand. "Got a car waiting. Let's go."

"See you later," Nora called out. "Ask him that thing."

Harlow took her hand back for a second, walked back into the room and flipped her friend off, making Poppy guffaw.

"For the record," Miles said once they'd gotten into the car, "you are nothing like one of many chicks with this look. There's no one like you in the world."

She smiled and sat back against the seat.

Miles held off until they came out of the first store, and he dropped their bags with the car, and they headed to the next place, just down the block. "What thing are you supposed to ask me?"

"I was expecting you to demand to know in the car."

"I was hoping you'd share."

"My brothers live here in Atlanta. I told you that earlier, remember?"

He nodded.

"I'm going to dinner at my oldest brother's house. And he said I could invite someone."

"Yes, I'd love to go," he said quickly.

"I feel like you probably need to know more before you make that decision. There's some tension between my mother's side of the family and me. This dinner could be fine, but if my biological mother shows up, it could go left really quickly. It's a lot for me and it's my problem. I don't want to dump it in your lap."

If it was a lot for her, he definitely wanted to be there.

"I'd be there as your boyfriend?" he asked and then added, "Which I'd like, obviously. I just wanted to check." Because he was her boyfriend. Or whatever word that conveyed the same basic thing. In the month since the tour had started, especially since she'd been in his bed every single night, he'd come to feel something pretty intense for her. And it felt like she returned that feeling.

"I'm not sure it's a good idea for you to come. If it's awful," she shook her head, "it could really ruin your night."

"Your not being with me ruins my night. Your going to this dinner without me so you have no one to have your back ruins my night. You brought it up so it would be super rude to rescind your invitation," he teased.

Harlow wanted to tell him everything while simultaneously running away from the subject and never speaking of it again.

She had her very close circle and even then, it was only Nora who she really talked to about it. Over *years*.

She wanted to be the Harlow who wasn't so delighted by the idea of Miles being with her at this dinner. And she wanted to be the Harlow who hadn't gotten all tingly and flushed when he asked if he was going as her boyfriend.

After catching her reflection in a window, Harlow called herself the liar she was. If she was the Harlow who didn't get tingly over Miles, there wouldn't be this lovely thing building between them.

And she liked it so much. Liked that she could look over at him no matter what he was doing, and he looked up too, like she'd called him in some secret magical way. Liked watching him sing his entire heart out. Liked the thing he did with his tongue and her clit. Liked that he wanted to be with her and didn't try to hide it.

"Yes." She opened the door and got out, heading to the shop, face burning.

He caught up with her inside, taking her hand and kissing it before letting it go. "Yes, I'm your boyfriend, and we're telling your brothers about us when we go over there for dinner tonight?"

She rolled her eyes. "Yes."

"Great. Now I need your help with an outfit. It's not every day I meet my girlfriend's family."

She poked him in the ribs laughing. "You've met my dad more than once."

"Still. Don't ruin it, Harlow." He sneaked close enough to kiss her right on the mouth, crushing the A line dress she'd just pulled off a rack between them.

A thrill zinged through her. That he'd make a claim like that at all was sort of unexpectedly wonderful.

An hour and a half later they were eating lunch at a secluded back table in a funky little place they found down an alley.

Her chile relleno was fantastic, as was the giant margarita, and Miles looked even hotter and slightly dangerous in the low light.

"Harlow," he said, reaching toward her holding a little gift bag.

Inside, nestled in tissue paper were three resin bangles she'd looked at a few shops earlier that day. She'd put them back after considering the cost and the stuff she was already going to have to lug around or send back home.

Two tortoiseshell and one black. They'd go with the outfit she was planning to wear that night.

"These are wonderful. Thank you."

He shrugged. "I just saw you looking at them. I hoped you hadn't put them back because you hated them."

"You pay attention." Worry eased into his features, and she shook her head. "No. In a good way. It makes me feel nice." Valued.

"Oh, well good. I like paying attention and you deserve it. So." He ducked his head.

Every time he reached for the chips in the center of the table she got caught up in the flex of his forearms and the movement of his hands. It wasn't the first time she'd found herself staring at him as he played guitar or ate chips at a Mexican restaurant.

"I'd really like to lean in and bite you right here," she said quietly, pointing out a spot above his wrist.

He dropped the chip, a look of surprise chased by sensual promise. God, she really liked this guy.

And his arms.

"What's stopping you?" he asked, teasing.

"I'm going to guess the management probably frowns on patrons just nibbling on one another. Even if one of those patrons has forearms that make a girl all fluttery inside."

"The world is very unfair," he said, taking another chip.

"So true." Laughing, she went back to her meal.

"How much time do we have when we get back? Before we have to leave for your brother's house?" he asked.

"I did some research earlier and I think it'll take about

forty-five minutes or so to get there from the hotel. I called a car service so they're picking me...us up an hour before. I figure just in case we hit traffic or whatever. It's going to take me an hour to get ready before that. How long do you need to get ready?"

He was most likely trying to figure out if they had enough time for sex. Which normally she'd be down for. But the closer the time for dinner got, the more anxious she was becoming. Anxious sex wasn't her favorite. She found it difficult to focus on pleasure when something was worrying her.

So she took a step closer to being a grown up and told him. "We have time after. And I'll probably be in need of some relaxation."

Miles took her hand and squeezed to let her know he got it.

Miles was grateful Harlow had helped him pick out what to wear for dinner. He wouldn't have worried so much if it had been her father, or any of the extended family Miles had. But this was different enough that it had his normally bold Harlow off balance. Which had knocked *him* off balance too because his reaction to her reaction was something altogether new.

He wanted to project that he had his shit together and that he was there for Harlow. So the outfit of dark trousers with a thin but warm cashmere sweater—one he'd push up to his elbows so she could see his forearms—was a signal to her family and to Harlow as well.

Tonight was about Harlow, not so much for meeting her brothers. He wasn't going to start anything. He wanted things to go well if for no other reason than to erase all the anxiety he could clearly see she carried.

Then when they got back, he was going to stop by her room with her as she gathered her things into an overnight bag so she would be in his bed all night. Then he could make sure she was all right, sex her up if that was something she wanted and watch that she had a good breakfast the following morning. They had a show the following evening, so he knew she'd need the care and the energy.

He escorted her to her hotel room and took his share of the bags. "I'll be down here to get you ten minutes before we go to meet the car, okay?"

She hugged him, staying longer than she usually did, so he kept her against him, telling her through his body that he was there. He wanted her to tell him more. Reveal the whole story. But he understood from her reaction that she didn't normally share this much even with people she'd known for years. He needed to be patient. And smart.

Back in his room he took the time to make a call home. Yes, he was a grown man, but his father always had good advice.

"Miles, your mum and I were just talking about you at breakfast. How are things?"

"Hey, Dad. Things are great. The shows have been amazing so far. Sold out every night so far. We're tight."

"Yeah, once you get past the first week or two, you hit that spot where you all know one another perfectly. It gets at little threadbare toward the end when everyone is exhausted so remember to take the time for you four to connect and reconnect."

That was why they'd insisted on a rest day at least once a

week. It cost more but Earthquakes would be on tour for nearly six months and they needed not to be exhausted and burned out. His father had been the one to suggest it, another reason Miles respected his dad as a businessperson as well.

"Do you have a few minutes?" Miles asked.

"Always. Your sister is okay? She texts daily and sounds fine."

"She's great. You were right to push me to hire her. She keeps us all in line. She's decided Above Me is hers to take care of too."

"Ah, I wondered when you were going to tell me about Harlow."

Miles sighed. "Did she tell you about it?" Meaning his sister.

"She didn't have to. Tell me and then we'll circle back to this," his father said.

"Well, it all started before I kissed her the first time. But once that happened, I couldn't seem to find any reason not to pursue her. And yes, I get that I am on tour with her band and that if things go bad it could mess things up professionally. Though, I'll say Above Me isn't going to do anything outwardly that would hurt this tour or their own trajectory. It's one of the things I like most about Harlow."

Once he'd been with her the first time, he'd understood just how much trust she gave him. She was vulnerable when it was just the two of them in a way he never saw outside that. It made him feel ten feet tall that she trusted him with her body and her heart.

"She wants to keep this on the low." Which, admittedly frustrated him.

"Is she ashamed of it? Is she with someone?" his dad asked.

"No to both. I think, and this is conjecture based on what she's said and *not* said that she's lived her life in the public eye because of who her father is and that she's trying to navigate in a way that makes her feel she's earned her success. And that she likes to have her personal life private."

His father sighed. "You know your mother feels very much the same way about our personal life so I expect you understand her in a way others wouldn't."

"That's true. We have a lot in common with growing up in a spotlight that belonged to someone else. She understands the industry like I do. She knows the bad and the good and she's determined to make her way through the minefield of the music business. She's good at what she does. Confident in her skills. It's very attractive."

"Doesn't hurt that she's beautiful," his dad teased.

"Well, no. But her beauty is something that's a magical combo of who she is inside and all that pretty on the outside. I...I thought I was in love before, but I didn't know shit."

That made Adrian Brown laugh. "Miles, I wish I was there to have this conversation with you face to face. You don't know what you don't know. You had that other experience to know precisely what it meant when something real felt very different. A good life is learning from our mistakes. That doesn't guarantee no new mistakes, god knows, but pain is easier to get past when you can spin it as a positive."

"You aren't going to say it's too early?"

"Do you think it's too early?" his dad countered.

"No. I...I started falling the moment I saw the footage of her on stage back in April. I'm still getting to know her, and we aren't getting married tomorrow. But I want to do this right. She and I are going to dinner tonight at her brother's house. I'm meeting that part of her family and there's some tension there, so I don't want to mess anything up. I want her to trust I've got her back. She's stressed about it in a way I haven't seen from her. There's just this spot inside me that's driven to soothe that anxiety. It's not so much that I want them to like me. I want them to like her."

His dad was quiet for long moments. "That's an important distinction. I'm proud you can see that. All you can do is go with her and be at her side. If something happens, you can do your best to protect her. Just remember her feelings count most here. Since you don't know exactly what the problem is, you need to follow her lead. For what it's worth, I have faith you'll do just fine."

That was exactly what he'd needed to hear.

"Thanks, Dad."

"It's my pleasure to be your dad. It always has been. Now, let's circle back to how I know about you and Harlow."

CHAPTER
TWELVE

"You look so pretty," Nora said, stepping back from where she'd been pinning the braided bun at the base of Harlow's head.

She'd chosen black herringbone patterned pants and a pale pink short sleeved sweater. Her, but softened. Harlow wanted to signal to her brothers that she wanted the evening to be soft and calm and hoped they did too.

Her makeup was classic, and she'd gone with a berry-colored lipstick.

"They see me in media where I'm supposed to be *on*. I just want them to remember I'm more than that. I'm proud of the work we do as well obviously." It took all her self control not to wring her hands. Nothing else in the universe made her so uncertain in the way dealing with her mother's side of the family did.

Nora met her gaze in the mirror they stood in front of. "I understand. You look perfect. And you and Miles together are going to look like the ten minutes before a baby gets made."

Laughing, Harlow turned and hugged her dearest friend. "You always say the perfect thing. I don't know what I would do without you in my world."

"That's good because I'm not going anywhere. I need you to promise me you will get your asses up and out of there if she shows up and it gets bad," Nora said, her eyes narrowed.

"If it gets to the point where I want to leave, I will."

"That's a dodge of what I asked you to promise."

"No it isn't." Harlow held up a hand to stop her friend from speaking. "What I mean is, she probably won't even be there. I haven't seen her in person in years. She's in no hurry to contact me unless it's one of her phone calls to yell at me about my behavior." Sadly, Gloria found a reason to leave shitty, judgmental voicemails a few times each year. Not for birthdays or anything important in a positive way. No, just sniping at Harlow from out of the blue to remind her Gloria never believed she was anything more than an easy lay and a failure as a person. She'd done so during their solo tour earlier that year after she'd seen some pictures of Harlow on stage. Called to let Harlow know she looked like a whore and was disgracing the family. There were times she wondered if her mother had some sort of internet alert set up for Harlow's name so she could find extra things to be upset over.

Harlow took a bracing breath. "She's got no reason to show up tonight. What I'm hoping is that it's just me and my brothers and their kids. If it's just us, it'll be fine."

Their mother might be viewed differently by her and her brothers, but Harlow loved them and their kids. Even though they hadn't spent a lot of time with each other growing up, she knew they loved her in their own way.

It needed to be enough, or she would slip out and stay gone. She was working on that part.

"And if she shows?" Nora asked.

"Like a dog with a bone," Harlow muttered, and Nora flipped her off. "If she shows and she's unpleasant, and I can't ignore it by moving away from her or changing the subject, I will make my excuses and say good night. I'm not going over there to be disrespected. I'm not a doormat, Nora."

"No, you're not. But...you want her to love you. And she doesn't. Not in the way you need her to. That hurts you. And I hate it. You deserve so much more. But I also understand you love your brothers and it's just dinner. But you're taking your *boyfriend* to meet your family. That's big. And it's a message to them and to Miles."

Harlow threw her hands up into the air. "A message?"

"Let's keep our chill, ma'am." Nora gave her a look that had Harlow quitting the dramatics. "You know what I'm saying. You're trusting your brothers with Miles and you're trusting Miles with that whole side of the family and all that comes with them, including the drama. I've seen you with a number of different suitors over the years. He's my favorite so far."

Trust Nora to make her laugh and stop taking herself too seriously. "Don't make me regret telling you the boyfriend thing."

"That train left the station. I already know his dick is pierced. And anyway, he *is* your boyfriend. You have a picture of him in your contacts and it's all schmoopy. You like him and that's okay. He's not going to eat all the groceries and live in your house for three months without ever cleaning or offering to help pay."

Harlow gaped and then stomped from the room. But it was mainly for show because as usual, Nora was right, and she came right back. "I kicked him out, didn't I? It was only two months. And that's a *lessons learned* relationship. Everyone needs one of those."

Nora said, "You wouldn't be letting Miles be your date tonight if you didn't know the difference after you kicked him out, now would you?"

He was different and yes, she had let him in further than anyone else. "I can't take you because you threw a drink in her face the time you met her," Harlow replied through a fit of giggles.

"She's lucky I didn't run her over with my car. Woman shows up at the hospital where her fifteen-year-old daughter is recovering from two surgeries after a car accident and she accuses you of showing too much thigh when the nurse came in to give you medication? She's a monster. And she only stayed ten minutes *and* didn't come back to see you a single time even though she was in the city visiting theme parks and hanging out for another week. You deserve better than Gloria Martin."

Harlow heard the knock at the door and looked at herself in the mirror before grabbing her handbag.

"Nora?" she said before opening the door.

Her friend cocked her head.

"Thank you for always being my friend. In the shittiest of times as well as the best of them."

Nora blew her a kiss. "Right back at you. You're way easier to love than Gloria has tried to make you believe."

Heart in her throat, Harlow opened up to admit Miles. He came in looking like a star. Charisma oozed from him. He smelled good and only had eyes for her.

"You look beautiful," he said, taking her in. "The bracelets." He grinned and she was extra pleased she'd worn them.

"You look pretty damned good yourself." His dark sweater was unbelievably soft and seemed to make the greenish brown of his eyes deeper. His pants, simple trousers that leaned away from black and into charcoal. It also said luxury, but given who he was and what he came from, that made sense. Not gold toilet, look-at-me-I'm-rich luxury, but an effortless elegance. And, deep down she couldn't wait to see what her brothers thought because he looked like any big brother's most fervent hope, minimalist and yet stylish bar through his septum and all.

"Okay then. See you later," Harlow told Nora.

"You definitely will let me know how things go," Nora replied. "You're amazing, Harlow. Don't let anyone convince you otherwise."

Miles was quiet for the first fifteen minutes, wrestling with what he'd overheard as he stood outside her door when he'd come to pick her up. He needed to tell her about the end of his conversation with his father, but she was already tense—and if what he heard Nora say was any indication of how Harlow's mother had treated her on a regular basis, he understood.

He took her hand, something that felt like second nature

to him by that point. It was a way to touch her and connect. Simple and powerful at the same time.

"I haven't been a hand holder really. I mean dating. In the past. The way past and not now," he added quickly.

Her features relaxed as she smirked at him.

"I like this." He squeezed the hand he held in his own.

"I like it too."

"There are pictures of us on Earthquakes fansites." He said it in a rush, like pulling a bandage off. Get the pain over quickly.

"Us how?" she asked, calmly. Sort of. He caught the concern in her gaze for a brief moment.

"There've already been some pictures. We knew that. But there are some from before the show in New Orleans. My arm around your shoulders. Then another of us embracing. And some from today. From the street of us walking. And through the window of the shop where I kissed you." He shrugged, hoping she understood he had no problem at all with it being known they were together. "It's pretty clear we're involved."

She pulled her phone out and did a social media search. "Nora must have known," she muttered. Miles knew Nora and Brian did a lot of the social media stuff.

Miles took the opportunity to get even closer to her to look at her phone screen. And there they were. The photos that had already been out were enough to get people speculating about the way he looked at her or how close they stood to one another. But the ones he'd been talking about were... well they were enough that anyone looking would see way more than two friends spending the day. Kissing, but it was also the way his hand was buried in her hair. Holding hands was one thing, but in one he'd been kissing the inside of her wrist and she'd been looking at him through half lidded eyes.

If Miles hadn't already admitted to himself just how intensely he felt for her, seeing it so clearly in the series of photos certainly would have made it impossible to deny. Those moments captured in the pictures had shown a deeply attracted couple. The sexual energy was palpable. Just looking at them again made his dick hard.

"They're going to ask you about this at your next media thing," she said quietly.

"Yep." And now he could finally be honest and move on when it did come up.

"I'm sorry."

Hurt speared through his gut. "What the fuck do you have to be sorry for? Being with me? Kissing me?"

Her features softened and she shook her head. "No, dumbass. But this is out now, and you have to deal with it. That's what I'm sorry about."

Relief replaced the hurt. "Oh. Well, I don't accept your apology because I don't care about that. And it's not your fault. We weren't trying that hard *not* to be seen together anyway."

It had been sort of reckless, but she'd done it regardless, knowing they took a risk every time. And wasn't that hot as fuck? Knowing he wasn't alone in this constant craving that made him pursue her despite the logic of waiting. It was impossible not to touch her when they were out and about together. She made him feel like he fit in a spot perfectly shaped for only him.

"It takes focus off your business goals to have to answer questions about your girlfriend."

He flashed her a grin and kissed her quickly at that last bit, and then sobered a little. "When they ask me, and they will. I'll keep it simple. I want to respect your privacy, but I don't want to pretend we aren't together. Yes, we're dating. Yes, it's serious. Yes, it's private. Now let's talk about our next single or show or whatever. Does that work for you?"

"I like that you asked me," she told him as she tucked her phone away. "You could just do whatever you wanted. That's sort of your vibe." She snorted and then she was the one who took his hand. "I notice when you pause to wrestle back all your bossiness and include me in things like this. Although, we're riding in a car you booked after canceling the one I already had scheduled."

"And now we don't have to be so wary. If it's out, I can hold your hand anywhere. Or kiss you, or whatever." He sat back against the seat, feeling very satisfied with himself. "As for the car?" What could he say? He'd done it because he wanted her to have a more luxurious experience, one he could afford far easier, and the driver also had a personal security background should they need it.

Harlow gazed at him, one corner of her mouth quirked up. Waiting for him to explain.

"Okay. So. I'm...not going to apologize because I'm not sorry I did it."

Her head whipped slightly and part of him inside stilled at the sight of the predator within her coming to the surface. She was no fragile flower even though he wanted to treat her that way.

"Is that so?" she said, an edge in her tone.

"What I mean is I'm sorry for surprising you. I should have told you up front. I just handled it without thinking. It's like the room service, right? You let me pay for that. I wanted to be sure you'd be the most comfortable and at ease as you could get. I know this is stressful. I'm not sorry I did something to protect and spoil you."

"It's not the cost, Miles. It's the audacity."

He had to fight so hard not to smile at that. She had him so dead to rights. "My mum says I've been audacious since before I could walk."

She harrumphed and looked away, but he caught the ghost of a curve on her lips and knew he'd charmed her out of being mad.

"I'm so glad you reached out," Mindy told Harlow as they stood in the kitchen an hour later. Miles, Hector, and Luis were in the dining room sitting at the table, drinking beer, and talking.

"I appreciate your inviting us. And for making dinner. I know you work all week."

"We don't get to see you very often so I'm glad we had this chance. The last few times we've all been together have been...tumultuous to say the least. It's good to have a quiet dinner where we can catch up."

Tumultuous. Ha! Yeah, that was a good term for Gloria's presence. Harlow relaxed a little, feeling welcomed by her sister-in-law in that subtle reference.

"Look," Mindy continued quietly, "I just want to say I see it. The way she acts toward you. You're not imagining it."

Relief poured through Harlow. Just having another

person admit they saw the same thing Harlow did, after an entire lifetime of pretending it away, meant more than she could say.

"Thank you," she said, desperately wanting to ask what had happened, but also not wanting to overstep in what had already been a really nice departure from her usual interactions with them.

"It needs to be said. Hector and I argue about this a lot more since Lulu came along. I'd like to talk more openly about the situation. Obviously not right now as this isn't the place. But when you get off this tour maybe?"

Harlow ruthlessly tamped down any embers of hope that there'd be a happy solution to the distance between her brothers and herself. She wanted to keep trying, but it hurt too much to have those hopes dashed over and over.

"I'd like that," she said.

"Oh shit," Mindy muttered as she looked up at the doorbell alarm monitor on the nearby counter. "Heads up, she's here."

"*She*? No. You didn't invite her too? Hector didn't mention that." Harlow should have gotten an explicit promise, but she hadn't wanted to rock the fragile life raft they were all on. Still, she wasn't surprised. Not really. Gloria would not pass up a chance to stir up some drama.

"*We* didn't. But Luis wants his mother's approval so much, he invited her. I'm sorry. I was hoping she wouldn't show up. Hector called and told her not to."

"He did?"

Harlow's head spun. There was a missing piece of information here. Had something gone down between her mother and Hector? Or Mindy given the way her sister-in-law just sounded?

"Yes. Like I said, this has been a topic of arguments between us," Mindy said.

Before she could ask, the doorbell rang, interesting, as her mother had just waltzed into her sons' homes on the other times Harlow had been there. Luis jumped up and headed to answer it. Mindy sent a scorching look to her husband, who nodded and held a hand out, indicating he had it under control.

Harlow knew that was impossible when Gloria Martin was in the mix.

Mindy turned back to her and said, "Hold your head up, Harlow. You don't deserve any of what she throws your way."

Well now. Something *had* happened.

"Let's get everything to the table," Mindy said, grabbing a platter. Harlow followed suit and took another with all the meat on it.

"I'll help," Miles said, moving into the kitchen as the sound of Harlow's mother carried from the entry.

"What do you mean she brought a man?" Gloria demanded. Not in a whisper or even a slightly lowered tone. "The one from the pictures where she's rubbing all over him?"

Hector growled as he looked toward his wife and then back to the entry where Luis still stood with their mother, explaining something. His voice was lowered, but that wouldn't stop Gloria from making a scene if that's what she wanted.

"Harlow, can you please go get Lulu? I hear her on the

monitor so she's awake." Mindy glanced at her mother-in-law quickly. "She'll be hungry."

Harlow scooted from the room to head down a short hallway. Her niece sat up, rubbing her eyes. When she saw Harlow she put her hands up in entreaty and Harlow said, "Hey punkin', you hungry? Your mom just finished making dinner."

Lulu nodded so Harlow swung her up to rest on her hip as she headed back out to the dining room.

Her mother had all her grandsons in her lap as she got kisses from them but didn't bother to look up when Harlow returned with Lulu.

At the sight of her grandmother though, Lulu didn't clap for joy, she burrowed deeper into Harlow's hold.

"Mom's here," Luis said to them like their mother wasn't right there not bothering to acknowledge them.

"Lulu, you want to see your grandmother?" Luis asked her and the eighteen-month-old looked over to where her grandma sat and then her whole face screwed up as she wailed, grabbing onto Harlow with all her might.

Miles moved to stand next to her and Harlow figured she needed to introduce him. For her manners, not her mother's.

"Miles, this is Gloria Martin. Gloria, this is Miles Brown," Harlow said as she swayed back and forth, running a hand up and down Lulu's back until she stopped crying.

Mindy mouthed a thank you behind Gloria's back and Harlow vowed to get whatever story was behind this situation.

"Some babies need to cry it out. If you spoil them with too much attention it's not good," Gloria said to Harlow, who continued the sway and soothing touch that had calmed Lulu down.

"Lulu is just fine, isn't that right?" Harlow asked her niece who gave her a smile. "Love isn't spoiling. It's letting her know the big people in her life listen to her moods and want to help."

Her mother harrumphed, clearly agitated that Harlow hadn't risen to any bait so she shifted her tactics. "I'm sure that's what your father did and why you turned out this way. Gloria? You call your mother by her first name now? Is that how you were raised?" Gloria, who'd been the one to insist Harlow call her that instead of mother, said imperiously.

Ok then, how about some radical truth? *Let's see how you like it.* "You told me when I was fourteen that it made you look old when I called you mom and to call you Gloria. It's a habit now. How are you?"

Her mother's eyebrows rose. Clearly, she expected Harlow to shrink under that tone, and maybe she would have if she hadn't been holding her niece who so clearly was not having anything Gloria was selling. And Gloria made no move to snatch Lulu from Harlow's arms which she found really confusing. Her mother wasn't one to sit around waiting for someone to comply with her demands.

Hector stepped between them and held his hands out. "Hey, baby, come give Daddy some love and I'll let you eat off my plate. Mommy made short ribs."

Lulu held Harlow's face in her tiny hands and left a slobbery kiss on her chin before she moved to her dad.

"I got a call from some media person today," Gloria said as she rose and headed to the table without acknowledging Miles at all.

"I'm giving this ten minutes and if it doesn't improve significantly we are leaving," she told Miles quietly. There was something with this call and when Gloria finally let it out, it'd be time to leave or confront whatever nonsense it was.

"I'll follow your lead. But remember you're here for your brothers, not her." He kissed her cheek, and they went back to the table where he held her chair out before sitting next to her.

"No one is going to ask what this media person wanted?" Gloria said like she was confused.

"Who wants mashed potatoes?" Mindy called out and sent a giant bowl on a circuit around the table.

"What did that person want?" Luis asked, doing the legwork of their mother so she could continue this fit.

Mindy sent him a scathing look that made him flinch a little.

"After *those* pictures showed up on the internet, naturally everyone is asking if Harlow is sleeping with her boss."

Harlow whipped her head to face Gloria. "Stop making a picture of me standing in a clothing store being kissed quickly by my boyfriend sound like it's a sex tape. And I don't have a boss. I'm my own boss. Anyway, why would anyone ask *you* anything about me in the first place?"

Gloria sneered. "*He's* your boss. You're playing on his tour. I guess we know why."

"Boys, can you please take your plates to the tv room?" Mindy asked and held a finger up to silence Gloria.

They were hesitant but when they remembered there were gaming consoles and sodas in the fridge in the garage, they scooted out with a backwards glance at their grandmother.

"I didn't come over here to not be able to spend time with my grandsons. You can't just withhold them."

"No one invited you to come over here in the first place," Mindy said through a clenched jaw.

Hector looked at his wife with a mixture of anxiety and pride.

"This is my family," Gloria said as she leaned in, using her iciest tone on Mindy. "I don't need to be invited."

Exhaustion washed through Harlow as the inevitable began to play itself out just as she'd dreaded. The last thing she wanted was to be there, feeling this way because of Gloria.

"Enough." Harlow stood. "Mindy and Hector, thank you for inviting us to your home. Luis, I hope this is rock bottom for you. God knows you should be ashamed of yourself for enabling her bullshit." She nodded at her brother who knew a scene was going to happen when Gloria walked in. He knew she was right because he cast his eyes down without an argument.

"Don't you speak to him that way," Gloria said.

Harlow continued like Gloria hadn't said anything. "I'm done trying to have a relationship with anyone who helps her harm me." She didn't say she hoped to see them the following night because the way she felt right at that moment was that she never wanted to lay eyes on Luis or Gloria again. Hector, who'd said *nothing* to defend her was up there too.

But Gloria wasn't done. Obviously. She was a world

master champion shit starter. "So it's true. You're opening your legs to your boss?"

Hector groaned.

"Who I do and do not *open my legs for* is absolutely none of your business despite your lifelong obsession with my sexuality. Do not insult Miles, who was invited to be here for a meal, not some sort of talk show set where half the family starts beating each other up. You've all embarrassed yourselves enough."

"If anyone leaves, it should be Gloria," Mindy said, surprising the hell out of Harlow. And everyone else from the shocked looks she was getting. "Go ahead and pretend you didn't know this exact thing would happen, Luis. But this is my house. And Harlow and Miles are invited guests and family who brought wine, presents for *all* the kids and a good attitude. Let's contrast that with you, Gloria. *Not* invited. Pretends your youngest grandchild doesn't exist for some reason I think relates to why you don't like your daughter. Or me. Whatever do we all have in common?" Mindy mimicked being puzzled while she tapped her chin.

In the tv room the boys hooted and laughed and had a good time and Harlow was relieved, so relieved, they weren't touched by any of this. Because she felt sick. Sick that her mother would make Lulu feel like she'd made Harlow feel her whole life.

Was it because she was a girl instead of a boy? And if so, why? Could it be so simple and yet utterly complicated?

"Let's all calm down," Luis said.

"Calm down?" Mindy thundered and Hector sighed heavily.

"Harlow and Miles, please, sit down. Let's all have a meal

and stop fighting," Hector said. "Harlow, stop letting her push your buttons. Mom, you need to rein this in. Your grandchildren are here. Think about the example you're setting."

"Don't talk to your mother that way! She's whoring it up out there and it makes us all look bad. Just like your father. Worthless. You and Luis you went to school and got training. She can't be bothered with that or hard work. Never has a regular job. You talk about my example? What about her? Allow this tramp around your boys and they'll think all women are just like this one over here. They'll trap those boys into marriage by getting pregnant on purpose. Just you wait and see. I had to protect you from her influence. Even when she was a baby she flirted too much. You can see how she is. A lazy slut."

Though she'd had years and years of dealing with Gloria, Harlow couldn't prevent the way she recoiled from her mother's words. Though she knew better, she paused to see if anyone would actually kick Gloria out for real, and after a few more loaded seconds, she knew that wasn't going to happen. She hated herself for the hurt that trickled past her shields.

Before she could say anything though, Miles tossed his napkin to the chair. "Harlow, let's go."

"No, please don't go," Mindy said before glaring at Gloria who was in her element having just set things on fire for pleasure.

"He's right. Nothing has changed here," Harlow said. "I wish I could believe otherwise, but I'm old enough to accept reality."

"Go get our things and say goodbye to your nephews," Miles said in her ear.

And leave him alone with them? No way. She shook her head.

"I'm good," he said firmly. "Go on. Give them some love and we'll leave." Harlow nodded a little jerkily before heading to the room where she'd left their things.

Mindy pointed at her husband. "This has gone on long enough. You need to think hard about the next few minutes and do the right thing or risk your relationship with your sister being broken forever." And she got up and headed after Harlow.

Miles wrestled back his absolute killing fury at the way Harlow had just been treated by her family. This wasn't about his feelings. "Now that she's out of earshot, let me go ahead and say a few things." Miles pulled his sleeves down with care before he looked to Gloria and then both Harlow's brothers. "You two," he said to Hector and Luis, "are the poorest excuses for brothers I've ever encountered. Do you know what I'd do if *anyone* spoke to my baby sister the way your mother just did to Harlow? It's a long list, but nowhere on it is make my sister responsible for the abuse heaped on her. Not that our mother would ever speak to her children that way because she's not a spiteful bitch."

Gloria sputtered and he didn't care. He held eye contact with Harlow's brothers until they both looked away before he looked to their mother again. He'd hoped against hope that at least Hector would do something, but he'd been wrong.

"Understand this. First, if you speak to the press and say *anything* disparaging about Harlow, I will make it my business to strip away everything that matters to you and set it on fire." He shifted his attention to her brothers. "That goes for you too. She loves you and your children. She came here tonight knowing she might be ambushed by this trash, and she came anyway. With an open heart because for some unknown reason she continues to love you despite the fact you do nothing to protect her from behavior you know is wrong. You don't deserve her."

"Who do you think you are?" Gloria demanded,

"I'm someone with more connections than you can dream of. I'm someone who cares deeply for your daughter. Someone who is absolutely shocked that any parent could be as cold and meanspirited toward someone as full of love and light as Harlow. And, I'm someone who will make good on all the threats I just made. Call your child a lazy slut? Get yourself right, you nasty cow."

Harlow came back down the hall and he moved to meet her and Mindy.

Lulu started crying and Hector murmured to her, trying to soothe her.

Gloria opened her mouth and Miles stood, waiting. Letting her see on his features just how much he hoped she would. Never in his life had he wanted vengeance more than against this person who had put so much sadness on Harlow's face.

"I'm so sorry," Mindy told them. "I would have warned you early on, but I honestly thought after Hector called her, she wouldn't come. Please don't blame Hector."

"But I do. And you know why. I can't always feel like a

choice was made and it wasn't me. It's never me. I don't know why. But Hector and Luis saw it my whole life and here we go, time eleventy million and it was you and Miles who defended me. I'm worth more than this. I have to go," Harlow said, and Miles stepped between them, shielding her as they left.

She made it to the car and a few miles until they'd gotten out of the subdivision until she turned her face into Miles's shoulder and started to cry.

CHAPTER
THIRTEEN

By the time they returned to the hotel, he had ordered a meal for them both and sent a note to Poppy. He asked her to coordinate with Nora to get an overnight bag packed for Harlow. So she could sleep in his room that night.

He wouldn't push it if she wanted to be alone. But he didn't want her to be all by herself as she was still reeling from that night's horror movie of a dinner.

She was on auto pilot, and he steered her into the elevator and then into his suite. "Dinner will be here in about ten minutes. Do you want to change into your pajamas first? Get your makeup off?"

Harlow's gaze cleared a little. "I should go to my room. I'm not feeling very sociable right now."

"That's okay. You can change and get into bed, and we can watch a movie, or you can read, and I'll get some work done." He pointed at the bag on the couch. "Nora packed you an overnight bag so you're all set. You can go down in the morning for your yoga and breakfast with your crew as usual. It's not like they don't know where you start the night out before you fall into your own bed."

She should resist. Go back to her room, eat a pint of ice cream while drinking minibar vodka and watching *Steel Magnolias*, weeping.

The shock of the night had settled in. Harlow kept replaying her mother saying she'd been flirty with men even when she was a baby and that's why she'd dumped Harlow off and walked away. When she'd been barely older than Lulu was!

Miles had heard it all. Every horrible, ugly word. She wasn't sure what he'd said while she and Mindy had been out of the room, but it had to be pretty harsh, because when she thought Gloria was going to talk some last shit to Miles and he'd just looked at her...Gloria had shut right up.

He'd stepped in and shielded her. Protected and defended her. And now here he was having ordered food and provided her with her favorite flannel PJ pants and her sleep tank along with her toothbrush and essentials like a change of clothes for the morning.

She took the toiletry bag and headed into the bathroom, closing the door at her back. She took her time getting rid of her make up, undoing and brushing her hair out. Her favorite pajamas brought her comfort, the cotton so soft after countless washings and so Nora had included them. Harlow needed to remember that. Remember there were people who knew her and loved her.

A deep longing for a hug from Marcella seemed to throb. When Gloria had tossed her away, it had been her dad's youngest sister who'd come to live with them to help Harlow's dad raise her.

It had been Marcella who'd taken her to the dentist. Who'd helped her with school projects. Who came to every performance, every play and musical. She remained a constant, and an example Harlow would have when and if she became a mom herself someday. Harlow would call her to reconnect and check in but she couldn't face the decision as to whether to tell her aunt what had happened or not,

Letting that love bolster her, Harlow gathered herself and went back to the main room where the food was being delivered.

Miles pointed her to what she had come to think of as her side of the bed. She obeyed, telling herself it was easier than arguing. And maybe it was, but she did it because she liked it that he was taking care of her.

Even as she was mortified that he'd been there to see that entire situation unfold.

Her phone buzzed as Miles brought in the food. A glance showed three messages from Hector and one from Nora. She opened Nora's, which was a few sentences saying she loved Harlow and that if she needed anything to let her friend know. She'd wait for Harlow to share what happened and urged her to let Miles spoil her some.

"Is that going to make you feel worse?" he asked, tipping his chin toward her phone. The look in his eyes told her he wanted to throw it out a window if it upset her.

"I'm not looking at the messages that might make me feel worse. I just read Nora's." Harlow put the phone on the nightstand, screen down.

When he pulled the heating dome from the plate, it

revealed a chicken sandwich she knew was only on the lunch menu. She'd tried to order one the night before and they'd told her no.

"I saw that you liked it when you had it for lunch yesterday," he told her, setting a glass of iced tea next to her.

"They said it was lunch only," she said before taking a big bite and moaning in pleasure.

He shrugged. "Well, not for you."

She grinned at him before dragging a crispy French fry through the spicy catsup the hotel restaurant used and she'd discovered she really liked. "I have to figure out what all is in this so I can make it at home."

"I'll see about getting the recipe for you," he said, and she realized he would do just that. For no other reason than that she wanted it.

Wow.

"So."

He got into bed and attacked the steak he'd ordered for himself. "If you apologize for anything someone else did tonight, I'm going to be annoyed," he said.

"I shouldn't have taken you over there. I knew something like this could happen. She's just...honestly, I don't know what she is. I like to think I'm mature enough to understand I'll never get anything I need from that woman. But here I am."

"You won't, no. But that's not maturity to be beyond feeling any type of way about it. She's your mother. I'd be a mess if my mum ever treated me or Poppy that way. Or even a shadow of that. And if I hadn't come with you, you'd be alone right now. So, I don't want you to feel sorry I was there because I'm not. I don't know how to begin to process a woman like her, to be totally honest with you. But it seems like this has been a lifetime of crap behavior from her."

Harlow took a deep breath and decided to share something to put the situation in perspective when it came to Gloria Martin. "When I was sixteen, the last year I had any regular visitation with her, I stayed at her house. She had a spare room with one of those pull-out couches so I slept there."

"Your brothers had rooms?"

"Of course they did."

"Did your brothers have their own rooms at your dad's house?"

She snorted. "Yes. They still do. But to be fair, my dad's house is far larger than the one my mother lived in. Anyway, so," she began again.

"What? I thought the making you sleep on a pull-out couch instead of a bed was the issue. It's worse than you not having a room of your own at your mother's house?"

She put her head on his shoulder a moment. She didn't know what she'd done to deserve him. Hell, she'd never had the experience of having some terrible scene with her family and having a person at her side, her romantic interest, being a shoulder to lean on the way he'd been. She understood why it was worthy of so many songs.

"In her house, on all the walls were framed photographs. My brothers at plays and theme parks, at birthdays and Halloween. All their school pictures. Santa's lap. All that stuff. There was not a single picture of me anywhere. She had a frame that said something like "My family" and it was her pregnant with Hector and Luis and their baby pictures. The whole house was just full. It was great. For Luis and

Hector, I mean. Because again, not a single picture of me. And I know my dad always sent them to her whenever he got any he thought were good. I had school pictures and Santa pictures and pictures from plays and musicals and dances I went to, but you wouldn't know it to be in her house.

"I didn't tell anyone. I went home after a week because she was too busy to be taking care of another kid. That was exactly how she explained it to my dad. He tried to shield me from it but he believed a kid should be around their mom, so he pushed for me to go there to see her, especially after she moved to Atlanta. Which by the way, we didn't know she had until she had her attorney send a change of address for the child support for my brothers. Anyway."

She ate the rest of the chicken sandwich and wished she had a milkshake instead of tea.

Miles wanted to speak so badly. But he knew right then, he needed to listen way more than he wanted to talk. His outrage was his burden, not hers.

At least she ate her food since they hadn't eaten more than appetizers as dinner had been finishing up. They'd been unable to have a single bite after that scene.

"Hang on a second. I want ice cream. They have peach ice cream here. Do you want some?" he asked. Though he knew she did.

"That's not a very good question, Miles. Who doesn't want ice cream?"

They looked over the menu and he placed the call.

But he knew the story wasn't over so once the call was

made, they settled back in, and he tried to be patient enough to wait for her to resume speaking.

"About six or seven months later, it came out during an argument with my dad, who was trying to make me go back to visit her again for spring break. I refused but he kept at it until I finally told him about the picture wall."

Miles hissed, imagining how that might have gone over.

"At first he was shocked. He made me repeat it once more because I don't think he believed he'd heard right. Then he hugged me so tight and said I never had to go again if I didn't want to. And I never did. He didn't demand to know why I hadn't told him. Then he asked me to leave the room and called her and asked her directly about it. I'm not going to lie, I listened on an extension. She didn't even deny it. She said since I didn't even live with her why should it matter? He kept trying to get her to see how it would have made me feel, the lack of a room that was mine, no pictures anywhere when he knew she had them because he sent them to her. She said she hadn't gotten around to it and that when I did something noteworthy and he took a picture of it, then she'd put it up. He doesn't know I heard her side of the conversation. He'd feel even worse and it's not his fault."

"Does he know she's still this way to you?"

"I think he's bewildered by it. He loves Hector and Luis, but they've been poisoned over the years about him. You heard her tonight about how he's lazy or useless because he didn't go to school like my brothers did. She used to say that about him all the time. How he was uneducated and therefore not a good person. My dad was a high school dropout. He grew up in a not so lovely part of Los Angeles and ended up doing construction work. That's when he and Gloria were first together, and she got pregnant, so he married her. Then he started the band with his cousins and friends, and they had success. Not at first of course, no one ever does right away. But he kept working construction while making music in every spare moment. Eventually they got a break and a record deal, and she had Luis after that. I don't know a lot about their early years. He never talks about it, and she only does in negative terms. But I know he's smart and I know he works his ass off to support not just his immediate family but also the extended family the crew depending on the band for their livelihoods made up." Harlow shrugged. "And I know a college education is great, but not for everyone and just because you don't go to college doesn't make you stupid or lazy."

All her points were correct, but she hadn't really answered his question, and he supposed, that was an answer in and of itself. "So you haven't told him. And he hasn't asked?" That was, to Miles's mind, weakness. If he hadn't asked, he wouldn't know and then there's nothing to be done and it left Harlow responsible for something an adult did.

"I don't *want* him to ask. I don't lie to him, and I don't want to hurt his heart. He has a good life, Miles. A wife who adores him. A great kid who knows how much she's loved and valued. His music still sells well. I'm on my own, supporting myself. My brothers have lives with kids and all that. He deserves peace."

Miles heard the defensiveness in her tone. And while he did have to wonder why any father would allow this to continue, he didn't want to put Harlow in a place where she had to defend her dad. That was Miles's to understand, and it wasn't cool to make her responsible for it.

"I'm sorry you have to deal with this. It should have been a fun night and it wasn't. Which is not your fault. In any way."

"I just wish I knew whatever it was that makes her hate me so much."

"You can't always make sense of things that are senseless, baby." He kissed her temple and she leaned into him a moment.

He used a pet name.

No matter how sad she was about the situation at her brother's house earlier, Harlow knew she and Miles had stepped into a deeper part of their relationship. He'd protected and defended her, took care of her when she'd been so very sad. She'd told him things less than a handful of people knew.

And he'd listened. Heard what she was saying and understood what she hadn't. There were so few people in the world she could say that about and it mattered far more than he could ever know.

Harlow knew she'd have to give him the same trust in return that he'd given her. Having the space to speak without interruption didn't always happen. It didn't even happen most of the time. Usually, it was about things that mattered less than what she'd just told Miles. But the safety in that sort of relationship was beyond alluring. It seemed very necessary now that she had it and it was impossible not to wonder how differently things would have gone in prior relationships if it had been there.

"Can you talk to your aunt about any of this?" he asked. "I know you and she are close."

Harlow told him, "I absolutely could. She's a person I can go to about anything. But, well, I don't usually. It's hard for her when I bring Gloria up. She and Gloria don't get along and Marcella considers me her kid and she gets super heated when Gloria makes me or my dad upset. Once when my mom still lived in So. Cal, I was at her house visiting but she'd taken my brothers out somewhere and I was there alone. I called because I got scared. Marcella drove out to Orange County to get me and as she was packing my stuff up, Gloria came back. But she wasn't mad I was leaving, just that Marcella was in her house. Whatever Marcella whispered to Gloria that day must have scared Gloria deeply because she *never* left me alone like that again. There were other things, as you can see." Harlow's laugh was rueful. "But I think Gloria is terrified of Marcella."

"I knew I liked your aunt."

"She's the best. I'm very lucky. Many kids don't have a backup mom or dad. They have the crappy ones they were born to and that's that."

"That's not lucky." Miles shook his head. "That's basic. Kids should grow up in a house where they're loved and protected. I know that's not what some kids have, and it's fucked up. But that doesn't mean Gloria gets points. I really do not like her."

"Me either." She clinked her spoon to his and then he, the cad, sucked all her ice cream off! "Cheeky!"

That made him laugh. "My mum uses cheeky all the time."

"Enough about my fucked up family. Tell me something about *your* life."

He snorted as he held up a spoonful of ice cream for her. "In exchange for what I swiped from you earlier."

That made her laugh but that didn't stop her from eating his ice cream.

"My family is fucked up in its own way. Like most families. I didn't know who my dad was for many years. Neither did my mum, who is biologically my aunt, but she adopted me when I was born. Anyway, I had a birth mother who avoided me, but my mum shielded me from it and loved me so fiercely and filled my life with other people who cared about me that I never noticed. It was when my birth mother died that we finally found out who my father was. My mother braved so much to go to Adrian to tell him about me. And she did it for me. Not for herself and not even for my dad.

"And suddenly my life was full of Browns. My dad made it absolutely clear from the start that he wanted to be an active part of my life. My aunt, Erin, and uncle, Brody, their kids, and partners all opened their lives to me and made a spot I'd be comfortable in. I used to be shy and quiet."

That made her laugh.

"Truly I was. And they respected that too even though they were loud and brash and full of music and art. The longer I was around them, the more I came out of my shell. It's still a little anxious before a show and I do like my privacy very much. But I'm a far more outgoing personality than I was then."

Who wasn't?

But she got his point. And liked very much that he had

this large family unit who had done nothing but love him with all their hearts.

It was on the tip of her tongue to ask him about other girlfriends or boyfriends in his past. She'd gotten a quick overview when she'd looked him up online. But so much of that stuff was half true or basically all rumor and it had felt sort of yucky to dig deeper rather than just ask him.

Harlow gathered all their dishes and put them and the tray out in the hall before returning to the bedroom. She paused in the doorway, just watching him clear off the bed and straighten everything.

He was beautifully masculine. Tall with long legs and delightfully muscled thighs. Wide shoulders. The line of his jaw covered by his beard was still sharp, his arms covered in the same dark hair as his chest. His ink was a work in progress, she'd noted, but it managed to cover so much of his back and shoulders without being too heavy. A Celtic dragon in black and gray with a tiny bit of white shading here and there. Quietly powerful. Sort of how Miles was.

When he had clothes on, he was absurdly gorgeous. Naked? He was magnificent. Either way, Harlow had to take a moment extra to appreciate the way he made her feel. He took care of things to make her life easier. He listened. He walked in front of her to part the crowd when they were backstage. She could do things for herself. Did so every day and would continue that. She liked being independent and self-reliant.

But she also liked being able to lean on someone. Had gotten used to it even as she remained grateful for him.

CHAPTER
FOURTEEN

"You should take your clothes off," she said, leaning her hip against the nearby desk.

"I should? Do you have dirty plans for me? Because that'd be great." He grinned.

"The day I don't have dirty plans for you is the day I'm unconscious. And even then." She pulled her t-shirt off and folded it before laying it over the back of a chair.

He matched her by disposing of his shirt and unceremoniously shoving his sleep pants down, stepping out of them and tossing them to the chair where her clothes had landed too.

And then he was utterly naked as he came toward her, stealing her breath because he was so much. It might have been too much for her even six months earlier, but where she was in her life right then? She looked upon just what and who Miles was to her and though she was anxious about it, about fucking it up, she welcomed it. Wanted the enormity of this person in her life. And she wasn't just thinking of his lovely dick with that delightful, thick hoop with those beads that hit everything worth stroking every time he thrust into her pussy.

He watched her through slumbrous eyes and she met that with a smile that told him what she was thinking,

Then he crooked his finger in her direction with a c'mere motion and she probably should have made him do the moving but why the fuck not move there to him so she could get her hands on the man?

The way he looked at her was nearly as much as a caress. It left her feeling beautiful and desired. Powerful that someone like him would want her this way.

He opened his arms as she neared and she walked into his embrace, pausing to bury her face in the curve of his shoulder, taking a deep breath of his skin. Of that scent that she believed she'd know in the dark. Just like she'd know the feel of his body against hers, the muscles in his forearm and biceps bunching as he moved.

"What you do to me, Harlow Martin, what you do to me," Miles murmured against her hair.

What *she* did to *him*? What about the way he waltzed right into her life and had her telling him things she'd only told less than three people before he came along?

All thoughts skittered away like a leaf in a breeze when he reached up and cupped her throat, holding her in place as he moved, kissing along her shoulder and then to her mouth.

The frantic beat of her pulse against his fingers as he cupped her throat called to him. Miles held her that way and she melted into him. It quieted everything outside, allowing him to focus on her. On Harlow and her pleasure.

On how simply by existing, she was his pleasure.

He turned, carefully and slowly so she didn't trip, and walked them over to the bed where he dropped her to the mattress and loomed over her while he looked his fill at her. Lips glossy and plump from where he'd been kissing them. Her nipples stood dark and hard, and he noted she wore a different hoop through her piercing.

"I like this," he told her as he traced a fingertip over her nipple and then tugged lightly on the jewelry until she gasped and arched into his touch.

"So do I," she said, her words slightly slurred from the state of pleasure that had washed over her.

He did that. Pride roared through him. This beautiful flame in his life came alive at his touch. This secret face she wore when it was just them two of them alone, bare to one another.

Dropping to his knees, ignoring her frustrated cry when his dick was out of her reach, Miles left a trail of open-mouthed kisses from her ankle, up her calf, behind her knee and over the velvet softness of her inner thigh. First one leg and then the other. Teasing not just Harlow, but himself.

Because he wanted to taste her. Wanted to kiss the heart of her in a way that would sear her memory forever. He craved her taste. The salty sweet of her pussy and the sounds she made when he went down on her were things he knew for sure he'd never forget.

When he spread her open with his thumbs, he leaned close to take several long, slow licks, triumphing in the way she shuddered, and her fingers slid into his hair and tightened.

He took his time. Building her up with nuzzles, licks and quick sucks of her clit between his lips. He'd loved learning all her cues, knowing that the flex of her thigh muscles meant she was close to climax.

He wanted it. Not as much as she probably did, but as much as he craved her taste, he craved her orgasms. Loved it when he made her come.

Miles used his palms on her hips to tip her up so he could get at more of her pussy as he drove her higher and higher until she arched on a snarl of his name and filled his senses with only her.

Harlow opened her eyes and stretched her muscles as little aftershocks of pleasure chased through her body. Her hips were a little tender where his fingers had dug into the flesh and muscle as he'd driven her mindless with pleasure. Her skin bruised easily and the first time he'd left a fingerprint bruise on her left ass cheek he'd been immediately sorry, but *she* wasn't sorry one bit. She liked it when there was a mark. It hadn't come from pain or anyone trying to harm her in any way. That was why she kissed him soundly on the mouth, told him she was just fine and to stop apologizing.

He was already putting a condom on, so she rolled up to her knees and bent, smiling against the blankets at the sound he made.

"So fucking beautiful I may die of it," he mumbled as he lined up behind her, his thighs against hers. He hissed as he slid into her pussy and she tightened herself around him, moaning as the bead on his piercing stroked against her inner walls.

Miles ran the edge of his nails down her spine and then back up again, then he tangled his hands in her hair and pulled her head back as he bent down, both straining to kiss the other as he began to stroke his cock deep into her cunt and back out again. Over and over and over until she was the one who thought she might die of pleasure as he left her there, right on the edge of coming again.

He kept control of the pace, even as she squirmed against him, delighting in his grunts and snarls as she pulled him closer and closer to his own climax.

More. She needed more of him. All he had to give and maybe a tiny bit more than that. She'd take what he offered freely, but with Miles there was always greed. Just one more kiss even moments after the last kiss had ended. When she watched him perform, she now knew what he looked like while he fucked her, and it had been impossible not to see one while he did the other.

"Make yourself come," he told her.

She had to redistribute her weight and balance to free one of her arms to reach her clit and that first touch told her it wasn't going to be very long. He must have known that because he sped up his thrusts, fucking into her, the sound each time his body met hers was a muffled slap and that was all she needed, that last nudge and she exploded around his cock.

"*Fuck*," he wheezed and pressed two more times before he came as well.

CHAPTER
FIFTEEN

"I know it was a shitty way to get to this point," Miles said to himself, "but damn if it's not fucking awesome to wake up to my bed warm from my woman."

Harlow was in the shower, singing an Earthquakes song, which eased satisfaction aside and replaced it with pride. Maddie had a great voice and she had pretty much no competition at her level, and Miles would be the first person to say so. But Harlow's smoky, whisky rough voice did something to him.

And she knew he would hear. A compliment to him in her own way.

Smiling, got out of bed, pulled on some pants, and went to get the breakfast he'd ordered when they'd finally been ready to sleep the night before.

While she was still in the shower, he took a moment to text Nora to let her know Harlow was okay.

But she called him. "Talking is better than texting. How is she this morning?"

"She's in the shower right now. Before she went in there, she said she wanted a big breakfast which just arrived."

"Tell me what happened."

Nora was bossy as hell. Probably needed to be to practically live with Harlow half the year when they were on the road.

Then again, she hit those drums *hard,* so she had her own fire.

Miles gave her a bullet pointed explanation of the whole situation at Hector and Mindy's place. He knew Nora had heard from Harlow all the shit Gloria had pulled, or part of it, Miles figured she kept the worst of it to herself. He also knew the two shared a deep loyalty and trust, so he didn't sugar coat it.

Nora cursed at the end. "*Lazy slut*? That fucking woman. I'm glad you were there and that you got her out of that place. This won't be the last she hears of it. Gloria has a long game planned. She'll drag out whatever this is to give maximum impact."

"What is her damage anyway?"

"Who knows? Over years Harlow has wondered the same. I can't ask Richie because he will definitely get involved."

"Well, maybe he should?" Miles walked a careful line here.

"You and I, and most likely Richie would agree. But Har doesn't. And she gave me her trust. I can't betray it."

"No, You're right." He didn't know Richie well enough to say how the man would feel one way or the other. But the way he'd built his life around Harlow's schedule when she was growing up so he could be an active part of her life was a clue.

"She just turned the water off. I need to go."

"Tell her I said to check in with me when she's done with breakfast," Nora said.

"I will. Do you think her brothers will show up tonight? Or should I tell them not to or?" Miles just wanted to make things better for her. She deserved it.

"Don't get in the middle of that part. Be there whatever happens. She loves them. Even when she knows they're weak and don't love her the way she deserves. We will *all* be with her tonight if they show up or if they don't. Someone might get hit in the head with a guitar, who knows?" Nora laughed.

Miles really liked Nora.

Harlow smelled coffee and moments later, bacon and so she quickened and got her clothes on before heading out to the living room where he'd set up breakfast at the table.

"Poppy just brought by dailies and stole a piece of bacon. Said it was her price for not complaining that you won't be at yoga this morning."

"Look at you tattling on your baby sister," Harlow said as she opened the curtains all the way to see the city outside.

"Hey, look, I know not to mess with your bacon. Poppy has to face that on her own. I'm no fool."

She noted the bottle of hot sauce, pleased he remembered she loved it on her potatoes and eggs.

Harlow needed to do a quick check of the calendar on her phone to be sure there was nothing more than signing some merch and a meet and greet with fans on her schedule that day. She hadn't turned it on yet, not wanting to face whatever might be there—or not—after that scene the night before.

When they'd finished and Miles had wandered off to do his own work, Harlow finally turned her phone on and waited for all the buzzing and dinging indicating texts and emails to stop.

"That sounds busy," Miles said from where he'd been at his laptop.

"I had it off. You know how it is," she said, looking at the screen. Multiple texts from Nora. One from Brian. Poppy saying she'd dropped dailies off with Miles instead of downstairs. Nothing from Gloria but two messages from Mindy.

The first was an apology that they'd been driven away from the house by Gloria. Harlow wanted to quibble with the brevity. It needed more than two sentences to be made right. But at the same time, these things should be said to her in person, or at least on the phone. And, most importantly, by Hector himself.

The second was a text saying she and Hector—but not Luis—were still coming to the show that night, and there was no way to stop the sound of disbelief that came from her lips.

"Harlow?" Miles asked, watching her while she scrolled through her messages.

"Mindy and Hector are coming tonight."

He didn't like Harlow's expression at all. Though she was trying to act nonchalant, he could see she was upset.

"I can deal with the box office if you want. Say no tickets are available. Or make sure they get no backstage access. Just the show and they go home afterward." He was on his feet and at her side before he'd even thought about it.

She sighed. "No. I can't uninvite them after she apologized and then said they were still coming. It'll look spiteful."

"The fuck do you care what they think of you? They're in the wrong, Harlow. And you deserve a little spite."

"I want a relationship with my brothers. Well, right now Mindy and Hector and my niece and nephews. I don't know about Luis. I don't need to be at war with him. Just for him to stay away unless or until he can apologize and truly understand where I'm coming from."

He wanted to argue, but instead he said, "So we'll get them up front and you can see them before Above Me goes on. We'll keep it brief. Hey hi, hope you like the show. Keep it moving. They have kids and they both have jobs so I'm sure they weren't planning on hanging out afterward anyway."

Harlow took his hands and brushed her lips over his knuckles. "Thank you for being so good to me." She pulled his head down and kissed him until they were both a little out of breath. "I have to go. I told Nora I'd be down shortly. I'll um, I'll see you later?"

"Absolutely you will. As usual, meet you at the elevator banks on your floor and we'll ride together to the venue." He paused and then said, "If you need me today, for anything at all, text or call. Please."

. . .

Nora answered the door and gave Harlow an up and down look before she hugged her. "Want to go for a walk?

"Yeah. Let's go grab a coffee and I'll tell you everything," Harlow said.

At the end of the telling, Nora sat back, sipping her iced coffee. "And you're letting them come tonight why?"

"She apologized."

Nora sighed heavily. "You are such a badassed bitch in so many other parts of your life but when it comes to these fuckos you're...not. Which makes me extra protective. Mindy apologized? Big fucking deal. Did *Hector* apologize? It's his house and his mother and brother who did all that. Did they kick *Gloria* out? No. You bore the weight of her bullshit like every other time. So, whatever to Mindy apologizing. It's her kid who is getting the Harlow treatment and Hector still lets your mother into his house? You don't need any of this bullshit. It's not yours. I will call them myself and tell them there are no tickets for them tonight and they know why."

Nora was incredibly protective of her closest circle, especially Harlow and Brian. She would absolutely call Mindy and say all those things. And in a tone that dared anyone to ask why when they should already know.

"My dad would be disappointed in me if I didn't try one last time."

"He most certainly would not be," Nora denied. "He'd be the first person to tell you to cut them off totally once you told him about this situation. I'm on your side. He's on your side. Miles is on your side. *You* should be on your side too."

"If there's such a thing as spite success, we are going to have it tonight. I can't uninvite them. It doesn't matter at this point that it was Mindy and not Hector who apologized. By text. I get it. I see it. However, we are going to play our asses off tonight because despite everything Gloria says about me, we are awesome. I want them to see it."

Understanding settled over Nora's features. "Ah. Okay. I get it." She leaned in and hugged Harlow tight. "I think we should play a cover of one of your dad's songs tonight. Don't you think?"

"Excellent idea."

Miles circled her, taking in every detail. She always looked fantastic before she went out on stage, but that night there was more going on. Earlier for soundcheck she'd been wearing jeans and a t-shirt but she'd changed into skintight metallic pants with pointy toed boots. Her shirt was sleeveless and lined down the front with little buttons that upon closer inspection, were tiny skulls.

Her hair was caught back from her face by sparkly pin things, but it was bigger than usual, and her makeup was stage perfect with dark lips and eyes. He only barely managed to hold back his hum of pleasure.

"I'm feeling a little like a bunny being stalked by a wolf," she said, making everyone standing around them laugh.

"You're no bunny, Harlow." He leaned in close and whispered in her ear. "But I do like to eat you."

She gave him an affectionate look and then sobered quickly. "You're messing with my game face, Miles Brown."

He paused, looking at her closely and then nodded as he understood. "I got you." He held a hand out and she put hers in it.

"I'm coming with you when you go out to see Mindy and

Hector," he said as they walked through the long hallways connecting their green rooms to the main stage. He'd spent most of the day thinking about her and the situation she was in. And more importantly how he could help, including staying out of it if necessary.

It wasn't necessary that day though. He was still surprised by the audacity of Harlow's brother in coming and leaning on her hospitality after what he'd done to her not even a full twenty-four hours prior.

So he'd stand at her side to let the other two know she had someone who would put her first. Miles had no reason to be nice or make them feel welcome. His purpose was to follow Harlow's lead and back her up.

"I'm having them brought into a receiving area near the stage," she said, and he heard nervousness in her tone.

"Okay."

"That gives a maximum of ten minutes. I won't invite them to dinner with us afterward. Well, okay, if he apologizes and means it I might."

He pulled her to a stop and the others kept walking.

"Hey," he said when they were alone. "You can handle this however you want. You know my feelings, but what matters here are *your* feelings. If you want them to come to dinner afterward, invite them. If you don't, that's okay too."

"I have to be a hardass so stop making me want to cry," she said, firming her mouth.

"That what you are, Harlow? A hardass?"

"No. But they don't deserve my soft parts and stop looking like that! I wasn't making a sex comment."

He laughed and pulled her into a hug.

"It's impossible for me not to think about sex when

you're concerned. But I'll control myself just this once. You're not a hardass. You have a beautiful, giving heart and you want to be loved and respected."

Poppy called Harlow's name from the end of the hall so they caught up with her. "I just sent someone to go get your brother and sister-in-law. You can talk to them right through here." She pointed to a room off to the left. "I had the chairs taken out. I can put them back, but I thought it might encourage brevity."

Miles nodded, approving

"That's good. Thank you." Harlow took a deep breath, squared her shoulders, and had just put on a megawatt smile when the doors opened up and Hector and Mindy came in.

When Harlow normally would have swept it all under the rug to keep the peace and keep anyone but herself from feeling uncomfortable, she thought about how it had felt that night before when no one but Miles had said much to defend her.

Mindy saw her and her eyes widened as she and Hector came into the room and Poppy left, closing the door, and leaving them. "You look amazing. Our seats are great. Thank you."

"Thanks."

Miles stood at her side but said little. Hector looked at him though, frowning before he turned back to Harlow. "Could we have some privacy?"

Miles looked not at Hector, but at Harlow and no, she wasn't going to send him from the room.

"Say what you need to say. Miles was there last night,

he's familiar with our family dynamic," Harlow said because it pissed her off that her brother would pull that. "Being rude isn't going to end up the way you think it will, Hector," she added.

"He's sorry," Mindy said. "He's embarrassed because everything happened, and he was caught off guard."

"First, he should speak for himself. Second, he *should* be embarrassed. Third, no he was not caught off guard." Harlow held up a hand when her brother opened his mouth to argue. "No. I'm not playing. You knew she might show up. Enough that you called her to tell her not to. And she did anyway. There was no *caught off guard*. Even I knew she might show up."

Time slipped away as Harlow stood there, waiting for... for what? Her brother to own anything? When had he or Luis ever? Their mother had always shielded them from whatever their behavior kicked up.

"You were in my house and then things got out of hand, and she wouldn't stop." Hector shook his head. "If everyone had just taken a deep breath and calmed down, we could have had dinner, but you left early and made it worse."

Mindy's sound of distress was echoed by Harlow's heart.

"Remember this moment and your failure to rise above it when your daughter is old enough to figure out her grandmother hates her but loves your sons. Save your money for therapy, I guess." Though Harlow wanted to cry, she stepped back and then took two more steps until she was at the door. Just outside the usher waited for them. "Can you escort them back to their seats, please?" she asked.

Poppy took one look at the situation and her brother's expression, and she bustled over. "Well then. Above Me is on in three minutes. Let's get you to the stage." She held her hand out to Harlow, who grabbed it like a lifeline. She left her brother and Mindy without looking back.

Miles waited a few seconds before he turned back to them.

"Just what the fuck did you think you were doing?" he asked.

Hector winced a little, but Mindy shrugged and looked at her husband like she didn't know the answer either.

"Oh, no words now?" Miles moved closer once he heard Above Me's set start and he knew they wouldn't be interrupted. "You had so many just a few minutes ago even though they were all the wrong ones."

"Hey!"

"Hey what? Go on, let's hear it?" Miles was so angry at that moment he wished Hector would come at him.

"She invited us tonight!"

"Before you abandoned her to the abuse your mother heaped on her while you sat there and did nothing. And you came anyway like you deserved to." He made a sound with so much derision dripping from it he was sort of proud. "You invited her to your home. You know—because you've watched—your mother has a shitty track record with Harlow. But Harlow trusted you. Oh sure, she knew it was a possibility Gloria would show up and she braced for it. But she trusted that you'd at the very least make your home a safe place for her. Though I don't know why she would because none of you have given her a safe space her whole life."

Miles held up a hand and shook his head when Hector opened his mouth to argue.

"You had your chance to talk and didn't rise to the occasion. Gloria showed up and from the first moment set out to insult and upset Harlow. Luis was her lapdog, tossing her whatever ammunition she'd need to hurt his own sister. And you...did nothing. You sat there and couldn't put together two sentences to stand up for your sister who had done nothing but accept an invitation to dinner with her brother and sister-in-law."

"I tried to calm it down," Hector insisted.

"How so? By blaming it on Harlow tonight? If she hadn't escaped a toxic situation where her mother was calling her a lazy slut because no one stood up for her everything would be okay? That's the reason Gloria says the vicious stuff she does with zero pushback?"

"This is family business," Hector said. "It's not your concern. My mom has overcome a lot."

"Fuck your mother." Miles squared his feet slightly apart, waiting. Wanting Hector to make a move because he'd never wanted to punch someone's face more than he did right then.

Mindy stood between them staring at Hector. "He's right. Gloria started all that. She always does. She treats Harlow terribly. I've said so for years and you've made excuses. I made them too even though I saw how she was. You need to apologize to Harlow. Genuinely. You're her big brother."

"She lives it up in this world and I'm supposed to what? Play nice so we get invites to places? Like she didn't get to have all the travel and money while we stayed home?"

Miles was so thoroughly disgusted. "She wanted to share this with you. Wanted you to be proud of her and see how hard she worked to achieve it. You're backstage right now while she's on stage and you're arguing with me instead. You could have said I'm sorry you got treated so badly in my home. Instead, you said *she* made it worse by leaving. Now get out. Go sit and watch her be amazing and you'd better tell her so afterward with your thank you. And then fuck off. Leave her alone because your absence is less painful than your presence when you abuse her just like your mother does."

He slammed the door as he left, not looking back at the usher who'd overheard that entire exchange.

CHAPTER
SIXTEEN

Just over a week later, Miles leaned against the stair rail and watched Above Me's soundcheck. He'd noticed that Harlow had seemed grumpier than usual earlier that day when they'd woken up, so he wanted to keep an eye out.

He'd hoped to entice her into a nice bout of morning sex to start the day right, but her phone had buzzed, she'd looked at the screen, her mouth lost that kissable quality and had turned down into a frown,

Probably had something to do with her fucking idiot brothers or their mother. There weren't a lot of things Miles actually hated, but Gloria Martin was one of them, right up there with homophobia and racism. She was probably both, come to think on it.

They headed straight into "Dark Heart", one of his favorites of theirs and now that he knew her better—and had met her mother—he understood who it was about and hearing her sing it tore him up every time.

Poppy bounced up to him and handed him a printed

email with all the numbers Jeremy had forwarded to them that morning. He nodded. They were doing great. One sold out show after the next. So much they'd added another night to several more US cities.

Someone in the audience shouted "Seek & Destroy" and Harlow grinned back over her shoulder and played the opening notes, but Nora followed up and so did Brian so they went for it, but it was Harlow who sang it.

And damn if she didn't know the whole fucking song, including the bridge where she and Brian kicked ass, and it wasn't the first time they'd played it either. They put their own spin, speeding it up slightly, slowing it down here and there. Miles was sad he'd missed her metalhead phase, but he could see the foundations of it right then as she played.

And she shined as she played guitar, clear on her face how much she loved it, and loved playing with Brian and Nora as she turned and played into the last part of the song.

"Haven't done that one in a long time," she said to cheers.

"Well, not all of us learn to play Metallica guitar solos from Richie Martin," Brian said of Harlow's father.

"Right?" Harlow gave the devil horns with her right hand.

"Is everything okay?" Poppy asked him as he broke his gaze away from Harlow back to his sister.

"Yeah. Yeah." He ran his hands through his hair after he handed the paper back to her. "Good news."

"Looks like it. More shows in Europe now too."

Selfishly, he'd tried to think on ways to bring her with him. Thought about how to have Above Me open for them in addition to the other bands scheduled.

But he knew she'd see it as him pulling strings for her instead of Above Me earning their spot. And he also knew she and Above Me were touring the festival circuit over the late summer and early fall when Earthquakes would be in Europe anyway.

Touring could be exciting and fun and fulfilling. He loved so many elements of it. It was also exhausting. And it was hard to sleep in different beds in different places every single night. It was stressful to be *on* every moment he was outside his hotel room. It didn't matter if one of them was sick or had a bad day. Fans paid good money and spent their time to attend a show and it was necessary to give them his best every time.

Harlow being there with him every day. Traveling with her. Experiencing this magical thing so few people every got the chance to at his side was fucking amazing. It made everything better.

"Before," he said to Poppy, "when I was with Sophie, I didn't have a deep sense of satisfaction like I do with Harlow. When we were apart, it didn't feel wrong or uncomfortable. With Harlow, I'm different because she's different."

"You've been free from that situation for over two years. That's enough space for you to see the difference and under-stand why. I wasn't worried you were going to go and marry whateverhernameis. She didn't want that either. She got her clicks. You got your kicks. It was fast and it burned hot and was done. And she helped you learn what it is you *need* and that wasn't her. I know the way she used all that personal information hurt you and makes you wonder just who you can trust. But that's about her, not about you. And Harlow is the opposite of that."

"You're pretty wise for a twenty-year-old," he told his little sister.

"I do okay. I was raised to listen more than I talked. Which is no mean feat in our family."

He laughed. "No shit." Miles glanced at his phone and saw the time. He had an interview scheduled in a few minutes and less than half an hour after that, they were due on stage. He and Poppy headed back into the warren of hallways to where he and the rest of Earthquakes had set up.

Omar had headphones on and watched a movie on his tablet in a far corner. Maddie was Facetiming with her parents so Miles waved at them as he walked by.

Silas was most likely off on a run. He liked to run the steps at whatever arena they were playing in as a good luck token. And to keep his cardio up because he was a monster beyond the drums and needed to stay in shape for it.

He'd find out whatever Harlow was bothered by later on when they were both alone.

"Gloria sent a cease and desist to me and your dad," Jenna, her dad's wife said after Harlow had been assured there was no emergency behind the call.

"What for? I don't understand." Harlow asked.

"He's doing press. You know how it is on tour."

Harlow made a sound to indicate she was listening, and yes, she totally knew.

"It came up that you were on tour now too. And he was talking about how proud he was of you and Above Me and then he told some cute story about how he taught you guitar as a reward for you getting your schoolwork done."

That made Harlow smile. "He did. It was more that it was one-on-one time than learning guitar chords, but I hope it was nice for him because it was everything to me."

"You're going to make me cry," Jenna said, emotion in her voice. "Yes, the way he told the story and the way the interviewer put it in the final edit made it clear it meant a lot to him."

"So Gloria is mad that...we were happy? She wants you to stop talking about your lives?"

Jenna snorted. "He mentioned that you and Marcella went on the road with him. He didn't actually say anything about Gloria, only that he was a single dad, and his sister was a huge part of why he could be out on the road with a young kid. Apparently, this set her off somehow. She considers it slanderous."

"That is so rich coming from her." Harlow was past being surprised when her mother did something terrible. But that didn't mean she wasn't seriously angry.

"You want to tell me what's going on? This was out of the blue and your dad is beyond pissed off. His attorney is already on it. But he doesn't want you put in the middle, so that's why he didn't tell you and I am."

"I'm not in the middle. I'm always on his side. I saw her recently. It didn't go well. But it had nothing to do with him."

"I know there's a really complicated history with her. I just want you to know your dad and I are always about you and Ry. I want to protect you. You can tell me anything."

Harlow ran a fingertip under her eye to wipe the tears and deal with what she knew would be mascara smears. "I went to Hector and Mindy's for dinner while we were in Atlanta. Gloria showed up and was a nightmare. I haven't spoken to her since. I've barely spoken to her over the last fifteen years. I'm not entirely sure why she would decide to make some sort of fuss now with my dad. I'm twenty six years old and I can't remember a *single* time in my life when she treated me like she wanted me around. She dumped me off on him when I was two and that's pretty much all the mothering I've ever received from her."

"This strike at your dad was about how people would perceive her. This has nothing to do with anyone but Gloria. I'm sorry. I'm sorry she can't be the mom you need her to be. You are loved. And you are valued."

"I'm sorry this has seeped into your lives." Like toxic waste.

"Sweetheart, Gloria doesn't scare me or your dad. Our worry here is about you. And how this makes you feel. You didn't tell him about the dinner in Atlanta? He would *never* blame you, you know that, right?"

"He's still selling out entire arenas! How many bands who've been around as long as AMJFJ has can say that? He's got a real relationship with a person who cares about him as much as he cares about her. And there's Ryder. Why would I bring anything about Gloria into that? He paid his dues. He gets to be done."

"That's not how life works, Harlow. You know that."

"I didn't tell him any of the details because he can't change what happened. He can't make her behave better. He can't do anything that would make her love me more. Or less, for that matter."

Jenna's voice was thick with emotion. "I wish I was there right now to give you a hug. Let him help you sometimes. I understand why you've kept some of this to yourself. I love that you protect him the way you do. But I love you too. And not just as Richie's kid or Ryder's big sister."

"Even if I'm a lazy slut?" Harlow said. She'd meant to tease but beneath that, she'd needed to say it out loud.

"She said that?" Jenna's voice had gone very hard.

"Among other things. Apparently I was a flirty slut even *as a baby* and I will trap a man into supporting me by getting pregnant so he has to marry me."

"Like she did? Oh I shouldn't have said that out loud. It wasn't like Richie was unwitting. He fucked her without birth control so it's not a surprise or a trick. Ugh, I'm sorry. *She* is terrible. And she is accusing you of things she perhaps feels she is or did herself. Thank god for Marcella. You got a way better mother out of the deal, but your heart still hurts and I hate that."

Harlow laughed. Relieved, so relieved at Jenna's response.

"I hate it too. I'm working on getting past it. Can you at least tell me if Hector or Luis are involved in this cease and desist thing?"

"Not that I know of. Your dad does talk about them in interviews, though not as much. He feels bad about that too. But that you don't know tells me maybe they weren't supportive when Gloria did whatever she did at this dinner?"

"No, they weren't. To be fair, Hector didn't participate in her attacks but there's tension now between me and them because I stood up for myself, and they're not used to that."

"They don't know you at all then. Which I guess is not only a pity, but the root of the problem," Jenna said.

"Not everyone wants to know me. I've got to deal with that like anyone else. And I've hit a place where I am unwilling to take a bunch of disrespect for doing nothing more than existing."

"Well, good. I'm sorry they're not being the brothers they should. I'm sorry about a lot of stuff."

Harlow blew out a long breath. "None of this is yours to feel sorry about. You can mention to my dad that there was a dinner where a falling out occurred and that's probably why Gloria is being like this. But if you can, as a favor to me, try not to make a deal of it. He's on tour. He's got to get up on stage and entertain over and over and this will mess with his mojo. There's nothing he did or can do now to make Hector and Luis be any different. She formed them into what they are, but Dad will feel guilty for it anyway."

"I'll do my best. Because you're on tour too. But when you're done and he's done, I think it's time for us all to have a long talk regarding your mother," Jenna told her.

Sounded fucking terrible. "If things change, let me know. She shouldn't get to decide the timing because she's feeling a way about me getting up and leaving the table where she is insulting me."

"I never turn my phone off when your dad is gone for work. If you need anything, including a sympathetic ear, call me. Promise," Jenna said.

"Okay, I promise. I'll call if I need you. Thank you for being there to answer."

When Miles came offstage later that night he was exhilarated and starving, so he went looking for Harlow so they could eat some late dinner together and he'd make her tell him why she was brooding. But she wasn't in their green room or around the stage either.

"She just went outside to get a breath," Brian said.

"She okay?"

Brian said, "Go find her and make her tell you."

"Harlow doesn't respond well to making her do anything," he muttered, and Brian laughed and laughed.

"Yeah, no shit. But you're alive and unbruised, so you've got something going for you because otherwise, she'd never tolerate it."

Miles thanked Brian and went back out.

They nearly crashed into one another when she entered the building as he was leaving. He caught her around her waist. "Hey. I was just looking for you. I'm starving. Come eat with me. The garlic is singing a siren song."

That's when he noted her expression.

"What's up?"

She told him about the cease-and-desist Gloria had sent her father.

The first three words that came to mind were those he thought of most often when it came to Gloria Martin. "What the fuck? How's your dad taking it?"

"It was Jenna who called, not him. He's trying to shield me from it. Like I don't already know how she is. I'm so mad he didn't tell me."

"You're both the same. He won't tell you to protect you and you won't tell him to protect him. Meanwhile, Gloria runs riot with her bullshit and hurts you both for funsies."

Her eyes widened and he wanted to apologize. Didn't really want to cause her distress but damn it, this fucking woman was a tornado, and she was dead set on hurting

Harlow. She needed to share this stuff with her dad and he sure as hell needed to share with Harlow. She wasn't a kid anymore. Their mutual secrecy hurt them both.

"Telling him changes nothing."

"I bet he'd say the same," he challenged.

She growled.

He brushed hair back from her face and kissed her temple, just breathing her in. He tried to tell himself he'd be just as concerned about this if they were only friends. But his heart thundered in his chest at her scent. He wanted to do anything and everything he could to make her stop hurting, including saying tough stuff because she'd listen to him, and she needed to hear it from someone she trusted.

"At least Hector and Luis don't appear to be involved," she said at last as they started walking toward the mess area for dinner.

"That's good. I'm glad he listened to me."

She looked to him as she skidded to a stop. "Listened to you when?"

Oops. He'd forgotten to tell her about that little exchange after she'd left for the stage. "Just a little back and forth that second night in ATL when they were backstage. I told him he owed you a real apology because you trusted him, and he didn't make his home a safe place for you. And then I told him to fuck off if he couldn't be a real brother to you."

"Hector and Mindy sent a text saying they'd been impressed with Above Me. They thanked me for the invite and apologized that things got heated backstage. That was only because you told him to?"

These people made him want to punch everyone in the throat. Even though he had told them to thank Harlow for the invite and to say she was awesome Miles hated that she thought they'd only done it because he'd made them.

Maybe they had for all he knew. But he didn't want her hurting from these people. Enough was enough. So he'd ease around the truth. "They should have thanked you so I'm glad they did. They should have apologized for that shitshow backstage *and* at their home, so I'm annoyed but whatever. I don't think they only did it because I made them feel guilty by telling them the truth. You *are* wonderful and talented so it's good they saw it and maybe understand you a little more."

He'd never forget the bitterness in Hector's tone when he'd made that comment about playing nice to get invited to things. Gloria had done a number on all her kids it looked like. But Hector wasn't a kid anymore and it was time to grow the fuck up or stay away.

"I know an attorney or two if you need someone," he told her. "Extended family. If you need someone tough to handle Gloria, they'd be good."

"Jenna said my dad's attorney was on it already, but thanks."

"You still hungry?" he asked. Miles had noticed she would go too long without eating when she was in the middle of work or was upset about something. Being on tour was grueling, he wanted her to stay healthy, so he wasn't above some nagging.

"Maybe."

"Come on then. Let's get dinner. You need the calories so you keep up in bed later." He winked at her and steered them both toward the scent of garlic.

CHAPTER
SEVENTEEN

Harlow stood in the audience, looking up at Earthquakes on stage at Madison Square Garden. Above Me had already played their set and she was still buzzing with excitement. Her first time playing MSG and it had been as incredible as she'd imagined.

And now she got to watch her man kick ass to a sold out crowd in a mythical arena in the city that never slept.

The place was absolutely packed with cheering fans who knew all the words to every song. Miles and his band were giving them every bit of their money's worth and more.

A silvery blue spot seemed to caress him as he leaned in to the mic to sing the lyrics to "On Your Back", a song about being taken over by a sexual partner. Having been taken over by the man currently singing about naked slide of skin on skin, she could verify it was not overrated at all.

"So fucking soft. Hard edged need like a knife. Pull it from me. Pour into you."

Yum. He dominated the stage, and she could see those sexy forearms of his from where she stood. Usually, she stayed stage left but some nights she got out in the audience to get the full experience and that night she wasn't sorry.

Their sound was perfect and every single member of Earthquakes was in synch with the others as they made an incredible storm together. It was so magical all Harlow could do was clasp her hands together in front of her chest, just so thrilled for him.

Thrilled enough to ignore all the exposed tits being showcased in his direction. After all, hers were the ones he paid attention to, and really could she blame anyone for trying to get some from him? As long as he didn't give it, she could find a way to deal with it.

He'd be sweaty and revved up and the moment the hotel room door closed behind them he'd pounce on her. Hot damn she was lucky.

"This one's for a certain dark-haired siren," Miles said into the microphone and they began playing, "Mine," one of the sweeter and still darkly sexual songs on their most recent release.

"Dayum," Nora said into Harlow's ear. "He's wants that kitty cat for real."

That made Harlow giggle even as she saw it for what it was. Miles wanted everyone to know they were together. There'd been pictures and enough talk that it was obvious they were. But this declaration from stage was sweet, yes, but also her dude staking a claim in front of the world.

He was a handful. Especially when it came to getting whatever it was he wanted. She was wildly flattered that what he wanted was her. Even while she was wary of the way he simply steamrolled through things to achieve his aims.

Usually it was about sex or getting her to eat or rest or sleep in his room, so he got away with it. But there were lines he skirted, and she realized more each day that she had to keep an eye on those lines, or he'd stroll right over them.

Still, she couldn't remember the last time she was so wonderfully, truly happy. And that bossy guy up there on their second encore was a big part of that.

"They're nearly done. Come on." Nora grabbed her hand and dragged Harlow backstage once again so they—really Harlow—cold be there when Miles came offstage.

Backstage was chaos as the band came off the stage, handing off instruments and ear monitors. Harlow would have waited for him back in their green room space, but Miles really liked it when she waited there where he could see her as he came down.

Harlow realized she liked making Miles smile and it wasn't a hardship to stand out of the way and take all the chaos in. Miles was still in charge. Speaking to his tech and their tour manager and sound engineer. Doing their nightly postmortem as Above Me had done earlier.

He was just so sexy and in charge as he focused on whoever he was speaking to. He listened before replying. The others looked to him all the time in myriad ways they probably weren't even totally aware of. He was so capable and steadfast even with all the sharp edges. A protector.

She liked it. Most of the time. So far, he was worth the effort it took not to let him get away with whatever he pleased.

"Holy shit!" Nora exclaimed, catching Harlow's attention.

"What?" Harlow tried to read over her shoulder. All she

could see were three bullet pointed things from Jeremy so she waited for Nora to fill her in.

"We hit gold record status. And now two of the singles are charting and getting a lot of play. Jeremy has been approached about using one of our songs in a movie Mercury Reid is directing."

"Holy shit is right!" She and Nora hugged, dancing around until Brian approached and then joined them for a moment after they'd told him the news.

Miles rolled up looking deliciously disheveled and sweaty. Goddess, she wanted to lick him to celebrate. Like a more carnal version of a tequila shot.

"Hey, beauty, what are we celebrating?" he said, a smile on his face.

She hugged him and instantly he wrapped himself around her in response. She was utterly surrounded by everything Miles. He made her heart sing.

Harlow told him the news and he hugged her again. "That's fantastic. Congratulations." He grinned. "Tell Maddie no," he murmured.

Before she could ask what he meant, Maddie came bounding up, full of energy. "Hey, everyone is going out. Silas knows all the afterhours clubs and stuff. We'll drink and eat and dance or whatever."

Nora and Brian nodded. "Yeah! We're in. We have a lot to celebrate tonight for all of us. You all sounded amazing tonight. Top show so far, edging Vegas into second place."

"I think I'm going back to the townhouse," Harlow said, understanding what Miles had meant. It wasn't like she hadn't gone to clubs and parties so far on the tour but having some quiet time to celebrate that whole day with him at her side sounded perfect.

"Oh, good yeah, me too," Miles said, all innocent-like.

"Fine. See you two tomorrow. Don't forget we're doing media in the morning," Nora told her.

"It's on my calendar and also the daily Poppy pre-delivered to me. Do not let her get drunk," Harlow murmured to Nora.

"There's no way they'd let her get hurt but I'll keep an eye out. I'd question how she'll even get into a club when she's not quite twenty-one, but I was not quite twenty-one and got into plenty."

"That and you're all famous. Nora, we are having a very good day. I love your fucking face."

Nora snorted a laugh. "Love you too. Have fun."

Miles took a shower and changed before they grabbed a car over to the townhouse Richie owned and had insisted she and Above Me use while in the city for the MSG shows. Still buzzing from that night's show and then all their good news, he was beyond relieved to have her all to himself in a quiet place to celebrate.

She toed her shoes off and headed from the enclosed front entry space and into the main part of the house. He hadn't expected all black walls and studded leather couches or anything, but the elegant and yet very comfortable layout and furnishings had been a nice surprise.

Then she turned and hugged him. "Nora was right. Tonight's show was stellar. You eye fucked that crowd, and they ate it up."

He grinned. "I did what now?"

"Come into the kitchen so I can get plates and drinks. Pizza will be here shortly. I've been dreaming of their sausage and black olive for weeks now. Champagne is going to make it even better."

She pulled a bottle from the fridge. "I checked earlier when we first arrived. Fully stocked fridge and there are good snacks in the pantry. Jenna is one of those ultimate host type people. Everything is organized and comfortable with great snacks."

Harlow's step-mother seemed like the polar opposite of Gloria. Generous and loving. But Miles was not going to ruin their night with the mention of that harpy.

"I'm pro-snacks if I'm being asked for an opinion," he told her, stealing a kiss and loving the way her mouth curved up as she smiled.

"If you want to open it, I'll find glasses." She twirled away and hunted through a few cabinets until she found what she needed.

"Can you take the plates and drinks up to our room, please? The pizza place just texted to say the pies were on the way. I'll bring them when they get here," she told him.

As if he'd just go upstairs and wait for her to answer the door to a stranger at nearly one in the morning?

"Oh, hey can you take this a second?" Miles handed her the bottle and once she was burdened by the things in her hands, he grinned. "I'll get the door," he called out over his shoulder as he heard the doorbell.

He heard her little growl, but it only made him smile more. She needed taking care of and that's what he'd do.

"So tell me how I eye fucked a crowd?" he asked as he kicked the door closed behind himself.

"You know exactly how you eye fucked a crowd, Miles. You know when you do it to me and it's just as distracting when you broadcast it to thousands. It's part of your persona for sure. But it's also part of the Miles behind the mask. You're an inherently sexual being and you know how to use it to your advantage. Like getting me all addled and handing off that champagne while you went to the door."

She changed into shorts and a barely there tank and then handed him a glass of champagne.

"To Madison Square Garden night one." She tapped her glass to his and they took a drink.

"To two singles charting." He tapped his glass to hers.

"To gold and multi-platinum and Mercury Reid," she said.

They drank and kissed and drank some more before loading slices on their plates.

"You know," he said after a few minutes, "Jeremy left me a voicemail earlier about a possible movie role. I wonder if it's the same movie the song is for."

"Whoa. Do you think?"

"I'm talking with him in the morning, so I'll find out for sure."

"Do you want to pursue acting jobs more now?" she asked.

"I've had two small film roles so far. It's fun, you know? Something totally different from this part of my life, but really, it's all acting in some way or another. Boosting a part of myself, lessening another. I don't want acting to replace music, but it's definitely a way to keep myself working across a few different fields. Money doesn't hurt either." He grinned.

"I saw both the movies you were in," she admitted. "You're good and the camera absolutely loves you. You have that something extra. It's not just looks. You have charisma. You know how to work a crowd. You're great with fans. You've got star power. People want to look at you, be around you. They want to buy your branded bass guitars and those spiffy watches you model for."

"Sometimes it feels like maybe I took something meant for someone else." He shrugged.

Truth was, there were times Miles was conflicted about taking modeling jobs. It seemed weird to profit off his looks. But as his dad had pointed out, it was just another part of his career. He didn't have to take jobs for companies he didn't like. But the money was good. It was a bit of advertising for the band, and it had gotten him other jobs from the exposure.

And truth be told, each successful gig he had was a way to prove to the world that he made his own success. That he wasn't a fluke or something made out of shadows his famous family had created for him.

She nodded. "I understand." Harlow, she got it. He didn't even need to explain it all. "Deep down you know that's bullshit. But it still can mess with your heart. I'm here to say there's no one I'd rather buy a watch from because I've seen you looking gorgeous in an ad. Not because your dad is Adrian Brown. But because you're Miles Brown."

He leaned over to kiss her because she filled him with so much happiness. "You're right. Thank you for reminding me. Speaking about the camera," Miles said. "I keep meaning to tell you how much I like your photographs. I follow your social media. I didn't even know who took all the pictures. I figured it was one person, but I realized the candids of everyone, but you were your work."

Her blush shot straight to his gut. "The official ones at the various social media platforms and on our website are taken by Phil's wife, Edda. She's fantastic, right?"

"Yes. I like the ones of you all performing. And the glimpses of Earthquakes are nice."

She looked up into his face. "Edda doesn't do those, I do. The ones I post I do get permission for, I promise. I know you have your own social media presence, so I don't want to overstep."

Overstep? He'd been practically begging for more space in her public life so those shots of Earthquakes had absolutely made his day. "It never crossed my mind to wonder if you got permission. I'm not worried about that. I just like it that I'm there in this other part of your life." Miles shrugged and realized she'd underlined a key difference between herself and his ex. He never worried that Harlow would use any part of their private life for her own gain. It just wasn't who she was or how she did things.

"Oh. Okay then."

"Will you post a picture of me when I'm still sleeping tomorrow morning?" he teased, and she guffawed.

"No, but I do have some on my phone. Those are for my own personal enjoyment. Reality is better anyway."

"I'll happily be reminded of that tomorrow when you wake up. Wake me up too." He paused. "How long do you think we have until Nora and Brian return?"

She put her plate aside after taking another bite of her pizza. "I think we have an hour or so."

One handed, he pulled his shirt off and put his plate next to hers before using his body to take hers to the mattress.

"Let's get to work, shall we?"

CHAPTER
EIGHTEEN

The last interview Harlow needed to do before the show that night was with some up and coming new music and media magazine. Women in rock and roll or something. As it was something she and Nora believed in and were a part of, they had agreed. Brian, at the merest suggestion he didn't have to be there, jetted so fast if he was a cartoon there'd have been little puffs of smoke at his heels, headed for a comics store near the townhouse.

Their names were at the front desk, so the guard swiped a card through the elevator panel and unlocked the fifth floor, sending them on their way.

The offices weren't huge, but the vibe was edgy and young, and they were offered fresh pressed juice or coffee when they were seated in a smallish conference room and told Sophia would be in shortly.

Though shortly meant twenty minutes late and tried not to let it show when their interviewer finally came in.

Tall and blonde, she looked very much like one of those perfect Manhattan influencers. Cute and slightly quirky outfit that Harlow was certain came straight from a designer showroom. Perfect hair and makeup that had to have been done professionally because she refused to believe anyone's eyeliner could be so flawless done on their own. Her entire being was a production and no lie, Harlow couldn't help but be impressed with what had to be a great deal of effort to be so put together.

"Thanks for your patience," she told them as she settled in.

Harlow's aunt had counseled her years back to never apologize for being late or whatever in a business context, but to thank the other party, so she saw it for what it was, and appreciated it just the same.

It wasn't like she could make a scene. Good press was important and if they were impatient or acted like assholes, that would come out.

"I'm Sophia and you're Harlow and Nora, right?" After they nodded and said their hellos, Sophia got right into it.

There were leading questions really designed to make the person asking look good and once Harlow figured out who this interviewer was, she adjusted her replies and persona to fit.

There was talk about their recent release and the themes of strength through vulnerability and both Harlow and Nora warmed up to that. The songs and the music itself were a love letter to messing up and being better and the power of female friendship.

"And you two are friends then? For real?" Sophia asked.

"Yes. Since we were thirteen or so. She's my human." Harlow smiled at Nora.

"Never fought over boys?"

Boys? What were they, twelve?

Nora cocked her head. "We don't have the same taste in romantic interests. Even if we did, I hope we could avoid being a cliché."

"So, you're not jealous over Harlow's new man candy?"

Well. That was unexpected. She'd been asked about Miles in interviews since they'd more or less gone public with their relationship, but the way Sophia was acting right then was over the top.

"I'm good, thanks," Nora said, and Harlow barely smothered a laugh.

"I guess that means she can share details. Miles Brown is incredibly inventive in bed, don't you think?" Sophia leaned toward them with a predatory smile, and Harlow realized she'd let the other woman fool her into believing she was generally harmless.

This was the ex-girlfriend everyone made a sour face about. Clearly, she hadn't gotten over Miles and frankly Harlow could understand that. However, Miles wasn't a piece of pizza she would fight over like a seagull.

And it wasn't that this person had sex with Miles before he'd even come back into Harlow's life. It was the way Sophia seemed to delight in this gossip. That they'd either bond over Miles or fight?

"I mean. A penis piercing. I did enjoy that. The septum piercing though, meh. He's more handsome without it don't you think?" Sophia said.

Nora stepped on Harlow's foot, and it surprised her enough to bite back what had been her first instinct. Sophia was a complicated little monster. And she'd feed on Harlow's response if she allowed her buttons to be pushed by this dumbass.

So she just looked at Sophia until the other woman cleared her throat.

But Sophia wasn't done.

"So how did Above Me get this opening spot on the Earthquakes tour?"

"Erin Brown is a fan. She passed on our music to Miles and told him we might be good to open for them. He heard our music. We share an agency. The band asked us, and we accepted. It's a great opportunity for us to reach a bigger audience, so it was an easy decision."

Sophia wasn't expecting Harlow to resist the bait. She frowned prettily a moment.

"But when you met him." She waggled her brows at Harlow. "I mean, just between us, it couldn't hurt that you're pretty."

"Thanks, I guess? Thing is, there are plenty of bands fronted by pretty people and most of them would happily jump at the chance to open on this tour. But thankfully, we have a sound they and their management liked, so we got the opportunity."

"Why not use what you have? Pretty face, famous dad, famous boyfriend with a successful band." Sophia shrugged. "It's rough out there. Competitive."

Nora put a hand on Harlow's arm.

Harlow took a deep breath and then answered. "We did use what we have. Talent. That's what got us this spot. As for the rest, I think what I'd say is that women have it hard enough being taken care of in the music industry without the calls coming from inside the house, you know?"

"Calls?"

"It's from a movie. The bad guy is in the house. It's her way of saying we should be supporting one another's work, not playing into stereotypes that they can't achieve success unless it's through a man." Nora fluttered her lashes.

"She's sleeping with one of the hottest men in music right now. She can't expect it not to come up as an issue. I don't hate the game like she claims to, but Harlow, you can't pretend it doesn't exist," Sophia said. "You sure can't pretend it doesn't matter that you're riding that dick."

Harlow rolled her eyes, not bothering to hide that response. "It doesn't matter to *you*. I don't need to share details with you like we're close. Or like I have permission to share anything about the private life of someone I'm with."

"Permission? Honey, men with dick piercings don't worry about that. He loved it when I talked about it. Got him more fans too. Did you sign a NDA or something? He might have gotten wiser after me." Sophia snickered.

"Are you interviewing us about our band and music or about my boyfriend's body jewelry?" Harlow asked.

"You already talked about your band. Now talk about your *boyfriend's* cock. Come on. Loosen up a little. This is part of the business you're in. The public wants to know about your life, and that *especially* includes when your life means you're sleeping with a rock star. Just because you can't get past that he and I were together you're going to act holier than thou?"

Harlow snorted. "Don't make this into something it's not. I don't give a shit if you fucked Miles a *thousand* times before I came along. I'm here now. That's all I need. This isn't some sort of fight over a guy. You're rude. We aren't friends. I don't know you and I'm not going to share details of my private life because you want me to help you get readers."

Beyond annoyed and utterly done, Harlow stood and Nora joined her. "We've got another appointment to get to."

"Well I was done with you anyway. Don't hold your breath that you'll keep his interest after the tour ends."

"Bye bye!" Harlow waved as she paused in the doorway. "Have the day you deserve."

Not wanting to catch the subway, they hailed a cab and headed back to the townhouse. Harlow looked at the time. "Do you want to text Brian to let him know we're on the way back?"

"He's a big boy. He'll see that when we return if his face isn't stuffed into a comic book. But we need to talk about what just happened," Nora said.

"Not the first time it's come up in an interview," Harlow said.

"The first time you've squared up with your boyfriend's ex who wants you to share details about your sex life. And who came out and inferred you have your success because you're pretty and have a famous dad. And you *are* pretty, and you do have a famous dad. And your success--"

Harlow interrupted, "I'd be lying to myself and everyone else if I claimed it had nothing to do with those things. It does. Jeremy heard about us because we had connections. We used our family connections to record our album. Jeremy is the one who sent the music to Miles's aunt Erin to start with. Yes, we work hard. But those other things she brought up are a factor."

"Not the same and you know it. She was totally off base. The whole thing was a setup. You know that right? She knew who you were, and not just the part about your music. She's kept tabs on Miles, that much is clear."

"If he wanted to be with her, he would be. That's literally it. I can't control any of that part about how she feels or what she does. Only what I do in response. She can't have him back. I already licked him."

Nora burst into laughter. "How are you going to explain this to him?"

"I'm not. He's got enough on his mind. I have enough on my mind. Some random ex-girlfriend from years ago isn't a threat to me."

"What if she's a threat to him?" Nora asked. "Like, sure he's got a pierced dick, but he's not out there shaking it at people. At least not that I've seen and since we've been on this tour, we've been around him a lot. He seems to keep his private life quiet too."

"Maybe because he dated that twat, and realized if he wasn't careful, his business would be all over the place?" Harlow cracked jokes, but also, that comment Nora had made got her thinking. "Still, that's actually true. It's well known he had a dark time when he was with her. I think their breakup was fraught and he learned a lot of those painful life lessons. But you're right. The Miles I'm with would likely be super uncomfortable. He hasn't mentioned her to me more than a reference to an old relationship. I'll do a little research when we're at the arena." During Earthquakes's soundcheck so he wouldn't happen to stumble in while she was cyber checking out his ex.

"Your saying that bit about not having his permission to share was important. I don't know if that part will make it into the final edit, or even if there'll be an interview at all, but I'm glad you thought about that. About how he'd feel."

"Nora, I think about how he'd feel about a lot of things." More than she really had before. In a different way than she had with her lovers in the past. Harlow chewed on her lip as they arrived at the townhouse and they paid for the ride before heading inside.

"Go check on Brian," Harlow said when they unlocked the front door.

"We weren't done." Nora was such a good friend.

"There's always more time to talk about all the rest. I'm going to be out on the patio. I want to call Marcella and my dad. Just a check in."

After a heavy sigh, Nora hugged her and headed up the stairs while Harlow grabbed some tea from the fridge and headed outside to the pretty garden patio.

Her chat with her dad was easy. He and the band were in Mexico, and she caught him before he'd have to go on stage.

She grinned because he always made her happy. "Hey, Dad! I'm in your townhouse eating all your snacks. Thanks for letting us use it."

"Makes me feel better knowing you're in a house surrounded by love. Tell Jenna you ate all the food she had stocked. That'll make her day," he said.

They meandered around. Talked about her music news.

Talked about his own news and tour stuff. He passed on his love to Nora and Brian and said the rest of AMJFJ send theirs to her.

At the end, he said, "We just added a show in Ottawa and it's when your tour will be there. Let's meet up. I want to take Miles's measure in person."

They talked some more details before he had to run. They'd avoided the Gloria topic, and Harlow was good with that. They'd talk after they were both off the road.

Then she settled in to talk to Marcella. When her aunt's face popped up on Harlow's screen, relief seemed to pour through her. Her anxiety ebbed and she smiled, truly pleased.

"What's poppin'?" she teased.

Marcella's smile echoed Harlow's. "I have missed your face so much! How are you? Good I bet. I read the reviews of last night's show at MSG. I'm so proud of you."

"Last night was so incredible I'm a little afraid tonight can't top it," Harlow admitted. "Everything about it was better than every dream I've ever had about playing there."

"I'm bummed we couldn't be there." Marcella and her wife were supposed to come out for the NYC shows but her father-in-law had gotten into a car accident and stayed back to help as he recovered.

"We'll see you both when we play the Gorge." The amphitheater in Eastern Washington was a few hours' drive from Seattle. "We hit gold yesterday. And two of our singles are charting. Jeremy is in talks to have one of our songs on a movie soundtrack. This is all just a lot."

Marcella laughed, pleased as she clapped a few times. "Gold? I knew you could do it. Congratulations! When you're done with this tour, we need to celebrate. Movies? Sweetie, you're meant for great things. You know I get to be your date on the red carpet at the movie premiere, right? Miles has to share you that night."

"So you know about Miles and me?"

"Hard not to. Pictures of you two all over the place. You look good together. Your dad tells me Adrian's a solid dude so I gotta hope he raised his kid well. And that I raised mine well enough to walk out on anyone who'd be careless with her."

"I really needed this call with you," she told Marcella. "He's...good. I like him a lot. I would not only walk out if he treated me poorly, but Nora would set his clothes on fire when he least suspected it."

Marcella laughed. "And then I'd get hold of him. So, you think this has staying power beyond the tour?"

"I'm trying to go week by week. I'm having a good time. He seems to be having a good time. He's not trying to have a good time with anyone else and neither am I. I understand him. I get this life in ways most others can't. I'd like it very much if this deepened and lasted past the summer."

"It's like that. Okay. Then I hope it does too. As long as he deserves you."

They chatted a while longer. Harlow realized her dad hadn't told Marcella about the cease and desist, so she didn't bring it up.

It was time, she realized, to give her aunt more details. But not when she had a father-in-law recovering from multiple surgeries to help care for and a wife to support emotionally through it.

They chatted a while longer before saying their *I love yous* and disconnecting.

Since she was alone for a little while, Harlow decided to give in to her curiosity and do some internet research on this Sophia person, and whatever the hell it was between her and Miles.

CHAPTER
NINETEEN

Miles had been called into one meeting after the next when he'd arrived at the venue that afternoon, so he'd missed Above Me's soundcheck.

Then he'd gone to get changed for their own soundcheck and meet and greet with fans and missed Harlow again. It wasn't like they weren't going back to the townhouse together or anything. He saw her every day, slept with her every night. He'd even been with her that morning. It was silly to be wistful when it had only been a few hours.

And still, as he stood in their empty dressing room, he could smell her on the air. Her ebook reader sat on top of her ever-present notebook with a pen clipped on it. He recognized her well-worn cardigan that she always brought with her even in the summer because backstage areas and hotels got cold.

He picked it up and smelled it before putting it back and heading out. At the very least, he could watch their show. That's when he saw the banana with a bright pink post it. Sitting where he'd see it if he came in.

Miles, eat a piece of fruit and drink something that isn't soda. Xox, Harlow

She did that. They'd just be going about their day, and she'd pull two apples from her bag and hand him one with orders to eat it because *you can't live on bacon and potato chips alone.* And he loved soda. Drank it all day long but she started bringing two water bottles to the venue instead of just one. She usually went through several refills each time, and because she encouraged—and nagged a little—him to drink more water, he'd probably tripled his regular water intake and had cut back on the soda too.

Just little things that meant a lot.

Miles couldn't have been too far behind them because he recognized one of the songs Above Me usually played during the first half of their set.

Pleased he hadn't missed the part of their show when they played a cover, he found himself a spot to watch after finishing the banana and tossing the peel into the trash.

The song ended and Harlow paused to drink some water. "Hey, Madison Square Garden. So we do a thing in our shows where we play a cover. Sometimes we decide ahead of time but it's also fun to get suggestions from the crowd. We love music and there are so many great songs we forget about them all. If we know it, we'll give it a whirl."

Shouts came from the audience for songs from across genres of music and Miles knew she'd be delighted by that. But what he heard more than once were Earthquakes songs.

Brian went and spoke in Harlow's ear, and she shook her head. Nora joined them. Shortly after that, Harlow said to the crowd, "I love "Can't Shake I" too, but we don't know all the chords."

Miles found himself walking out, totally surprising Harlow, who grinned at him, filling him with relief because he realized too late that she might not want him out there.

"I don't know the bassline," Brian said in his ear.

"I know the chords," he said to Harlow. "As long as Brian is cool with it." Brian shrugged and nodded.

"This guy's name is Miles. He says he knows the chords," she told the crowd.

Nora did a few drum rolls.

In the background, the crowd had gone wild, chanting the name of the song over and over. Brian, laughing, bowed. Suddenly Miles's guitar tech thrust his bass into his hands and backed off.

"You okay with this?" he asked them.

"Don't expect us to pay you your regular rates," Harlow said. "We're on a budget here. And I'm singing it."

"I think I can work with a payment plan." He waggled his eyebrows, gave her a sexy look, and she giggled, shaking her head at him. "As for you singing? Yeah, I'd dig that."

She began playing the opening to a song Miles had written about addiction and obsession and he came right in behind her. Not singing the song was a totally new experience, but holy shit he loved Harlow's vocals and the direction she took the song in. Growly, low snarls, whispers, and desperate explanations. It was like hearing the music from the perspective of the audience.

It filled him with pride and also humility that he'd come through a wild and dark phase in his life and was stronger for it. Proud that he'd opened himself up that way and poured it all into a song he loved even more at that point.

Harlow took care of his words. Took care of the song that

had come from that dark, healing part of himself. It was astonishingly intimate.

The audience sang along with her, letting her lead them through it, through the pause at the end of the first two choruses, down to the depth of pain near the end and then brought everyone up, higher and on solid ground at the end.

When it was over and everyone cheered—including Miles—he looked her way and blew her a kiss before he left the stage on slightly rubbery legs.

Because an unassailable truth had punched him in the gut. He was absolutely, positively in love with Harlow Martin. No more *falling* in love. He was there.

By the time they'd come off stage, Harlow was buzzing with energy and excitement. Not just because had been such a great show, but because Miles had come out and they'd played music together. It had been so ridiculously wonderful she was a little bit drunk with it.

"Wow. You two were like, combustible out there." Nora put her arm through Harlow's as they headed away from the stage and back to the dressing room area.

"It felt nice. Singing with him I mean. I didn't even get nervous that I was singing his song and his words. Until the end when I had that realization, and then it was…okay. More than okay. That's not a fair word. I hope he appreciated our treatment."

"I watched him the whole time. He was totally down with the way you sang it. He looked at you like he wanted to take a bite."

Brian, who was to her left, leaned in close to say, "I like

that you're happy he came out on stage. I know you're wary about what people might think about how you achieve the things you do. I'm real fuckin' proud of the Harlow out there with the dude she's caught feelings for, not giving a fuck about anyone who doesn't wish her the best. This guy is good for you. But better than that is how you are good for yourself."

Harlow came to a halt and then threw her arms around him. She couldn't say anything without risking tears, so let the hug speak for her. He teased her from time to time. They argued too, didn't talk to one another for a day or two until it was forgotten or worked through. But mainly he was part of her family. He knew more about her, cared more about her than her biological brothers.

And instead of feeling the lack of what her brothers had given, she felt the blessing of having such wonderful people in her life. That Brian, who didn't often have conversations about feelings, would say that to her meant so, so much.

Nora grinned at them both as they headed the rest of the way back.

Miles met them as they turned a corner and she found herself skipping the last few feet to him and jumped into his arms. "Hi."

He smiled at her as she eased back to the ground before he fell, or she broke something he needed to play music.

"Hi. Thanks for letting me come out tonight. I had a great time." He kissed her quickly. "I loved the way you sang my lyrics."

"I'm glad you didn't mind that we covered you."

"Are you kidding? I'm totally flattered, and you killed it. Everyone else thought so too."

The other three members of Earthquakes caught up with Miles. After calling out their compliments on the cover Above Me had just done, they headed to the stage so she stepped away from him knowing he had to move too. "Going to clean up and then come back to catch your show. Kick some ass."

"Okay." After another quick kiss, he turned, and she watched him walk away for a few seconds before they both disappeared beyond the opposite corner. Seconds later he jogged back to her. "Hey, I was...do you want to spend the four days between shows up in Montreal with me? Just me and you? I thought we could, you know, maybe get a rental somewhere."

He blushed and she went to her toes to kiss him. With Nora and Brian going back to Southern California to visit family during that time, she'd definitely like to spend it with him. "Yeah, I'd like that a lot."

"We'll talk details later. See you in a bit." He kissed her once more, and moved away again quickly to catch up with the rest of his band.

"Looks good coming and going. Damn," she muttered with a smile as she caught up with Nora and Brian.

CHAPTER
TWENTY

Miles looked Harlow up and down slowly. God damn, she was sexy. "See, now I'm regretting making these dinner reservations. I'd much rather stay in and dine on you."

She wore a body hugging deep blue dress that ended mid-thigh. Her very long legs were bare, and she wore strappy heels. He loved that. Loved that she was an amazon, tall and strong and wore high heels not caring that she was already tall. It was another example of the fearlessness she had that called to him.

Her hair hung in pretty curls that framed her face and she had her lips painted what he considered his favorite red on her. He wanted to see that on his cock.

"You know what that lipstick does to me," he murmured as he got close enough to press his lips to the side of her neck and breathe her in. He heard her soft intake of breath and saw the flush creep up her chest and neck.

The power of it rode his spine. *He* could make her

breathless. She was his to please. A high bar, and one he gladly put energy into meeting.

"You're one to talk. Look at you," she said, pressed against his body, her head tipped back as he licked a path down her throat. "Not that my eyes are open," she whispered. "But it's burned into my memory."

A buzz from his phone was the text telling him their car had arrived and was out front. He'd arranged for an apartment with a private elevator and enough security he felt they'd be safest and away from any paparazzi.

"I was about to suggest we order takeout so I could bend you over that couch and take you from behind. But our ride is here."

"There's plenty of time." She smoothed her palms down the buttons of his shirt before straightening his tie. "You really do look delicious in a suit."

"Gotta keep up with you," he said, guiding her into the elevator once she'd grabbed her handbag.

The mirrored walls of the elevator car reflected them back. With her heels she was the same height as he. The two of them looked really good together. Dressed up and ready for dinner in a quiet, dark, and very well reviewed restaurant that had been around forever.

She pulled her phone out and took a photo of their reflection and then a selfie with him.

"We look awesome, Miles. I'd fuck us."

He laughed, keeping an arm around her waist as they headed to the car at the curb out front of the building. The driver opened their door, and Miles took a moment to watch Harlow get in, those legs of hers visible as the hem of her dress rose.

. . .

The place he'd brought her was old school elegance. She used her serviceable French and wished she'd taken a few more semesters of it. Still, it was enough to order a drink and some appetizers.

The chef came out to let them know he had a multi course meal planned for them based on whatever Miles had told him before they'd arrived. Harlow figured it'd be great because Miles paid attention to what she liked and didn't.

He clinked his glass to hers. "To the most beautiful woman in my world."

She was already all worked up from their little interaction before they'd left the apartment and when he was this way it only made it harder not to jump on him.

"You're so good for my ego," she told him with a laugh.

"It's not hard to say nice things about you. Believe me, Harlow, you're on my mind pretty much twenty-four-seven, and it's all good." His expression said a lot of that thinking was probably sex related, and that was totally okay with her.

"I'm glad we have these days all to ourselves. I like everyone else, don't get me wrong. But I do like not having to share you. No media. No interviews. No shows. Just us." Sure, people looked at him. How could you resist those good looks? Harlow really couldn't blame them. As long as they kept their distance there wasn't a problem.

"I'm always all yours," he murmured, and she smiled again. Good lord, he was irresistible.

Harlow's phone vibrated and she ignored it. Everything could wait. The outside world was far less interesting to her than this brief and magical time she had with Miles.

Then dishes began to flow from the kitchen. Small plates full of deliciousness. The first were thin slices of buttery soft smoked salmon she managed—barely—to eat with perfect sized slices of slightly toasted bread instead of inhaling them on their own immediately.

Bites of smoked meat came next, along with some sort of crispy potato thing and some delightful roasted vegetables.

Her phone vibrated several more times. Enough that she excused herself to look at the screen and make sure no emergencies had come up.

There were two voicemails from...her mother. Three missed calls from her as well. A text from Hector and another from Mindy.

"What's wrong?" Miles asked, snagging her attention as she read her brother's words.

An interview came out and it's got Mom furious. Watch out for her call.

Mindy's was similar though there was another apology for what had happened back in Atlanta, and the things Hector had said before the show. As well as a warning that Gloria had gotten worked up over some interview.

"Family crap." With forced calm, Harlow turned her phone off entirely and tucked it away. Whatever it was, it'd hold until after their date.

Naturally though, Miles Brown was not used to being told no when he wanted something. And Harlow knew by the way he looked her over so carefully that he wasn't just going to let anything go.

Damn it.

"Gloria?"

"Yes. Gloria crap and it's not going to ruin this lovely

dinner so let it go. I have. Phone is off. In an emergency, my dad, Nora, and Brian know they could call you and you'd know where I was. So. No need to do anything but enjoy this lovely meal." Her smile was probably a little feral, but he paused. At least for the time being.

"Fine," he said at last, refilling her wine glass. "But you'll tell me about everything once we're back at the condo."

Harlow didn't bother telling him she didn't even know just exactly what Gloria was upset over. There was no way she was going to listen to those voicemails and let them ruin her meal.

Miles frowned at the mention of Gloria. He'd hoped she'd slink off and lick her wounds and leave Harlow the hell alone. Gloria didn't seem to want contact with her daughter so why the fuck was she trying to upset her?

Still, Harlow had that stubborn set to her mouth and even though he wanted to kiss it, lessening whatever it was she was holding back, he nodded and let it go. For the time being.

He wanted a nice night out too.

"You realize this is a date, right? We've eaten in restaurants and gone places, but this is just me and you. I like it. I think we need dates. Plus it allows me to show off the gorgeous woman at my side and let the world know she's mine."

Harlow smirked at him. "Doesn't hurt that we're in a whole different country that feels less obsessed with you than the one to the south."

"Obsessed?" He snorted.

Harlow just raised a brow, daring him to argue.

"I think obsessed is maybe not the best descriptor, though." That was a whole different subject and not one he wanted to get into in public.

"If you say so," she told him before trying the mushrooms that had been delivered to the table. "Jesus these are incredible."

He tried them and then nodded his agreement. "It's the tarragon."

She took another bite and shrugged. "Whatever it is, I could eat a bucketful. If this was on toast or pasta, I might never eat anything else."

Miles made a mental note to get the recipe so he could try a hand at it once he'd returned to Seattle after the tour was over. He'd make her mushroom pasta or whatever and they could eat it in his bed.

"You live on Bainbridge too?" she asked.

He nodded. "I do. My parents have a few acres and wanted me to build on their property but I chose a place far enough away but still close. It's quiet on the island. Like a small town in a lot of ways really. Private. I grew up there. People know me but they leave me alone when I'm home. It's something hard to find in other places. I use the studio at my parents' house when I record." Just like she did, he knew.

"Saves a ridiculous amount of money. And it sounds good. For your dad and for Earthquakes."

"Exactly. My dad was sure to instill in me an understanding that even after I signed a recording contract, I'd be charged for everything I used or needed back against any profits. The wiser I was with the services I used and where, the more money I'd be saving myself. I'm betting your dad told you the same."

Harlow nodded. "It's why he built the studio at his house. He faced the same thing with his contracts so once they had the ability, they took control of their music recording. *Control equals choices, Harlow Michelle*, he said. And he was right. I can't afford to build my own recording studio, but I don't feel bad using his. And when we use that studio, I'm not obsessed with getting every possible thing I can out of every second because it costs so much. We can experiment. Get things wrong. Getting things wrong is the best way to find out how to get them right. But it costs time and money to make mistakes."

Miles hadn't really had to worry in that way. Not in the last five years or so. Earthquakes's success had been pretty swift, which kept the lights on and the cost of failures turning into victories hadn't been an issue.

More food showed up as the empty plates were whisked away.

"My parents are coming when we play the Gorge," he told her. "They'd like me to see if you'd want to come to dinner the afternoon after the last show. They've rented a house not too far away. Maddie's parents will be there too. Her uncles and their wives. Probably cousins. Plus my aunt and uncle, their spouses, and several of my cousins." He'd talked to his mother about this just the morning before. She'd been excitedly planning for a huge celebration as it was the end of the tour and the whole freaking giant extended family would be in the area. She'd poked around for details of what he and Harlow were to one another, though it wasn't that difficult because Miles had told her how special Harlow was to him. She'd told him to invite Harlow and the rest of Above Me to the party too.

"My dad and Jenna and Marcella and Cherry will be at the Gorge show. His tour will be done by that point. I think Nora's family will be too though probably not Brian's parents because they're going on a trip and he's joining them when the tour ends."

"They're all welcome. My mum will happily feed an army if it meant she got a good look at you and I together. Well, not personally. But arrange it."

That made her chuckle, and he was glad for it.

"When we're in Ottawa, my dad and the rest of the band want to do a big lunch. Same deal, you've been invited. The other day, Marcella told me my Pop let her know he thought your dad was a cool guy who probably raised a good man. But he obviously wants to peep that himself."

He really liked it that she was including him in this stuff. Sure, that was what people did when they dated and got more serious. They met the family and all that. But he liked Richie and hoped lunch with him and the rest of the band would be far better than dinner with Gloria.

"Sounds good." He paused, weighing his thoughts a few moments. "If I asked you to visit me when we were on our Europe leg, would you?" he blurted out before he changed his mind.

"Are you asking me?" she replied.

"Yes, I am. I know you have work here in the U.S. doing festivals at the beginning of our tour, but maybe for the UK shows at the end since you'll be in Europe at that time? We wind up in London at the O2. Before that we'll be in Edinburgh, Cardiff, Leeds, and Manchester. Whichever and how many days you can be there I'm happy to take." They could fly home together at the end. Maybe he could cajole her into staying at his house for a few days when they returned.

Her expression was something he'd remember for a really long time. Pleasure to be invited and at the idea of their being together. "I'd like that. By late-September our shows both here and in Europe should be finished for the year. Looks like we finish up in Amsterdam. Quick flight to London from there."

Miles smiled, happy as hell. There was more for them both once this US tour was done. He'd wanted that a whole lot.

On the way back, in the car, she listened to the voicemails Gloria had left, and it had been impossible for Miles not to have heard all the screeching about that fucking interview with Sophia. Harlow was a whore who showed it off to the world. Miles was her sugar daddy. She was godless and unfeminine. The usual except for the sugar daddy stuff. The interview had played into that like it was her mother's favorite song.

And it meant she'd have to tell him about the interview even though she knew it would make him feel bad and it wasn't his fault at all. Fucking Gloria. Fucking Sophia. Fuck, fuck, fuck.

"I'll tell you when we get back," she told him quietly, knowing he was impatient to hear what was going on.

He grunted, obviously displeased with having to wait, but he took her hand and squeezed it, agreeing.

Still, he said, "What the hell is she talking about?" once they'd returned to the apartment.

Harlow took a deep breath. "Your ex-girlfriend interviewed me and Nora in New York. I read it after. Most of it was decent." And it had been, surprisingly enough. Sophia said complimentary things about Above Me and their music, notably the songwriting she and Nora did.

It hadn't been about wanting Miles back, Harlow had realized as she'd read the piece the first time. It had been about using Miles to push her own star a little higher. Which made Harlow mad in a different way, because she found herself incredibly protective of Miles and through him, those in his family.

"*Ex girlfriend*?" Miles paused a few seconds. "*Sophie*? Sophie interviewed you last week and you're just telling me now?"

"She's calling herself Sophia now. Yes, as I said, she interviewed us last week. I didn't tell you because those just in two days alone we had eleven different interviews. It would have been pointless anyway."

"It *slipped your mind* that my ex interviewed you?" His voice had gone a little chillier, which succeeded in pissing her off because she was in a no-win situation and had done her fucking best not to hurt him.

"What is it you think I should have told you? Do you think I haven't been confronted by someone you put your dick into before? You've put your dick in quite a few people, Miles. If I told you every time I brushed up against one of them we wouldn't be together." It was one thing to accept that they'd both had other partners before they'd gotten together, another entirely to talk to him about it every single instance it came up that he'd had sex with someone. It would drive her into a state of perpetual comparison and Harlow understood herself enough to know that would have eaten her alive and eventually killed their relationship with jealousy.

He blew out a breath. "I'm sorry my past bothers you." He wasn't being an ass about it, but the hurt was clear in his tone.

"Your past doesn't bother me."

"You said you wouldn't be with me because of it." God, he was handsome when he was pissed off. It made her want to hit him with a couch pillow and then climb aboard and fuck the grumpy right out of him.

What she *didn't* like was that he wasn't listening as close as he usually did and beating himself up over something she never intended him to think. "I *said* if I had to talk to you every time it came up because someone you had been with crossed my path, we wouldn't be together."

"What's the fucking distinction then?" he demanded.

He didn't even have sense to fear when she cocked her head and narrowed her gaze at him! She held up a finger. "*One*, do not speak to me in that tone," she told him. "I'm not a wayward child or a pet. *Two* the distinction—as you put it—is that if I was coming to you every time it happened, it'd emphasize all those other experiences as somehow about me. And they're not. What you did before me isn't something I can or want to control. It's not part of what you and I have and it's not an interaction I want to have with you. If I thought you were still fucking other people we'd have a problem. If I thought you harbored feelings for any of them I'd be concerned and jealous as hell. But I'm not worried about that." They'd argue because they were both strong willed people. But the weight of worry that he'd stray wasn't one she had or would take on.

The rigidity left his spine as he sucked in a breath and blew it out, centering himself, she figured. "Oh. I'm sorry about my tone. I was being defensive."

"And not listening even though you asked me to tell you what was going on," she added.

His mouth flattened again. She got it. He was spoiled as hell. Everyone went out of their way not to upset him. Everyone around him bent to his will and made his life easier.

This thing between them wasn't going to last if they couldn't disagree well. That'd take some effort. Learning one another in a new way. Harlow very much thought he was worth it. And that *she* was worth it too.

"I'm sorry," he repeated. "Can you please tell me the whole story?"

"Sophia didn't reveal that she was your ex until toward the end. And then she tried a *we both nailed the same guy isn't that fun* thing, but of course she didn't think it was fun. She was trying to push my buttons and make me jealous but also talk about intimate details and I refused to go there." She gave intimate details to Nora and that was it. Harlow wasn't one to giggle over dirty girl talk with strangers.

He stared at her, surprise on his features. And, if she read him correctly, the flush on his cheeks was embarrassment. "Christ. It was a dark time for me in a lot of ways. I never hurt anyone. I never lied about what I was."

She shook her head and kicked her shoes off, angry with Sophia anew. "I don't want you to be ashamed of that. You and she were adults. Everyone consented. Obviously, you're different with me because I am a vastly superior human being. She's cute and interesting. I get why you'd be attracted to her. But she's not me."

He snorted a laugh and kissed her forehead. "No one on earth is you, Harlow. Thank god. I'm…I'd say I was surprised but that's pretty much on brand for her. I didn't know she was doing music interviews, or I'd have warned you. She's got few filters, especially if she thinks she can use whatever it is to further herself."

"I refused to talk about our sex life because that's private and it's ours. Whatever she had with you is not my business but what you and I have is no one else's business either. I told her your body and sexuality weren't hers and mine to talk about. Especially without your permission. I respect your privacy and she doesn't."

His expression softened. "Protecting me?"

"Well of course!"

Miles leaned closer and kissed her. A soft brush of his lips over hers. "You don't know what that means to me."

Harlow figured she had a pretty good idea. But it was never a chore to be appreciated by a person you cared for deeply.

"I'll get back to the protecting me thing in a bit. But for now, how does Gloria come into this?" he asked.

"She saw the interview. In it, there are several places I discuss what certain songs are about. She took issue with some of that. And in another part of the interview the "not good" part, my sexuality is discussed. You're part of it. Sophia mentions your piercing and your history with other people, including men. Gloria has decided my whorish ways

—you're also my sugar daddy—have shamed her and her family."

He blinked at her, disbelief on his face. "Each thing she does I tell myself that has to be the worst of it and she'll fade away because she doesn't want to be around in the first place. And then she doubles down."

"Gloria is no quitter. Hector texted and said she's been worked up since I walked out of that dinner. And the legal reply from my dad apparently sent her into a rage." Harlow rolled her eyes.

"Legal reply from your dad?"

Oops?

"Didn't I tell you about that?"

"Harlow! No, you haven't. What the hell is going on?"

"I told you about the call with Jenna! I know I did."

He frowned. "But not the reply part."

She was pretty sure she'd told him her dad had an attorney on it. But maybe not that it had happened. "I thought I had. I thought that it had finally shut her up but apparently, she's been stewing in her bitterness, waiting for an opportunity to strike. I'm not hiding things on purpose. Some of this I forget, think I already told you or in some way I'm embarrassed and want to pretend it away."

He stepped close. "Baby, I know it's complicated, but I want you to share this stuff with me. You never have to be embarrassed over something someone else does. Especially with me."

"Yeah? That why you're so unembarrassed about whatever Sophia said about your piercing? Do you tell me everything going on in your world?"

"If I got interviewed by your ex and he wanted to talk

about our sex life? If he said so in a printed excerpt? If one of my parents called yelling at me over it? Yes, I'd tell you. Also, fuck Gloria. She can't just call you like this and say all that stuff."

"Sweet summer child. Miles, she's been calling me and yelling about what a whore I am since I was a kid."

"Harlow..." He closed his mouth on a leashed snarl.

"There's more. Since I'm telling you all this, you should know the interview also has a bit about your aunt Erin and your uncles Todd and Ben." Gloria had ranted about *lifestyles* and a bunch of homophobic bullshit in response to reading three lines about someone she didn't even know, who was happily married and involved in a relationship of three and had been for over two decades. Her comments about Miles dating men had been similarly laced with hatred.

"I never should have let her into my life," Miles said of Sophie. Sophia. Whatever.

"Yeah? And I should have never taken you over there and exposed you to Gloria."

He made a sour face. "Bullshit."

"It's an open fact that Erin is in a polyamorous relationship. You can't blame yourself because someone else used that for attention. You know *now* Sophia would have been sniffing around for every bit of information she could get. But you didn't know that then. I don't know your aunt very well, but I am pretty sure she'd agree with me. And you sure can't take responsibility for getting someone like Gloria angry. This is Gloria's drug. She wants to be mad. She seeks it out like an addict." Harlow had become convinced of this. Gloria Martin was an anger junkie. Nothing made her happier than being mad at something or someone unless it was sitting back and watching everyone be miserable because of her anger.

"How come you can believe that, but not that you need to block her from your life and move on?" Miles asked. "You're right. Sophie didn't find out about Erin through me. I never even introduced her to Erin. But then *you* don't make that next logical step." He put his hand on her chest, over her heart. "Protect this. Protect your big, beautiful compassionate heart and cut this woman from your life. She brings you nothing but heartache."

No, she hadn't blocked Gloria's number, but she would that very day. In the month and a half since Atlanta, Harlow had done some soul searching about her relationship or lack of one with her biological mother.

She didn't know why Gloria hated her so much. For a long time, she'd believed once she figured it out, it could be fixed somehow and she and Gloria might be able to have at least a civil, non-toxic connection. Harlow didn't believe that anymore. Yes, she still wanted to know the reasons, but Gloria was Gloria and there would be no tearful apology and reconciliation.

Harlow licked her lips. "I'm trying. It's not second nature to cut off family but I know it's the choice I need to make."

He took her hand. "I can help you. We can do this step by step. Who on that side of your family is salvageable for a relationship? Would your maternal grandparents cut you off?"

"I've...I have no relationship with them. I've only met them twice. Gloria told me I looked too much like my dad and they couldn't stand that."

What a mess. She was riding that line between anger and

embarrassment at having this level of her disfunction revealed to anyone, much less Miles, who was just so kind and good to her.

Miles wrestled his instincts back as much as he could. The words he wanted to say, castigating her fucked up mother and brothers and even her grandparents. God damn, he hated these people so much. Including Hector and Mindy, who only popped up when they could benefit from something.

He could see how mortified Harlow was by sharing all these details and that made him even angrier. None of this was about her or anything she'd done and yet, she was ashamed of things these assholes did to her.

"My maternal grandfather murdered someone," he told her quietly. Her eyes widened with that information and then she took his hands in hers.

"Oh my god. Miles, I'm sorry."

He waved it away. "I never met him. But my mother was manipulated and hurt repeatedly by that story. A reporter tried to break my parents up over it because she hadn't told anyone about it, and it came out at the worst possible time. I'm only telling you this, so you understand you're not alone in being related to monsters. And to underline it's not about you. Like the people I've been with in the past aren't about you," he said, reminding her of that earlier part of the conversation. "Family isn't about who you are. It's not about DNA. Family is about what you do. They don't deserve you. Any aunts or uncles or cousins?"

"No. Gloria has three brothers. I've never heard anything

from them. Ever. As for anyone else? I don't know. I love my niece and nephews. I'll continue to send them things as long as that's okay with their parents. I still love my brothers even though I don't know if I can have any sort of healthy relationship with them at all. Hector and Mindy both texted me today to warn me about Gloria. That gives me hope that one day in the future I might be able to be in their lives in a healthy way. Luis? Maybe never. They're all a big question mark."

At the crack in her voice, Miles pulled her into a hug, stroking his palms up and down her back. "Each new thing I learn about them makes me sicker. Did your dad and she fight? Did he...hurt her?" Miles couldn't understand why they would hate one kid so much but accept the other two just fine. Though everything he knew about her dad told him Richie wasn't the type to put his hands on anyone weaker, it needed to be considered.

"I'm sure they fought. How do you not? I did some searching to figure out what happened. I couldn't find anything in their divorce papers or in the tabloids pointing to him being abusive. Or drugs or alcohol or side chicks. He led a fast life so I'm sure they suspected he was up to no good. People do bad things. Just because he was always gentle with me and everyone else he considered his to protect doesn't mean he couldn't have hurt her. But to be completely honest with you, Gloria would have said. If it were true, she'd have shouted from the rooftops that he'd hit her or fucked around. She complained a lot about being neglected when he was on tour, and that I can believe. Gloria has no issues talking shit and making people look bad. She said plenty about my dad as I grew up, but it was that he was lazy and stupid, not abusive."

Miles hurt for her. Hurt to hear she'd been treated so badly by her grandparents as well as her mother and brothers. He wished he could get her the answers she deserved. He wished to his toes that he'd never given Sophie a second glance. Embarrassment burned in his gut that Sophie had used details she'd learned from their involvement to mess with Harlow. And that she sensationalized his aunt Erin's relationship to get clicks and sell sodas or whatever else was outside his control.

Worst of all, Sophie could have damaged his relationship with Harlow, and that infuriated him more than it embarrassed him.

"My uncle Ben runs a personal security company. If you ever wanted to do some deeper checking on a professional level, I'm happy to make that connection with you two. He's really good and he knows others who are equally good at investigating," Miles said

"Investigate my *mother*?"

"Not her finances or anything like that. But if she won't tell you and if you won't demand your father tell you everything he knows about their break up, find out what you can on your own. An investigator can find police reports if there are any. Talk to possible witnesses to anything between your parents or between your mother and her family. You deserve to know, Harlow. If for no other reason than to finally accept that none of this is your fault. Plus, with Ben, I'll get the family discount. You may get answers. Or not. But what's the harm in trying?"

"I'll think about it. In the meantime, I'm blocking her

number." She looked down at her phone as she said it, so he hoped she was doing it right then.

"I'm going to read that interview. Is that okay with you?" he asked. "I want to see what Sophie said." He needed to explain to Harlow what the end of that relationship had been like. What it had left behind. But there was enough on her plate right that moment, so he'd wait a day.

"Hang on. I'll text you the link," Harlow told him moments before the info showed up on his screen.

"I will read this and then you and I are going to put this away for the night. I have plans for you and none of them involve Gloria and her bullshit."

"I'm glad to hear all this hasn't made you want to run for the hills."

He shook his head, pulling her close. He was glad for the same thing. "You and I are just fine. None of this is about you and me, Harlow."

After a kiss, he settled on the couch and opened the interview to see just what Sophie had said and why Gloria was so up in arms over it.

CHAPTER
TWENTY-ONE

As he finished the interview, she put music on in the background. Interpol, he recognized and smiled. She'd told him they'd been an influence on Above Me. They certainly had been on Earthquakes.

He was about to frown, remembering the piece he'd just finished reading, but she came out from the bedroom wearing...nothing at all except for the shoes. She leaned against the doorjamb, one eyebrow raised, her bottom lip caught between her teeth.

"Before dinner we had plans. You made some promises, Miles Brown. I'm here to collect."

Going hot all over, Miles tossed his phone to the side and stood, moving to her because what else was there on earth he wanted more than to touch her?

"I love the shoes," he told her before he kissed along her jawline. "You're wearing my favorite outfit on you."

"Yeah?"

He traced along the vines and lavender-toned blossoms of the clematis tattoo on her side. A symbol of mental strength and will, she'd told him. So very indicative of what she was, who she was. Strong, always climbing to reach her goals. Beautiful and unique.

He took her breasts in his palms, loving the shape and weight of them. Loving that no one else had this privilege but him. Loving, especially, the way she arched into his touch.

"New jewelry?" he asked, bending to look at the opalescent bar with onyx beads. "Pretty."

She hummed her assent right before she raked her nails down his back through his shirt and circled her caress around his waist until she reached the button and fly of his trousers. "I like this too," she told him as she pulled the zipper down and the edge of her blunt tipped nails dragged over his cock through the thin material of his shorts before she pulled him out carefully and then shoved his pants down, his cock still in her grasp.

Already so hard his pulse seemed to boom through his dick, that touch brought a bead of semen that she ran her fingertip through, and he watched, rapt, as she brought that finger to her mouth and licked it off.

That sound of desperate longing came from his gut and brought a sexy smile to her lips.

Yep, she was going to kill him.

And then she dropped to her knees, and he had to grab the doorjamb to keep his legs because the sight of Harlow there, naked except for heels, on her knees as she looked at his prick like it was the yummiest thing she'd ever seen, was a sensual punch to his gut.

She leaned in, brushing her cheek against his thigh and across, over the head of his cock where she paused to lick through more precome. The molding around the door creaked slightly as he gripped it, so he made an effort to ease up.

Harlow licked over his piercing and tugged slightly with her tongue, and he groaned. She looked up the line of his body, her lips already glossy and slightly plump. "If you lean back against the doorway that might help."

Miles wanted to laugh but instead, he turned slightly to do as she'd suggested. "Whatever makes this easier on you," he managed to say around a tongue that felt four sizes too big for his mouth.

She helped him out of his shoes and then slid his pants and shorts off his legs before she moved back.

"Wait." He managed to make his rubbery legs walk him over to the couch and grab a pillow from it that he handed to her. "So your knees won't hurt."

Harlow had been in the bedroom as he'd read that damned interview, trying to figure out what the hell to do about everything when she'd realized all of that outside shit could wait. She had this brief time with him, and she'd be damned if she allowed Gloria or anyone connected to her to ruin that.

He'd gotten her all sexed up and silly before they'd left for dinner, and she had every intention of making good on his promises. She had a few promises of her own to keep and as she'd been thinking about how powerful it made her feel when she sucked his cock, Harlow had gotten rid of all her clothes, put the shoes back on and decided to take Miles's attention from anything in the universe but her.

He was so hard the surface of his skin seemed to buzz just slightly, as if his sexual energy was a tangible thing. She wanted him to know just because some chick he nailed a while years before she came along didn't have the power to lessen anything between them. Sophia might want to cash in on her knowledge of this piercing, she thought as she played along it in ways she knew drove him crazy, but Harlow loved the way she made him feel.

This was none of anyone's business but theirs.

She cupped his balls and slowly sucked him into her mouth, careful not to snag on the metal but giving enough pressure she rocked the piercing from side to side.

He snarled her name as she took him as deeply as she could and pulled back, swirling her tongue around the head before swallowing him again.

Over and over, she took him deep and pulled nearly all the way free only to do it again and again and again. The muscles in his thighs began to tremble and his hips began to thrust as he lost his control bit by bit.

"Stop," he said in a harsh whisper as he tunneled his fingers through her hair, tugging.

Without moving, she flicked her gaze up and locked to his. The connection of that moment clicked into place.

"I want to fuck you," he managed to say, though she heard his breathlessness.

"Plenty of time for that," she told him before she licked across the crown without breaking eye contact.

He groaned, but she knew he'd lost motivation to make her stop. As if he didn't have excellent recovery time? He'd be inside her soon enough. But she was in the middle of something she had no plans to stop until he came.

. . .

What the fuck had he done to deserve her? On her knees, his cock in her mouth, greedy for him to the point she refused to let go.

The naked carnality of the picture of this woman pouring all her sensuality into him rendered him slightly faint and certainly not in the sort of control he usually was when he wanted to sex her up.

He was at her mercy. And what mercy it was as each lick and suck, each nibble and tug combined to absolutely devastate him. His climax began to tingle in the balls of his feet as a flush seemed to flow from his scalp to his cock while he clenched his jaw, attempting to hold back. Wanting to draw out every single second of this absolute pleasure until there was nothing else to do but let go as he came so hard his teeth tingled.

He thrust his hips, meeting her mouth in long strokes as he came.

She continued until he finally pulled back and turned to the side. The sensation rolling through him in wave after wave of hypersensitive pleasure, ebbing just slightly until he had the presence of mind to bend, grab her upper arms and haul her up to her feet so he could kiss her.

"My turn," he said between kisses as he maneuvered them both to the couch. "Going to eat your pussy right now and while you're still juicy and fluttering from climax, I'm going to bend you over the couch like I've been wanting to."

"Shirt off," she mumbled as he pushed her to sit.

Not bothering with finesse, he pulled halves apart, sending buttons flying. She protested but once he fell to his knees in front of where she sat, she quieted, her pupils so large they nearly swallowed all the color.

Her skin was velvet soft as he kissed his way up from her very pretty shoes, pausing to lick behind her knee before continuing to her pussy. Miles breathed over that sensitive skin but didn't quite touch, instead starting at the other ankle and kissing up that leg.

Then he spread her labia, exposing all that sweet, slick flesh, dark pink with her desire. "Look at you. So pretty and so, so wet."

Her hands fisted, grabbing the edge of the couch cushion as he took a slow, leisurely lick, circling her clit with the tip of his tongue until she gasped and then growled, tipping her hips slightly to get more friction.

"Patience. We'll get there, I promise. Let me love you," he murmured, his mouth against her.

He kissed up her belly, up to her breasts. So fucking sexy. Her nipples hard, drawn tight, called to him. "Can't forget these," he said before he sucked hard, flicking his tongue back and forth until she squirmed, her hands on his shoulders as she slid her fingers up his neck and then into his hair.

The scent of her rose between them and he wanted to rub all over her to cover himself in it.

Sex with Harlow was never boring. She never gave anything but everything. Their connection seared through him as he realized it had changed his perspective in ways he'd probably still be discovering years from then.

That she demanded her pleasure was one of the hottest things he'd ever experienced. He kissed her mouth, drowning in her taste, hissing when she nipped his bottom lip hard enough to sting.

Her grip on his hair changed as he continued to kiss her until she went soft and a little dreamy. Soon enough though, she placed her palms on his shoulders and pushed.

Chuckling, he obeyed her command to get back to eating her pussy. Fucking into her with his tongue, groaning himself when she put one of her legs up on his shoulder and arched, stroking herself against his mouth.

He grabbed a healthy bit of her ass and held her to him to get the angle he knew would drive her higher. Harlow was greedy for her pleasure. Impatient to come as she kept a handful of his hair in her fist, holding his face to her.

She wasn't quiet when it came to sex. Soft moans, snarls, a squeak from time to time and lots of orders to go faster or slower. Damn it, nothing else could compare to this.

Kneeling between her thighs, his mouth on her pussy as he held her in place, he was surrounded by everything Harlow. Her scent, her taste, the softness of her inner thighs against his ears and the side of his face.

He'd leave beard burn on that extra sensitive skin and instead of guilt, he'd remember at different points all day long. Smile as he thought about Harlow moving or having her clothes brush against that tender flesh and recalling just how he gave it to her.

Her clit was swollen and firm, and when he licked it she shivered over and over until her legs began to shake. He slid two fingers inside her and she fluttered all around him. His cock had already come back to life after his last climax just at her taste and the sounds she made. When he sealed his mouth around her clit and sucked over and over, she cried out and wrapped her legs around his head as she came on his mouth. He heard nothing but the rush of blood in his head and the pounding of his pulse until she went limp, and her legs slid open.

He kissed her belly and then remained on the floor, resting his cheek on her as they both caught their breath.

Harlow had to blink her eyes a few times to clear her vision after that climax roared through her system. Her limbs felt like noodles as she wiggled her toes to get the feeling back. Miles's hair was soft and so very cool against the fingers of her left hand, still tangled in it.

He rose and she watched as he stalked, naked and gorgeous and absolutely fucking hard, into the bedroom and then out again moments later holding a condom.

Thank god.

"Awesome. I'm not sure I could have walked that far," she managed to say as he approached.

The grin he gave her in response was wicked and it sent a chill—the good kind—down her spine.

"Do you have the energy to bend over the back of the couch?" he asked, silky and really sexy.

She managed to stand and move around.

"The shoes put you at a perfect height," he said as she listened to the rip of the condom wrapper and the crinkle and stretch as he pulled it on.

He could have been giving a weather report and she'd still be panting, needing whatever it was he wanted to deliver. He drove her wild with the way he touched her, with the way he used a toe to spread her feet wider. The front of her body brushed against the nap of the couch fabric. Enough sensation to be nearly too much.

"My hands smell like you," he said as he lined up at her back and bent to kiss her where her neck met her shoulder. "I love it when I fuck you before we show up at the venue so I can have you all over me."

Wordless, she pressed back against him, wanting more.

"Shhh," he said, kissing her again. "Patience. We'll get there."

She growled, hating to wait when his cock was just right there and ready to be in her. He traced through the folds of her pussy, and she squirmed, pushing back toward him.

"Just wanted to be sure you were ready," he said.

As she was still wet after he'd gone down on her, she was quite sure she was more than ready, but it never hurt to double check.

And then, blessedly, the head of his cock bumped against her, sliding slowly into her pussy as she breathed through it, stretching around him as he got all the way to the root and paused as they both got some control.

"Nothing on earth feels this good. In you so deep, with your pussy so tight around me, so hot I'm scalded through the damned latex. Mmmm, perfect. I never want to leave."

When he withdrew a little, the bead on his piercing stroked over all her best, sensitive spots deep inside, sending little arcs of pleasure pinging through her system.

She closed her eyes as she rested her cheek against the couch, holding on and bracing as he began to fuck her. First it was slow and so, so deep. The rhythm of it hypnotic. He petted his palms down her back and over her hips, gripping there as he sped slightly and made shorter digs of movement that seemed to spark up all the nerve endings inside her.

"More," she wheezed.

He shifted a little, bending over her body a little more and it changed the angle slightly. Her eyelids flew open as she realized she was on her way to climaxing again. Twice in such a short period wasn't usually this easy.

Apparently, everything was easy when it came to Miles and his dick.

Miles took one of her hands and led her to her pussy. "Make yourself come again, beauty."

She didn't need to do much more than touch her clit with the tips of her fingers, letting him do most of the work as he continued to thrust into her.

Harlow let her eyes drift closed again as she gave over to how good it was with the fat width of him so deep, with that piercing, with the way his muscled thighs felt against the backs of her own. He was so strong but she knew he'd never use that to hurt her. Would in fact go as far as he could in the opposite direction.

"So close. I can feel your cunt gripping me tighter and tighter. You're so wet, baby. It's driving me to distraction."

His movements got a little less controlled and she knew he was close too. Concentrating, she tightened herself, working those inner muscles around him until he grunted, and she knew they were in a race to see who came first.

The sight of those fingerprints where he gripped her hips while he fucked her made her lightheaded with delight.

Orgasm built and began to yawn wide, sucking her in and with her, Miles as well. He pressed so deep she gasped, pinned between him and the couch as she came so hard she saw stars against her closed eyes and felt the jerk of his dick inside as he climaxed.

He put an arm around her waist, pulling her back to the bedroom as he helped her onto the mattress and went to dispose of the condom before joining her.

"Give me fifteen minutes and then I'll make us drinks while you scoop us both some ice cream," she said as she snuggled into his side.

"You've got a deal." He kissed the top of her head.

CHAPTER
TWENTY-TWO

Harlow couldn't stop smiling. She and Miles were on the back of a golf cart being driven through a large festival space to where her dad's band had lunch set up.

Metal festivals hadn't changed much since she'd toured with her dad. The usual suspects of food and drink stands, of people everywhere dressed every which way. So much hair. "Best hair in the industry. Hands down," she told Miles as they passed by a group of teenagers, some with hair to their asses, one with a mohawk, a wide variety of colors too.

This had been her summer camp. Her weekends at the lake or a family reunion. "Being here just feels comfortable, you know?" she said to Miles.

"When it's not my band it feels like I'm at a theme park. I can dawdle here and there, see whoever I want. I know where everything is. Yeah, I totally get it. I feel the same." He kissed the top of her head.

"It is weird though that one of your godfathers is the lead singer of Dark Divine," Miles said. She'd just told him that a few days prior when he'd made some comment about Marky Archer's ability to hit those high notes and still be metal as fuck.

Dark Divine had started playing shitty little clubs in Pittsburgh in the mid nineteen seventies and never stopped touring. Most rock bands playing there at the festival had been influenced by them in one way or another. Marky had seen something in Harlow's dad, Richie and his band A Martin James Family Joint, AMJFJ as they more commonly went by, and had become a mentor of sorts. At first. But then, her dad and Marky had become close as brothers and he'd just been Uncle Marky to her.

"My cousin Xander loves rock and roll and metal music. When I told him I was coming here today with you, he was so jealous," Miles said.

"Xander is the tattoo artist cousin, right? Erin's son?"

"Yes, that's him. He's ridiculously good at tattooing. My uncle Brody owns the shop Xander works at. He and another artist, Raven Warner, trained him from when he was like fourteen or so until now. He's the one who's doing this dragon." Miles indicated his shoulder.

"I'll get him some tickets when the tour rolls through Seattle," she told him.

Miles's wide open, happy smile was her prize for the offer. "Thanks. He'd love that. He wants to meet you. I've been texting him about you. He's more like my little brother than a cousin. I tell him the good stuff."

"Aw." She was the good stuff.

They'd reached the tents where the different bands had set up to hang out or eat in, so Harlow began looking for her dad. She knew he'd have been told when they came through the gates and would be waiting outside for them. He did the same thing when she was coming to his house. It always said to her that he couldn't wait to see her.

And there he was. His formerly dark brown, waist length hair now trimmed short, shot with silver at his temples, he wore jeans and an Above Me tour t-shirt that had her grinning as hard as he was once he'd caught sight of their approach. He was, like the man at her side, a star. But more than that, he was her dad.

She hopped down and skipped over into a big hug. "Punky, you're here. I missed you," he told her.

"I missed you too," she said as she squeezed him tighter for a few seconds more.

He took a look at her and smiled. "You look good. Healthy. I'm glad you're taking care of yourself." He kissed her cheek and hugged her one more time.

"You remember Miles."

They shook hands while her dad gave him the dad look. Friendly but also with an edge of parent who wanted to be sure this person would treat their baby well. "Hey, Miles, good to see you."

"Thanks for including me today." Miles looked effortlessly cool. It was sort of annoying because she had to put a lot of effort into looking effortless and he just rolled out of bed that way.

But he was also sweet and warm and good with people and her dad was smiling and looked relaxed, so there was that.

"Come in. Lunch just got set up so we're ready to go. I made everyone stay in here, so I got to hug you first," her dad said as she was then hugged by a line of her honorary uncles.

"Punky, you're there in the middle of the table. Miles is on your left and I'm on your right. That way everyone is close enough to you to visit but I still get to be right next to you." Her dad pulled a chair out and she sat in it, pulling it in herself.

Soon enough, smoked meat sandwiches showed up with two different salads. This smoked meat thing was something she really liked about Canada.

Once everyone started eating, her dad made them stop pelting her with questions. "Let her tell everyone at once. Go on, Punky," her dad urged.

She told them the song they'd just contracted for a movie, their gold record, singles charting and that they'd been added to two more summer music festivals in the U.S. and nearly cried at all the wonderful things they said in response.

"Tell me good things about Harlow," Miles asked everyone at the table, making them like him for it because they loved her too.

"We all watched Harlow grow up," Stuart, her dad's closest friend, said. "Remember your gig out in San Bernadino? Still in high school if I remember correctly. Y'all were babies."

Miles turned to her. "God, let this be one of your stories," he said crossing his fingers, making her laugh.

"I don't remember what the name of the festival was. We were still in high school and didn't have licenses yet, so Marcella drove us." Harlow and her dad both laughed at that. "It was hot as balls. Dusty. We were on the new talent stage at eleven in the morning or something like that. I think the crowd consisted of my dad and the band and a bunch of other dudes who were also dads and wanted to support us. Adorable."

"That was a very short story," Miles said, disappointed.

"Tell him the best part," her dad said.

She cocked her head, trying to remember anything notable other than being sixteen and having a bunch of dads rocking out to their music.

"The thing you said to the guy from that other band. I can't remember the name. Seems we're both getting old, Harlow."

"Oh! That guy. I don't know the name anymore. One of those names with the super fancy gothic looking fonts. Murder Stains or Satan's Taint, whatever." Harlow waved a hand because she did remember what her dad alluded to.

"So, as I said it was the up-and-coming stage at a time most of the musicians weren't even up. But lots of young bands were there and there was a strict timekeeper to keep things going or there'd have been nine minute guitar solos, and half the bands wouldn't have been able to perform because everyone went over time.

"Satan's Taint played before us and went overtime. It was early enough in the day that the timekeeper dude wasn't super grumpy yet, so he gave them two chances before he pulled the plug. No working mic, nothing. But there's beef and the lead singer is yelling about being silenced and we're just doing our thing. Roadies—not even theirs I don't think —have shown up and are taking their gear away. There's more whining and the other members of the band have accepted this and are off the stage.

"We plug in because *we* deserve electricity, thank you

very much. And then the lead singer comes up to me and *tries to take my mic.* I mean. Timekeeper is pissed and naturally the dad filled audience isn't pleased and there's rumbling and dad looks. I take my mic back. He wants to explain to me why he has been wronged like I wasn't there when their band went six minutes over their time and wasn't wasting our band's time. Which I said to him and told him to back off or I'd back him off. Then he told me to calm down."

Harlow wanted to laugh at the gasps in the room. They'd all been there but they still knew what a thing it was to say to a woman.

"So you did time for murder and didn't tell me?" Miles teased.

"Ha! No. I said into the microphone, *when a man tells a woman to calm down, a deep, dark fissure to her meanest, angriest self gets opened up a little deeper. Do you want to be the one calm down that finally releases all that lava all over you? No? Don't tell women to calm down. Now get the fuck off this stage.*" She shrugged, pleased by that memory. "Nora counted off and started playing and he slunk off."

"That's my girl," her dad said.

Not too long before they had to leave, Miles got a chance to speak one on one with Richie, so he took it. He knew how much Harlow respected her father and he deserved that respect. Miles wanted Richie to like him and support his relationship with Harlow.

Richie gave him a sideways look. "Tell me about the situation in Atlanta with Gloria. Jenna said very little, but that you'd been at a dinner where something terrible went down."

Miles shook his head. "No sir. I don't think I can. You need to ask Harlow. She's the one who needs to talk to you about it."

"She's trying to protect me by not telling me a lot of very bad things that came her way from Gloria, isn't she? I should have known. She was a terrible chapter in our lives, and I just wanted to close that book to protect us both."

Sure. Miles agreed that in retrospect Richie should have known. Should have pushed Harlow to tell him more. But Miles also heard the way the man spoke about his child. And he'd seen over and over how much he loved Harlow. Richie might have fucked up. But he did the best he could at that time, Miles was beginning to believe.

But there was something there. Something more than Richie trying to protect his kid by pretending away the bad shit and being the best he could to make up for it. Miles could feel it. And it had to be connected in some way to whatever the hell had ended their marriage and had Gloria dumping Harlow off without looking back.

"Look. You need to talk to Harlow about this. She's on tour and you're on tour, but at some point you both should sit down and talk," Miles said trying to be careful. If he had said nothing, he'd have felt like he failed to protect Harlow. Richie needed to know the whole story about Gloria as a mom. And Richie needed to tell Harlow the whole story about his situation with Gloria too.

Miles simply wasn't willing to watch Harlow suffer for other people. She could get mad at him for it, but someone needed to put her first and if it was him, that was worth the fight they'd have over it.

"That sounds ominous."

Miles thought hard about what to say. "I think you know there's more to it than a bad dinner with Gloria. And of course she knows there's more to this entire situation with Gloria than she's been told by you. You're both so important to the other you're holding things back, thinking you're protecting one another. Silence sucks, Richie. You know it. It's hurting you both."

Richie clapped Miles on the back. "You care about her a lot."

"Yes. I'm in love with her." Saying it out loud made it so much more real. But not scary. "That's why I'm urging you to talk to her. I'll tell you one thing, because it was between me and Gloria and your sons. I let her know that if she persisted in her bullshit to harm Harlow, I would take away everything she holds dear. And I will. Gloria is a bomb waiting to explode in Harlow's face and the longer she doesn't know the whole story, the greater the opportunity Gloria has to use it to hurt her."

Richie ran his hands over his face a moment. "Yeah, okay. You're right. I want to ask you more about this, you know that right?"

Miles laughed. "Yeah. I get it. I would too. And if it were up to me, I'd tell you everything. But you made Harlow into the person she is, and you know she'd skin us both. She already says I'm bossy because I do thinks like deal with the door when there's a food delivery or whatever."

"You do that?"

"Yes, sir I do. Not because I think she can't do it herself.

But because I can do it for her, and I like taking care of her. She doesn't need to go answering a hotel room door to anyone she doesn't know at some ungodly hour of the day."

"You'll do just fine, Miles. I like you, kid. Don't fuck my daughter over or dozens of metal dads will hunt you down and beat your pretty face in."

It wasn't until they'd gotten back to the hotel that she turned to him. "What did you say to my dad?"

He could have pretended he didn't know what she meant, but he said, "I urged him to talk to you and be honest about the Gloria situation and to ask you himself about the dinner because he wanted to know more."

"I made it clear that I'd talk to him after he was off tour but now he wants to talk sooner." She put her hands on her hips, her eyes flashing, mouth set and goddamn he wanted to kiss her.

"He asked me a direct question. I told him he needed to speak to you. He's not stupid. He loves you. He knows there's something more going on with Gloria. Every day this goes on the potential for you to get hurt by some fucking secret is greater. Nora told me Gloria played the long game and she's right. I don't want this threat hanging over you."

"*I was handling it.* Now he's going to get upset during his tour. There's no reason it couldn't have waited," Harlow's last few words were so sharp they could have sliced skin.

Miles shrugged. "If you expect me to feel bad for answering a direct question and *not* telling him everything he has a fucking right to know, it's not going to happen. I should have told him. I wanted to tell him. But I didn't. Because you asked me not to."

"I didn't want to bring this shit into his tour! Let the man have some damned success for five minutes without some of my bullshit."

Miles couldn't stop the, "Ah."

There it was. Gloria's abuse went deep into the place where Harlow wanted to please and protect her dad because she was terrified of losing his love too. That was why she protected everyone else at her own expense, and *that* was something Miles could not abide.

Her gaze snapped up to his and though he loved her, he didn't miss the frisson of fear that slithered through him momentarily at that expression. "Ah?"

"You see, Harlow, I want to protect you and that means you having the information you need. And giving that information to your dad because he needs it too. To protect you as well. He's a grown man. A father. He has the responsibility of dealing with a situation in his family life even while he is working. Millions of parents do it every day."

"What about what I want?"

"If what you want is to shoulder everything so no one gets inconvenienced, I'm not going to help you achieve that. Your father loves you, Harlow. He regrets that he didn't push you harder about her as you were growing up. He doesn't love you more if you never make any trouble. You know that. He shreds that guitar and sings and does his thing, and he will do so after the two of you finally share this fucked up tale. And so will you. I expect some new songs will be written."

"This is my life, Miles."

He took her hands. "Yes, it is. Your one, beautiful and precious life that deserves to be free of this bullshit. That's why I care so deeply about it. And why I did my best not to reveal what *you* need to. But I was there at that dinner, and I'm allowed to speak on it, so I gave him one detail and that was something personal."

She frowned. "I don't like it."

"I know."

She gave him a glare but there was less heat than before. "What detail?"

"When I told her I'd strip away everything she held dear if she continued fucking with you. And those calls she made to you definitely qualify."

She blinked at him, speechless. Finally, she took a deep breath. And grinned. "What did she say back?"

Relieved by that response, he laughed, hugging her to him for long moments.

"She asked who did I think I was. And I said I was the guy who'd do it. I also told Luis the same."

Her eyes went wide. "Miles!"

"What? Fuck him. Fuck Hector too. Weak ass. I'd go to war over someone treating my sister that way and they helped her hurt you. They're lucky I'm not calling my attorney right now to figure out how to ruin her." Though she didn't need to know he actually *had* called an attorney to give a heads up that they might be needed.

"Hector is trying. Not as much as he should, god knows. But he warned me about Gloria this most recent time. Luis is a jerk, but he's got kids. They don't deserve that," Harlow said.

"You're right. Kids don't deserve that. Like you didn't. So, moving on. Next time our tours are near one another is in San Diego. I think this is a face-to-face thing, but that's up to you."

"Oh, is it? Is that up to me? Nothing else is up to me but that is?"

Okay, so she was still pissed at him.

"At the very least, spend a few hours with him, Jenna, and Ryder. After you two talk privately, that is. That'll be good for you all."

"You're very bossy. I don't like my wishes being ignored like I'm not a whole ass adult capable of making her own choices."

He took a deep breath, wanting to choose his words carefully. This wasn't about winning an argument; this was a thing between the two of them they had to work on or it would destroy them.

"I know you're an adult capable of making her own choices. I didn't tell him anything more than what I said to Gloria when you were out of the room. I'm doing the best I can to find a way between respecting those choices and keeping you safe. So yes, I'm bossy. I know what needs doing. And I'll do it when it comes to protecting what's mine. Not because you're less, but because you're everything."

"*What's mine?*" she said, her eyebrows high.

"You arguing that point?" he asked, daring her to deny it.

She harrumphed but didn't. Didn't argue with his reasoning either. He needed to let that be enough or they'd re-ignite their argument and he really just wanted to snuggle her.

CHAPTER
TWENTY-THREE

Miles saw the caller when he checked his phone and smiled as he answered, "Hey there. Everything okay?" he asked his aunt Erin.

"Blue! Miss your face. I wanted to check in to see how you were. I've been keeping up with all the tour news. Your dad is ridiculously proud of you so he's pretending not to spy on you, but I'll own it." Her laugh was like a hug.

"Spying huh? Find out anything good?"

"Your dumbass ex, whatserface wrote some words. I read them."

Embarrassment flashed through him yet again. "I'm so sorry."

"Fuck that. You aren't responsible and let's be real, she didn't make any of it up. Xander is a grown up now, so it's not like we make any effort to pretend we are anything but what we are. Todd, Ben, and I have been together for a minute or two and it's no secret. How are you? And how is Harlow?"

After their lovely four days in Montreal were over, they

were back to it. They'd hit Montreal, Ottawa—including that fight and amazing make up sex—and Toronto before they dipped back into the US to play Minneapolis and then had come back to Canada to hit Calgary, Winnipeg, and Edmonton. That night they'd play the last of two shows in Vancouver before they went back to the States.

Canada had been a pleasant set of shows. Great fans. Great venues. Privacy was nice too. And best of all, Gloria was in a whole different country, and he knew—though Harlow didn't say it—that was a comfort to his best girl.

"She's…" Miles paused because he wanted to think about how Harlow would feel about whatever he told his aunt. Harlow would trust him, and he strived to keep being worthy of that. "It made a whole mess with her biological mother." Miles gave a brief recap of *that* situation.

"Harlow isn't mad at you though, right?"

"I wondered if she would be, but no. She said it had nothing to do with me, or with us. She's not upset really about the rest of the interview."

"Well, Sophia douchenozzle did say some nice stuff about Above Me. I hope that sells some albums for them after the mess the rest of it has made. Are you going to talk to Ben? He's right here if you want to."

"I'm trying to let Harlow make that choice. No matter how curious I am. No matter how much I want to show up at Gloria's door with an attorney and paperwork forbidding that bitch from ever uttering a single word to or about Harlow ever again," Miles told her.

"Well now." Erin paused. "Your dad told me he thought you were falling in love with her. He was right."

"What gave it away?" Miles asked, laughing.

"You're very protective of your friends so I'd have expected your concern about Harlow and her mother. But it's the way you thought about what you were going to say to me about her, the way I know you weighed what you thought she would want you to reveal to anyone else. That's a different level of connection. And then the threat to show up at a woman's door after you called her a bitch."

"I respect women!" he protested. "This particular terrible person happens to be a woman who is also a bitch."

"If I thought for half a second that you didn't, I'd show up at your hotel in ten minutes with your mum and we'd both kick your ass. Hell, I might even bring Raven along for that. This Gloria character sounds like an absolute miserable bitch. She's got all my mom hackles up. But she's got your *this is a threat to the person I love* hackles up. You're more intense than I've seen you over anyone you've had in your life."

"There's no *falling* about it. I'm there."

"I really can't wait to meet her. Your mom and I are here in Vancouver. I probably should have led with that, but I wanted to take the temperature first."

He snorted, unbelievably pleased. "You're *here*?"

"Okay, well, it's not just me and your mum. Todd, Ben, and your dad are here as well. Kelly and Vaughan too because they want to see Maddie."

Miles waved at his sister to call her over.

"How many of you so Poppy can let the box office know?" he asked, thinking it shouldn't be that hard to accommodate seven people.

"Is this going to be too much? The most of the entire crew is here including part of Hood River and Bainbridge. It took us four giant SUVs to fit everyone. We want to get a look at you and Poppy and obviously Harlow, but there are twenty people. Will that be way too much of us and scare her?"

So much for seven. "Hang on." He looked up at Poppy. "Mum and Dad are here along with pretty much everyone else. Let the front know we've got twenty guests coming tonight."

Poppy's eyes got wide a second and then she laughed. "I knew it. I knew they couldn't wait for the Gorge shows."

Erin interrupted, "Miles, we'll be there for Above Me's set too. We're staying at the same hotel you all are apparently. Jeremy hooked your dad up with the info and also got us all seats."

"Of course he did." He and his sister gave one another a look. "Poppy's going to doublecheck and make sure everything is in place. Text when you arrive at the venue so we can come meet you."

"So you think this will be okay for her? Last chance," Erin said. "We're a lot. We want you to keep her, not freak her out."

"Just use your manners and don't rush up to her all at the same time asking questions. No one gets to ask her what her intentions are with me. And please don't mention this ugly business with her mother." Harlow felt enough guilt that didn't belong on her shoulders because of Gloria, Miles didn't want to make it worse.

"I think we can manage not to act like animals," she told him and in the background, Miles heard his mother's voice asking if he said they could go.

"I didn't ask if we could come see him. We're here,

Gillian and that's that. I just asked if all of us would freak the girlfriend out," Erin told Miles's mum.

Harlow came into the room and his heart lightened.

His mother got on the phone. "Hello, darling. I would apologize for all of us showing up here, but that would be such a terrible lie. We miss you and Poppy and after all the pictures we've seen on the internet, we want to meet your Harlow."

"Everything is fine, Mum. We'll see you all later."

"Later? You didn't tell him we were already here?" his mom asked Erin.

"I don't need to *now*, do I?" Erin said.

"You're *here*? At the arena? Now?" He stood and Harlow backed up toward the door and he pulled the phone from his ear. "No, wait. Not you, Mum. Poppy will bring you—are you *all* here?"

"Not all. It's me and your dad along with Erin, Todd, and Ben. Everyone else will wait another two hours or so. Your uncle Brody wanted to be sure we told you he agreed to stay back at the hotel, but he got the first hug after you came off stage."

Miles didn't even know how much he needed to see his family until right that moment as joy crashed through him.

Over the line, Miles heard his sister's voice which meant she'd already reached the front office. "Mum, we'll see you shortly. Poppy will bring you back here." He disconnected and took two steps and Harlow took another back. "I guess you heard part of that?"

"Your parents are here right now? Here at this venue?"

A little bit of panic edged her tone, so he took her hand and pulled her to him. "I only found out myself about five minutes ago. A whole crowd of them will arrive in a few hours. Right now, it's just my parents and Erin, Todd, and Ben."

"Go be with them. I'll see you later."

He frowned at her, edging even closer so he could wrap his arm around her waist. "Don't leave. They want to meet you. You'll like them, I promise. You've already met my dad."

"I look like crap." She squirmed. As she currently looked beautiful, he had a differing opinion.

"Hush. You're gorgeous. Also, you know they've all been backstage before a million times. They're not expecting anything fancy."

"Miles, I look like a racoon. My hair is a mess and I'm in sweats."

She wasn't usually this nervous about stuff. "Are you all right?" he asked quietly. "You were okay going to the big dinner with everyone at the end of the tour."

"I'm just going about my day, no makeup, hair in a messy ponytail, wearing sweats and a ratty shirt when I *meet your parents*. How does that equal all right? I probably have a mustard stain!" She kept her voice low because she must have realized they'd be coming any moment as well.

"I didn't know until right now or I would have told you. They're going to see you perform at your set. You'll be fully made up and dressed up and all that then. But it won't matter. They aren't going to care about that. And I repeat, you look beautiful." Her idea of ratty and messy were in a different universe from his.

He heard Poppy's laughter and then the rumble of his dad's voice. He might be fully grown and living on his own but hearing his parents' voice still filled some empty space inside when he was away from them for long periods of time.

They came around the corner and Harlow let go of his hand, but he kept hers. Did she think he'd just forget she existed the moment he saw his family or something? She knew she meant more to him than that.

She held on again and he relaxed as he moved them both out into the hallway fully.

"Hello, darling," his mother said as she approached him with a big smile and a sparkle in her eyes. Since Poppy had moved next to Harlow and he knew she wasn't going to run away, he did let go to hug first his mum and then his dad.

Erin waited, mostly patiently, for Adrian to finish before she hugged Miles and kissed both of his cheeks. Naturally, when Todd and Ben hugged him, Miles was reminded that while he was considered tall, both his uncles were giant, broad shouldered, and could be scary as fuck when they were protecting someone, including Miles.

"I wasn't expecting you," he told his dad.

"Well, you should have." Poppy snorted. "I told you this would happen." She slung an arm around Harlow's shoulders and Miles figured his sister had picked up on her nervousness, he'd noticed the two getting closer at the tour had gone on.

It was probably where his family was getting their information from.

"Everyone," Miles said as he took Harlow's hand and pulled her a little closer to his side. "This is Harlow. Har, that's my mum, Gillian. You know my dad already, my aunt Erin, my uncles Todd and Ben."

She blushed and freed her hand to hold out to everyone,

ending with his dad. "It's really nice to see you again, Adrian."

His dad gave her a charming smile, designed to put her at ease. "Thanks for letting us crash your show tonight. Even though we didn't ask so I guess there's no *letting* involved," he teased.

Harlow laughed and it wasn't strained, so that much was going okay. He hadn't seen her nervous like this except... before they went over to her brother's house. "After touring with Miles for the last few months, I can see where he gets that from now, I guess."

His mum's scoff made Miles snort. "Yes, Mum, I guess you're not the only one who makes that comparison."

Gillian said to Harlow, "To be fair, you'll have to see Adrian with Erin and Brody. You'll meet him later tonight. He's the original who taught it to them. As for Miles, bossiness is in his DNA."

Miles could see Erin wanted to hug Harlow and he gave her a subtle shake of his head. She was nervous enough, so he wanted to give her a little time to adjust.

"Come through." He indicated the room Earthquakes had set up in.

"I'll be back in a bit," Harlow told him quietly.

"Oh no you don't. Don't run off," he said as everyone else got settled.

"I was on my way somewhere when you grabbed me just now. I just came in here to say hi and drop off some grapes on my way to procure some chocolate. Nora and I are working."

"You brought me grapes?"

"Yes." She pulled some out of the tote bag she had and handed them to him. "I told Nora I'd be right back."

Well, he didn't want to interrupt her work. He knew they'd begun working on songs for the next album.

"I'll be back by the top of the hour," she reassured him, and he felt better. Without waiting for him to reply, she looked around his body. "I'll see you all later. I know Miles and Poppy are pleased to see you."

"We don't mean to chase you off," his mum said.

"Oh no, it's not that," Harlow said. "My drummer and I are in the middle of something. I just paused to say hello."

"She said she'll be back by the top of the hour," Miles said.

His dad said, "Understood. We'll see you in a while."

Miles followed Harlow into the hall. "Go be with your family," she repeated, sounding annoyed.

"They didn't mean to be overwhelming," he murmured as he pulled her close. "They just are."

Harlow kissed him quickly. "Everything is fine! I've got to go. Nora is going to kill me, and I'll owe her a cookie."

He reluctantly let go and watched as she jogged toward the end of the hall where Above Me was at.

"Jesus, did you fuck him or say hi? You've been gone *fifteen minutes*. And I don't see any candy in your hand," Nora said accusingly when Harlow walked in.

Brian was off in a far corner on a couch wearing headphones and a sleep mask, curled up napping.

Harlow said in a loud whisper, "His *whole fucking family* just rolled in. All surprise, we're here and look impossibly perfect!" And they did. Every one of them was beautiful and at total ease with one another. A tight, loving family who adored Miles.

And there she'd been, unprepared and looking like she slept in her clothes.

"Are we nervous about meeting them? Why?" Nora's question was absolutely free of judgment. She would get the information and would support whatever Harlow wanted.

"What must they think of me?"

"Did anyone say something?" Nora's gaze narrowed and it filled Harlow with relief. Her friend would throat punch anyone who hurt Harlow.

"No. No. They were nice. Friendly."

"Tell me what you mean about that comment then? What do you mean what they must think of you? That you're a successful musician their son is involved with? You're ridiculously pretty and have great taste in best friends and men?"

"I'm on their son's tour and sleeping with him. And that interview with all that stuff about his aunt. What if they think I had anything to do with it?"

Nora made a derisive sound. "Your band is opening on another band's tour. I'm sure Mud Bay opened for other bands before back when Adrian and Erin were starting out. As for you and Miles, ma'am, it's way more than just sleeping with him, and they must know that if they have any sense at all. As for that stupid bullshit from the interview, if they blamed you, they'd be wrong. But Miles doesn't so why would they? They're in this business too, they know how this works. But if they're mean to you about it, Miles will address it. And if he doesn't, I will kick him in the scrote."

That started the giggles and before long they were both laughing.

"If I thought for even one second that Miles wasn't the one for you? If I thought he didn't see the absolute best in you, but also the worst and he loves you because it's all you, the good and the bad? I would have said. I would have told you and we probably would have gotten into a thing over it because you are goofy for him right back. But I think he would go to the mat for you." Nora shrugged.

"Loves me? Dude." Harlow's scoff was a poor attempt to cover her fear.

"Don't dude me."

"Dudetrix."

Nora flipped her off. "You are physically tuned to one another. He comes into a room, and you light up. Same goes for him. He watches you, watches out for you. When you're performing, he is so into it. He listens when you speak. He hates Gloria as much as I do. He loves you, Harlow. And you love him."

"God." Harlow tugged her hair free of the ponytail and put her hands over her face for long moments. "It's not like I need to be with him every minute of the day. He does his thing and I do mine. We work on our own stuff. And while I'm doing my stuff, I'm not pining for him. I like sleeping in the same place every night, but I don't *have* to. But I find myself thinking a dozen times a day about him. What he'd think of something. That he'd like this or that song or coffee or hat. It's...I thought it would be different. Falling in love, I mean."

Nora just watched, not interrupting.

"I thought it would be all consuming and that I'd suffocate or not measure up. That I'd need my own work and my own successes and my own friends and art, but it would come second to someone else's. I expected it to feel like I didn't know where he ended and I began."

Harlow grabbed her water and took several long drinks before she spoke again.

"I know where I begin and end. I am my own country. My own universe. I do not need to be attached to anyone else's."

"Of course you know that. Love doesn't mean you have to drown in someone else. It doesn't mean you live through someone, or that someone thinks you should live through them either. You and Miles are not the same person. That kind of love isn't for you, Harlow."

Harlow nodded. Okay that was good.

"You don't have to love like anyone else does it. There's no rulebook, though there are red flags, and you know those. We're not in red flag territory."

"No." She shook her head. "He's not that guy at all. I know where my borders are. But I know where he is too. And while I'm happy to hang out with you and do band stuff and work and all that stuff that is not Miles related, I know he's somewhere. I know he's doing his thing and that he probably thinks of me from time to time. I am aware of him out there in the world being beautiful and talented and sexy and funny.

"I'm not suffocating or drowning but sometimes I'm off balance and anxious because things are so good, and I am so happy and I'm scared of screwing it up. Scared something out of my control like Gloria or this interview or other internet nonsense will happen, and it will split us apart."

"That sounds like you love him to me. He doesn't want you to be his fan. He wants you because you're independent and talented and funny and pretty. You and he know this world," Nora indicated all around them, "in a way that connects you. There's understanding and commonality. You're both creative. You sure do share a whole lot of physical chemistry. But if it was just that, you wouldn't be panicked his mom might read an interview and think badly of you. You light up when you're with him, or when you talk about him. And you love yourself more. You have finally drawn real boundaries with Gloria and your brothers. Because you believe you're worth it. And his family is going to be just as happy to meet you as you are to meet them. They have to know how he feels for you. They raised him into the person he is today. He loves them and is close like you are with your dad and Jenna."

"He asked me to visit him at the end of their Europe leg. I think I forgot to tell you."

"And you said?"

Harlow snorted. "I said yes, obviously. I said we'd have to work around some of our festival dates but those will be done by then. And you and Brian are going to Italy in the fall anyway, so it's a good time."

They'd started writing new material already and were hoping to begin recording the next album after Thanksgiving so time with Miles in London would be really nice after being away from him for a month and a half.

Then she knew to her toes. "Oh my god. I'm in love with him."

Nora snickered as she patted Harlow's shoulder. "You sure are! Isn't it wonderful?"

"Yeah, it doesn't suck. I want to be so awesome tonight, especially now." Harlow had said it in a quick barrage of words, a confession before she changed her mind. "I just really realized that his dad is Adrian Brown, and his aunt is Erin Brown and they're going to be watching us perform tonight. Like, they're royalty! My stomach hurts."

Nora said, "You're spiraling. Breathe. *You* are rock and roll royalty! And our little band is amazing, and they will think so because it's true. And even if they didn't think so, they'd never say that because they're not assholes. We will all hang out after the show. I'm sure Poppy has already found a space to accommodate us all if there are so many of his family members here. It'll be fine. Now. Let's use this in this chorus, shall we?" She tapped the yellow lined pad in her lap where she'd been writing lyrics. "It needs a little angst I think."

CHAPTER
TWENTY-FOUR

"It's so good to see you," his mum said again, hugging him once more. "You look healthy and well rested. Especially for someone who has been on tour two months already. I'm guessing Harlow has something to do with that."

"She always grabs extra fruit for me when she's out and then has it in her bag so when we're waiting around, she'll just hand me an apple or a banana." He held up the linen bag she'd brought. "Or grapes. Pokes at me to drink more water. Called my preference for soda *juvenile*."

His aunt burst out laughing.

"While she's gone, tell us more," his mum said.

"I'm head over ass in love with her. She makes me so happy. She makes me frustrated sometimes too. She has this giant heart. Always giving and supporting everyone around her. She makes me feel like the luckiest person around. I'm better when I'm with her."

"I saw a photograph of you on her social media," his dad said. "Black and white, in profile."

Miles knew the one because she'd asked him if she could post it. He stood next to a speaker stack, stage lights up casting shadows over his body. His bass was in his hands while his eyes had been closed. Maybe thirty seconds before he walked out so he'd been going over the setlist in his head and probably thinking about the way he still tasted her kiss.

"I showed it to your mum and told her it was taken by someone who saw straight to your heart. Someone who loved you. It was an unguarded moment. A glimpse of the man who wore the rock star persona."

He found himself swallowing back emotion. "Yeah, that's my Harlow."

Erin grinned at him. Even in middle age, his aunt was bright and colorful and full of energy. Her hair was teal blue with darker blue tips. A pixie cut that showed off all the piercings in her ears. How she managed to look the way she did but also project a sense of safety and home, Miles would probably never know. But he'd been very close to her since the very beginning. She'd never steer him wrong or hurt him. Erin Brown always had the best interests of those she loved at heart.

Poppy spoke quickly, answering a question before anyone asked, "Harlow didn't know who Sophia was when the interview first started. And when Harlow did find out, she told Sophie that she wasn't going to talk about personal details about Miles because it was private, and he hadn't consented to her sharing anything intimate. Sophie brought up her own experiences with Miles to try to egg Harlow on to get her to share."

How could he forget that Poppy and Harlow were friends and that Harlow shared stuff with her because of that?

"She's nervous you'll think poorly of her because of the interview. Especially the stuff about you, Erin." Poppy turned to Miles who was relieved she'd shared those details but a little concerned because he knew Harlow was sensitive about it. "You're not going to want to tell them this stuff because you also want to protect her privacy and I like that. But I can share because it's different."

Erin shook her head. "Well, that won't do at all. I'm not blaming her for any of that. God knows we've all had interviews worse than that one where things came out we were mortified by. Tell her we aren't upset with her at all. I'd tell her, but Ben informs me I can be a little *much* for a newcomer."

Ben chuckled. "You tend to leave people looking like a deer in the headlights when you're on full Erin mode."

A minute later Poppy started telling them a story about what had happened in Edmonton and Ben leaned closer to Miles.

"I know Erin mentioned that I could help look into Gloria's story. Whatever help I can give, you know I will. I did a quick internet search a few minutes ago on her mother. She put up some rambling video about Harlow. Looks like it went up yesterday. It only has four views at this point so there's no reason for alarm. Especially until we can listen to see exactly what it is she says. I just got a few highlights, but I'll watch it in detail."

"Please don't mention this until after the show. I don't want her to get upset before she performs. She's already nervous about meeting everyone. I did mention you, let her know you could help. There's a lot she doesn't know. It hurts her. Maybe if we found some answers, it would be easier to let go."

"That's not always how it works, Miles. Sometimes, hell, more often than it should be, people just do shitty things because they're shitty. And their *reasons* aren't really reasons at all. It's some imagined sleight from twenty-five years back or whatever. Some people are just bad parents. Selfish and narcissistic. I'm sorry. I just want you—and more importantly Harlow—to know that going in. If that's what she decides. It may not make it easier, but it's a step toward closure of one type or another."

"You'll watch it? And tell me?" Miles knew he should probably watch it, but he didn't have the control not respond and he wanted to keep the knowledge about the video away from Harlow until he knew exactly what it was.

Ben answered, "Yep. There's no reason for you to watch it at this point. I'm not connected to it the way you are so it won't bother me the way it might you."

Relief washed over him. "Thank you."

Ben gave him a one-armed hug. "That's what family does."

Miles came straight to her as Earthquakes left the stage. He kept an arm around her shoulder like he worried she'd run away. Where the hell would she go where Browns, Keenans and Copelands weren't going to just pop up?

There were *so many* of them! She'd thought the group that had shown up earlier was a lot, but by that point there were at least twenty or so of them and all seemed turned up to twelve on the dial.

They milled around backstage, so full of love for Miles and Maddie and by extension Omar and Silas too that it made Harlow wish it weren't already so late so she could call her Marcella to tell her she loved her.

"We're headed back to the hotel," Miles told her. "We've got some space reserved so we can all have some dinner and visit a while. You okay with that?"

She wanted to snort. So badly. What if she *did* have an issue with it? What could she do that wouldn't wreck this thing she and Miles were building if she didn't want to be around his family? This giant cast of characters came along with Miles. Part and parcel, and if she didn't like being around them, she may as well break things off right that night.

Yes, they were loud and full of energy and obviously adored Miles, and that was why she knew that no matter what, Harlow would find a way to get along with them all. Whether she truly liked them or not—and so far she really did like them—they were part of him. And as she'd admitted hours before, she loved Miles, and that was that.

"Go with them back to the hotel. I'll ride with Nora and Brian."

He frowned at her. "Plenty of room for everyone to ride together."

"Miles, it's a fifteen-minute trip. We'll be right behind you all. I'm going to change clothes before I go to dinner with everyone anyway."

He gave her a long look and she rolled her eyes at him. "I'm just worried about you."

She snorted. "Why? Did something happen that I don't know about?" Harlow had been teasing but then it hit her that maybe that was actually true. Then it was her turn to give him scrutiny.

"I want you to get to know them," he told her softly. "But I hate that you're overwhelmed."

He hadn't really addressed her comment but as it had been put in a teasing manner, she wasn't concerned.

It wasn't that she was overwhelmed by their presence. She'd grown up around crowds of people and was fairly used to them. And his family had been nice to her. But she'd gone from having a regular day to admitting she was in love and then meeting not just his parents, but pretty much his entire family at once all in the matter of a few hours.

All while she was terrified they'd feel she was responsible for the things in that interview. Would they think she was using him for the spot on the tour too?

That's what the interview had done to her head. Sure, it was complimentary for the most part, but that last bit about Miles had left her unsettled. Yes, she did think about what others might assume about her relationship with Miles. But it was different now.

If Sophia had felt it enough to toss it out like it was *normal* and acceptable to trade her pussy for fame, that meant she hadn't been imagining it from others. Not every time, at least. People out there would assume it, no matter how hard she worked. Gloria assumed it!

He framed her face with his hands then and kissed her with such softness a swell of emotion thickened her voice. "I'm not overwhelmed by your family. I'm not running away. There are lot of them, yes. But we're okay. I just want to change my clothes and give myself ten minutes to prepare."

"Baby," he murmured, "you're riding with me and that's

that. Then you'll change your clothes, and we'll catch up with everyone shortly after."

They were going to think she was the type who couldn't do anything unless their boyfriend was there. Ugh.

But she didn't argue with him over it. Everyone swirled around them, chattering and hugging, filling the narrow hallway with energy. It was good energy. Happy energy, and she wasn't going to do anything to dampen that. Miles glowed with happiness.

"Fine."

He laughed and kissed her quickly, pleased he'd gotten his way.

Miles Brown only looked easygoing. Beneath the surface was a spine of steel and the soul of a person absolutely used to being in charge.

They paused long enough to grab their things and then loaded into a row of vehicles that would ferry them all back to the hotel.

Nora stood at her side by that point. "It's like they keep multiplying. I turn around and there are more. And they're all like a big happy army," she said, easing Harlow's nervousness.

Miles leaned forward a little to see Nora around Harlow. "Resistance is futile."

"Oh my god. Did you just make a *Star Trek* reference?" Brian asked, incredulous.

"When my dad toured during school breaks, my mum and I came along in a pretty swanky tour bus. It had a DVD player and we had stacks and stacks of multiple seasons of television shows. Mum is a big science fiction and horror fan, so *Star Trek* in all its iterations was definitely on our list."

Brian gave Miles an up and down look and then nodded once. Like...conferring an honor or something. "Cool," Brian said.

By the time they'd arrived at the hotel, the others had already gotten there and had texted that they'd see Miles shortly.

"This isn't all of them. Just so you know," Miles told her when they'd gotten into their room and she looked through her clothes, pulling out a few things.

"Your family?"

"Yes. At least twelve more when you count all my cousins. And Maddie's family is now mine by association and by marriage as my aunt Mary is with her uncle Damian. That's three more couples and oh yes, some more kids there too. Last year we all spent Thanksgiving together at Sweet Hollow Ranch in Oregon. That's where Maddie's from. We bunked in every open bedroom and then we rolled up in several tour busses for even more beds. Utter madness." He laughed and then watched as she tossed clothes aside, grabbed others and created an outfit.

His family wouldn't expect that. But he understood, which is why he took a quick shower as well, though she gave him a long slow look as he undressed, she stayed out of the bathroom, which was for the best. Probably.

He hurried though, coming back out, clean and dressed, not ten minutes later.

She looked so pretty there in nothing fancier than jeans

and a short-sleeved blouse, but he could have been surrounded by people in couture and he'd have been drawn to her no matter what. She seemed to emanate a frequency only he could hear.

"Hey. Your phone buzzed a few times and then Poppy texted me. She said to come on up to the top floor when we're ready. Nora and Brian are stopping in for a few minutes but he's getting over a cold, so they won't stay long."

He moved to her and wrapped his arms around her waist. "Whatever's best. Does he need urgent care or anything?"

"Nah. He's drinking those fizzy vitamin C things and chugging as much water and tea as possible. He's already better than he was yesterday. But thank you for asking. I think he's decided you're okay."

"It was the *Star Trek* reference, wasn't it?" Though it was a joke, the truth was, Miles was very relieved to hear her close friend liked him. Brian and Omar had developed a friendship over the last few months as they shared a deep love of merch and D&D. Nora and Poppy and Maddie were all friends with Harlow so now that he'd passed the Brian test, Miles felt better.

Harlow laughed and Miles loved the way her entire being seemed to light up. "I'm not going to lie, I think yes."

"Good. Whatever it takes," he said, spinning them both to orient them toward the door. "Ready?"

She looked at her reflection in the mirror near the front door and tucked her hair behind her ear.

"Let's do this. I'm starving."

CHAPTER
TWENTY-FIVE

The following day, Harlow woke up before Miles—not unusual, he slept like a rock—and went to do yoga and breakfast with Poppy and Nora. Maddie was hanging out with her parents so she was passing on that day's gathering.

"Hi!" Erin and Gillian both smiled at her as she entered Poppy's room.

"It's not an ambush," Poppy said once she'd closed the door. "They just wanted to hang out this morning. Maddie is with Mary and Damien and everyone else is still sleeping."

If it *had* been an ambush, there was still not much Harlow could have done about it. These two women she faced were the most important people in the life of the man she found herself in love with.

But Gillian Brown was just...well she was fucking lovely. And it was impossible not to really like her. Erin, Harlow had a feeling, would simply make you like her.

"Good morning," Harlow said to everyone, pretending it

was just another day in the life instead of yoga after she'd rolled out of the bed she was just naked in with Miles.

Nora winked. "Let's get this done. I'm hungry."

They all rolled out mats and began.

"By the way, I wasn't able to get two minutes alone with you yesterday," Harlow told Erin a few minutes later, "but thank you for sending Miles our music."

"Jeremy felt I'd like your stuff and he was right. I thought your sound would fit with Earthquakes." Erin gave Harlow a searching look. "I didn't quite figure on the rest."

Gillian gave a disapproving grunt and Erin blushed.

"I don't think Miles figured on it either," Harlow said. "I sure didn't."

"Why not? Look at the boy!" Erin exclaimed and this time Gillian said her name sharply.

"You can't plan for things like this," Gillian said quietly. "Yes, my boy is handsome and talented and all those good things. But what you two have, well, that's not really about good looks."

"It doesn't hurt," Harlow found herself saying, bringing a surprised laugh from Miles's mother. "I'd be a liar if I said it wasn't easy to take a look at Miles and want to know more. Or if I listened to his lyrics and didn't think, *hey that guy is interesting.* He's absolutely gorgeous inside and out."

"What's your favorite thing about Miles?" Gillian asked.

"He's always feeding me." Harlow snorted a laugh. "If I'm tired and I take a shower, when I come out there's food waiting for me. After soundcheck he shows up to corral me and make sure we go to the mess and eat together. He makes sure I drink hot tea for my vocal chords and when he found out I liked blackberry honey he special ordered it so I can have it with my tea."

Gillian's smile was a little shaky.

"He's nearly always calm at the center of a storm. There can be total chaos and upset everywhere and he just handles things. He's steady, but not cold." Harlow blushed furiously. She desperately wanted Miles's aunt and mother to understand she cared about Miles not for fame or power but for how he was with people.

"Adrian is that way too," Gillian said. "It's Brody."

The night before Harlow had finally met Brody, who Miles considered a second father, and she could see why. She'd watched Brody manage everyone, herself included. Had noticed everyone defer to him at one moment or another. And she'd definitely noted when Miles and Adrian had stood side by side, laughing at something Brody had said, just where some of the physical tells Miles must have gotten from the Brown men.

"Miles told us that it's you who feeds him," Gillian told her. "I think you both take care of each other quite nicely. I approve of that. He easily gets caught up in whatever he's doing and forgets to eat. He doesn't sleep enough sometimes. He's got a hard time saying no when anyone asks something of him."

"Don't get me started on that," Harlow grumbled.

"Oh, pet, please, that's exactly what we want. Do get started. Tell us," Gillian said and Poppy groaned.

Harlow said, "Everyone wants a piece of him. He doesn't owe the world a piece of himself. He gets to say no. His job is to go out every night and give a great show to fans. Above and beyond that? I think sometimes he's too nice. Luckily, between me and Poppy, we try to remind him it's absolutely his right to not take every single opportunity that gets tossed at him."

"The promoters came to Earthquakes last week and wanted to add another hour of meet and greet before the show. But for VIP ticket holders who weren't necessarily fans, but influential people who post pictures online. You know how that goes," Poppy said to her aunt. "She makes sure he guards his time better."

Harlow scoffed. "Well, I think Poppy is downplaying just how much she does. I can make sure Miles lives on more than soda and food from vending machines, but it's Poppy who lulls them all into thinking she's just so sweet and innocent and then boom, she's setting boundaries and pushing back to give Miles space."

Gillian smiled at her daughter and then back to Harlow. "Seems you see the best in both my children. That they both feel the same about you tells me everything I need to know."

Miles showed up five minutes later, right after they'd rolled up their mats. "Thought I'd find you here," he said to Harlow as he came in.

He dropped a kiss on the top of her head before he greeted everyone else. She wondered if they'd be upset about that. After all, she'd only been in his life months! But no, Erin and Gillian seemed very pleased and Harlow relaxed just a little bit.

"I just got a text from dad. He made arrangements for us to go get lunch on Granville Island somewhere."

"Oh yum. Bring me back something tasty," Harlow said as she stood.

Miles took her hand and pulled her to a stop. "You're

part of the *us* that's going to lunch. Nora, you, and Brian too. Depending on how he's feeling?"

"Better this morning. I'm probably going to urge him to stay here though. Just get him rested as much as possible before tonight's show," Nora said.

"Guess we'd better go change and get ready then." Gillian surprised Harlow by hugging her. "See you both in a bit."

Harlow indicated her outfit. "I need to get changed too since they probably look down on people coming in wearing ratty yoga pants and a tank top with a stain on it from the poutine I ate in Montreal," Harlow said.

Miles shrugged. "That was damned good poutine though. I'll come back up to the room with you. I need to get ready as well." Then to Nora he said, "If you change your mind about coming, we're meeting to leave in an hour and a half down in the parking garage. Otherwise, we'll bring you back something."

"How long does it take you to get ready for a lunch?" he asked, trying to sound casual.

"A lunch with three hundred of your closest loved ones?"

"That's a tiny exaggeration," he told her, trying not to laugh.

"I'm sweaty so I need to shower."

"Okay. Go on," he told her as the elevator slowed to a stop at their floor.

"Forty five minutes. Maybe closer to an hour depending on how my hair goes," she said as they walked down the hall.

"Okay. Then we'd have forty-five minutes to do *other*

things." He opened the door and motioned her to go in first, hanging the do not disturb sign on the handle and using the slide lock.

She turned and in two steps he'd backed her to the wall, holding her there with his body pressed to hers. Her breasts heaved up at the neckline of the top she wore so he leaned down to lick over first the right, then through the crease where they met in the center and then the left.

He groaned at her taste.

"Let me shower first," she said, breathless and not trying to leave his embrace at all.

"I'm only going to get you dirtier," he said, nibbling over her collarbone. "I promise to wash your back. It's a very large shower so we'll both fit."

"*Yes, it is*," she gasped when he sucked her earlobe between his teeth.

Then he got what she meant.

"You're very resourceful," he told her as he pulled her toward the bathroom.

"Multi-tasking!" she said, laughing as she managed to get her shirt off one handed leaving her standing there wearing a sports bra. It was plain. Not created to inflame desire but to hold her tits while she worked out. And yet, even the simple gray fabric made her more beautiful.

He stood there for the longest time, just looking at her, at this unexpected and yet essential part of his world.

"Do I have spinach in my cleavage?" she asked after a bit.

"Just taking a second or three to realize how lucky I am." He opened the door to the shower stall and turned the water on.

"You're about to get even luckier." She snickered. "Sorry, I had to."

He whipped his shirt off and stepped free of his pants and boxers. "Don't apologize," he told her, his hands moving to her hair where he freed it from the ponytail she'd had it in. He dug in to all that dark softness, pulling her close to him so he could slant his mouth over hers and take it for a scalding kiss.

Her taste rocketed through him, filling him with a near frenzy to have her. Her arms were free and he noted—without breaking the kiss—that she shoved out of her leggings and underpants before she planted her palm on his chest to push him back slightly.

He panted, watching as she peeled the bra off and then grinned at him before she took a step into the shower, groaning as the three different showerheads hit her with hot water.

"I'm in here, all wet and pliant," she called out.

He'd been attempting to gather his patience and control to take it slow but her voice and the blatant suggestion in her tone had him snarling and getting in with her.

CHAPTER
TWENTY-SIX

"I know it's a lot to have nearly two dozen of us show up in the middle of your tour. You're taking it well," Ben Copeland told her.

"You love Miles and Poppy and wanted to see them. It's three hours from home. I think it's nice. They're certainly happy to see you all. I'm glad I got to meet everyone. Makes me miss my family too."

They'd had lunch in a restaurant overlooking the water, their party took up pretty much the entire place. After the meal, she'd headed to the deck to get some fresh air and stretch her legs and Miles's uncle had followed.

"There's more of us back home. We seem to grow exponentially every few years," Ben told her.

"Miles told me about Thanksgiving in Hood River. It sounded fun."

"We like being together. It's weird, but it works. I imagine you'll see for yourself. Listen, I wanted to speak to you in private."

Harlow's stomach lurched. "I'm so sorry about that interview. I swear to you I had no idea she was going to say any of that, or I wouldn't have gone. I didn't even know she was Miles's ex until near the end."

Ben paused and then ran a hand down her arm. Just a brief, reassuring touch. "No, please don't apologize. That wasn't the first time our relationship was brought into an article or interview. Won't be the last either. We know you didn't have anything to do with it. But what I wanted to talk to you about is connected in a way. Todd and I run a personal security firm and part of what we do is background investigation. Miles talked to me a little about the situation. He told me he'd mentioned to you that if you wanted, we could look into your mother's life. See if we could find anything that might help you understand her and her choices. We can look for things like police reports or activity. I'll check what documents regarding their divorce and custody agreement if it's not sealed."

Her face flamed and she wanted to dig a hole and hide in it.

"He did mention it to you, right?" Ben asked gently.

"He did, but I didn't know that he'd spoken to you about it in detail." He certainly hadn't mentioned to *her* that he'd spoken more specifically about it to his uncle. She continued to watch the birds wheel about in the sky over the water, diving for fish, struggling not to be pissed. Struggling to see this offer in the spirit it was being made. She and Miles would discuss the rest later when they were alone.

"You have nothing to be embarrassed about," he said, obviously understanding her discomfort. "Miles only shared enough to give me background. An idea of what was happening and what we might do to help."

She blew out a breath. "If she would just stop, I could let it go. Probably. But I never know when she's going to pop up to wreak havoc. And I don't know why she seems to want to punish me. I've asked and she doesn't explain. That interview got her worked up but I'm unsure how to deal with it, or even if I should. I don't want to make it worse. I just want her to leave me alone. And leave my dad alone."

"I know that video she posted must have been upsetting, but it only has a handful of views," Ben said softly. "Anything we find out, as long as it's not a crime she's covering up, will be confidential. I wouldn't even tell Miles what I found unless you gave permission."

Nausea coated her like a cold sweat. "*Video*?" What the fuck?

"You didn't know. I thought...I'm sorry."

"I blocked her number after a string of calls and voicemails. I've been trying not to think about her." Harlow pulled her phone out, but Ben put a staying hand on hers.

"You don't need to look at it. I already told Miles what was said, but it's nothing for you to be alarmed about. She's a middle-aged woman who's railing against the modern world and using you as her cudgel. No one is going to care unless for some reason it gets more notice. If we make a fuss, that gets more notice. Let it die by giving it the attention it deserves. None."

No wonder Xander seemed to be such a great person. His dads had given her nothing but kindness and a solid strength.

Still, she was mortified that anyone else knew about this ugly chapter. "This is about me because of that interview?"

"I'll tell you all about it if you promise not to look. I'll be honest and won't leave anything out. But you don't need to hear your own mother talk about you that way," Ben said.

"I know it's such a cliché. Boo hoo my mom is terrible. Meanwhile I have an aunt who raised me and is very much my mother figure. And my dad is great and supportive. I went to great schools and live in his house rent free when I'm in Southern California. It's stupid to be upset over this." Her voice wavered a little and she hated that weakness.

He waved a hand. "My father stopped speaking to me when he found out I was in a relationship with Todd as well as Erin. He refused to go to any of the parties when Erin was pregnant with Xander. He's never *met* Xander. Didn't go to his high school graduation. Never shared cake with his grandson at a birthday party. He's never stayed up late with me to put together toys on Christmas Eve. We can't choose our parents. And just because we have a life full of others who *do* love us and accept us doesn't mean it isn't painful when our mom or dad are failures at parenting and reject us."

"I'm so sorry." And she was. Though she wasn't a parent herself, the way some parents just threw their kids out like garbage infuriated her. It put her own situation into perspective.

"There's nothing for you to be sorry about," Ben said. "My mom is great and has been. They divorced over it nearly twenty years ago. I hated that part because it was about me. When I told her that, she said she tolerated it for so much longer than she should have. Hoping he'd see what he'd done and want to fix it. She asked me what I would do, in her place, if Todd or Erin rejected Xander the way my father had done with me. I love them. Todd and

Erin, I mean." He grinned a moment and it lightened her heart. "We have a good life. A close, loving family. It's a blessing. But I'm Xander's dad first. Always. And yes, I would leave either or both if it meant protecting my child."

They were both quiet for a few minutes.

"I'm telling you all this for a few reasons. Your dad and your aunt love you and you know that. You know it's a gift to have such support. But you should apply that standard to your bio mom. You may not know her reasons, if she's got any, but that still doesn't make you responsible for how a grown person acts. The weight of this is not yours to carry, sweetheart. No matter what she said on her little video, it doesn't matter to anyone who cares about you."

Not trusting herself to speak without crying, she blinked tears back and turned, resolutely looking at the birds again while she found her self control.

"Tell me," she said at last.

Miles realized Harlow wasn't anywhere he could see inside the restaurant. There were plenty of people around and any of them could be with her somewhere else. He wasn't worried. They'd all be fine with her and if anything came up, someone would come to him about it.

So it wasn't worry that had him getting up to cruise around the place. But a need to connect with her.

"She's outside with Ben," Erin told him as she must have guessed why he was looking around.

Shit. He was probably talking with Harlow about the whole mess with Gloria.

"He's not going to hurt her, you know," Erin said. "He's good with people."

"He's not the one hurting her anyway, Erin. If it were only that simple."

"You can't stop other people from hurting her. It's impossible, and she'll end up resenting you for controlling her. And you'll end up resenting her for needing to be protected. She's made it this far in her life without a man fixing her."

Miles snorted. "I'm not trying to be her white knight. I know she's strong and capable. But she doesn't always have to be. I'm here now to help. And there's no reason Gloria should be allowed any access to her to hurt her further."

"What are you going to do when you're in Europe working for six weeks and she's here? You both travel all the time with your work so you can't always be at her side. What then? If you start doing everything for her, you're going to make her weak when she's on her own. And you're telling her she can't do it herself."

His aunt had a way of saying just exactly whatever it was a person needed to hear most. It was a little spooky.

"I know I *want* to be there all the time to protect her. I also know neither of us needs that and in the end that would hurt our relationship. But I love her. And this business with Gloria rips her heart to shreds. Believe me when I tell you if it were up to me I'd have a slew of expensive attorneys stripping that bitch of everything dear to her until she got the message to keep her mouth out of Harlow's business. I actually threatened Gloria with that very thing and the following day I also called my attorney to give him a head's up."

His mum joined them and gave him a raised brow at his words.

"She'd hate that if I went through with it," Miles admitted. "She's embarrassed but doesn't want to admit it. And if I did that, it'd be calling attention to the situation and that would hurt Harlow even more. But the more crap this woman does, the closer I get to doing it and apologizing afterward."

"How's she going to feel when she finds out you've already paid for Ben's services?" his mother asked.

"I'm the one who suggested Ben to her to start with," he said, defensive. "And I had to make a detailed argument to Ben to get him to agree to take money, so don't think he hasn't already spoken to me about this. Once I paid him and she became a client, he told me he can't share anything without her permission and I agreed. As for the rest? She does okay financially. Not from the band really, we all know how that goes. But the music is beginning to take off and she's got a great reputation for her studio work. But there'll be hard times to come with the good and she's got a mortgage to cover. I have the money."

He had ridiculous amounts of it. His father had seen to that, despite his mum's strenuous objections when he'd been younger.

"She has *not* asked for any," he hastened to add. He didn't want his mum or aunt thinking Harlow was using him for anything. Possibly sex, he smiled inwardly, but that wasn't something to share either.

"She comes from money. Like you do." Erin looked him over closely, but he'd just noticed where Harlow and Ben had been standing outside and at the sight of her back, his anxiety at not knowing exactly where she was melted away.

"Well, yes. And she doesn't want to take it from her dad

as an adult any more than I do. And, she hasn't told her father about most of this bullshit with her mom." Harlow had plenty of support in her life and she'd be the first person to say that. But she was also wary of sharing details with her aunt or father because she didn't want Gloria to hurt anyone else. Hopefully this conversation with her dad would help.

"So why did you pay then?" his mum asked softly.

"*Because I know*. Her dad doesn't. Her aunt doesn't. She's protecting them even though neither would want that. But because I know, because I've seen the wreckage Gloria leaves each time she pulls some shit on Harlow, I couldn't not move on this. I want her to have answers. I want Harlow to at least know why this is happening. Or if there's truly no reason other than Gloria is a terrible person. I just want to protect her in ways I can."

His mum's frown slid into a smile that made his heart overflow. "Your dad and I are so lucky you're ours. We're so proud of you."

"But she's still going to kick your ass when she finds out you paid Ben," Erin said with a lopsided smile.

"Probably." But he'd deal with that when it came up.

"Wait, back up a moment," Harlow said to Ben as she figured something out.

He paused, looking to her to figure out what she needed.

"You said you and Miles talked about the video Gloria made?"

"Yes. Last night at the dinner. As I said, if you do go forward with this investigation everything would be confidential. I can tell Miles if you like, or you can. Or whatever.

He and I only spoke at this point because he was giving me background.”

“How long?”

“How long what?”

“How long has Miles known about this video?”

And not told her.

“He brought the situation with Gloria up, saying he’d talked to you about hiring me. So I did some quick searching of the web and found it. This was only yesterday. He didn’t tell you,” Ben said. It wasn’t a question.

“He did not.” And they’d been together alone plenty of times since then in which he could have said. And decided not to.

But he’d shared with this person who despite being lovely and all, was a relative stranger.

“Harlow, he only wants to help. I’m sure he expected to talk to you about it or have me talk to you about it. I explained when he paid the retainer that if you went forward with this, it would be up to you to share whatever you chose.”

“He paid a retainer to you? For me?” She hadn’t intended to sound so pissed, but there it was. Miles just pushed and pushed and pushed and apologized afterward, and despite his intentions being good, it really made her mad.

Ben cursed and pinched the bridge of his nose. “I’m usually better at this,” he said at last. “Then again, I guess I never expected Miles to be clumsy like this either. He’s not… I’ve seen him be protective of many people. Our family definitely, but also his band members. But never once a romantic interest. That’s the only reason I can imagine him not telling you. He's not underhanded like that. He respects you and wants you happy."

No, he wasn't underhanded. But.

Harlow wasn't about to make a scene over it. As pissed off and hurt as she was by Miles's paying a retainer without even consulting her, they'd work it out and that would need to be done outside the view of his fan club.

"How much is the retainer?" she asked Ben.

"He took care of it. Don't worry."

She just looked at him until he sighed. "Work this out with him. Then whatever you need, you're the client and we'll handle it if you want to pay instead. I informed him when I accepted the retainer that once that had happened, you were my client and what I found would be confidential. He agreed to that."

"Oh, I do want to pay. It's my issue, not Miles's." She had money to pay her own damned bills. It was one thing to stay in his swanky hotel suites and take advantage of the offers he'd made of things like sharing their transport to the venue and the like. Another entirely for him to pay her fucking expenses like he was her sugar daddy as her mother had screamed in one of those voicemails.

"I'll have an invoice sent to you directly," Ben said at last. "And I won't share anything else with him from this point on."

She scrubbed her hands over her face a moment. "This is already more complicated than I want."

"I apologize," Ben said. "I have messed up here because he's my nephew and he's so fucking in love with you he can't stand knowing you're hurting. He just wants to take care of you. I should have been clearer up front and not shared any of this with him. It's not professional at all."

And now she was in an impossible position.

"I think I'll watch the video on my own. You don't need to be part of this. It's not fair for you to have to take responsibility for something Miles did. No matter his reasons. That he hasn't shared with me."

Ben put a hand on her arm to stay her. "Please don't. He fucked up. I fucked up. I absolutely understand why you're upset. Can we start over? Please?"

What could she say other than yes? Even though she wanted to leave and be alone for the hours before they took the stage, she couldn't. Because she was with someone now who came with this big extended family.

It felt like manipulation if she were to be totally honest. Ben knew that too. He knew she cared so much for Miles that she wouldn't risk alienating him or them.

"I dislike being manipulated with my feelings," she told him, and he nodded.

"I'm not trying to manipulate you. I wouldn't do that even if you weren't with Miles. I'm not that guy. But I understand right now, Miles and I have given you reason to feel that. I can only apologize again and promise you to be better. I truly do want to help."

She blew out a breath. He was a genuine guy and she liked him. And importantly, she believed his apology and his reasons. He loved Miles and Miles loved her and that was what made this all so complicated even as it was generous and wonderful.

But she was pretty sure she wasn't going to keep him on the job. If she even had the job done at this point.

"Fine. Tell me what was in that video. And I don't want you revealing *anything* to Miles. *I* will let him know if that's what I choose to do. They are my details and I have every right to do that myself."

Relief flashed over Ben's expression. "Fair. So very fair." He looked back over their shoulders to the restaurant and then back to her. "Gloria is a narcissist. She's the kind of person that if you say you broke your toe, she'd interrupt with a story about her own health. There's no subject she will allow anyone to shine with and will always center herself in every conversation. All while telling everyone how much she cares about them. And when she gets called out, I bet she tries to pretend it's that she's truly just awkward and is only trying to connect."

Bullseye.

"She blames your father and the liberal elite for your scandalous behavior. She claims you were purchased from her and then made into his image. Says you were sexually forward from an early age and trained to be by your father and his minions. And that's why you're so successful in the music business."

Harlow swallowed hard and willed the tears away.

"According to her, Miles is your sugar daddy and is using you and your youth and beauty to further his own success."

Well, he did just pay on her behalf without even discussing it with her beforehand. If anyone like Gloria found out Miles had paid for this investigation into her background it would only lend credence to the sugar daddy theory.

He sighed. "There's a bit where Gloria talks about Miles.

His piercings and his variety of romantic interests as evidence of how far you've fallen."

"That he's bi? Like that's a big shocking secret?" Harlow waved that away.

Ben grinned at her briefly. "Yes. I know you wouldn't be surprised by the way some people still think about that. But that attacks your foundations. And the foundation of your happiness, right? She wants you to doubt all the things that empower you. Then you're weak and defenseless."

She wanted to run away from everything. Fighting the urge not to bolt took all her concentration and control. All this internal struggle was not something she wanted to deal with in front of all these very important people in Miles's life. All while she was pissed at him.

Harlow needed to make herself some pro and con lists and try to process everything but there wasn't the opportunity for that right then. Which left her anxious and feeling trapped.

"I have to think about all this," she said at last.

"Fair. There's a lot going on. I'll create a report for you with everything as I go," Ben said.

"I also need to think about whether or not I'll use your services. I'm sorry. I know this is so rude." She fought back emotion.

"This was the worst possible way for me to bring this up. I apologize again."

"You want to help. I see that. And I appreciate it. I truly do. But this is...well, I'm not prepared to..." She shook her head, not having the words.

Ben took a deep breath and sent her a conciliatory smile. She felt like the worst, meanest person alive not to jump on this chance. But Harlow had hit a wall and ill-timed or not, it was her moment to stand up for herself in the midst of all this chaos being orchestrated by *everyone but her.*

"How about this? Take your time to think about everything. If you have questions, just ask them. Text or call, whatever is best. I'll hold off on anything else until I hear from you. I will urge you not to respond to Gloria's video at this stage. Protect yourself," Ben said.

"Dessert is here," Erin called out from inside.

"Be right there," Ben replied.

Miles looked up from where he'd been chatting with his mum and a chill ran down his spine when he caught Harlow's expression when she and Ben returned for pie. It only got worse when she seated herself where he couldn't weasel in next to her while not allowing him a single second of eye contact.

Then while he was fussing around over the check, Harlow jumped into the first car to go back to the hotel.

Ben saw it and shook his head, taking Miles aside. "What the fuck is going on?" Miles demanded of his uncle. "Am I imagining it or is she pissed off?"

"You're not imagining it. We fucked up, Miles. You and me both," Ben said and explained the whole situation that had happened on the deck.

Damn it.

He stood to the side, making a quick call.

Harlow didn't answer her phone. It went straight to voicemail.

"I know you're mad at me and you have a right to be. I

didn't do it because I thought you were incapable of handling it on your own. I just wanted to help you because you have so much on your shoulders, and I hate to see you suffer. I would have talked to you about the video. I wasn't hiding it like that. I figured we'd talk about it once you met with Ben. As for the retainer? We can talk about that later on. Look, Harlow, I'm in love with you. It makes me stupid sometimes. My emotions take over and I want to protect you and I mess up. I'm coming to you now. So take the time you need to process between now and then."

He disconnected and shoved his phone in a pocket before returning to his family, all the while itching to be done so he could go to her and reassure himself they were okay.

CHAPTER
TWENTY-SEVEN

She wasn't in their room when he returned. A quick, frantic check of the closet showed her clothes still hanging there and her things were all over her side of the dual sink area in the bathroom, so she hadn't run off. He'd gotten used to her being with him in the month plus since she'd finally given in and agreed to share his room nightly.

Ben had stressed several times that he did not think Harlow was going to break up with him. She was pissed, but she'd told Ben they would work it out and he fell back on that even if he wanted to run down to Nora and Brian's room immediately to see if she was there. Nora had stayed back from lunch to keep an eye on Brian, who was still feeling poorly, and as she was Harlow's best friend, that's probably exactly where she'd headed.

Instead of going down there, he decided to text her.

Where are you?

She replied a minute later. *At a coffee shop near the venue.*

It was about an hour earlier than they all usually went over, and he knew it was to avoid him.

Alone?

I'm fine.

Oh shit. I'm fine rarely ever meant I'm fine. Like *whatever* rarely meant that person was letting it go.

We should talk. I'm going to come over now.

No. I'm here with Nora and we're working. We can talk tomorrow.

Though he knew the answer, he couldn't help but ask. *Are you breaking up with me?*

The little dots indicating she was responding seemed to taunt him for a terribly long time.

I know I told Ben this wasn't a break up offense and that we would work things out.

He winced, waiting for more but it didn't come. *So let's work this out.*

I'm working. Don't bring this shit to me tonight and fuck my mojo.

Despite his annoyance, he smiled. If she felt well enough to send back that little verbal middle finger, she'd be okay. Yes, she was sad about this bullshit, but Harlow wasn't cowed for long and her spine was still just as steely as it had been before.

She'd make it. And so would they.

You said tomorrow. We'll talk this out tonight after the show. I don't want to go to bed with this unsettled between us.

You have a real issue with boundaries sometimes, Miles. Your family is here. Spend time with them before they leave later. Tell them I said to travel safe.

He groaned and tried to Facetime her. She didn't pick up.

I'll see you at the venue in two hours. He also sent a selfie. Couldn't hurt to remind her how handsome he was.

Miles would spend this last time with family and wouldn't rush over to the arena even though he really wanted to.

"Why can't they just listen when we tell them something?" Harlow asked Nora.

"Don't ask me. I have a non-alpha male boyfriend. Brian listens when I tell him to back off," Nora said.

"Because you had to train him, though. Maybe that's it. Plus you were babies when you first got together so you grew up with one another. Hopefully, after some time and some reinforcement of boundaries Miles will figure it out."

Nora thought that was hilarious. "Sure. Let's pretend we're done talking about that. You two are going to hash this out and have make-up sex and then he'll go back to doing whatever because he's a bossy person who is used to being in charge. As are you. So, tell me what Gloria said on this video."

Nora met her at the coffee shop after Brian went to the venue and Harlow was telling her friend the story of her day. Harlow had watched the video in the cab on the way back to the hotel and had been even sicker to her stomach since.

"Let's see, first she says my dad bought me from her. Then she says he made me in his image. You know, left wing lesbians on the west coast, witchcraft, and shit. I've been slutty since I was a kid and now, I'm shaming my *innocent* family—she means her side—with my promiscuity and association with my sugar daddy who is paying me to fuck him so I can be on his tour. Oh and worse, his pierced penis has touched another penis at some point in his life."

Nora blinked; her mouth opened to speak but she closed it again as she shook her head.

"I know. It's like trail mix of terrible takes. Ben said something that makes a lot of sense though. That if we react it might get more attention to the video, which makes things worse. So do I shut up and hope it goes away, at least until the tour is over? Do I sue and make her take it down?"

"I totally agree that Ben could have handled this better. And I really agree that Miles could have. Are you going to let Ben continue to advise you on this? He seems to truly care."

"I'm struggling with that. The reality is, he's so close to Miles. It becomes a Harlow and Miles issue. And it's not. Ben is *absolutely* a very nice person. I appreciate that he got on this so fast. And I appreciated that he shared some very personal stuff about his father. He said he saw himself in me and got tripped up and that's valid, you know? But he loves Miles. Miles is his family and everything we say or do, regardless of whether it is about Miles, will be brought to him or compared to him or measured as to what he'd feel. It's not that he's a bad guy. He isn't. But this whole thing is about me standing on my own and finally rejecting whatever this Gloria thing is. Right? I'm wondering if it's better all around if I don't use his services. Obviously, I'll pay for his time. But I can talk to Jeremy. He'll know people I can hire, and they won't be connected to Miles. I'm worried this will cause a problem with his family no matter what I decide to do. Which makes me pissed. Because this is my shit, and I shouldn't have to feel guilty because other people messed up. But here we are."

Nora grunted. "He better *not* have been angry. He shouldn't have brought this whole thing up to you at that lunch. I'm so sorry I wasn't there."

"Most of the lunch was fine. They're all interesting. Ben was just being nice." Harlow paused and then just blurted, "What do you think I should do?"

"My opinion is that I'll support you no matter what. That said? Yes, you can talk to Jeremy, and he'll have multiple suggestions to you, all with details about their specialties and the like within twenty-four hours because that's how he is. They will all be qualified and if you hire one, you'll have total control and there'll be no connection to Miles except what you choose."

Harlow just waited. She'd already come to those conclusions too.

"If you go that way, you'll be dealing with a relative stranger. Which isn't necessarily a bad thing. Or, you can continue on, at least a bit more, with Ben. Do you think he'll tell Miles anything after you and he spoke?"

Harlow thought about it carefully. "No. I don't think so."

"Ben has gone through some of his own shit with a fucked up parent. And he shared that with you. That's not necessary. He didn't have to do that. But it makes a difference that he did. And it makes a difference that he understands what you feel like first hand." She took Harlow's hand a moment to squeeze. "And he's already part of a circle you trust." Nora shrugged. "Do what you feel is best. There are pros and cons to each decision. But in your position, given all the stuff I know, and you've told me, I'd at the very least try to work with Ben. At the first sign of anything you don't like, kick him loose. He wants to help. He's already helped, you said. The real question is, will he be professional and keep his mouth shut when it comes to his beloved nephew."

Harlow blew out a breath. "I totally think, after this talk with Ben, that the idea of an investigation is a good one. Not that I think she's hiding a criminal past or anything like that. But the fact is, I don't know much about her, and no one seems to want to be up front and tell me. So this will get me some details. Maybe I'll actually find out something to help me understand her choices better. I just want to try. It's not a *should* I hire an investigator, but *who* should I hire."

She'd call Ben to talk to him. See if they could both get past this situation. See if she could truly believe his claims of keeping Miles out of things unless and until she said it was okay otherwise.

Nora agreed that was a good choice.

It was coming up on soundcheck so they paid for their drinks, grabbed one for Brian and headed out.

Naturally not even three minutes after they'd arrived and were in their green room, Miles came strolling in.

She gave him a look that dared him to talk about anything before she was ready. He grinned and plopped down on the couch next to her.

"I've been looking for you. I brought you an extra slice of pie."

As apologies went, pie was a great start.

"Where is it?"

"It's in the fridge in our room. You can eat it later tonight after the show."

She harrumphed.

"Harlow..."

She turned her head to look into his face. Letting him see just how much she didn't want to talk about it right then. As she'd told him already more than once. He paid that retainer without even discussing it with her first. He knew about that video and said not one damned thing and *now* he wanted to talk about it? On his schedule? Because he got caught out and she was holding him accountable to *her* schedule to work it through? No, sir. Not today.

You wanted me. Now you've got me. But only if you respect my boundaries.

"My family says they'll see you at the Gorge," he said at last. "They really liked you."

"That's nice. I liked them too," was all she said.

"All of them?"

"Dude! What did I say? Four times. Four. Times."

"I wasn't trying to discuss the things you promised we could hash out later tonight. I just wanted to be sure you were okay with them."

"Just because you like to eat my pussy doesn't mean I'm going to give you a pass for steamrolling over my wishes," she said in a quiet voice.

It was true. Mostly. He was really good at eating pussy! But still.

"I just want to know things are okay," he said before kissing her forehead.

"Yeah, well you don't get to know everything exactly when you want to. Especially when I already answered that goddamned question. I'm really pissed at you. Leave me be."

"And you didn't even respond to me telling you I love you."

"You said it on *voicemail* so unless you're my nana or my dad, fuck off with that."

He laughed then, pulling her into a hug. "Harlow?"

"What?" she asked, annoyed.

"I love you."

Oh. Well.

It would serve him right if she said thank you, or that's nice. But she was pissed at a choice he'd made, not really him, and withholding love wasn't the response.

She settled on, "I love you too."

"Yeah?"

"Yeah. Don't let it go to your head."

"Too late."

"Go." She made a shooing motion with her hand. "We have soundcheck in fifteen and I need to get my shit together."

"You keep pushing me away." He frowned.

Harlow made a very heroic effort not to roll her eyes at this gorgeous, spoiled baby.

"*This is my job*. Though people like to think I have it because of you, I work really hard, and I deserve my success. It's not pushing you away. *It's not about you at all!*"

Miles finally *heard* what she was saying, and shame washed over him. He'd been flirting and trying to charm his way out of her being mad. But that response told him about something deeper.

Motherfucking whatserface! She'd stirred her pot of toil and trouble to get herself some attention and clicks but had also amplified something that hit Harlow in the confidence.

"I know you work hard, and I apologize for insinuating otherwise. Can I still watch your soundcheck?"

She looked him over carefully, measuring her answer and he wanted so badly for her to say yes that he ruthlessly tamped down his instinct to kiss her or attempt to sway her in any way.

"I need you to understand something."

He nodded.

"When I set boundaries it's because they're important to me. When you bulldoze over them it makes me feel like they don't matter to you. Frankly? I don't care if they don't matter to you. That's your problem. They matter to me. And that's the point. There will be plenty of times in our relationship that one of us will set a line we don't want the other to pass. It's one thing to blunder over it because we're human and we care about each other and want to fix things. But I'm not a problem to be solved. Mainly, I want you to respect me and my independence and when I tell you something like, *we will hash this out but not until after I've finished my performance,* I expect you to do that. Whether you want to or not. Whether you like it or not. Whether you agree with my reasons or not. I get that you are bossy and spoiled and very much used to people following your lead. And I get that it's a heavy thing to be that person everyone looks to in times of trouble. I'm proud of you for that."

It was that last bit that felled him. She saw him to his soul and got him in ways no one else did. It mattered so much. And it was just another sign that they were meant to be together.

"Thank you," he said first. "For sharing that and for the compliment."

"We can talk about the rest later. Yes, you can come to soundcheck."

He did give in to impulse and kiss her then. Far more briefly than he wanted, but he wanted to show her he heard her and respected her boundaries.

"I'm going now," he said, heading to the door. "I'll see you at soundcheck."

He made himself leave and ended up bumping into Maddie as she came out of their green room.

"Hi there," he said to her. "Nice to see everyone, huh?"

"It was. My parents brought proof of life for Carl."

Carl was Maddie's cat that her parents were sitting while she was on tour.

"He's gained weight," Maddie said with a snicker. "My dad spoils animals too much. My mom said he gives Carl brie. Who gives cats expensive cheese? Vaughan Hurley apparently. He's a big old softie."

Bits and pieces from home life helped when you were out on the road, Miles had discovered very early on. Even though they were all adults and out on their own, calls from parents or pictures of pets could really help the loneliness.

Miles realized he'd gotten some much appreciated love from his family, but also that he hadn't needed that touchstone as much as in the past. Because his heart was on the tour at his side.

"Going to catch Above Me's soundcheck. Wanna come with?" he asked.

"Yeah. Hang on a second. I want to grab a hoodie. It's freezing down here."

CHAPTER
TWENTY-EIGHT

At the end of Above Me's set, Harlow was suddenly so tired all she wanted was to go back to the hotel and rest. It had been a lot since that damned interview had come out. A lot of stuff that had been revealed when she had no choice in it. And she knew that was just the way of things.

Emotional stuff rarely cropped up when you were ready for it, or prepared. It nearly always came out of the blue and hit hardest and deepest because you'd been trying to pretend it away.

Nora took one look and shook her head. "You don't need to be here. Earthquakes performs perfectly every night and that's not because Miles's girlfriend is watching."

"No. But it means something to him that I am." Which was the truth and why she chose to guzzle a bunch of water, eat some fruit, and changed out of her stage clothing and into something more comfortable.

"You and Brian should go back though. He's getting better but you both have been running ragged. Eat something healthy and sleep," Harlow told Nora when she'd finished.

"I don't want you to deal with this alone." Nora watched her closely.

"It's not him," Harlow said. "It's Gloria and all this other stuff. He fucked up, yes and we'll deal with that. But his response was a misstep. You can't protect me from either. Not from Gloria and not from Miles being a pushy control freak. Go take care of yourself. Thank you for being such a good friend. It means more than I can ever say."

Even after she and Miles cleared the air the situation would still exist. Her triggers and sensitive parts would be part of her, and it wasn't up to Miles or Nora to heal her or support her through it. That wasn't how it worked. If only it was.

Brian approached and gave Harlow a hug. "I love you, Har. We're here at your side. Not to fix you or protect you. But because you're our family and that's what family does."

"You're going to make me cry and I can't. I need to hold it together until it's safe for me to let it go," she told him quietly.

He nodded as he stepped back. "Okay. I understand. We'll see you later. Text to let us know you return to the hotel, so we won't worry."

She agreed and as they made a right, heading to the back of the venue where they'd get a car to take them back, Harlow took a left, heading to the stage.

If she'd been hoping to get there without an escort or notice, that fell away when Miles, who'd obviously been waiting at the base of the steps leading toward the stage, caught sight of her and smiled.

"I was hoping you'd want to come watch us." He held out a hand and she took it; glad she'd decided to stay.

Harlow ascended the steps at his side and settled herself in her usual place, out of the main line of sight from the crowd but a great view of the stage so she could watch him do his thing.

The rest of the band waited, and she waved. "See you in a bit," he told her before a sweet kiss and then he joined the others and the familiar sound of their opening came up, along with the change in houselights.

The roar of the crowd when they all stepped out made her smile.

It was three hours later when they finally arrived back at the hotel. Earthquakes was still buzzing from the energy of being on stage, so Harlow contentedly sat back and let it wash over her until they finally got to their room.

Blessedly quiet and absent anyone but the two of them.

"I'm going to shower," she told him and closed the door to the bathroom. Hoping he got the message because she didn't want to be swayed by stellar sex right then.

And when she came out a few minutes later, wearing pj pants and an old t-shirt, he was waiting.

"I'll shower too. Be right back."

They were both being so careful. It made her happy and terribly sad at the same time.

Finally when he'd come back, she'd settled on a chair in the small sitting room attached to the bedroom. He'd have chosen the couch to be next to her if she'd been there. And it would have been harder to keep her concentration if all his delicious body heat mingled with hers.

He frowned but pulled the other chair up so it was directly across from her, close enough that their knees touched.

"I only found out about the video thing yesterday," he said. "And I only learned exactly what she'd said last night at the dinner upstairs. I should have told you, but I wanted you to be able to rest. And this morning, first you did yoga with my mum, and I didn't want to ruin that. Then we did other stuff that truly made me forget. Then lunch." He winced. "I'm sorry you found out the way you did. Ben feels terrible that he brought it up. He knows it was the wrong place. I think he just wanted to help and got in his own way."

"You could have just ended that sentence. Left it as, *I should have told you.* As for how it got brought up, by a total stranger? It was a massively stupid miscalculation." She caught his blanch, but it had to be said. "I understand he's your uncle and he cares about you. I even like that about him. But it was a lunch with your entire family, only the second time I met them all. What they must think between that article and that situation with Ben." She tried not to wring her hands at the anxiety that brought.

He shook his head. "Obviously he'll tell Erin but that's because they're married, and she'll see his upset and demand to know why. But he's not mad or upset at you at all. He's pissed at himself for how he handled everything. And at me for not being more up front with you."

Harlow stared at him, torn between feeling bad that Ben was upset and being angry that she was feeling that way because he'd brought it up the way he had to start with.

"He'd very much like it if he could continue the investigation," Miles said. "He won't say anything to me. You'd be the one to share whatever you felt I needed to know."

"He said stuff designed to make me feel better and stronger. And most of it did. I've been wrestling with whether or not to continue with him." Harlow shook her head. She wasn't going to tell him just yet that she'd already spoken to Ben, and they'd laid out a very clear set of boundaries and he would continue his work. For Harlow

"He's the best at what he does. And just because he told me the stuff at the start doesn't mean he won't keep his word going forward."

Harlow just stared at him, stunned that he continued down this path without even a basic gesture toward what she'd just told him.

"Let's pretend you didn't just make a point against me hiring Ben. Because you did. If I had an investigator I hired and I paid, you wouldn't be involved. You wouldn't be arguing that I continue to keep someone providing a service in a way I do not like. You'd poke your nose in because that's how you are. But if I'd said I wasn't satisfied with someone's services, you'd accept that as my choice to make. But here you are, *arguing* with me about it and only because he's your uncle."

"But we laid ground rules now."

Never had she wanted to hit someone in the face with a pillow more than she did right then. "*You* discussed my case like it was yours. *You* gave him personal details. *You* paid a retainer. Neither of you thought it was important to include me at the start. He was defensive on *your* behalf. As your uncle, that's great and I love it. As a person supposed to be working for me? *That's* a problem."

"I have the money! Why does it bother you so much that I want to help you? Someone should be protecting you, and since no one else has, I sure as fuck will. You mean *everything* to me. In the time we've been together I've watched her attack you a dozen times. It wrecks me to see it, so I know it's a thousand times worse to feel it. I was told I was reckless for pursuing you during this tour. And then Maddie said something that made total sense to me. She said that when I was with Sophie, I was out of control but with you I was reckless. And I am, because I will do everything I can to take care of you and shield you from pain you don't deserve. Even if you get mad. And I hate it when you're mad at me."

The emotion in his voice had her taking his hand a moment. There was plenty of reckless on both sides. She'd broken a dozen of her own rules for him as well.

"It's incredible to me that you're so protective. That you care about me so much you'd start a relationship in the middle of a tour. That you want to be seen in public with me. That you'd brave my wrath because you do what you do to keep me from being hurt. I accept your bossiness and the way you do whatever you want most of the time. You can't own what Gloria does to me. All the money in the world can't fix that."

He sighed, squeezing the hand she still held. "This would be easier if you'd be less rational and just admit I'm right about everything."

She snorted.

"I need you to understand that if you don't respect my boundaries it will kill us. Not your over protective bullshit, not your bossiness or the fact that you're spoiled. But when I tell you something is important to me and you don't listen and argue with me when I call you out, it breaks something in my heart. I love you, but I'm not going to be in a relationship with someone who doesn't see me as a fully formed person who makes her own decisions. I respect your choices and I need you to do the same."

She held a hand up to keep him from speaking. She wasn't done.

"Here's what's happening. Ben and I have spoken in detail about this issue. He will continue on as my investigator. I considered asking Jeremy for names of people for me to hire, but Nora made some good points about why I should stick with Ben, and I agreed with them. I'll share the information I get back. I'm not trying to keep you out of my life, Miles. I want you at my side, not driving while I sit in the back seat."

Miles took a deep breath, but she saw his smile of relief that she was keeping Ben. "This is our first big fight," he said, and that smile turned down into a frown. "I don't like it."

"I don't like it either. But we can make it through if we're honest with each other. And we listen when the other says something is important to them. You're used to everyone going along with whatever you say. You're a leader. Super sexy. Great when it comes to fucking. Not always easy to handle when you're with a person who is never going to let you run their life, even if it's the best, safest way ever. You don't like being told no and I rather like saying it."

"I don't want to break this thing, or any part of you. I just want you to be surrounded by love and support. I promise to do my best to listen and respect your boundaries. Again, I'm sorry. Ben is sorry. It was a mess and one that could have been avoided if I'd listened to you better. I'm relieved you gave him another chance. He really is awesome at this stuff. You'll share what you find? Promise?"

They'd make it. She wasn't stupid enough to think that would stop him from getting up in her business, but if he listened and paid attention, they'd be okay.

"Yes. Unless you turn into a control freak and ignore my very well defined boundaries. Then we might have to rene-gotiate."

He held out a pinky and she clasped it with hers.

"I will do my best to not take over. Even when I might have a better plan and do it a certain way because that's best."

She smirked a moment. "Oh, okay, well good talk."

"And I'm sorry I was high handed." He laughed. "I love you. I'm sorry the first time I told you was over the phone." He snickered and she flipped him off.

"Remember what I said. Oh. And I love you too. Sucker punched me yesterday. Nora knew before I did."

Miles laughed. Only Harlow could describe falling in love as being punched.

"Yesterday? And you still love me after all this?" he teased. Sort of.

"Must be love that I'm still here now."

Blushing and absolutely pleased at everything she was telling him, Miles rolled his eyes. "You're absolutely gorgeous and smart and funny and you make me stupid with happiness. They saw it. Whatever you said to my mum turned her into your number one fan." As much as he wanted to drag her into the bedroom and sex her into oblivion, there were some other things he needed to share. Wanted her to know so she understood him better. Not to excuse what he'd done, but to give context.

"Your mother is a delight. Also, who knew she cursed like a sailor when she got mad?"

"It's adorable when it's pointed at someone else. Not so fun when she's pissed at you."

Harlow watched him for long moments until she finally said, "There's more. Tell me."

Of course she'd sense that. "It's that she's involved that makes it worse. Sophie I mean."

Harlow paused, cocking her head.

"Will you tell me why? I'm not going to get jealous that you're still emotionally connected to her."

He snorted, shaking his head. "I *am* emotionally connected. Not how you might assume. Can I tell you about her? It?"

Harlow looked at him with a sad smile. "Of course you can. I want that."

"And can we do that snuggled up? You've been mad at me for hours. I hated that."

She held her hand out and he tugged, pulling her up so they could relocate to the bed and under the blankets facing one another.

He took her hand. "When I was the Miles who was with Sophie, I was a different person. A lesser version of who I am now. Weaker. It wasn't a great love affair or anything like that. When we met, Earthquakes's success was just heating up. It seemed fun to go out and be wild. After all, I'd earned it hadn't I, with all my hard work." Miles shook his head.

"Sophie's world was different than mine had been. There were drugs everywhere all the time. I came to rehearsal high more than once until Silas took me aside and said none of them wanted to see my face unless I was ready to do my job. I thought, fuck that! They just want to kill my fun. The sex," he peeked at Harlow, but she didn't look upset. "Threesomes and more. She didn't care if there were other people with us, so I didn't care either. I stopped caring about a lot of things, mainly how the truly important people in my life saw me and what I was doing. It wasn't that I was a junkie, or that I'd physically harmed anyone. But I was a wreck. A juggernaut of chaos and instability until she got bored and cheated and I got ashamed and finally broke things off."

Harlow squeezed his hand but said nothing. Just letting him get it out.

"Then, after the breakup, Sophie took things, private things, between us and she threw out all the details. She gave all these breathless, giggly little bits about us to get more attention and to raise her profile as a celebrity adjacent person. This stuff was everywhere. She bragged about my piercing and how high capacity I was when it came to drugs and alcohol. She posted pictures of my dick on the internet. I had to face my mum knowing she'd heard I did coke. That she knew I'd smoked dope with heroin. People knew all my weakest moments and I had no defense other than pretending it didn't bother me."

He pulled his hand away to scrub it over his face.

Harlow continued listening to him with nothing more on her features than empathy.

"I don't mean to say she made me do it or that she was a bad influence, because that's not true. I allowed her into my world and then I wallowed in the way we dirtied it up." The words had been ripped from him. Something he'd thought dozens of times but had never given voice to. "It took me a really long time to trust anyone new after that. And I can't say it wasn't hard even with those I did know and had no reason to suspect."

He pressed the heel of his hand against his chest, against the pain. "Because of me, she slithered into your life and did to you what she did to me. I hate that it was her who brought Gloria's attention back to you in such a visceral way. I hate that it made you upset. I hate that it makes you believe you're not deserving of your success. She's a shallow person who doesn't care about anyone above what they can do for her. Obviously, she sees you and thinks you had to fuck your way to success because it wouldn't occur to her otherwise. I hate that she's in between us because she's stirred her pot again." He'd worked so hard to get past that part of his life and his worst mistake had come back to do harm to his best thing in the world.

"Miles, I feel this way because of years and years of being taken less seriously because I had a famous dad. Or because I'm female. And attractive. With boobs and a brain. It's part of this industry and *I loathe it*. But it's not because of whatserface. Sophia is an archetype. There are many of her. You can't own that. In fact, you've gone out of your way to be the opposite with me."

She kissed his fingertips.

"Thank you for trusting me enough to share this. It helps me understand you so much better. I'm sorry she betrayed you. I'm sorry she messed with your trust but I'm so grateful you gave it to me."

He blew out a long breath, letting go of the guilt and the anxiety that Harlow might react badly. Let himself accept the fact that she loved him. She wasn't going to hurt him like that. Would, in fact, go out of her way not to.

"Are we at the make-up sex part?" he whispered.

"Probably," she said. "If you've got the energy to pleasure me well, let's get to it!"

CHAPTER
TWENTY-NINE

Harlow spun in a circle as she took in the master bedroom of the house Miles had rented for the next several days. Floor to ceiling windows fronted the entire space with a large deck just beyond. The ocean glittered to the horizon past that as the setting sun set the sky afire in oranges and pinks.

The light on her skin was a lure. God she was magnificent there in a short sun dress of blue gingham. Sexy and sweet all in one.

La Jolla was one of her favorite places. She'd mentioned it once, months ago at the beginning of the tour. He'd remembered because it occurred to him they'd be in San Diego for shows. It'd been a pleasure to choose this house for her. A base for the next several days. A way to spoil her, which was one of his favorite things.

"I had Poppy text the address and basic directions to your dad and to Jenna. There are groceries in the fridge and pantry. Poppy took the initiative to stock up on things we'd all like. She's really pleased you invited her to stay here with us," he told her.

"Well of course I did. She's your sister and my friend. Also, she's exceptional at taking care of people."

"Sometimes you have a tendency to assume the things you do for people are things everyone does. Even though there are few enough people who do those same things for you. You're a beautiful soul and very much a nurturer and fixer."

He met her in the middle of the room, just looking into her face and letting her smile ease every heavy thing on his mind.

"You're one to talk. You take care of me all the time. And the band and your friends. Your family. My friends."

Miles warmed at her words. "In all the world there's nothing for me to do but take care of you. Then I know for sure you're okay because I'm the one who helped make you that way. You're pretty easy to take care of. I don't do all that much because you usually beat me to it because you're taking care of me." Which was frustratingly true at times. As problems went, it wasn't a bad one to have really. But as he loved spoiling her it did take creative thinking.

"I have very few riders in my contract." She grinned. "This house is stunning. And we're here because you remembered something I said months ago. So my dad and Jenna and Ryder can stay here too. And Poppy to balance it."

Yes, he'd done it because he'd tucked away that detail when she'd been talking about her favorite places. But he'd also done it because she could meet with Richie there in the house instead of some other place where Miles would have to remain behind. In that house he'd be near enough to step in in necessary. Or to lean on. Whatever. He didn't mess around when it came to her, damn it. If that made him pushy or bossy, well, yeah it did make him both those things.

He promised to do the best he could to respect her boundaries, and he was! But that didn't mean he had to give up attempting to protect her entirely. Just that he'd be better at keeping it below her radar.

"You look so pretty," he told her, inching the hem of her dress up little by little. "You'd look even prettier riding my face."

The intake of her breath and her blush rocketed straight to his already achingly hard cock.

"I don't know if you noticed, but the headboard looks like it's bolted to the wall. I think you could brace yourself there. And make all the noise you want because for the next few hours we're all alone."

It didn't matter that he'd already had her that morning when they woke up. Or that he'd have her again when they got home later that night. He wanted more. Always. Greedy for her.

"You can even leave the dress on. I'm all about your ease."

Her delighted laugh stroked over his skin like a caress. A little husky from desire. Like a secret she'd whispered.

"I noticed it has these little buttons." He flicked them open one after the next, all the way to her belly button. "I've been thinking all day about how I could open the front of this dress up and free your tits from that bra." As he said it, he'd done it, popping the front clasp.

In addition to pretty much always wanting to fuck her, Miles figured it would help her not be so nervous about the upcoming conversation if he kept her busy climaxing, napping, and eating.

He'd start with the climaxing, then they'd go to dinner with Omar and depending on what the mood was when they got home, he'd probably top up the orgasm tank so she'd sleep deeply.

One handed—the other was slowly twisting the bar through her nipple back and forth—he was able to grab the waistband of her underpants and pull them down so she could step free.

She was already wet as he slid his fingertips through her labia and up to her clit.

But before he went any further, he took several steps back. His shoes were already by the front door so he laid on the bed and beckoned her.

She straddled his body as she moved toward his face. He stopped her when she tried to undo his jeans. If she touched his cock he'd lose it. And he wanted all his focus on her. Then he'd free his cock and fuck her so hard her tits bounced.

There were no words between them just then. Just the soft sounds her knees sliding over the bedspread and their breathing. But when she got close enough, he grabbed the tops of her thighs and her ass, holding her in place.

Her hair slid forward, partially obscuring her features as she looked down at him. Her pupils were huge, lips wet from where she'd licked them. Christ, every little detail of her reaction to him unraveled all his control.

He urged her up. "Grab the headboard to brace yourself," he said and then groaned when she immediately obeyed and her pussy was just right there. "So wet already." He pulled just a bit more so he could reach easier and then he settled her, partially supporting her weight with the grip he had on her legs.

Eating pussy this way...no...eating *her* pussy in this position was his favorite because he loved the way she trembled as he did. Her thighs and belly started first as he began to lick and nuzzle.

Her clit was swollen and each lick sent a shiver through her.

"I'm going to break this headboard," she gasped.

He doubted it. He'd given it a quick look earlier just to see if it was sturdy enough for this purpose. But he liked the idea of making her so hot she broke things.

"If you did, it'd be worth it," he murmured against her pussy. That would be an expenditure he'd gladly pay for.

She giggled and it faded on a groan as he tickled the underside of her clit with the tip of his tongue. *Yes, ma'am, this is what I bring to the table.*

Harlow struggled to stay balanced as he absolutely devastated her with his mouth. He was just so damned good at oral sex he took it to the next level. She held on so tight to the spindles of the headboard they creaked slightly while her entire body began to tremble.

He did this thing with his tongue and upper lip against her clit that had her upper body jerking like she'd touched a live wire only instead of electricity he sent a bolt of pleasure searing through her system.

It wasn't too long before she found herself churning her hips, stroking herself against him with abandon as little waves of pleasure washed through her, preparing for the tsunami of her climax. He'd never content himself with a small orgasm for her. No. Miles paid attention to detail, and he was a perfectionist. Which meant every time he put his mouth on her pussy, he made her scream his name by the end.

There was nothing else but sensation as she let her head drop forward after closing her eyes. There was no hiding. No pretending away the things he made her feel. With Miles she could be wanton, and her desire was beautiful and worth the effort.

That freedom was something she didn't take for granted. It was more than sex with nice orgasms. Wanting more, demanding more was part of this connection she shared with him. Another layer to their affection and trust. Private and absolutely perfect.

Soon there was nothing else to do but let loose the sounds from deep in her throat as he sucked her clit between his lips over and over and over again until she came so hard her lips tingled and her hands hurt from gripping the headboard.

She opened her eyes as he helped her to lay down next to him, the muscles in her legs still jumping here and there. He kissed her and she wrapped her arms around him to hold him to her for long seconds. He was warm and firm and tasted like her. He was safe and strong and someone who would always be on her team.

So absolutely sexy.

"We're supposed to meet Omar in an hour," he said, starting to roll from bed. Lightning quick, she grabbed him, pulling him back to her.

"Where are you going? You're not done," she said and sounded slightly drunk.

"I didn't want to rush," he said.

"We can rush out the door to meet Omar. After you put your dick in me."

"An offer I cannot refuse, my good lady," he said, reaching under his pillow to pull out a condom.

"So prepared," she said, very much pleased he was.

"I confess that I like to put condoms in places we might need them. Under my pillow, in the bathroom near the shower."

And then he rolled her over and situated himself between her thighs. Again.

He thrust, entering her body in one movement, stealing her breath. Then he grabbed her ankles and pushed her legs up, holding them at the knees where he pushed them further up and apart.

It kept her open for him to get extra deep. Each time he bottomed out, she grunted with him. There was little else she could do because the position kept her in place for him but she was bent in a way that kept her stationary. It was over-whelming in the best sort of way. Helpless but not really. Just enough to get the thrill without the fear.

It didn't matter that they should speed up so as not to be late. Miles would take his time. And once he started fucking her, he often teased about never wanting to leave. But beyond the teasing was the way he touched her, the way his eyes took in every detail of her face. He *didn't* want to leave her pussy and showed her without hesitation. He touched her—always—as if she were precious. Like there was nothing he wanted more in the universe than to be touching her.

He kept deep, allowing most of his body weight to hold

them in place. His kisses were feverish, a gnash of lips and tongue, swallowing one another's breath. Here with him she could lose herself. Give over to whatever it was they created together.

Miles shifted a little, breaking their kiss and Harlow took that opportunity to stare up into his face. In the shadow of the dying daylight, he looked a little dangerous, his dark hair tousled, lips swollen. His eyes had gone glassy and fuck-drunk. His beard, the ink on his shoulders and chest and the septum piercing combined with the snarl as he got closer and closer to climax pushed all her bad boy fantasy buttons. He looked reckless and sexy and mysterious. It sent a thrill through her.

He added a circular grind to the end of each thrust as he pressed against her clit. Each time was nearly percussive as the wave of sensation echoed through her. Miles was all about her pleasure and he wasn't going to let himself come until she did first. A very fine quality.

She dragged her nails down his back, careful not to leave marks as he took his shirt off at the pool and ocean and on stage and she didn't want to announce to the world that she'd dug her nails into his skin because he fucked her so good.

Each tortuously slow circle, over and over was a slow dance that left her panting. Left her so fucking close to climax every single cell in her body seemed tense and ready.

He knew it of course, she realized when his gaze cleared and focused on her face before smirking a moment.

Miles hummed low and obviously pleased. "Do you know you just got hotter and wetter? I think someone finds confidence very hot," he teased while doing the aforementioned circle, sending little jolts of pleasure skittering through her.

There'd been a smart assed comment on the tip of her tongue but that last sex swirl had stolen her words. All but one. "Please."

He groaned. "I'm helpless to deny you anything," he murmured, increasing the pressure, and driving her higher and then right up over the top as she came in a hot rush that would have bowed her spine if she wasn't pinned by his weight.

A snarled curse and he came, continuing that slow press for a while afterward until he rolled free with a sigh. "Don't move," he said as he disappeared into the bathroom and returned shortly.

"Like I could even if I wanted to," she told him lazily as he got into bed at her side and pulled her close. It was a good thing the dress she'd had on resisted wrinkles.

"I love you," he said, kissing her with aching sweetness and she melted.

CHAPTER
THIRTY

Miles stumbled into the kitchen the following morning, following his nose and the sound of Harlow's voice. She stood at the stove while Ryder perched on a nearby step stool watching as Richie and Harlow cooked.

Harlow looked up from the bowl she held, smiling widely when she saw him there. "Hey." She put the bowl aside and came straight to him for a hug and a kiss. "Morning."

He breathed her in and let that settle his worry. "Morning. Smells good down here." He kissed the top of her head. "What can I do to help?"

"Nothing right at the moment. Come get a cup of coffee. Ryder's been looking forward to seeing you," Harlow told him with a wink.

He smiled a hello at Jenna as he grabbed a mug from the cabinet over the coffeemaker and filled it.

"Morning, Richie." He put his mug down and squatted a little to get face to face with Ryder. "Hello, Ryder. I really like your pajamas. Your sister told me how much you love Bigfoot."

"I watch with Pop!" Ryder said of the endless Bigfoot television shows Harlow said she watched with Richie every night when he was home. "Haryo too."

"Yup. When I'm around, we watch together," Harlow told her sister with a wink. "Oh, Poppy will be back shortly. She went for a swim earlier."

"A poppy is a flower! She pretty like that!"

"Right now, nearly every sentence ends in an exclamation point. I'm hoping it's a short phase," Jenna muttered, making Miles laugh.

"It is a flower. Very good. My mum had a baby doll when she was a little kid, and her name was Poppy. When my sister was born, our mum looked at her and said she was as pretty as a doll and that's the name they chose," Miles told Ryder.

"I didn't know that story," Harlow said. "I love that."

The moment Miles had seen Poppy's sweet little face he'd appointed himself her protector. Sometimes though, it snuck up on him that she was the one doing the protecting.

"Did I hear my name?" Poppy came in, her shoulder length dark brown hair pulled into a bun. She looked more relaxed than he'd seen her in a while, clearly at ease around Harlow and her family.

She paused to give Miles a hug before grabbing a cup of coffee and waving at Ryder, who waved a spatula back.

"Let's start taking this food to the table," Richie said, pointing to several platters and bowls. "Ry, go with Mommy so you can supervise everyone."

Ryder skipped off with her mom and they joined her shortly. Harlow sat on one side and Poppy the other.

There were pancakes, bacon and chorizo, fried potatoes, scrambled eggs, oranges fresh from the tree in the back yard along with strawberries, and some sweet breads Jenna had brought from a bakery nearby.

"I'm going to need to nap after breakfast," Poppy said as she filled her plate.

Miles had wanted to get a chef in to prepare some meals, but Harlow had said she liked cooking with her father, and she thought it would be better if they just had groceries delivered. The following day they were all headed over to Omar's house—he lived in San Diego when they weren't recording or on tour—for a barbecue before their first show that night and Miles looked forward to time when Harlow was with his friends socially. Yes, they all hung out regularly backstage, but it was different and far more relaxed in someone's back yard.

And the invitation while Omar hosted meant he accepted Miles and Harlow's relationship. That made a lot of worry go away too.

That day however, Miles and Poppy were going to watch a movie with Ryder and Jenna while Harlow and her dad finally talked. The more they ate, the heavier the air became. He wished he could make this easier for her, but the only way out on this was through. So, he'd be nearby just in case he was needed.

Finally when all the food had been eaten, Miles stood. "Poppy and I will clean since Richie and Harlow cooked. Ryder can supervise."

·   ·   ·

Harlow settled on a chair across from her dad in a library just a few doors down from the master bedroom. Earlier that morning she'd put a pitcher of water and some muffins along with an electric kettle and the ingredients for tea if they wanted.

She nearly told him he didn't have to do this. More than once. But if she did and he accepted, it would have broken something between them. Harlow needed to know.

"I'm just going to start," her dad said. "Jenna gave me a bunch of advice after she kicked my ass for letting this go on so long. I'm sorry for not telling you more when you were growing up. I guess I didn't want you to feel bad if I brought it up." He shook his head. "There's a video Gloria put up. Most of what she said was a lie. But not all of it. I paid her over three million dollars. For you. To get custody."

Miles looked up from where he'd just put away the snacks they'd had during their movie as Harlow came in.

"Jenna is going to play in the pool with Ryder awhile. Poppy's joining them. You want to head to the beach? Just me and you? If you're done, that is," he said.

He knew she was done. Harlow had been crying, but the heaviness that had been around her that morning had gone. There were still shadows in her gaze, but clearly, she and Richie had talked and worked through things. Otherwise, she'd be frantic to avoid everyone.

"There are so many steps, Miles. Going down will be peachy. But coming back is going to hurt." Her tone was faux outrage, but there was a thread of truth in it too.

"It'll be my workout for the day."

"Okay." She rustled through the pantry and held up an insulated tote bag and filled it with some juices, cheese, crackers, chocolate, and a container of the fruit leftover from breakfast. Then she added towels, sunscreen and pointed at everything. "I'll let you carry it. We have nowhere to be until dinner. I'm wearing my bathing suit beneath this dress, so I just need to get my shoes and I'm ready. Get sunscreen on," she told him as she plopped a wide brimmed hat onto her head.

About halfway down the steps, Miles agreed with Harlow's joke about the climb back up. But he wasn't going to complain because he had her all to himself. The little cove they headed to had beachgoers but nowhere near a crowd. Miles just went where she pointed and waited as she put out a big blanket to sit on.

Though he was dying to ask about the conversation, he forced himself to be patient and wait for her to tell him.

"Turns out Gloria wasn't lying about everything in that video. My dad paid her a settlement of three million bucks to essentially take full custody of me," she said at last.

Miles was grateful to be wearing dark sunglasses and a hat that hopefully hid some or most of his shock.

"He left her because of me. He denies it," she said before Miles could speak. "But he said he noticed she was never affectionate with me. Never paid attention at all aside from the basics of clothing and feeding. I had a speech delay because of it."

Cold washed through him at Harlow's words. Gloria was a fucking monster.

"So he wanted out and wanted custody of me and my brothers. She handed me over, he said right there on the spot when he told her. But she said she'd fight him on my brothers. And take me just to punish him. He fought as hard as he could to be sure he got visitation and access, but he feels guilty, like he chose one child over the others."

"He did." Miles reached out to slide a fingertip down her cheek. A brief touch to comfort. "Baby, he looked at his children and saw that for two of the three, Gloria was a decent mother. They'd be safe with her. But you were absolutely not. He knew it and got you out. That's what a parent is supposed to do. He wouldn't have gotten full custody of you three anyway. He was a musician. On the road half the year. Having met Gloria and seen her in action these last months, I can say I believe she absolutely would have kept you from him just to be spiteful. He made the best choice he could for everyone given his circumstances. It's not a perfect choice. But there weren't perfect options. I'm certainly not going to be anything but grateful your father pulled you out of an abusive household."

"He also said some stuff that leads me to believe what I'd suspected. She grew up in a strict household. One where all women were sluts. He said she always had negative reactions to other women. Even at the beach. Always covered me up too."

"Fuck Gloria. Really, Harlow, she's absolute poison to you and your life."

"I told him about the stuff she used to say and do. I hurt him a lot. He blames himself for this situation. He doesn't have a close relationship with two of his kids because of me."

"Bullshit. You didn't make Gloria into who she is. Sounds

like she grew up that way. And you didn't make Gloria abuse you to the point you had a speech delay." The thought of it made him sick. That she was still abusing Harlow was not acceptable. At all. "She moved to another state and didn't even tell your dad. *Gloria* is the reason they have a strained relationship with your father. And, let's be real, your brothers are assholes. While I'm bummed your dad feels bad, *they* watched you grow up and be treated differently and haven't said boo about it. No, you can't blame a kid for their parent's behavior. But they aren't kids. And they haven't been for a long time. And they still treat you like shit."

Her mouth wobbled a bit, and he regretted the vehemence he'd used. He meant everything he'd said, and it needed to be spoken out loud. But he knew she was upset, which pushed his buttons and made him upset. But his tone only made it worse.

He took her hand. "I shouldn't have snarled that last bit at you. I know you're overwhelmed right now. Relieved probably. But it's years' worth of stuff and you can't process it as quickly as it was revealed."

"He wants to have his attorney deal with this. In the divorce agreement, she wasn't supposed to say anything about the payoff," she told him, not addressing anything he'd said. She would be mulling it over, he knew. That's how she dealt with the big stuff. He blurted, but she was more measured.

She felt more guilt about it though. And that had to stop.

"What do you want him to do?" Miles asked.

"If he does push back, she'll use my brothers to hurt him. I hate that."

"What do you want him to do about Gloria continuing to

abuse you even though he paid a huge amount of money and spent your whole life trying to prevent that?" He couldn't have cared less what her brothers thought or felt. But he thought his question to her was nicer than saying it how he really thought it.

"I don't need an investigator any more at this point. Now I know the truth. But, Ben and my investigator said the more fuss you make with Gloria, the more attention she gets. My dad already had his lawyers respond to her cease and desist. Now he's going to slap at her again. I'm worried about what she'll do next. Selfishly, Miles, god, I just don't want to have to deal with stories about me being a fame whore latching on to famous men for advancement. I don't think my heart can take it."

Miles realized that what his heart couldn't take was watching the woman he loved being broken hearted over what a bunch of assholes who'd never buy her music anyway thought.

"So then what? Let her keep it up until it does get attention for whatever reason? Let her abuse you whenever she gets bored or whatever it is that strikes her fancy? Forever? Because she gave you away at two, which means she's had twenty-four years not to be an asshole and she hasn't made that decision yet."

"What do you suggest then?" she asked, frustrated that he wasn't going to support any plan that had her taking one moment's worth of shit from Gloria.

"I suggest you let my lawyers step in and do exactly what I told Gloria I would do if she kept her bullshit up. First, she needs to be reminded she's in breach of that divorce agreement. Then she needs to be informed in cold, hard, very concise terms that she needs to keep your name out of her mouth. If she wants to blather that she sold you, fine. Let the world know this bitch sold her fucking kid after neglecting her to the point it delayed her development. People want to threaten you with the facts when the facts make them look like a goddamn movie villain? Okay then."

Harlow's eyes were shaded behind her big sunglasses and most of her face was partially obscured by her hat, but she'd gone very still. She wasn't angry, he knew—from experience—how her body language changed when she was pissed at him.

"That could be the end of my dad's relationship with Hector and Luis."

"If Hector and Luis stop speaking to your dad because you told your mother to stop calling you a whore and me your sugar daddy, why would you want them in your life anyway? What do they bring to you that you'd continue being silent in the face of this abuse? Why is it your responsibility to stop protecting yourself so she can continue hurting you? To what end? Keep your brothers comfortable? I will not sit by while you make another choice that puts your own wellbeing behind the wellbeing of people who never think of you anyway. And, since I'm all worked up now, your brothers act like the way your mom treats you and your strained relationship as a result is none of their business. And they expect you to accept that as a reasonable excuse. But you can't expect the same in return? You can't set boundaries with Gloria because they'll have a tantrum and be mad at...your dad? Who they barely acknowledge anyway. What kind of love is that?"

She stood, tossing aside her hat so she could pull her

dress up and over her head. Leaving him utterly mesmerized by the black bikini emblazoned with cherries. Decidedly vintage in feel with bottoms that came to her belly button while the top kept everything covered while framing what wasn't.

"Are we swimming?" he asked.

"I need to be in the ocean for a few minutes," she said.

He dropped his hat, ditched his shirt, and followed her to the water. It was all he could do to watch as she got far enough to dunk herself, coming back up with her hair plastered to her head. She met him in waist deep water, droplets clinging to her skin like diamonds.

"You're the most beautiful thing I've ever seen. I love every part of you. Your vulnerability fills me with awe but also fear that someone will use it to hurt you. I know you love your family. And it doesn't matter if I think they deserve that love or not. You are a person full of love. It's one of the many reasons I find you gorgeous. But it also awakens every single one of my protective instincts."

She wrapped her arms around his waist, and they stood as the ocean swirled all around their legs, a solid unit in the midst of leashed chaos. The white noise of the surf wrapped around them both like an embrace.

"Secrets I have held in my heart, are harder to hide than I thought," he sang to her.

"Maybe I just wanna be yours. I just wanna be yours, wanna be yours," she sang the Arctic Monkeys lyric back.

"You are, you know that, right?" He kissed her, tasting salt.

"Yeah. Same goes."

He grinned at her. "Thank god for it. I'd get into so much

more mischief if I wasn't yours. Now all my mischief is carnal."

She laughed and the sound filled him with joy. "And getting up in my business."

He nodded, solemn for a moment. "Yes. I can apologize, but we both know I'll do it again. Not because I don't think you can handle yourself. I know you can. But because damn it, Harlow, I can't watch you suffer. Not without pitching in at your side."

She hugged him and kissed his neck before diving back under the water and popping up again. "You're a water baby, huh?" he teased.

"I love the beach and the pool. Beach is too cold in Washington, but it's only a two hour flight to get here. Hotel pools are fine depending on the hotel. I've been able to swim regularly during this tour. But this is so much better." She threw her hands out to her sides and tipped her face up to the sun.

His parents had an indoor pool. He'd lure her over for a swim as often as he could because he loved this Harlow. Carefree and splashing, even after the difficult conversation she'd had that day.

After another half an hour or so, they headed back to the shore.

Though it was a hot day, the water had been refreshing enough that it felt really good to lay next to her on the blanket and let the sunshine dry them off.

Miles sat and after a quick rummage through the tote, he found the sunscreen and began to rub it all over her skin. The big sunglasses were back, but her mouth had quirked up into an amused smile when he took extra care to get her cleavage and thighs covered.

Then she answered the question that'd been asked before she'd headed into the water. "I tried to convince myself that if I ignore this she'll go away. And she might. For a time. But she'll come back. Always. But I'm so afraid I'll fuck things up with my dad and brothers."

Miles reapplied his sunscreen as well and laid back down next to her, seeking her hand and trying to hold his tongue.

"But you're right. And my dad is right. If we don't push back now, she'll just take that as a sign that she can do more. She's got some respect for authority, so I think the only way to get her to stop, or even consider stopping, is to use an attorney to say so. They can threaten to expose her with the same information she's using in violation of the agreement. But make it sound fancy. And legal. And it won't be personal so her most effective weapon is useless against them."

Relief coursed through him. He'd called his attorney while she'd been in the shower the day before, just to see, obviously via hypotheticals, what were some options and he'd liked several things he'd heard. Obviously he'd need to tell her about the call. Maybe just fold it into the convo somewhere she wouldn't notice too much.

"Agreed. Would you consider using my attorney? Or not her, someone else at her firm who deals with this type of stuff. They're very good and have a great reputation." He'd done some research on that too. But she didn't need to know that part. "I gave a head's up that you might be contacting them. I do think it needs to be as soon as possible since that video has been up weeks at this point." There. He'd told her about the call.

"Yes. Maybe. Let me think on it for a little while. Not days, so get that look off your face. I'm trying to process and don't think I missed that part about the *head's up* to an attorney on my behalf."

He hated that she had to, even as he understood the need. So he'd do his best to help and not make things worse, no matter how much he wanted to step in and handle things. "Okay. I get it. So while that's processing, can we talk about how Gloria makes you feel like your success isn't yours even though she barely knows you and is a terrible judge of character in any case?"

Her look radiated surprise and a little hurt. He was sorry for the second, but he'd needed the first or she'd have had time to erect excuses between them, so she didn't have to face what had happened.

She was the bravest person he knew, but if she had the choice between dealing with her own shit or someone else's, she'd choose the latter. And the longer he knew her, the more he understood that.

Miles used to think her hesitation at the beginning with being seen together was an overreaction. Sure, he figured some would think she was on the tour because of her dad. But the group—small though it was—who brought up some whackadoo theory about her fucking her way to a tour slot had no problem making that claim all the time.

When one of the people shouting that stupidity from the rooftops was your mother, it hit differently. Deeper. And he wasn't willing to let her wallow in this unnecessary pain any longer.

"That's why you were so mad about me paying the retainer. Not that I wasn't out of line." He put his hands up. "I was impatient and wrong to do it without asking. And I see how it played into the narrative she was trying to put out.

I'm sorry for it." He leaned over to kiss her. "But, you're still vulnerable to her attacks on that. And because of her years of abuse, she's turned an opinion of a bunch of people who don't know you at all into a weapon against you. That can't continue."

"You're very full of pronouncements today," she said.

"Are you new here?" he teased.

"I know I work hard for my success. I know she thinks otherwise and that yes, she doesn't know me. But it's hard to be out and about and know strangers have an opinion about my life that's so…awful."

"I get it. Not to the extent you face it. I know as a woman it's far harder and way more common to have to deal with this stuff. But it's not true. You know that. Your album sales say otherwise."

"I'm trying to think about that. You know, when I start feeling shitty about someone's opinion, I need to pull out some high point as a reminder that random people's perception isn't reality. I'm trying."

He nodded. "Your dad will love you even if you make waves. Especially when it's to protect yourself. Oh don't get that face. Kids who grow up with parents like Gloria often have issues like this. They want to be perfect because they were denied affection and told it was a result of bad behavior. But all it is, is a result of abuse. She's fucked your head up and of all the things worth hating her for, that's the one at the top of my list. Your dad loves you. I love you. Your friends love you. Your fans love you. She doesn't because she's incapable of it. That's not you. That's her. Every time you find yourself pushing your own feelings down because you're worried they make you unlovable, I want you to try to remember this conversation and stop it. You're not unlov-able. You are absolutely loveable for countless reasons."

She huffed a breath and he smiled but kept his eyes closed and deliberately did not think about what a garbage human Gloria Martin was and how she'd tried so hard to destroy Harlow's heart.

CHAPTER
THIRTY-ONE

The Columbia River Gorge was one of the most beautiful places in Washington to play live music. She'd made the several hour trip from Seattle to see shows more than once since she'd relocated to the state. She'd been backstage with her dad at multiple shows AMJFJ played.

Nothing could have prepared her for what it was like to be on that stage looking out at the crowd instead of the other way around. The river and gorge at her back as the sun began to set made the whole moment surreally perfect.

And hot. August in Eastern Washington wasn't like the milder summer weather in the greater Seattle area on the west side of the mountains. No, this was real summer. Nuclear ball of fire in the sky and dust stuck to the sweat on her skin summer.

"The last time I was here," she said into the microphone, "me and my friends," she indicated Nora and Brian, "sat up there on the lawn." Harlow pointed to the higher point of the bowl, past the floor seats and the second level seats beyond that. The lawn was the outdoor venue version of the nose-bleed section of an indoor arena. "The time it took to get from there to here was long. But oh, so worth it. How you doing up there on the grass tonight?"

The cheers of the crowd made her smile.

"It's awesome to be ending this tour here. We promise to give you all we've got tonight. Keep an eye on your neighbors, okay? It's hot. Stay hydrated and remember beer doesn't count as water."

Nora counted off and they launched straight in to "Dark Heart" as Harlow began to sing. Her dad and Jenna were in the front row along with Marcella and Cherry. In fact, the entire front row was family of one sort or another. Parents, aunts, cousins of not just Above Me, but Earthquakes.

Harlow had been pulled into a hug right before they came out on stage as Erin Brown had tracked her down for that reason. Miles's aunt had taken a deeper interest in Harlow and had begun to text here and there with various questions or comments.

Gillian had quietly and sweetly let Harlow know that if Erin got to be too much it was okay to tell her so, or to contact Gillian. Erin was a lot. As were all of Miles and Poppy's family, but they all seemed to come with good intentions.

Still, it was pretty impressive to be hanging out with Sweet Hollow Ranch and Adrian Brown and half the most important musical influences in Harlow's life. Sure her dad was one of them, but it was mind blowing to consider just who all the people she was surrounded by were. Not only to her, but to musicians and music lovers everywhere.

Right then though, they were dads and aunts and moms and uncles and the like.

"So," Harlow began as their set neared the end. "Wanna hear something new?"

The crowd roared and she looked over at Brian, who grinned wide, and then back to Nora, who'd been the one who, along with Maddie's help, had written the song with Harlow.

"This one needs an extra guitar and I know you'll give her a big welcome. Maddie Hurley."

Maddie came jogging out, already holding her guitar. She waved at the audience, who renewed their excited hooting and shouting.

The opening lines were, "*Yeah and I am my own country. I know where I end and you begin. Don't stop me from wanting. Won't stop you from taking as much as you give.*

Miles stood there listening to a song she'd written about him. She'd told him she had a surprise for him toward the end of their set and that Maddie was part of it. The reality of that promise was…so much better, so much more than he'd imagined it.

"She wrote a song for you," Silas said quietly at Miles's side. "Gotta admit, Harlow is the fucking real deal. I'm going to miss her after today."

Miles snorted a laugh. "Right? No need to miss her though, Si. She's going to be part of my life and since you're also part of my life, we'll see her as often as we can around our work." This opening gig, being able to see her and be with her every day for three months had been spectacular.

Had given him a chance to really dig deep and get to know her but also lots of time to play and have fun.

Chances were, they wouldn't on the same tour bill again. Maybe big, multi day festivals in the future, but he had the distinct feeling Above Me was going to be the one having opening acts on their next tour rather than being an opening act again.

From now on, they'd both have to make a different sort of effort to stay connected. A new step in their relationship, but he realized how totally okay he was with that.

They came offstage but the lights stayed low to let the crowd know there'd be an encore. That's when Miles saw Richie coming toward them, his guitar tech at his side. The look on Harlow's face as her smile transformed her concentration, brow furrowed, to total joy seemed to sing through the air.

Miles stepped back and simply watched Richie Martin fist bump his daughter and then strap his guitar on.

The crowd roared when Nora bounded out and back to her drums. Brian followed and then Harlow, holding an acoustic guitar. Then there was a hush as they wondered what Above Me was going to play.

Then she started playing the open to Monster Magnet's, "Space Lord" and Brian began to sing. Richie waited in the wings and then stepped out as he began to play, and the fans went apeshit.

Including the whole backstage area that erupted into wild cheers as they all hit the first chorus and the song exploded.

Miles's dad showed up at his side, bumping his shoulder a moment before they both just watched Richie hit that guitar bit at the crescendo of the song and shred the fuck out of it as Harlow sang along and moved her body.

"Richie Martin, everyone!" she said after the song had ended. Richie made a bow and then pulled his daughter into a hug before they all took one last bow and headed offstage for the last time on this tour.

As the crew loaded off Above Me's gear, everyone seemed to congregate in a huge knot of excited people, congratulating them on their performance and being wowed by the new song as well as Richie's appearance at the end.

"Quite a surprise," Miles told Harlow as he hugged her. "I hope you three are proud because I've watched you play nearly every day for three months and tonight's show was your absolute best."

Harlow didn't say anything. She just hugged him again.

"Going to be hard to top that," Silas told them.

"Somehow I think you kids have a future in the music business," Harlow teased. "All joking aside, I really can't wait to see what Earthquakes has in store."

He grinned. He was pretty amped up about it too.

And then Miles walked out on stage as the lights swiveled up and created an aura of blue around him and the anticipation and excitement in the air hit his lungs like a drug. Fuck yes. This.

This was an addiction he could be okay with. This and Harlow. And there she was, instead of backstage, she'd taken a seat up front and bounced around, dancing as the band ripped into *Beg Me*.

"Well how the hell are you?" Miles asked the audience

once the song had ended. He looked side to side to lock eyes with Omar and then over to Maddie.

"It's good to be home again after being away for months. We're going to have to work hard to top Above Me tonight."

The fans cheered at that.

"We've been lucky to have them opening for us this tour. And we got bonus Richie Martin. Score," Miles said.

People in the crowd started to shout Harlow's name and Miles just grinned at them all. "Well, she's my bonus too," was all he said.

And then Maddie started the opening to "Collide", a song Omar had written for her to sing.

The rest of the show had been a blur. They'd synched in with one another and had run with it. They'd already decided on the setlist the afternoon before, and it seemed to click with the audience in a magical way.

They sang every word. They cheered and were so loud before the second encore it had echoed into his gut.

And then it was time for the double whammy of a final encore as another drum kit and several more mic stands were placed.

Ezra, Vaughan, Damien and Paddy Hurley waited, Maddie next to them as they all got their monitors set.

Adrian caught up to them and tipped his chin at his son and they went out to the stage, first just Earthquakes. "This is a special place for me to play. It was the first time I'd ever played for a crowd other than for jazz band in high school."

There was laughter and Miles grinned at the memory. "The first time I was here, I played this one." He began the bassline to Radiohead's, "Creep." The first song he'd ever learned to play with his dad.

Then Adrian came out and began to play and Miles had to force his smile away so he could sing.

"This one's for Harlow," he said and then sang, *"I want you to notice, when I'm not around. You're so fuckin' special."*

At his side, Adrian Brown kicked ass and played the fuck out of his guitar and Miles had never been happier the entirety of his pretty damned happy life.

And right on the heels of that Maddie started the open to "Show the Way" as Hurleys filled the stage and hooked into one of Earthquakes most popular songs like they played it every night.

During the break, Miles stepped back and let the guitars take over as he caught sight of Silas drumming like his life depended on it right next to his personal idol Damien Hurley.

Ezra began to sing, and the audience began to say his name, leaning into the Z sound and Maddie's smile seemed to light her whole being up. Her dad and her uncles had showed up and showed out.

Miles's father rocked alongside them, part of his journey as he'd been from the moment he'd learned of Miles's existence.

They all sang the last chorus together, backing Ezra's lead vocals and as the last notes died, Miles caught Harlow's movements, hands up in the air, singing along with them, Poppy at her side, doing the same.

For a reckless move, he'd sure gotten lucky.

CHAPTER
THIRTY-TWO

After what had been the best night of her entire life, Harlow wasn't ready for what it looked like when all their friends and family had joined up for the most massive family gathering she'd ever been to.

"Jesus, Miles," Harlow said as they stood on the covered porch of the massive house many of them were staying in. Just beyond the house the yard was absolutely awash in musical legends.

He laughed, putting an arm around her shoulder. "I know. I'm with these people regularly and yet I still find myself stunned by all their talent and energy. I nearly combusted on stage last night at one point."

"Speaking of last night."

He laughed again, kissing the top of her head. "Yes, my beauty?"

She hadn't said anything about the call outs to her he'd made during the previous night's show. Or the way the crowd had reacted by chanting her name.

"I'm your bonus?"

He turned so he could give her a real hug. "They said your name. They know who you are and what we are together. As for the bit in Creep? Like I said, everyone already knows we're together, so I get to shout it from the rooftops. It's not a secret. Plus you liked it."

He spun her and then pulled her back to his side.

"How do you know that?" she demanded, trying to stay stern but failing.

He bent to speak quietly into her ear. "Because I wouldn't have put my cock anywhere near that sweet mouth if you'd been snarly."

Blushing at the memory of their hushed coupling the night before when they'd returned home. With the house being full of family and friends, they'd had to keep it down. Which had added to the experience.

"I see Ezra over at the drinks area." Miles nudged her. "Go on. He's alone."

"It's weird!" she whispered back.

"If you were him and someone said they loved something you wrote, would you think it was weird?" Miles asked and had Harlow moving over there like an adult. Which she was. Mostly.

Waving in a hopefully nonweird way, she smiled as she approached him. "Hi, Ezra."

"Hey, Harlow. Y'all were fantastic last night. Congratulations. I'm biased, but the song you played with Maddie? I really dug it."

Omigod! Did he just really compliment her songwriting? When he was...well, that's what she was there to tell him.

"Wow, thank you. That means more than you can know. You're sort of a personal icon for me. Um. All your songs are favorites, but the songs you wrote on *Sometimes We Forget* are lyrical perfection. The depth of emotion kills me. It's so timely but also timeless. It's a beautiful album."

His easy grin fell and remade itself into a smile that made him a thousand times hotter. And he already had that silver fox thing going on to start with.

"Thank you. Wow. I'm very touched that you think so and that you'd tell me. It was a horrible time in my life, but I'm really proud of those songs. Sometimes you turn your pain into something better."

"Songwriting as therapy. Absolutely."

Fortunately, she managed to avoid an embarrassing incident and excused herself a few minutes later, absolutely glowing with pleasure.

The morning activities were done, and everyone had gathered on the large back lawn of the house one or another of them owned. Her dad had Ryder on his hip as he listened to something Adrian was telling him. Marcella and Cherry sat with Jenna and Elise, Brody's wife, the four of them had settled at a table, chatting like they'd been friends forever. Maddie had her mom on one side of her and her dad on the other as her sister—also ridiculously gorgeous—told them all something that had them laughing.

There was enough food to feed an army, or the assembled group of creatives, weirdos, goddesses, demigods and randoms that made up this large and colorful crowd.

Miles was in his element, loving up on everyone, reconnecting with a hug or a grin. Every few minutes though, he'd look up from whatever he was doing and search her out, only relaxing once he caught sight of her.

She figured she only had a few minutes left of solitude. He'd frowned when he'd caught sight of her tucked away in a gazebo at the edge of the garden. Harlow had waved a hand at him to mind his own and have a good time. She wasn't hiding! Just watching the ebb and flow of the group had filled her with happiness and several lyrical snippets she'd had to get in her phone before she forgot them.

In the end it was her dad who'd come to find her. He sat next to her and looked out on the party beyond.

"Hey, Punky. Great party, huh?" He put an arm around her shoulders and squeezed her to his side a moment.

"It really is. Seeing everyone with their family makes me so happy." She put her head on his shoulder a moment. It wasn't that she couldn't make do otherwise. She would have. There were plenty of people there she liked and would have enjoyed spending the day with. But none of them were her dad.

"Ryder has been talking incessantly about seeing you," he told her. "And naturally I can't ever pass up some time with you. And I get to know Miles a little better through his people."

"Hang on one second," she told him as she jumped up to grab them both a beer and some food and returned with it.

"Uh oh. You must be planning on telling me something difficult," he teased, but his eyes were serious.

She clinked her bottle to his and took several long pulls. "I met with my attorney. My new attorney. Whatever. She's the badass who is going to take Gloria on. "She had some stuff to say that helped me put this in perspective."

"Like what?"

She took a deep breath and a few more drinks while they ate yummy meatballs.

"I like this Bella already," her dad said.

"I think you would. She's great. But I should warn you, she's not worried about this hurting Luis and Hector. She says they're either with me or against me and I fought that for a few weeks. Miles was pissed at me for taking so long to see the truth."

"He should be pissed at me then," her dad muttered.

"He was in his own way. At first. But he knows you love me, and he knows you did your best. He's the one who told me that right off. You made the best choices you could at that time given your options. They weren't perfect. But no one is perfect. You kept growing and learning and I hope I do the same. I'm not mad at you. But if I have to protect myself from her and it hurts them because they refuse to accept the truth that's on them. You're their dad so I know it's different for you. But I wanted you to know up front that it might happen."

"I regret—deeply—that I'm not close with your brothers. They're my sons and I love them. Nothing will change that. But it doesn't mean I don't see the situation for what it is. And I'm choosing you, Harlow. Because you've been so hurt, and no one chose you. Fuck that."

The tears in her dad's voice brought her own in response.

"I've spent the last two weeks really thinking about everything. What my part in it is. What your part is. How what she's said and done has shaped me even though I didn't live with her for most of my life. Miles said some stuff to me the day you and I talked about everything. He asked me how long I was going to let Gloria make me feel like I wasn't good enough to be loved."

"Ouch," he murmured.

"Right? He's cute and all, but he knows stuff. And he was correct. I'm working through all that. Hooked up with a therapist I can connect with online. I wasn't sure how I'd feel about that part, but it's been good. Helped me put things in perspective. It's going to take me a while to reject everything I know is wrong, but I'm trying. Because I'm worth it and healthy relationships are worth it."

"You are, Punky and I'm so happy to hear you're rising above all this bullshit to keep being the amazing woman you are. Do whatever you need to shut Gloria down. I'll help however I can. I tried to connect with Hector and Luis but neither will take my calls. I don't want them to hear the story from Gloria about the custody situation. I want to explain it."

"You can't if they won't listen. Dad, they know she's cruel and petty and they think it'll never turn on them. And maybe it never will. I'll always have love for them, but from a distance. Maybe that's the only way it's possible. I've had some limited texts back and forth with Mindy. She sees this for what it is. Knows what Gloria is. But Gloria is her mother-in-law so it's a lot of pressure on her marriage. I don't know how that'll work out. I hope he chooses his wife and kids. But." Harlow shrugged. "I'm sorry for it. She's in a tough spot. But maybe you can check in with her? Just a note that you want to talk. It might go nowhere. But if anyone can get him to listen it'll be her."

Her dad sighed, sadness in the sound.

She turned to him, putting one of her legs up on the seat. "I'm great," she said. "I'm in love. I'm experiencing more success than ever. My friendships are strong and important. I have a *loving* and involved father who I adore and who adores me. Aside from this Gloria drama, things are a-okay."

They watched Ryder run and play but when she caught sight of them, her entire being lit up and she ran toward them, her arms wide open.

"That's the prime example of what a great dad you are," Harlow told him as she stood and grabbed her sister, pulling her up and into her arms for a hug.

"Are you going to be okay now that this tour is over, and Earthquakes will be in Europe for the next six weeks?" he asked as Ryder played with Harlow's hair.

"I'll miss him. But I was fine before he came along, and I'll be fine when he's away for work. I have my own work too. Our first festival date is in four days. He and the rest of his band leave day after tomorrow for Spain. He and I will call and text and if we can't make it work, I guess it's better to know now. But I think it'll be fine."

"Backstage can be a horror movie for anyone worried about their partner straying," her dad said.

"Truth. But I'm not worried about it. I can't be. If he wants to be with someone else, he will be. I can't be with him every moment to make sure he never gets the chance to mess around. It's what you do when you're not being watched that counts, right? He's not messy like that. If he wanted out, he'd do the respectful thing and say so before he stepped out." And if he didn't, he wouldn't be the man she loved anymore.

"I've seen the way he looks at you. I don't think you need to be concerned. But I do think it's good to know what you're facing," he said, grinning at Ryder, who started singing her ABCs.

They wandered back to the heart of the party. Harlow filled a plate with the things Ryder pointed at and then they found seats at one of the many tables set up around the yard.

After four bites, Ryder caught sight of her mom and ran off to tell her all the things. Harlow snorted and pulled the plate over. Waste not want not.

"Mind if I join you?"

She looked up at Brody Brown. Harlow waved at the empty chairs. "Have a seat."

"Having a good time?" he asked.

"I am. Gillian and Mary did a great job setting this whole thing up. It's nice to be able to celebrate with people you love when you finish a tour."

Brody nodded. Harlow didn't know him very well. But what she did know was Brody was instrumental in the man Miles was.

"When you're done with your summer and fall dates and Miles is finished, Elise and I would love to have you over for the weekend. I'll fire up the barbecue and we'll hang out and get to know you. It's hard in a setting like this. Too many expectations and people watching."

"Expectations?"

He laughed and she saw Miles in the movements and his expression. Saw Adrian too. This man—Erin and Adrian's older brother—had dropped everything to step in and raise his siblings after their parents had died. They all spoke of him with a sort of reverence. At the same time, he was flesh and blood like anyone else. And yet he radiated an effortless calm and sense of competency few others could.

"We've never seen Miles in love before. Oh yes, there was *the interviewer*, but he didn't bring her around. For the best, as we'd have seen her for what she was sooner. While you're making a mistake, sometimes you do all you can not to see what a mistake you're making. You know on some level, so you hide from anyone who'd tell you otherwise. He learned."

"She's awful. I mean, she's very pretty and I can see she'd be fun at parties. But scratch the surface and she's totally about herself. And she ran through your lives with scissors. I'm so sorry about that interview. I didn't know who she was until toward the end and then it was too late. I never meant to have your family get hurt."

He patted her hand briefly and stole a chip off her plate. She understood now where Miles got that too.

"She's no threat to us. The world already knows Erin has two husbands. Frankly, you've met her, do you think one mere human could manage that?"

Harlow nearly choked on her surprised laugh, and he winked at her.

"Sophie never cared about who Miles was beyond his status. She encouraged his most self-destructive behavior, but he did those things himself. Miles kept telling me he wasn't looking for love or forever. And I said forever didn't care. And then you popped up and he understood what I meant. You see him. Not just the rockstar part. Not just the jetset life. You see his family and his heart. You understand he's so much more than those few hours he's on stage. He deserves to be loved by someone and I'm glad it's you."

The men at this party were bound and determined to make her cry that day apparently.

She tried not to make a big deal out of her sniffles but he handed her a napkin so she must have failed. "Sorry."

"For what? Loving Miles so much you're touched when someone who loves him too says they appreciate you?" Brody asked. "Life's too fucking short, kid. Look. Miles is a great guy and I'm not just saying that because he's my nephew. You survived a legit Brown/Keenan/Copeland swarm like a champ. Even when Ben fucked things up." Brody snorted. "He's a kind man who loves his family. I'm glad you worked it out. Takes guts to give someone a second chance."

"Well, for heaven's sake, he didn't mean to be anything but kind. I wasn't mad. He and I both had too many sore spots. But he was kind and he helped me. Doesn't take guts. Just compassion. Anyway, it was more Miles than Ben. And Miles and I worked that out too," Harlow told him. "Mainly. Your nephew is very bossy. He's a work in progress."

He grinned at her. "See, this is why I think you and Miles are perfect for one another. You don't take any of his bossy or controlling shit."

"Well, not all of it. It's sort of impossible to stop Miles from being bossy. It's part of who he is. I don't want to change him, but sometimes he needs to be told no in a very firm voice. He loves me very well. He wants to protect me from everything and everyone. I'm told he and his father get it from you."

His surprised laughter caught attention and soon enough, Miles wandered over.

"He wants to keep an eye on us both," Brody said with a wink.

"I've been looking for you," Miles said and sat next to Harlow, putting an arm around the back of her chair.

"I'm just here finishing what's left of a toddler's food, hanging out with Brody. Talking about you," she said dragging a breadstick through some hummus.

"It was all good. Don't worry," Brody told Miles. "Elise and I are really proud of you. This tour has been hugely successful. But more than that, you look good. Healthy. Like you love what you're doing."

Miles practically glowed as he smiled at his uncle. "Thanks. Best year of my life." He looked over at Harlow and she blushed.

"You ready for Europe?"

"Yeah. First show in four days. We leave day after tomorrow. Wish I had a few more days to rest up and spend with Harlow, but Above Me has shows coming up too so they're leaving when we are."

He started talking about all the cool venues they'd be playing, and a part of Harlow that had been worried, eased. She'd been concerned he'd try to downplay the tour details to save her feelings or even because he was sad about not being together. But she was going to enjoy the hell out of her tour dates, and she wanted him to as well.

She could have gotten up to walk around and chat with everyone else, but it felt nice there next to Miles as he talked about something he loved so much to someone he loved just as much.

Marcella came to them, sitting on Harlow's other side. "Cherry has been drafted into what I think is a very fast and loose game of horseshoes. The rules? I don't know what the hell is going on. But everyone seems to be having fun,"

Marcella said. "As I get a little alarmed at pieces of metal being thrown all around, I removed myself from the danger zone. Those Hurley brothers are pretty rambunctious."

Brody laughed. "They make me, and my siblings look positively sedate by comparison."

Harlow looked over at Miles, so very pleased to see their loved ones mixing and liking one another. He winked and then stole a quick kiss.

All through the afternoon and long into the night, there was so much music—both what they made themselves and also over speakers from other artists—and dancing that by the time the stars winked above them and yet another meal had come and gone, Harlow was absolutely bone tired. But in the best way.

His parents had insisted they sleep in the house, and she was so glad when all she had to do was walk for less than four minutes and close the door behind her with a sigh. A shower, some earplugs and bed was just the ticket.

Miles had been with Harlow and noticed she'd begun to flag. He got it. He was tired too and he was used to all these people and their constant noise and activity. She'd thanked his mum and aunt Mary for everything and had quietly made her way to the house and inside.

He'd made his own goodbyes with promises to see everyone the following morning and went to their room, following the Harlow scented steam to the bathroom where she'd just gotten out of the shower and was putting lotion on.

"You're wearing my favorite outfit," he told her.

"I put it on with you in mind," she told him.

He stepped to her, taking the tube, and setting about rubbing it all over her skin. He only had one more full day with her before they went their separate ways to work for the next six weeks. Not like he hadn't counted the days. Ha! Of course he had.

He ran his hands over her skin, so soft and supple, all his. It still hadn't quite sunk in that she was his to touch this way.

Right then he wanted to commit every part of her to his memory so he could carry it with him while they were apart.

"Gonna miss you so much," he murmured at he put the tube aside and took her hand, pulling her close.

"I'm going to get lotion all over your clothes," Harlow protested, and he snorted. As if he fucking cared about that.

"I should probably take them all off then," he said, pulling her into the bedroom.

"Okay!" she agreed heartily.

Laughing, he managed to get out of his clothes but while he was on one foot to kick off his shorts, she pushed him back to the bed and scrambled atop his body.

"Well now. Good evening, Ms. Martin," he drawled. "You up to something? God, I hope so." He reached up to twist the bar in her nipple, delighting in her hiss of delight. Even more delightful was the way she ground her pussy against his cock, her breath hitching when the bead in his piercing slid over her clit.

She was hot and so wet already and the feel of her honey as it nearly scalded him was so good he had to fight to keep his eyes from rolling up into his head as she rendered him utterly witless.

Over and over until the need to come dug into his spine.

Especially when her whole body tensed and relaxed each time her clit brushed against the piercing.

He moaned as he gripped her hips. This skin to skin contact was amazing. When they were done with touring and were back in the northwest, they'd get STI tests and once they knew it was safe, he'd be able to fuck her without a condom.

Fucking her in any way was a delight, but he was *very* much looking forward to being able to ditch condoms.

"You feel so good," he told her around a gasp of pleasure when she reached behind her body and ran her short, blunt nails over his balls. "That works," he wheezed.

Her smile in response sent a shiver through him. Supreme woman expression, utterly sure of her sensual appeal and it yanked him far closer to orgasm than he'd planned to be at that moment.

"I want you to have something to think about when we're on different continents."

As if he wasn't already going to think about her all the time?

"I'll add this to the myriad other moments that make me love you," he told her and watched as she blinked back emotion.

She dropped closer, still stroking herself over his cock, to kiss him. At first it was sweet and gentle but soon enough, as they both drew closer to climax, she added the edge of her teeth to nip his bottom lip.

He hummed his delight because he fucking adored it when her control wisped away because of the pleasure he'd given her. Although, in this case, she gave it to both of them. Making it even hotter.

She was the most gorgeous erotic wet dream wrapped in skin he'd ever beheld as she rose again, her body blocking out the light at her back, casting her face in shadows that rendered her more beautiful and mysterious.

That she was as astonishingly gorgeous inside as she was on the outside was a miracle to him and something he woke up thankful for every damned day.

"I'm so glad we found each other," he told her, looking up into her face.

Her smile did him in. Vulnerable and touched, proud and confident. All a swirl of Harlow's most alluring qualities.

He arched up and one of her eyebrows rose imperiously until she rolled her head around and stretched her shoulders like she was getting ready for a marathon. Then she tightened her pussy around him, bathing him in that hot, sticky honey, stroking over and over until her breath went uneven and her gaze glassy.

Orgasm built in his belly as he continued to arch up right when his piercing brushed her clit. Her nails dug into his sides sending a wave of pleasure/pain through him and when she came on a gasped whisper of his name, that was all. He couldn't hold it back another second as he joined her.

She continued to move over him for a while afterward until she rolled off his body. "Uh, I think we both might need a shower," she said with a laugh at the mess on his belly and her thighs.

"When I can work my legs again, that's a plan."

She jumped up and returned with a warm, wet cloth she cleaned him up with. Why that should have filled him with such tenderness he didn't know, but it did. Like everything else, when she took care of him in little or big ways, it centered him, reinforced that he'd made the right choice falling in love with this person who sought to comfort and enrich his life.

"It's only six weeks," she said later. "And it'll go fast because we'll both have so much work."

Problem was, he'd gotten used to working with and around her. He'd deal. Just as she would. But he'd miss her terribly.

"We'll text and call and chat via video. Then we'll have our time at the end of our tours, and the rest of the year to spend together," he said.

It wasn't like their jobs would end when the tour was over. There was always new music to be made and she'd told him earlier that day that Jeremy had already started negotiating with the label for more from Above Me. That would take more effort from them too. Then there would be awards show season and all that other stuff and Jeremy was in talks for a movie role for Miles that would start shooting the following spring.

Their lives would continue to be busy, which was better than the alternative of it being quiet because they weren't selling albums well enough to get picked up for a new contract. But he was certain they'd get through it and work around their schedules because their relationship was worth it.

He might have been nervous leaving another person for six weeks at this point in a relationship or be wondering if they had what it took to survive the chaos of the entertainment industry. But he...wasn't. Their connection was so real and so deep and she was not dependent on him as much as she was the boss of her own world and made room in the front seat for him to join her.

The damage Gloria had done notwithstanding, Harlow was his partner because she was bold and confident and talented. In her own right. Worries about what others might think aside, two artists in the same business could make it work if they were both in the right headspace. Lucky for him, they were.

CHAPTER
THIRTY-THREE

They walked offstage, holding hands. United as they'd been the first night of their solo tour back in January. Their bond—emotional and musical—stronger than it had been back then. Nine months on and off the road would have destroyed them or made them tighter and it had been the latter.

Harlow tried not to cry but it had been an amazing show and the last one until the next year. They'd kicked ass through festival season, played several solo gigs that had been added after their successful open for Earthquakes, and had flown to do their own European shows, albeit a much smaller version of the tour Earthquakes was finishing.

It was the last time they'd walk down a hallway to and from the stage until their next show the following February. Back in their dressing room after everyone had cleaned up and changed, they got all their things ready to go. Gear would ship back to the United States to be stored in a warehouse. Most of Harlow's stuff would be shipped back to Seattle and Nora and Brian would head out to Italy in just a few hours so they'd take clothes and send the rest home.

The trip to the airport they'd mainly looked at one another, started to speak and then began to cry. Even Brian. So they'd eventually quieted down for the rest of the trip.

They paused at the area on the other side of security at the airport, each heading in the other direction. "I'll see you both in a few months. Have a great time in Italy." Harlow hugged Brian and Nora. "Text me when you get there so I know you're safe."

Nora sniffled, hugging Harlow tight as they both cried ugly tears. "This whole year with you recording and touring has been magic. And I can't think of anyone I'd want to share it with more than you. You're my soul mate, Harlow. I love you and I'm so proud of us that we pulled this off. We've got a song being used in a movie. We just got a new deal from the label because the numbers were so fantastic. Four singles have charted. All that cloud talk from high school came true. How rad is that?"

That made Harlow's tears come harder. "No flying cars yet. But otherwise yeah. Even the part where I have my very own rockstar to love like you do. Thank you for being my best friend and for always being in my corner from the first day we met. I love you."

"I'm so proud of the way you stood up to Gloria. And the way you let yourself love Miles. You need to be the one to text when you get to London, okay?"

"All right. It's less than an hour so I'll get there first and wait for your text soon after." She needed to go but she gave

Nora one last hug. "He loves me like I need to be loved," she whispered into her best friend's ear.

She allowed two steps backward before she waved one last time and turned, heading toward her gate.

It had been seven weeks since she'd seen Miles, watching his back as he and the others had moved through airport security, and she'd been on the other side of that line. That extra week had meant more shows for both bands, but those seven days had felt like an extra month. Seven weeks of texts, short Facetime calls and little packages he sent to her via her aunt.

No Miles snuggles in the middle of the night when she woke up cold and her bed was empty. Funny how fast she'd gotten used to sleeping with him and sharing space. She had to order her own room service, though Nora did let her steal part of her food like Miles always did. But it wasn't the same.

Still, once Earthquakes had headed to their own festivals and the Europe leg of their tour, Above Me's star continued to rise. Their album sales had continued at a rate that pleased Jeremy and had clearly impressed the label, so they had the amazing experience of signing a new contract. The press they'd gotten was positive for the most part. Harlow had given in and had hired on a PR firm to deal with any negative backlash from Gloria. But Shelly, her rep, was fucking awesome and Harlow was convinced the peace of mind alone was worth the money. The *fucked her way to success* brigade got quiet and the *riding her dad's coattails* had been spun to a *rock royalty* thing.

A drink would have been nice, but the flight was so short and she still needed to get to the house she and Miles would be staying in for the next several days. Earthquakes was playing the O2 that night to close out the tour. She'd really wanted to be there but when the Amsterdam shows got scheduled it had given her no time to do both.

Travel had become such a regular part of her life that she'd quickly deplaned, grabbed her bag, and headed out to grab a cab on auto pilot. On the drive, Harlow texted Nora, Marcella, and her dad to let them all know she'd arrived in London safely and would connect with them all later.

And then she was on a doorstep facing a black lacquer door with a fancy gold knocker. Her heart pounding, she knocked but only got one rap before she heard her name being called.

He got out of a sleek black car at the curb just a few feet away and everything in her stilled and then exploded to life. Clicked back into place because there he was. Her person.

"You're here," he said as he pulled her close. She wrapped herself around him, squeezing tight as she breathed him in.

"You're here too. God, that's good. It's so good to see you and smell you and feel you. I missed you so much," she told him as she pressed her face into his neck. "You better still love me," she threatened.

That made him laugh and squeeze her tight before setting her back. "I do love you. Until the sun burns out." He pulled a key out and then punched in a code once the keypad slid down. "Let's get inside. You need food. I bet you came straight from the show without anything to eat or drink."

The townhouse was posh as fuck. Elegantly classy. It didn't scream wealth, but it sure whispered it in every finish and element.

"You know some swanky people, Miles," she said. "I knew this was a fancy neighborhood, but this house is dreamy. It's like a spread out of *Architectural Digest*."

He took her bag and her hand and dragged her along. "Let's put your bag in the bedroom and then have food and a cocktail to celebrate the end of both our tours."

She grinned, up for whatever he proposed. "Okay."

The master bedroom and attached bathroom were done up in navy, gray and bright white. The bed was massive and she gave him a sideways glance and a smirk.

"When I was here earlier to leave my things, I had to jerk off afterward just thinking about you and me in this bed," he said after pressing a kiss to her temple and getting her worked up.

With a moan Harlow reached up to encircle his neck with her arms and rubbed herself all over him. "I'm marking you like a cat. Just so everyone knows. You probably need to reenact that jerk off situation. Just so I can be sure it's okay with me."

He chuckled. "Ah." And shrugged. "Only if you do it too so I can watch. Not because I need to be sure I'm okay with it, I'm more than okay with it. I just want to see you make yourself come."

She hugged him tighter.

"I missed holding you," he said, kissing her forehead. "And since I'm going to show you some other things I missed and that will demand calories for energy on your part, food first. I have nowhere to be for the next three days. And then back in Seattle, you and I are going to spend some quality time just hanging out."

He spun her and marched her out and downstairs where

she volunteered to get them both a drink while he set about making them both sandwiches. Naturally the fridge was stocked full of delicious food and drinks, so she made them a fruity themed cocktail from the guava juice that tasted freshly made.

Then they sat at the table in the small garden out back and clinked glasses. "Forever," he said, and she echoed, agreeing.

"Now," he said as they began to eat—and she was hungry and had already drunk two big glasses of water. "How did the show go tonight?"

They talked about their closing gigs, and he updated her on where Maddie, Silas and Omar were headed. They talked about plans for the next few days. Her suitcase was pretty empty because London had great secondhand shops she wanted to visit and knew she'd need the room for all her new treasures. There were some restaurants Miles wanted to try and she was always game for eating stuff.

It had been a great show. The O2 had been packed full. They'd been a fantastic crowd, one of the best of the whole tour, though he was pretty sure nothing could compete with that last night of the tour at the Gorge. The band was tight, easily drifting along with one another, stepping aside here and there for the others to shine.

He'd said his goodbyes to his bandmates before the show because right afterward, he'd grabbed his stuff and jumped into a waiting car to head to the townhouse he'd borrowed from a producer friend of his dad's.

What he'd really wanted was to get there first and light

some candles and get the place ready with some snacks because he knew she would have rushed to him just as he was doing for her. But that meant she would either have shoved a granola bar in her face or told herself she'd eat when she arrived.

Traffic had been a nightmare though so as the minutes ticked by he tried not to fret. She could get in with the keypad if she got there first. There was food in the fridge, Poppy had told him, so she could be comfortable while she waited.

But he hated the idea of her showing up to an empty townhouse when she was excited about seeing him. Just as he hated not being with her right at that moment.

They'd driven up the street and he'd been barely controlling his urge to jump out and run when he saw the doorstep and the most beautiful woman on earth standing on it. Her name came from his lips like a prayer, and he was out of the car, yelling his thanks over his shoulder and rushing to her.

The feel of her against him filled him with calm. Everything would be fine now because she was there in his arms and he no longer felt like he'd left something important behind, always patting his pocket and remembering there were six weeks without her stretching ahead of him.

He hadn't liked her being so far away and that fact hadn't changed one bit in the time they were apart. At the same time, he wasn't panicked or worried. She was out there in the world kicking ass and making music and that's what he was doing too. Every night as he'd walked those halls back to the dressing room all those hungry gazes from people lining them had barely registered except he knew she'd hate it.

None of them could have mattered to him the way she did.

He knew *he* hated the idea that she walked down similar hallways lined with people giving looks, thinking about her naked. Understood, too, that she didn't give any of them a second thought.

Because she was his.

He desperately wanted to ask her to move in with him, but he held back. Best to wait until they were stateside again. He'd fill his house with things she loved best and have her over as much as possible to charm her with the idea. Then he'd ask.

"By the way, the way your attorney handled Gloria has been helping me sleep well every night." Harlow had finally let go of her hopes about her mother and had let experts step in to handle things. "Your regular updates on the way they slap her down whenever she tries anything have given me life." He snorted.

"Combined with the stuff Ben dug up that pretty much confirmed my dad's story and all her weirdness about women, Gloria appears to be complying with the non-disclosure again. After she made those comments to the media after being told not to, the correction my attorney sent regarding what she'd said made her look terrible. Which is what they told her would happen." Harlow shrugged. "I guess the embarrassment and the proof that no one was playing games with her was finally enough. For real, Miles, I feel so much better for your career that these people are your attorneys. They're fantastic. I know how hard it was for you to step back and let me handle all this. I'm grateful to you for it."

"I knew you had to do it on your own. It drove me up the wall. Thank god I was on a totally different continent or it would have been impossible." He flashed her a smile. "I know myself and when it comes to you, it's hard to let you take any hits. This was difficult on you. Not being there to hold you through the tough parts sucked. But I never doubted you could. Do you understand the difference?"

She nodded. "I do. And it means a lot."

"Don't get too used to that sort of disinterest. I had to fake it and throw myself into work to keep from getting on a plane to you. Pretty much daily," he admitted.

Her smile went a little wobbly and he felt it to his toes.

"I'll try to schedule my shit while you're out of the country," she said, tears in her voice.

"Please don't. Let me in next time."

She was up and in his lap, hugging him tight, before he could blink. He held her against his chest, soaking it in.

"I wasn't shutting you out. I had to know I could do it."

"Anything new with Hector and Luis?" he asked, hoping there was something positive.

"I don't think there's much to salvage with Luis. Maybe never. But he's said nothing about me to the media and that's all I can ask for at this point. Hector? Mindy and I text regularly at this point. I want to be part of the kids' lives so if I'm cool with their mom, it'll be easier. He hasn't said anything directly to me though and from what I can tell, he and Mindy are going through some stuff, but she hasn't given up, which is a good sign. She talks to my dad now, by the way. Sends him pictures of their kids. He's cautiously optimistic. I hope to hell Hector doesn't break his heart. Now, enough about her. It's in the rearview."

He smiled even though she wouldn't see it. "Good." He stood, still holding her. "Let's lock up, tidy the kitchen and head upstairs to get to the next part of this reunion."

"The naked part?"

"Yep," he told her, putting her on her feet in the kitchen.

"Well okay then."

They cleaned up, locked up and headed to the master suite.

Thank god he was reckless back in March when he'd kissed her the first time. Thank god she was reckless and kissed him too, even though she knew it might come back to bite her in the ass. And it had with all that sugar daddy nonsense. But she'd risen above it and deepened her connection with him and he let himself fall for this woman he'd never tire of touching and tasting.

She whipped off her shirt and he sighed happily at the sight of her tits encased in pretty dark lace.

"Come show me how much you missed me," she said quietly.

And he did.

RECKLESS TRACKLIST

F.Y.R – Le Tigre
TKO – Le Tigre
Particles – Nothing But Thieves
Real Love Song – Nothing But Thieves
Impossible – Nothing But Thieves
Amsterdam – Nothing But Thieves
Futureproof – Nothing But Thieves
This Feels Like the End – Nothing But Thieves
Get Better – Nothing But Thieves
If I Get High – Nothing But Thieves
Graveyard Whistling – Nothing But Thieves
Painkiller – Nothing But Thieves
Smile – Wolf Alice
The Beach – Wolf Alice
Lipstick on the Glass – Wolf Alice
How Can I Make It Ok? – Wolf Alice
Heavenward – Wolf Alice
Yuk Foo – Wolf Alice
Don't Delete the Kisses – Wolf Alice

Space Lord – Monster Magnet
Gimme – Banks
Fuck With Myself – Banks
Propaganda – Banks
Waiting Game – Banks
Lovesick – Banks
Judas – Banks
Seek and Destroy – Metallica
Feuer und Wasser – Rammstein
Four Letter Words – K Flay
TGIF – K Flay
Nothing Can Kill Us – K Flay
High Enough – K Flay
Black Wave – K Flay
Toxic – Kehlani
Can I - Kehlani
Bad News – Kehlani

ACKNOWLEDGMENTS

Special thanks to Frauke at Croco Designs, who is always such a great help, and seems to know how to do everything.

Tony Mauro graciously agreed to create a cover for the book after doing so many for me for my Brown Family and Delicious books. I adore this cover and can't wait to see what else is in store.

I love music to my toes. It's absolutely part of my creative process! Thanks to all the bands I've seen live, I have a great idea of what it feels like to be at a show and to the magic it creates. And thanks to YouTube, I was able to watch countless videos of concert set ups of massive shows of the type Earthquakes has, backstage antics and sound-checks. I walked away with even more respect for how hard a job it is to be a musician, especially one on tour.

Nothing But Thieves and Wolf Alice were on constant repeat as I wrote this book. Both happened to be on tour as I did, so there was a fun bit of magic involved with that. Thanks to both bands for helping keep me firmly in the universe of my characters

Megan Hart – you've been my friend though a lot of highs and lows. I'm grateful I don't have to know what I'd do without you. Thank you for being someone I can be my true self around.

SIGN UP FOR LAUREN'S NEWSLETTER

Don't want to miss Lauren Dane's latest book? Sign up for Lauren's newsletter and get notified when she has a new one out.

www.laurendane.com/newsletter

COMING UNDONE

INSIDE OUT

NEVER ENOUGH

LAID OPEN

DRAWN TOGETHER

————

CASCADIA WOLVES

Paranormal Romance

RELUCTANT MATE (formerly *Reluctant*)

PACK ENFORCER (formerly *Enforcer*)

WOLVES' TRIAD (formerly *Tri Mates*)

WOLF UNBOUND

ALPHA'S CHALLENGE (formerly Standoff)

BONDED PAIR (formerly *Fated*)

TWICE BITTEN (formerly *Unconditional*)

————

CHASE BROTHERS

Contemporary Romance

GIVING CHASE

TAKING CHASE

CHASED

MAKING CHASE

CHASE BROTHERS: COMPLETE COLLECTION

————

CHERCHEZ WOLF PACK

Paranormal Romance

WOLF'S ASCENSION

SWORN TO THE WOLF

————

CO-WRITTEN WITH MEGAN HART

Contemporary Romance

TAKING CARE OF BUSINESS

NO RESERVATIONS

————

DE LA VEGA CATS

Paranormal Romance

TRINITY

REVELATION

BENEATH THE SKIN

———

DELICIOUS

Contemporary Romance

SWAY

TART

LUSH

———

DIABLO LAKE

Paranormal Romance

MOONSTRUCK

PROTECTED

AWAKENED

———

FEDERATION CHRONICLES / PHANTOM CORPS

Sci-Fi/Futuristic Romance

UNDERCOVER

RELENTLESS

Phantom Corps:

INSATIABLE

MESMERIZED

CAPTIVATED

————

GODDESS WITH A BLADE

Urban Fantasy

GODDESS WITH A BLADE

BLADE TO THE KEEP

BLADE ON THE HUNT

AT BLADE'S EDGE

WRATH OF THE GODDESS

BLOOD AND BLADE

GODDESS WITH A BLADE VOL.1

GODDESS WITH A BLADE VOL.2

————

HURLEY BOYS

Contemporary Romance

THE BEST KIND OF TROUBLE

BROKEN OPEN

BACK TO YOU

————

INK AND CHROME

Contemporary Romance

OPENING UP

FALLING UNDER

COMING BACK

———

METAMORPHOSIS SERIES

Sci-Fi/Futuristic Dystopian Romance

ALL THAT REMAINS

ALL THE LITTLE PIECES (*coming soon*)

———

PETAL, GEORGIA

Contemporary Romance

ONCE AND AGAIN

LOST IN YOU

COUNT ON ME

———

WHISKEY SHARP

Contemporary Romance

UNRAVELED

JAGGED

TORN

SUGAR

————

SINGLE TITLES

BELIEVE

CAKE

LAND'S END

SECOND CHANCES

SENSUAL MAGIC

STRIPPED

————

ANTHOLOGIES

THREE TO TANGO

(including *Dirty/Bad/Wrong*)

ABOUT LAUREN DANE

The story goes like this: While on pregnancy bed rest, Lauren Dane had plenty of down time so her husband took her comments about "giving that writing thing a serious go" to heart and brought home a secondhand laptop. She wrote her first book on it before it gave up the ghost. Even better, she sold that book and never looked back.

Today Lauren is a *New York Times* and *USA Today* bestselling author of over sixty novels and novellas across several genres.

For more information:
www.laurendane.com

www.ingramcontent.com/pod-product-compliance
Lightning Source LLC
Chambersburg PA
CBHW051209130726

47988CB00001B/31